# Scandal

*The Sweets of Pimlico*
*Unguarded Hours*
*Kindly Light*
*The Laird of Abbotsford*
*The Healing Art*
*Who Was Oswald Fish?*
*Wise Virgin*
*The Life of John Milton*

# A. N. WILSON

# Scandal

or
## Priscilla's Kindness

Viking

# For John Blackwell

VIKING
Viking Penguin Inc.,
40 West 23rd Street,
New York, New York 10010, U.S.A.

First American Edition
Published in 1984

Copyright © A. N. Wilson, 1983
All rights reserved

LIBRARY OF CONGRESS CATALOGING IN PUBLICATION DATA
Wilson, A. N., 1950–
Scandal, or Priscilla's kindness.
I. Title.  II. Title: Scandal.  III. Title: Priscilla's kindness.
PR6073.I439S3  1984    823'.914    83-40663
ISBN 0-670-62007-6

Printed in the United States of America
Set in Sabon

*Why should good hours of sunlight be wasted on the judgement seat by those who, presently, will take their turn in the dock?*

BARON CORVO

# Author's Note

Every now and then, a British politician resigns as the result of a public scandal. The characters in this story are all caught up in such a scandal, but they are all completely imaginary. The story happens in a real place, and in recent times, but it is wholly fictitious. Derek Blore belongs to an unnamed political party which is not to be identified with any of the four or five major political parties in Great Britain today. This is not a *roman-à-clef*.

# One

Bernadette Woolley was aware that her name was professionally inappropriate. She tended to get a lot of jokes about it. There had even been recommendations that she should change it. The pious connotations put men off, it was averred. Non-Catholics recognised her allegiance at once because of the label, and scorned her for it; while co-religionists, reminded inappropriately of the Virgin apparition at Lourdes, blushed, or sniggered, or asked for another girl.

But – one of the many false impressions under which Bernadette teetered through life – she always felt you couldn't change the name you were born with.

The other girls were luckier. Either they had perfectly acceptable names like Charmaine, Rita or Cindy; or they were shameless enough to be known by parodies of the professional nomenclature: Lulu, Fifi, Busty, or Miss Caine.

Bernadette's name was only one of the many features which marked her out, in her own words, as 'a bit of a loner.'

She had never particularly wanted to sell her body. Her ambitions all those years ago, at the time of the quarrel with her mother, had been to become an air hostess. She had dreamed of travelling to Bangkok and Los Angeles. She would have worn smart uniforms, and been given free make-up and hair-does. Like the girls on the Qantas adverts, she would have been good at bringing the passengers their trays, and smiling at the executives as she supplied them with drinks or smoked salmon.

These blessed ones, who stood about with gleaming white teeth collecting their passengers at Gatwick or Luton, and jetting with them across the hemisphere; who were probably adored by the pilots, and treated to proposals of marriage every few months, had possessed the edge over Bernadette from the beginning. 'O' levels, diplomas, even typing, were accomplishments which she had never managed to acquire in the admirable government school at Bognor Regis.

1

Her mother worked in a hotel as a cleaner and chambermaid. They had come to Bognor from Liverpool when Bernadette was a baby. Her dad – formerly a cook in the Merchant Navy – had got a summer job there. It was not a summer to which Mrs Woolley very frequently referred. An infidelity, and an elopement, had occurred. Bernadette had never seen him, although he was believed to be running a hotel of his own in Blackpool and 'doing well.'

Such good fortune had not been enjoyed by his abandoned wife and child. They had few friends, and little money. Mrs Woolley, exhausted by long hours of hotel work, had never wasted much conversational energy on her daughter. The first fifteen years of Bernadette's existence had been fraught and dull. A failure, during her last year at school, to obtain employment, was written down by her mother as fecklessness. They had got on each other's nerves. A domestic dispute of some triviality – an inquiry whether Bernadette expected Mrs Woolley, after a hard day at the Excelsior, and only fifteen fiery bloodstained minutes for her morning refreshments, to scour out a frying pan, which had been left dirty for several days – caused their final parting. Bernadette had not expected her mother to clean the pan. She had not noticed it was there. She was an imperceptive girl, not gifted with prescience.

A girl from school, a Wendy Jenks, had been fortunate enough to obtain employment at an emporium called Pants Plus in Oxford Street. Hearing of Bernadette's misfortune, she had asked her manager if her friend might not be employed in the same establishment. The answer had been no, but Bernadette gave an opposite impression to her mother, and left Bognor on that pretext for the capital.

A similar shop, selling jeans and cheesecloth blouses, *did* employ her for a few weeks in Notting Hill, enabling her to rent a small bed-sitting room in the environs of All Saints' Road. But a fundamental lethargy had made the conditions of work uncongenial. The boutique opened at ten every morning. Bernadette discovered in herself an inability to appear at this hour. It wasn't as though she *did* much with her evenings. She had soon lost contact with Wendy Jenks, and spent her evenings sitting alone with a transistor and a bag of chips, allowing the hours to slip past in a melancholy haze. Sleep mercifully blotted out consciousness some time before the close-down of Radio One, and held her, as though drugged, in its powerful embrace until the sun was high in the sky. She tried alarm clocks. She tried going to

2

bed earlier. It got no better. Half past ten, eleven, it was sometimes nearly dinner time before she arrived at the shop.

Sandra, the manageress, said it wasn't fair on the others if Bernadette turned up at all hours. She wouldn't be pleaded with. After five weeks, Bernadette got the sack.

Day after day, during those weeks of employment, Bernadette had walked to the shop past a newsagent in Pembridge Road, displaying advertisements on a glazed notice-board outside the shop. A little huddle of men were always peering at the cards there, and it was some time before Bernadette recognised what the advertisements had to offer. FRENCH LESSONS GIVEN: BIG CHEST FOR SALE: VERY YOUNG, QUALIFIED MASSEUSE. Telephone numbers – even, on occasion, an address, were scrawled beneath these legends in felt-tip pen.

Coming out of the newsagent with her True-Life Romance and her packet of Silk Cut, just after her dismissal by Sandra, Bernadette started thinking. She went on thinking all the way to the Wimpy, and by the time she was squeezing ketchup from the plastic tomato on to her cheeseburger, she was doing some hasty sums.

The bedsitting room cost £18 a week. On the half-landing near her room there was a payphone with a number on it.

At the boutique, Bernadette had been paid £60 a week. But they had given her much less than that in her envelope. Sandra had explained it all to her. By the time she had paid her tax, and her national insurance, it only came to £41.70. Take out the rent and that left her with £23 each week to live on. She had no idea what people charged for Bubble Baths, Strict Riding Lessons or Instructions in Swedish; but it was surely possible to learn the value of these things as she went along. Moreover, it would be a way of meeting people. She might even make a boyfriend.

Bernadette had been brought up strictly. She had been shy of boys at school, and her mother would never have had one in the house. Other girls had had boyfriends. She never had. There was a difficulty in knowing what to say to them. In the previous five weeks, as she sat alone in her room and listened to the love songs on Radio One, Bernadette had been desperate for someone to take her out to the pictures and kiss her afterwards under lamp-posts. But no one had ever asked her. She did not know anyone. And now that her job was finished, there was no chance that she would ever meet anyone again.

Life had been hard on £23. She wondered if she dared ask as much

3

as £10 for a visit from one of the men peering at the advertisement-cards. Supposing she did, and she had four such visits in a week? There would be no tax to pay on it, and she could start saving. One day she might even have a jeans shop of her own.

By the time the cheeseburger had been consumed, her mind was made up. If she could have remembered the number on the payphone, she would have gone to the shop directly. As it was, she had to go back to the bedsit and write it down on a card. She sat on her bed and contemplated a suitable wording for the advertisement. She did not feel capable of anything too clever or fancy. One of the cards was a drawing of a spider's web, with a little fly caught in it, and COME INTO MY PARLOUR written in big letters at the top. Bernadette did not feel equal to that sort of poetry. And fear prevented her from putting an esoteric message which she did not quite understand herself. In the end, she simply wrote BERNADETTE and the telephone number. In the afternoon, she paid the shopkeeper £1 – rather a lot she thought – to put it in the window. When she and her mother had been hard up and wanted to sell some furniture, they had put a card in the local shop at Bognor and it had only cost a few pence.

In readiness for her first caller, she took a bath and made up her face with her limited supply of lipstick, blusher and mascara. She was not bad looking. Her complexion was pale and freckly, and there was nothing anyone could do about being somewhat flat-chested. She worried a bit about the spots on her shoulder and back, which no amount of Clearasil seemed to shift. But her fair, sandy hair looked pretty, as she combed it down over her shoulders. By the time she had finished painting herself, endeavouring to make her thin pale lips more sensuous by a rather smudgy application of pink, she looked more like a child who had been playing with her mother's make-up box, than a professional woman about to embark upon a profitable career.

She sat for hours, smoking a lot and too nervous to eat; and, as time passed, she felt a growing sense of failure. It had not occurred to her, once the card was in that window, that she would not have men queueing on her staircase almost at once. The next night passed equally miserably, and the next; and it was only on the third day that she discovered that the shop had not yet displayed her card, and that she would have to wait another two days before it did.

There was no money left in her Post Office account by the time the

4

card went in and she received her first call. It was a very foreign man, and when he arrived, she was frightened by his being rather old. She tried to get £10 out of him, but he claimed not to have more than £8, and when he had gone, she felt sore and bruised and ashamed. Why did women willingly do this? Why did they want to get married, so that men could do it to them all the time? No one had ever told her how much it hurt, or of how terrible men looked as they writhed about on top of you.

Still, £8 was £8. The next day, she had only two callers. One was quite a young man, handsome. She felt she wouldn't too much mind him doing it to her. He paid his money and took his trousers off, but it just wouldn't work. She was too shy to say anything, and so was he. The thing just dangled there like a funny little sausage. And she had thought the man was crying when he hurriedly got dressed again and went down the stairs. It was quite a contrast with the next man, after whose visit she thought she would have to go to the doctor in case she had torn something or had been done an injury. Again, there was nothing remotely pleasurable about the experience. He had kept up a flow of really smutty talk, and she had just tried to smile politely, but hadn't known what to say. Even so, adding up the minutes actually spent on the job, she had earned twenty-eight pounds in the space of about two hours' work.

A week had passed, and another week. On some days, she received no telephone calls. On one day she had eight visitors. She was still too shy to say much to them; and she remained completely baffled by the fact that anyone could consider this activity pleasurable. During a pious childhood, week after week, she had been warned against sin. The priests at mass preached about it. They spoke as if everyone would be doing it all the time if it wasn't a sin. She had had to buy some cream from the chemist because it made her so sore. Some of the men were too big for her, and even the ones who weren't could be a bit rough.

After about fifteen visitors, she began to wonder if £10 wasn't quite cheap. The next time a client called – a dignified man, an executive probably, with a nice suit – she had told him it was £15. He had paid up without complaining. He obviously went with a lot of girls. He wanted to do it a bit different from the others; but in the end he paid her £20 so he could stay rather longer. By the end of three weeks she had been visited by sixty-three men and she had £740 in her Post Office savings account.

5

She had never dreamed of possessing such riches. Already, however, she was surprised to discover that it was not quite enough. On a sum like that, she could have bought herself some nice clothes, and still had enough to spare for a holiday until she found the next job in a jeans shop. But it was hard to contemplate going back to a bossy woman like Sandra, for little more than £23 a week.

She wandered through Soho one day and had her hair done at a really posh place. Then she went into a shop and bought some things which should be useful in her job: red satin knickers trimmed with fluffy nylon fur; bras to match; fish-net tights and naughtie nighties. She spent about £150 on all this. The hair-do had cost £23 and she spent a further £40 on make-up. Then she wandered in the Tottenham Court Road and bought herself a cassette recorder and a portable television. A few more sorties like this – new frocks were bought, and a white fur coat – and she found that she only had £47 left in the Post Office.

But the clients kept on coming. The more they came, the bolder she grew. Some of them were talkative; they wanted to tell her about their wives, or remember scenes from their youth. Others were rather quiet and shy, and concentrated on what they were doing as though something might go wrong. Quite a few of them were like the handsome young man and didn't manage to make the sausage go all big. It seemed funny to pay good money when you knew you couldn't do it; though, years later, Julie told her that they were trying to cure themselves, poor old darlings.

The £47 became £250, and she was beginning to set her heart on a new bed and an electric blanket, when she was visited by Mr Costigano.

There was nothing about him to warn her of danger. He was a squat little man, with Brylcreemed hair, well combed back from a rather blotchy red face. He was, perhaps, less obviously respectable than some of her visitors. He was conspicuously unembarrassed about discarding his flashy blue and white tie, his silky blue shirt, and his check trousers and blue blazer with silver buttons. While he did this he continued to smoke a cigarette and stare at her as she lay back in her newly acquired tarty outfit. At first she thought he was going to be a limp sausage, but everything went quite normal when he had stubbed out his cigarette. While he enjoyed himself, he chewed gum and sang quietly to himself, 'Thanks for the Memory'. He didn't seem to know many of the words, but he repeated the

6

words that he *did* know quite often.

It was only when he had finished that he lay back and said, 'So, Bernadette, what's your real name, then?'

'It is my real name.'

'Oh dear, oh dear, oh dear.'

She wondered what was wrong. He lit another cigarette as he put on his underpants and began to reclothe himself more fully. As he stared at her he grinned and blew smoke into the air.

'Bernadette, eh?'

'Yeah.'

'Little Saint Bernadette.'

'Can't change the name you're born with.'

Mr Costigano sighed and repeated, 'Oh dear, oh dear, oh dear.' When he had hoisted his round little belly into the check trousers and was buckling them up at the belt, he said 'You and I will have to have a little confabrication, Saint Bernadette.'

Her heart leapt as he said this. She realised that he had come not as an ordinary client, but as a predator. Was he a policeman? She knew that what she was doing was against the law; but she was not sure how *much* against the law.

'You shouldn't be doing this, my darling,' he said, no longer troubling to aim for the ash-tray, but flicking ash hither and thither on her carpet. 'I mean this modelling's a dangerous business, know what I mean? You get all the nutters coming here, I expect, don't you? All the old sex maniacs.'

'I'm all right,' she said lamely. Perhaps he was not a policeman; perhaps a social worker.

'I mean you need someone to look after you, don't you?'

So he *was* a social worker. She wondered if he would find out that she was only just seventeen, and whether she would be taken into care.

'D'you mind my saying this, Bernadette? Don't get me wrong, but this isn't a game for amatures. Amature, that's what you was just now. I'm not trying to be nasty, but you was. Now, when you get amatures coming in on an act, it muddies the water, dunnit. You see what I mean, Saint Bernadette?'

She didn't. She tried to smile, but she felt that she might be about to cry.

'Now take your case just as an example. Supposing one of these loony buggers comes up your stairs and starts getting nasty, know

7

what I mean? Supposing he wanted to rough you up nasty?'

She became frightened at the menace in his voice. None of the men had been 'nasty'. Some of them had hurt her, but that was only because she was a bit small for them, and not because they meant to. The thought of being roughed up had not occurred to her until Mr Costigano mentioned it.

As he spoke, he wandered round her little room, and picked up an almost empty milk-bottle which reposed by the gas fire and the jar of instant coffee. He cracked the top of the bottle on the fender so that it became jagged, a dangerous weapon.

'Supposing someone was to come at you with this,' he said. 'Supposing they was to change the shape of your lovely little face, eh, Saint Bernadette? What would you do, eh? Scream, would you? And who d'you think'd come and break the door down? Eh? The fuzz, would they? D'you think Old Bill'd come to your rescue? To help a whore? You must be joking.'

On the contrary, Bernadette intended no pleasantry. She had never felt less like joking in her life. Her lip trembled with panic as he brought the broken milk bottle closer and closer to her face, until she could feel its jagged edges against her cheek.

'No need to be frightened, darling. Not now I'm here to help you.' He lowered the bottle. 'I'm just warning you, see. Of the *kind* of trouble you girls get into. No, you're all the fucking same, you amatures. You think you can get by on your own and you can't, right? You're just a bit too greedy, aren't you, right? And it happens to all the amatures. Oh yes, I've known hundreds. Hundreds. D'you know what happens?'

She shook her head in terror.

'Some fucking loony comes up those stairs, right? He comes in here and rapes you, right? And then he's not going to stop at that, oh no. Not this fucker. He picks up a broken bottle and puts it in your face, don't he? And then he has a cigarette, don't he, or maybe a cigar.' Mr Castigano blew smoke in her face and brandished his Rothman's King Size threateningly. 'And he stubs it out on your beautiful little body. Oh dear, oh dear, oh dear,' he concluded contemptuously. 'Amatures!'

As he spoke, the dangers and folly of the last ten weeks suddenly swept over her and she collapsed into tears. But, even as she wept, she felt a sort of gratitude to Mr Costigano. If he had not made his terrifying speech, she might have gone on for weeks, and never

8

realised the dangers she was in. As it was, she made up her mind to leave London tomorrow and go back to Bognor. She could throw herself on her mother's mercy; say that the idea of working in the jeans shop had been unsuccessful; try to get work as a chambermaid in the same, or a similar, hotel.

'We'll have to take you in hand, I can see,' he said, putting his arm round her to comfort her.

Mr Costigano had taken her in hand at once. He asked to see her National Insurance Book. When Sandra had given her the sack, she had hardly had the time to collect any stamps, but she had her 'cards' and these were shown to Mr Costigano, who peered at them.

'Where's your social security then?'

'I don't have social security.'

'Oh, dear, oh dear,' he said once more, sending a chill into her soul. For she knew that she should have her documents in order, but could not face going to the social security office and filling in a lot of forms she did not understand.

'You could get yourself into trouble, you know, not paying no stamps,' he said with a wink. But, before she could ask him further about it, he had slipped the cards and documents into his pocket book. 'Get your things together,' he said.

'What?'

'Your toothbrush, your teddy bear,' he leered. 'You're coming with me.'

'It's ever so kind of you,' she faltered. 'But I shall be all right.' She thought hastily of the lies she would have to tell at the social security about losing her cards. 'I'm going away,' she said. 'I won't do this any more, I promise. I'm going back to me mum.'

'You just come with me,' he said quietly, tightening his grip on her arm.

In the event, he did not even give her the chance to pack. When she was dressed, she was bundled down the stairs, along the street, and into a motor-car which was parked on the corner of All Saints' Road. Huddles of disconsolate Negro youths dawdled and gangled on the pavement. But there was no one else about. She could not cry out. The nig-nogs wouldn't help her.

They drove through the afternoon traffic down to Soho. Mr Costigano parked the Fiat raffishly on the pavement in Berwick Street, quite near the shop where she had bought the naughty nighties. She could easily have run, but by then she knew it was too late. He led her through a dark alley, and pushed open the door on which the orange paintwork was crumbling and faded. He showed her into a room where a stout woman of about fifty was eating a chocolate eclair and licking the stubby fingers at the end of which scarlet nails protruded like the claws of some exotic crustacean.

'I'm just having a cuppa tea,' she said, 'd'you want to join me? Hallo, dear, who are you?'

'This is Bernadette,' said Mr Costigano. He explained that the plump consumer of eclairs was called Muriel.

'Where have you been then, down the convent?' she shrieked with merriment. 'Come in, dear, no need to be shy.'

A rather leathery smile lit up her moist red lips. She was less frightening than Mr Costigano, and, after she had had her tea and smoked a cigarette, Bernadette felt more at home. He left them alone together eventually, after a certain amount of conspiratorial chat which Bernadette did not fully understand. She gave him the key of her room and her Post Office book, and he promised to send on her things.

Muriel revealed to Bernadette that she was now going to live in a nice house in Meard Street, with lots of other girls for company. She was slightly formidable and worldly, but Bernadette began to feel that, perhaps, after all, it was for her own good.

'Much safer, dear, and more friendly. They're nice girls, and you'll get your money. No need to worry.'

That was how the second phase of her London existence began. She needed a certain amount of training. Her job, it was explained, was that of a hostess. The older girls sat at the window of the house and waved to the gentlemen as they walked up and down. Bernadette, more timidly, sat downstairs in the bar drinking bitter lemon. When a client had been assigned to her by Muriel, she sat with him at a table in the tiny basement. Muriel brought them drinks – egg-cups full of sweet wine – for which the men paid £20. When she insisted on another round for the same amount most men seemed to pay up.

'Just to clear it with the police, lovey. It has to be seen to be a drinking-club, you see.'

When the £40 had been pocketed by Muriel, regular clients were shown upstairs, where they paid a further £20 for what Bernadette had to offer on the low-slung divan.

'Make it more if you can, dear,' Muriel would say. The other girls,

Charmaine and Lisa, for instance, who were from Jamaica, would often come downstairs again with as much as £50. They explained that you make them pay an extra £10 for taking all your clothes off; and then £15 a go for different positions. Bernadette was learning, but not very fast. Muriel always pocketed the funds, and it was a poor look-out for any girl who tried to keep anything back for herself. But they were paid a weekly sum of £75 in cash and – as they said – there was plenty of time off to enjoy themselves.

But she had only been there for a few months before she became ill. At first she thought it was just the ordinary sort of pain she had felt from the very beginning: the soreness it caused, to have these gentlemen endlessly poking away at her. But then she had become inflamed and she knew it was more than just ordinary soreness.

Muriel turned quite nasty when she heard the news. She had cuffed her and accused her of not being careful to make sure all the clients wore sheaths. They had sent her off to the clinic for pills and ointment and assured her that if she gave her real address she would be found by the police and put in prison.

It only took a few weeks to heal, but that was the end of the second phase. During the third phase, she was moved from Muriel's house and went to lodge at Julie's, on the other side of Mayfair in Shepherd Market. Mr Costigano arranged for her, while she still had the disease, to do other sorts of work. She posed in 'photographic studios' and gallivanted about with no clothes on in 'peep shows', finding her way back to Julie's house each evening in time for a meal and a few hours of tellie. When she was better, and had been 'cleared' at the clinic, she was free to work again, and she was able to do this without giving up her room at Julie's.

They were, in many ways, the happiest three years of her life. She did not enjoy the work any more than she had ever done. It was still a mystery to her why some women said that they enjoyed sex, but she had no longer any feelings of embarrassment about it. She managed to do most of what the customers wanted, though there were a few 'house rules' about 'positions' which it was considered unwise to adopt.

It was not the work which made life in Julie's house so agreeable. It was the companionship. Julie herself was a jolly, friendly woman with dyed peroxide blonde hair and false eyelashes dripping with mascara. She had been working in the Market, as she always called that part of London, since the war. Some of her clients had been

11

famous. There were lots of funny stories about the black-out and the Blitz.

'Oh dear, I'll die!' she would exclaim, exhausted by her own merriment, when she recalled a customer in disarrayed colonel's uniform running up Shepherd's Market without any trousers during an air-raid.

As well as Julie to amuse her, Bernadette had the companionship of all the other girls. On her landing there were Cindy and Lulu. At the top of the house, there were Melanie, Colette and Fifi. Cindy had wanted to be in the Ballet Rambert, but the ambition was thwarted when she had her 'accident'. The scars on the edge of Cindy's face, revealed when the make-up came off, and her misshapen elbow, which had been wrongly reset by the doctors, were a visible reminder of the truth of Mr Costigano's assertion that it was a dangerous profession. Fifi was really called Linda Murray and had been a waitress in Glasgow before she came south. Colette really was French. She said it made her feel at home to have another girl around with a French name; and on Corpus Christi, one year, she had even reminded Bernadette that they should have gone to church. Neither of them did in the event, but it made her feel at home to have the suggestion made.

On and off, Bernadette was still in touch with her mother. They had not seen each other, and neither of them was addicted to letter-writing. But short epistles had been exchanged. Bernadette had filled her letters with lies about the success of her career in the boutique, her continued aspirations to be an air-hostess. Her mother's replies hinted at poverty and complained about a bad knee. Neither of them was Mme de Sévigné, but at least communication of a sort was maintained, and, on Bernadette's side, at least, a feeling of guilt. She knew that her present way of life was wrong. She knew equally that her mother would flay her if she ever found out. The feelings of guilt rankled, eating into the reassuring pleasures of jokes and laughter with Julie and the girls.

One Sunday afternoon, when things were quiet, she sat with Julie watching an old film – *The Lady Killers* – and she decided to have a bit of a talk.

'I've had a letter from me mum again,' she said.

Any comment to Julie was likely to set her off in the performance of some old song, rendered with throaty gusto as she waved her habitual glass of vodka and tonic in the air.

'On Mother Kelly's *door*-step!' she intoned.
'I think she's a bit worried about me,' said Bernadette, 'and she has a bad knee.'
'Do you send her a bit, dear, now and then?'
'No.' It was shameful. It had never occurred to Bernadette that her mother could profit from her metropolitan activities. She felt it would somehow taint Bognor to send immoral earnings there by post.
'Are you still telling her you're working in a shop?' Julie asked.
'She must guess. I don't know why you keep it so dark, I don't really. But then I was born into the trade. My mum was doing the Market in *1920*. Come the black-out, she went back to it. They didn't notice how old you was in the dark!'
She roared with laughter and sipped her vodka. Bernadette wished she was a bit worldly like Julie, who had by now started to sing, 'I've danced with a man, who danced with a girl, who danced with the Prince of Wales.' Neither of them was really watching the film, so Bernadette blurted out:
'But I want to give it all up, Julie. I've had enough, I have really!'
'What's stopping you?' asked Julie sharply. 'You're always free to come and go as you choose. You know you are. I've never heard anything so silly.'
Bernadette thought that was the end of the matter. She had been rather astonished at the reply. The memories of Mr Costigano's first visit to her room in Notting Hill were still so strong that it had not occurred to her that she might now be free. All the time, it seemed, she had been sitting in a cage of which the door was not locked. Mr Costigano still came down to see her from time to time, and to pass the time of day with Julie. Once Julie had said, 'Stan said he wanted you for something special, but I've told him he's not having you.' Stan was what she called Mr Costigano. What the 'something special' entailed had remained unspecified. It had passed by, unnoticed, as she imagined that her confession had passed by that she wanted to leave.
But, the next time Mr Costigano was drinking in the bar downstairs, he turned to her, as she was waving goodbye to a client, and said, 'Well, now, Bernadette, my darling, what's all this I hear? Leaving us, are you?'
She had settled on the bar stool at his side and explained about her mother's knee, and said she was starting to feel she'd had enough of the job. She did not explain about not enjoying *it*. She did to the other

13

girls. It was very usual apparently, but not something you could talk about to a fella.

'And we'd all been getting so fond of you, know what I mean,' said Mr Costigano. He held a small cigar between his thumb and forefinger and grinned at her with a mixture of menace and amusement. 'You've come on a long way, Saint Bernadette, since we first bumped into one another.'

She hastened to say that she felt very grateful to him for all he had done. As she did so, he felt an awkward pang of pity. Stan Costigan (who, not sharing Bernadette's view that you can't change the name you are born with, had added an O to his surname to make it more exotic) was not really any more in control of his destiny than the girl he was addressing. He moved, as she did, casually and myopically through the world, obedient to those whom he feared, but seeing no further up the hierarchy of things than his own immediate superior. Being a lazy man, it suited him to live on this casual basis: nominally the proprietor of a pornographic shop, he was sometimes a bouncer in clubs, sometimes a driver. When need was, he could make a quick £500 by doing a rough job. But Mr Van der Bildt, the man from whom Mr Costigano took his orders, had expressed himself of the view that 'Stan was clumsy.' The victim had lived, needing to be finished off unambiguously the next week by another of Van der Bildt's henchmen.

Costigano did not know precisely who Van der Bildt was; still less, who he worked for. He had formed his own impressions, and kept them to himself, and as he viewed the matter, they scared the balls off him. Van der Bildt represented himself as a shop-owner and organiser of amusement arcades. Costigano was aware that there was more to it than that.

When Van der Bildt said that he wanted a girl for a special job, Costigano knew that he had to find one. Most of the pert young women under Muriel's and Julie's supervision would have had the wit not to do what he required. Few could be relied upon to be sufficiently discreet. He needed someone as retiring, timid and unworldly as little Saint Bernadette, although it grieved him to have to approach her. He had put off doing so several times. But, now that he had found her on the bar stool at Julie's, he knew that there was no escape.

'I'd really rather do something with more regular hours,' Bernadette was saying dreamily. 'Shop work or something like that.

14

Then I might even try and do a few CSEs and see if I couldn't become an air hostess after all.'

'Cards all in order are they?' asked Mr Costigano, grinning at her.

'How d'you mean?'

Bernadette remembered that he had taken away her National Insurance card. The terms of her present employment did not seem to involve weekly payslips, PAYE or any of the tiresome business with which Sandra had been concerned in the jeans shop. She was simply paid her cash each week and kept it hidden under her mattress.

'You don't mean,' said Mr Costigano with mock concern, 'that you have been getting behind with paying your stamps?'

She blushed, feeling herself once more sinking deeply into his clutches.

'Oh, that was *stupid*, Saint Bernadette, very stupid. As a matter of fact, it was worse than stupid. You was criminal, my darling, not buying your stamps. Who's going to pay your Old Age Pension? Uncle Stan? You must be joking.'

With great deliberation, he explained to her that it was illegal to opt out of paying for National Insurance. Not having a card and not going into the post office every week was something of which the authorities took a very dim view indeed. He'd known, he averred, a man be put in the nick for twenty years for not paying his stamps. Bernadette's skill at mental arithmetic extended to the capacity to add twenty to her present age of twenty-one. By the time she came out of prison, she would be forty-one, and her mother would be dead, and her entire life would be in ruins.

That afternoon, as she lay beneath the writhing form of a businessman from Saudi Arabia, she thought with horror of her own folly. It was criminal, sending people to prison like that. She was frightened at the idea of being locked up. She thought of the strict, lesbian prison guards. Fifi had been inside for a short period for soliciting. She said all the guards were lesbian, and sadists.

It was an act of supreme courage when Bernadette went, the next day, to the Social Security offices to see if she could not throw herself on the mercy of the State and regularise her position. One of the women there pointed out where you could get the leaflets – information about Pensions and that – and regulations for the Self-Employed. Bernadette did not understand any of it, and she was told she could not see anyone without an appointment.

15

'What is it, love, you wanted to know about? Social Security?'

She had not dared to say that it was to do with National Insurance stamps. She thought they would guess and have her arrested at once. So she made an appointment the next day to discuss what she said was a private matter to do with Social Security. When she got there the next day they gave her a token with a number on it and said that she was to come forward when the number was called. There were thirty-eight people in the queue in front of her and she was sat on that chair from half past two until twenty to four. When her number was eventually called, she had to go up to a glass booth, a cross between the counter at the post office and one of the peep-show cubicles where she had been obliged to work at the time of her indisposition.

Sitting there all afternoon had given her time to work out her story carefully. It was a bit of a shock to find that it wasn't a woman at the booth, but a Paki. In her childhood, Bernadette hadn't liked coloureds, and her mother said that the Pakis were the worst, worse than the Jews the way they bought up shops and post offices and made money while our own people were out of work. But, since working at Julie's, Bernadette had found her racial prejudices evaporating. Many of the clients were wogs. And, although she had now reached the stage of feeling that one man was very much like another, there had been none of the crudeness from the foreigners that you sometimes got from the whites; and a bit less of the kinky stuff. Anyway, this Paki at the Social Security was quite nice and polite. He wore a sort of pale blue-grey suit and rather carefully groomed side whiskers and a thick gold ring on his little finger.

'I'm just asking – for a friend like,' she assured him. He smiled sympathetically. Had he guessed, when he asked what the friend wanted? Bernadette explained that her friend hadn't been buying her National Insurance stamps. As a matter of fact, this friend didn't know you had to.

Paki seemed puzzled by this. How did the friend live? Was she self-employed? Bernadette said she wasn't sure, not exactly. Paki said it was most peculiar not to be sure. Employed people had their stamps bought for them; self-employed people had to buy their own. You could buy them at any post office. When you had been paying stamps for six months you were entitled to unemployment benefit. If, however, you found yourself out of work in less than six months, then you must apply for supplementary benefit. It was inevitable, Paki had said, that Bernadette's friend was doing one of these things.

16

Well, Bernadette said, her friend was self-employed really.
'Doing what?'
'You what?' she had replied, feeling herself blush.
'Your friend. What is she doing, please? How is she self-employed?'
'Oh, she's an air hostess.' Bernadette knew it had been silly to blurt this out. She couldn't think of any other jobs on the spur of the moment.

Paki scratched his head and smiled. 'Whoever heard of a self-employed air hostess?' he had asked.

She had gathered her things together and fled at that point. He must have guessed all along. Her only concern was to get out of the Social Security office before he set the fuzz on her. She chose a roundabout way home to Julie's, and wasted £2 on a taxi to throw them off the scent.

'Hallo, stranger,' said Julie, 'where have you been?' She was lolling in front of *Crossroads* with her vodka glass half empty. Mr Costigano was by her side, his puffy little hand resting on her lap.

'Been up South Audley Street?' Mr Costigano asked. The girls were not encouraged to solicit on the streets. Sometimes they would be picked up by the police and then there was trouble getting them bailed out. As Julie said, it got the place a bad name and discouraged the gentlemen.

'Come and have a drink, darling,' said Julie. 'Stan wants to tell you something.'

Bernadette eyed them suspiciously. Did they guess where she had just been? Would it anger them? She wished that there was someone she could turn to for advice. She did not understand any of what the Paki had told her. She only knew that she was in the wrong, and that They were going to get her if she wasn't careful.

Mr Costigano grinned awkwardly and stupidly at her, rather as he had done the other day, when he had reminded her of the dangers of not paying National Insurance.

'You'll have to tell 'er, Stan,' said Julie briskly when she returned with three glasses of booze. But he seemed to have lost his tongue, for Julie was obliged to continue, 'Stan was wondering whether you wasn't bored, darling, just seeing the gentlemen like Cindy and Lulu and the other girls do.'

'Oh, no,' said Bernadette automatically, hating it to be thought that she had cause for complaint.

17

'You was saying the other day that you wanted to leave us,' said Julie, her false teeth clinking against the ice in her vodka.

'Well, yeah, I'm not complaining though,' she faltered.

This remark prompted Mr Costigano to throw himself back into the fray. 'Complaining? Who said you was complaining, my darling? Not I, my duck. Not Julie. All we was wondering was whether you wasn't wasted here. You know, wasting your talents and that. I mean it's *repetitive*, isn't it?'

'Stanley was wondering – well, we both was, weren't we, Stan – whether you shouldn't branch out, like,' said Julie. 'Be a little bit more of an artiste, you know.'

'You'd have your own flat and everything,' said Mr Costigano; and Bernadette realised with a start of fear that the Julie phase of life was over. In that moment, she realised she did not want a flat of her own any more. She wanted to sit and watch Julie get sloshed on vodka; she wanted nice little heart to hearts with the other girls, and occasional jaunts to the cinema with them, or sandwich bars. She wanted the communality and the reassurances of working in a group.

'It's exclusive,' said Julie. 'It's a step up. More diverting in a way, dear. You don't have them clambering all over you, know what I mean? There comes a time when you say, *Enough's enough*. Look at me.' She was standing to refill her glass, and tapped her pointed toes as she intoned, 'I'm just a girl who can't say no . . .'

'But what have I got to do?' asked Bernadette.

'I've got all the gear, and we can teach you, like,' said Mr Costigano. 'Won't we, Julie?'

'With or without the mistletoe: I'm in a holiday mood.'

Julie and Mr Costigano had driven her to the new place next day, with a suitcase full of things. She was told that she would have a week to 'settle in' before she had customers; in the meantime, she was to learn some new tricks of the trade.

'You need to be just that more outgoing,' said Mr Costigano. 'I mean this is more your acting, know what I mean. Like Julie says, you are being now an artiste, this is something really professional.'

The apartment was in the furthest reaches of Hackney, but as far as Bernadette was concerned, it might have been anywhere. She was to be paid £100 a week, Mr Costigano provided her with the costumes, canes, riding whips and other equipment, and she was given a few days' intensive training. She felt that she was very bad at it. They told her that she did not talk enough. Eventually she got the hang, and she

18

found within herself enough anger and resentment to make the job almost satisfying. She thought of all the pain and boredom of the previous few years: the countless selfish, dirty-minded, horrid little men who had, as Julie said, been clambering all over her. It was an odd way of getting her own back.

She was not to have many customers. It was all to be much more exclusive. If she did well, Mr Costigano promised, there was something really big in it for her. Had she ever thought of being a star, acting in the movies? She thought he must be kidding. And then he had brought round Mr Van der Bildt to see her. He had a really smart suit, not a cheap one like the Paki at Social Security, but a proper executive one, with good shoes and a display handkerchief. He spoke rather foreign and smelt of scent. He told her that he was a film producer on the look-out for talent. How would she like to see her name in the bright lights as she went down Shaftesbury Avenue? He might even get her a part in a film with Sting or Jeremy Irons. He was that big.

She had to do as he said. She wondered as he spoke whether he wasn't a star himself. He had rather swept-back blond hair and a sun-tanned face. He explained that they were setting up a camera in her room, so they could get a few shots of her in action with her clients. Sometimes they would use a tape-recorder as well. He was telling her this because he trusted her, took her into his confidence. But she wasn't to tell any of it to the clients. If she did, she would be finished. Mr Van der Bildt hated to think what would happen to her. She understood. She would be discreet. If she worked hard, and if she was sensible, she'd see her name up in the bright lights within a couple of years. If she started to be silly, she could be sure that they would shut her pretty little mouth for ever.

19

# Two

The electric bulb – she never *did* get round to buying a lampshade – had gleamed nakedly from her Hackney ceiling ever since Bernadette had got up. That January day, the flat grey rain-laden sky seemed to give no light. It was as though London were covered with an enclosure of grey metal, a congealing meat dish which the lid of the firmament was failing to keep warm.

The Hackney apartments, some three years after she had taken up residence there, had failed to acquire an atmosphere of home. A poster of Groucho Marx, plastered above the chimney-piece by a previous inhabitant, had been harshly removed at Mr Van der Bildt's direction, leaving a tear on the joyless wallpaper, and revealing a little ashy patch of damp. There were no decorative concessions now, apart from a calendar from a neighbouring garage which hung beneath a photograph of a young woman revealing one of her breasts beneath a T-shirt. The furniture in the living-room was sparse: a boarding-housey settee, a war-time utility table, a number of upright chairs, from whose plastic-covered seats dribbled decaying foam rubber. The beige tiles round the fireplace ascended in the semi-castellated form which had been popular at the time of the Festival of Britain. The chimney itself had been blocked up. Two bars of the electric fire glowed from a warped asbestos board casting an orange reflection in the glistening black of her thigh-length boots.

She saw very few people now except her clients. The regularity of visits to the cinema with Cindy or Sylvia (girls from the Shepherd Market days) had somehow petered out. It was not a profession in which one made friends easily. She was, moreover, 'a bit of a loner.' Mr Van der Bildt said that it was better that way. Where would Garbo have been, he had asked her, had she not wanted to be alone?

The whole of the flat, unattractive as its furnishings were, had its professional uses. There was one gentleman who paid to be locked in the little broom cupboard behind the telephone. He paid £50 an hour for this, and hardly needed any attention, so long as one yelled the

20

occasional word of obscene abuse at him through the locked door and claimed that, if he wasn't good, he would be shut in there for ever. Another man merely wanted to be chained to the Baby Belling in the kitchenette and told to scrub it out with Brillo pads. Billy Bunter, this afternoon's client, had more histrionic tastes. He liked to howl as she stood there in front of the electric fire, hitting him with a cane.

'Ouch,' he squirmed.

'And, if you're not a good boy, I'm going to hit you again,' she said, prodding him gingerly with the stiletto of her boot.

The figure who grovelled at her feet on the hearth rug was a man in his late forties or early fifties. He had a round, pink, fleshy face and thick-lensed spectacles which he seldom removed. He wore shorts, a grey-flannel shirt, a school tie and a boy's cap. These items of equipment were kept in a drawer in Bernadette's bedroom for the purpose of his visits. For her part she wore her boots, a leather bodice, a short black scholar's gown and an academical square perched on her now over-hennaed and somewhat lank hair.

Billy Bunter, as they nicknamed him, was a client of particular interest to Mr Van der Bildt. He, or Mr Costigano, had been more than once, to see him chastised. There was a spyhole rigged up between the box-room and the living-room which gave them a perfect view. Another gentleman, foreign – she never caught his name – had been from time to time to adjust the electronic equipment. They had taped her conversations with Billy Bunter and taken photographs of him unawares. They had even primed her with topics of conversation which might be explored, though they never meant much to her.

She knew now that they did not intend to make her into a film-star. It had all been a trick. The sense of disappointment was slow in dawning. But she discovered with it a capacity to accept life as it came. None of this had been what she had planned when she first quarrelled with her mother and left Bognor. One thing had led to the next. She knew that she was partly to blame: Sandra's intransigence in the jeans shop, and the unhelpfulness of the Paki at Social Security had also contributed to the development of her life. But, in a way, she felt it had all been meant. Her upbringing conditioned her to believe that things do not happen all by accident. Only heroic feats of prayer or self-sacrifice could change Fate, as when miracles happened at Lourdes. For the most part, you just had to put up with things. Saint Teresa had gone for thirty years without experiencing a single ecstasy. That was one of the funny things she remembered from childhood instructions in the faith. An eager nun had told it to her. She did not know what it meant. She just remembered it. She remembered too that St Joseph was the patron of the dying. She did not pray much. But, when her lips formed the homesick imprecation *Pray for us sinners now and at the hour of our death*, she knew that it would one day all be over. Mr Van der Bildt, and Mr Costigano and the tedious routines with Billy Bunter would be over; there would be no more sickening dread about her failure to buy National Insurance stamps. In purgatory it would somehow be worked out and the slate wiped clean.

'You're being naughty again,' she said. Billy Bunter's face glistened with sweaty pain now. 'Take your trousers off at once.'

When this stage of the ritual had been reached, she knew that they were into the home stretch and it would all be over again for another week. The little travelling clock on the tiled chimney said ten to twelve. By the time it was noon, the game would be finished.

The ten minutes passed, as usual: the pleading with her to stop, her continued thrashings, his grunting and squealing, the final revolting little conclusion.

While he was tidying himself up with Kleenex, she went to make tea in the kitchenette. As she arranged the mugs on the Jubilee tin tray, from the centre of which the Monarch smiled up at her, she wondered whether she dared ask Bunter again about her insurance stamps. She prodded the tea bags in each mug with a fork as she contemplated the problem. Whenever she mentioned it, she knew that Mr Van der Bildt would hear her request on the tapes. It would not do to give the impression that she was planning an escape. It was always necessary to frame the inquiries within the prescribed lines of conversation about the news. But it was hard not to talk to Billy Bunter at all about the stamps. He was educated. He was a business man and if he didn't know about such things, who would?

She teetered back into the room with the tea. She was still in the same state of supposedly alluring undress, but by the time she returned he had swiftly exchanged the schoolboy outfit for dark pin-stripe trousers, string vest, gleaming white shirt and stiff collar and a really expensive looking dark silk tie with shields all over it.

'Never seems to get light, does it,' she said. She abandoned her cross, schoolmistressy tones for these chats. He always smiled back at her, as if he was relieved that the artificial nightmare had receded.

'Yes, yes,' he said, 'but it's been a mild winter.' He had a funny

22

sort of voice. He really said 'yas' instead of 'yes', and his words were delivered with punctilious emphasis.

'Here y'are.' She proffered the steaming mug.

'A good cuppa.' She could tell this phrase wasn't natural to him. There was an enforced jocularity about it, transparently false. His hand shook as he took the mug and sipped its syrupy contents.

'Like a ciggy?'

'No thanks.'

'Spect they'll be going up again in the Budget,' she ventured. He looked taken aback at the suggestion.

'That's a long way off. Three months to be exact. Quite frankly, anything could happen between now and then.'

'Is the Government going to survive, d'you think?'

Bernadette had only the haziest sense of how her country was governed, and would have been hard pushed to guess at the name of the Prime Minister. This was a question which Mr Van der Bildt had wanted her to ask.

'That's a very dicey one,' said Bunter. 'They're not doing very well on this latest round of wage settlements. The balance of payments doesn't look good, doesn't look good at all.'

'D'you hope they do lose, then?'

He stared at her with a bit of the blush which came over him at the beginning of their sessions. For a horrible moment she thought he was going to get undressed and suggest they start the whole boring business over again.

'I think it would be better for this country if they do,' he conceded.

'You know those National Insurance stamps I asked you about,' she said, as casually as possible.

'Oh, yas, yas, the Insurance. Did you go to the Department of Health and Social Security as I suggested?'

'I feel daft, see, not having paid them so long. I'm a bit scared to tell them the truth.'

His lips pursed. They were very thick and wet. They steamed a little in the ill-heated room.

'If you are behind in your payments, there would be the possibility of paying anything you owed over a number of years,' he said. 'In all probability that would not be necessary.'

'But I could get into trouble, couldn't I, for not paying them?'

'Everyone is meant to pay contributions,' he said, 'but you should talk to them about it. They are there for your benefit. What is the

23

point, frankly, of having a Welfare State if, at the end of the day, it isn't interested in the *welfare* of the ordinary men and women of this country?'

'Well, there was this coloured bloke I told you about. Paki, he was.'

'Yas. I remember you mentioned him.'

'He said as how I ought to be self-employed.'

'Well, so you are, so you are,' he chortled a trifle obscenely.

She could never tell him that she received her pay in cash from Mr Costigano. It was a matter where she was sworn to secrecy. If she suggested to Bunter or to the others that there was any such arrangement, they told her it would be curtains. She had no reason to doubt their opinion.

'It's awkward, see. When I was an air-hostess, they paid all our taxes and that for us. It was smashing. I went all over – Bangkok, America. D'you think it would be all right if I said I was still an air-hostess, only made redundant like recently? I feel a bit shy about saying what I do now.' Her voice trailed off into a giggle.

'You could, I suppose, say that you were now out of work,' he said dubiously. 'It would entitle you to assistance. They would help you with the rent on this flat, for instance. How much rent do you pay, as a matter of interest?'

This was an unexpected question. It was years since she had paid rent – for the little room in Notting Hill. That had been £18 a week.

'About twenty,' she said.

'About?'

'Twenty-two,' she added. She did not know if this was a lot or a little for a one-bedroomed apartment in Hackney. He raised his eyebrows, but he did not comment.

'I don't know why you think I should know anything about it.'

'You're educated, aren't you?' she asked. 'You liked your schooling anyway.'

There was a conspiratorial laugh between them as she twirled her academical square on the end of the cane. Her almost crimson hennaed hair fell loose about her face, which had grown paler and pudgier with the years. About her brow and the crown of her head, the hair was quite moist.

'I must leave this happy scene,' he said, rising to his feet, and putting the mug, half empty, back on the tray. He struggled into waistcoat, jacket, and British Warm overcoat, and picked up a hat

24

and umbrella.

'Next week at the usual time?' she asked.

'Yas, yas.'

'Be good,' she tittered, 'or else.'

When she had closed the door, her client descended the staircase of the crumbling house in Ardleigh Road and opened the front door with caution. He was always very careful about arriving and leaving, and he did his best to vary his routes. Today, he made briskly through the drizzle for a bus, and alighted near Highbury and Islington Station. Coins in the slot produced his ticket for the Victoria line. The ticket inspector did not give him a look. Nor did anyone on the sparsely populated platform stare at him.

But he knew that the days of his anonymity were numbered. So, too, were the days when he could snatch a few hours at the end of the morning and disappear into Hackney for his games with Bernadette. He shivered as he thought of this. Intense cold could have explained it, but he knew it was fear, an odd sort of fear to which he was somehow addicted. When he became truly famous, when there were cartoons of him in the newspapers and imitations by Mike Yarwood on television, it would be necessary to abandon his secret life. Then, even the moronic Bernadette would recognise him.

He sat on the train as it purred southwards, inwardly congratulating himself on how well the Bernadette side of life was calculated and managed. She was a perfect treasure for his purposes. Until he met her, he had taken silly risks. He had even picked up women on street corners and answered advertisements in newsagents' windows.

He had a twenty-year history of patronising tarts. It had begun during his phase of pupillage, when he would wander north from Gray's Inn and patronise the 'hotels' in the region of King's Cross station. There, for as little as an extra thirty shillings in those days, he had first discovered in himself the taste for 'something kinky.' The boot, the heel, the cane, the gown were now necessarily components, for him, of emotional gratification. A masochistic streak – if such it was – had been awoken gradually, and, he now felt, entirely artificially. But he was addicted to it, and saw no way out of the problem.

Only when he had discovered Bernadette had he managed to put his taste on a regular footing. He had proceeded with admirable caution. Not for him exposure to the blackmailer or the swindler.

25

The magazine containing the advertisements had not been bought in central London. A shop near the station in Brighton, which he happened to have been visiting when going to address a conference, had provided him with a number of 'contacts'. His system of false names and accommodation addresses, when answering the various advertisements, had been elaborate in the extreme. Any reply he received was passed through at least three intermediaries. It would have been a triumph of research to find him out.

He alighted on Bernadette with eagerness. She was obviously very stupid, almost to the point of insanity. And it was clear she was a pervert who shared his delight in ritualised acts of brutality. He very much doubted whether she had ever been a prostitute in the formal sense of the word, though clearly she took money for his services. He did not imagine her life very clearly when he was not in her company. He imagined that she drank a certain amount and had probably been on drugs. Her hair was in a truly appalling condition. Hackney was far from any of the usual scenes of vice. It was not as if he was ever going to be glimpsed coming out of a doorway in Soho or Shepherd Market. Were he spotted in the environs of Bernadette's bower, there could always be some innocent explanation: a desire to inspect housing conditions, a simple interest in the way that the other half live, being explanations as innocent as the idea that he had been driven miles out of his way and dropped there by a rogue taxi driver.

By the time the train reached Warren Street, the Billy Bunter self had almost wholly evaporated, and he sat there, a shadow of a person, waiting to climb back into his better recognised public role.

It was always depressing, the first hour or two after he left Bernadette. In anticipation, his visits to Hackney enhanced his self-esteem. They fitted his view that he was something of a 'dog': only the Edwardian phrase would suit these esoteric goings-on between a highly respectable man and a less respectable woman behind suburban lace curtains. At the time (a fact he forgot, week after week) he did not really *enjoy* being punished. It was something he felt he must do. And its oddity set him apart somewhat from the herd. It proved to him that he was really rather an exceptional character.

Then would come the dreaded boredom of her little conversations afterwards; the terrible droning on about her National Insurance stamps, or the pathetic attempts at general conversation – football, politics or the economy. And then, after that, the feelings he experienced now as they stopped at Oxford Circus: a sinking feeling

26

of misery. It was not guilt. There was nothing, in his view, to be guilty about. It was an uncontrolled melancholy. A post-coital wretchedness which was not even, strictly, post-coital: just smuttily, grubbily, after-sex. It was extraordinary how often he was capable of forgetting it. Week after week, his excitement and anticipation seemed all pleasure. There would be the tingling moments of ecstasy, and then this crushing sense of flatness.

At Green Park, he got out of the train, glad to be in the air. By mischance, he had found himself in a smoking compartment. He considered smoking a disgusting habit. But, as he strolled past the Ritz, and turned right into St James's Street, the cold moist air refreshed him, banished the unappetising effects of Bernadette's tea and made him ready for luncheon.

It took him six minutes to walk to his club in Pall Mall, and it was five past one as he had a glass of sherry in the smoking-room.

'There you are, Mr Blore, dry as you like it,' said the butler.

He was back in the world where he was known. Judges, diplomats and journalists milled about the long yellowing room. Many of them nodded or murmured 'Derek' as they saw him. There were not many parliamentarians in the Club; nor was there a great tradition of *talking* there: two reasons why he liked it. Staring out into the gardens, and beyond the twiggy trees to the rich creamy façades of Carlton House Terrace, he exchanged a few words with an aged clergyman in a frock coat. The moment was a helpful one. In the cavernous security of the Club, he was bizarrely remote from the horrors of Hackney. The faded, fudgy pilasters, the heavy leather arm-chairs, the dark oil paintings and the grandiose electroliers provided a pleasantly dingy narcotic; and the frock coat of the cleric added to the illusion that not much had happened since the days of Trollope or Sherlock Holmes.

When his glass was empty, Derek Blore climbed the gradual, well-proportioned stairs to the coffee-room and sat at a table alone. On the pad in front of him, he wrote what he wanted to eat: chops, creamed potatoes, cabbage, treacle pudding; apart from a glass of club claret, it was a school luncheon. When it was finished, he drank coffee silently in the library and read *Country Life*. At two, he donned his hat and coat, retrieved his umbrella from the stand in the hall and went out into Pall Mall for a taxi.

Architecture no less designed to keep the modern world at bay – the work, in part, of the same man who had designed his club – swooped above him as he trod the green carpeted corridor into the

27

Chamber at exactly half past two. The Billy Bunter self was now completely discarded. Fed with his club luncheon, and greeted now on all sides by colleagues, the erotic melancholy which had seized him at Oxford Circus evaporated in his self-important glow. He was, once more, the Rt Honourable Member for Wheatbridge East.

The Chamber was not very full for Prime Minister's Question Time, nor was anything very dramatic discussed in the course of the afternoon. It would fill up later in the evening for the second reading of the Energy and Supplies Bill, but Derek would miss that because he was presiding at a private dinner party. He bayed and jeered as much as was necessary at the Prime Minister, refreshed himself in the tea room with some colleagues, and when he returned to the Chamber at about half past five, he listened to a number of tabled questions to the Minister of Education about a school where allegedly brutal discipline had been inflicted on the children.

It gave him ridiculous pleasure to hear these matters debated publicly so soon after his morning with Bernadette. A very waffly and ill-worded question about the school was being put to the Parliamentary Under Secretary (it was too minor a matter for the Secretary of State to deal with) by a notoriously long-winded back-bencher. When the opportunity arose, Derek got to his feet, unable to resist a contribution.

'The Government,' the Under Secretary was trying to say, 'the Government . . .' (Laughter.)

'The Government does indeed view with the greatest concern the matter to which the Honourable Gentleman refers. And I do assure the House that we shall do all in our power . . .'

(More laughter.)

'In our power . . .'

'Order, order.'

'To see that the truth is arrived at. It does no good at all, no good at all, to prejudge the issue . . .'

(Hoots and catcalls from Derek's side of the House.)

'To prejudge the issue, I repeat, until we have heard the findings of the Committee of Inquiry.'

When Derek was called to speak, he felt waves of pleasure running through his body which exceeded the delights of the morning with Bernadette. He felt himself to be more than a passable parliamentarian. Not to beat about the bush, he believed himself to be brilliant. He liked to talk about the 'mood of the House', and was adept at sensing its whims and changes. This afternoon, a little bluff common sense was called for.

There was no reason why he should have been contributing to a discussion about education. When he had held office in the previous administration, he had been involved with aspects of trade and the economy.

'The wisdom of one generation differs in this regard from the wisdom of another,' he pontificated, gratified by the number of voices which said 'hear hear' behind his shoulders. 'And, speaking purely for myself, I have always thought that there were far crueller ways of punishing a child – far crueller – than the short, rough justice of the cane or the strap.'

There were more 'hear hears' at this from his own supporters, who continued to bay and shout for the rest of the afternoon. Derek wandered out of the Chamber again, glowing with the idea of his own common sense. Matiness overtook him in the bar – he was limbering up for the evening's dinner party – and he stood imbibing whisky and putting his arm round colleagues for about an hour and a half before turning for home.

While he had been so democratically employed, absolute darkness had descended on London. Parliament Square was dankly misty. The sky was a dirty orange haze giving way to a cloudy blackness. Where there was light – from the headlamps of cars, from street-lamps and shop windows – it seemed to be a fuzzy, half-hearted sort of light, almost conspiring with the dark to lose itself in blackness. The windows of the Abbey glowed dimly like old jewels. Behind them, the choir, Dean and Chapter had recently acknowledged that they had followed too much the devices and desires of their own hearts. Further west, up Victoria Street in the Roman Catholic cathedral, a stately Latin Mass had been sung, imploring the mercy of the Lamb of God, who takes away the sins of the world. But in the fuzzy enclosures of light, and under the cover of dark, the sins of the world went on. Beyond Whitehall and Trafalgar Square, the rowdy little neon-lit shops of Soho purveyed pornographic videos and magazines. Bored girls took off their clothes in crowded rooms to audiences of office workers and foreign visitors. In upstairs windows, pink curtains concealed sordid rooms where the act of coition was endlessly repeated throughout the evening and late into the night. Meanwhile, in all the public lavatories between Soho and the river, men stood furtively at the urinals, some hoping for lovers, some merely waiting for a glimpse of another man's nakedness as he stood there. Some of these loitered in these smelly places, cold and damp, for hours.

Juri Kutuzov, not yet abandoned either by the masters of espionage nor by the Bolshoi Ballet, but not deemed very successful in either area of life, hovered in the lavatories off Piccadilly Circus. He saw a handsome man in an anorak, and felt flattered that the man was staring at him. Ten minutes later, out in the street, the man was taking his name and address; and then asking him to accompany him to the nearest police station where anything he said might be used in evidence against him.

Other constables paced the streets in uniforms or drove about in cars. They heard that a sub-post office in Vauxhall Bridge Road was being attacked by a man with a sawn-off shotgun; that a middle-aged woman had been found shop-lifting in the Army and Navy Stores; that two men, drunk and disorderly, had found their way into the service flats in Ashley Gardens and that one of them had set off a burglar alarm.

They had not yet been told that a Chinaman was being knifed in Old Compton Street, and that one of the drunkards on the Victoria Embankment had just died of exposure. Nor had they been informed that beyond the murky Thames, in Lambeth and Wandsworth, other sins were being committed under the shadow of night. An old woman stood aghast in Wandsworth Road, watching two young men run away with her handbag containing £17.43, her pension book, her rent book, and her only surviving photograph of a son killed in the war. She never bothered to report this crime. Another woman, aged sixty-four, was unable to report the fact that three boys of fifteen were at that moment invading her house in Mabey Street SW8. After they had tied her to a chair and smashed up her things, they all raped her and then hit her over the head with a piece of lead piping. But a man called Mr Jimson, in Lollard Street, SE11, was able to report that his car had just been stolen, and it was found a few days later, abandoned near a building site in Camberwell.

These were among the sins happening at six o'clock that evening in London. Everyone was hurrying home. Some of the wives queuing in front of Derek Blore for an underground ticket were not going to tell their husbands with whom they had eaten luncheon. And some of the husbands were not going to tell their wives that they were involved in shady business dealings. The secretary just in front of Derek had stolen her copy of the evening newspaper while the vendor was serving someone else. The chemistry graduate just in front of her, now working for a bank, did not know that he had syphilis and was going home to make love to his wife. He had resolved not to commit adultery again. While they queued, two Turkish women slipped past the barrier without having bought a ticket.

Derek took the train to Sloane Square, and walked the pleasant distance to his house in South Eaton Place. He, his wife and his children had lived there for the previous ten years. There were two children. Kate, aged eighteen, was spending the year with a French family in Paris. Julian, her junior by some years, was at a prep school in Great Malvern. Priscilla, his wife, would be there when he turned his latchkey and went inside.

# Three

Priscilla heard him entering the hall. She was in the kitchen. Her very long fingers held a clove of garlic with which she was smearing the enormous salad bowl. She was a tall woman of almost too perfect beauty and elegance, who did not look her thirty-seven years. People were not being polite when they refused to believe her old enough to have a daughter of eighteen. She had naturally blonde hair, large plaintive blue eyes, and shapely lips which just stopped short of being sensual, partly because they were rather thin, and partly because she appeared to be keeping them under very firm control. It was a fundamentally round face, with a very good jaw and bone structure. Round shoulders were covered with a well-tailored dark blue shantung dress, over which she wore an apron. Her legs, concealed by the kitchen table, were long and slim. Her feet glistened in hand-made court shoes.

Some people felt faintly intimidated by Priscilla, but there was no one in the world who disliked her. Some of her friends, she knew, felt sorry for her, being married to 'that frightful man', but she had never hinted that she so much as knew of this opinion. Verbal disloyalty would have been impossible to her fundamentally decent nature. Besides, 'frightfulness', if a tangible property, was not what she found objectionable in Derek. What she minded – and the truth appalled her when she allowed herself to reflect on it – was his success. When she had first met him – in 1957 – he had been so very red and gauche, and ill-adjusted. She was little more than a school-girl, and he was a barrister on the local circuit; but there had been no doubt in her mind he needed protecting. She was just a Japanese maiden in the chorus and he was playing the Lord High Executioner. To this day, her brothers could be relied upon, should Derek come into the room with some important guest, to hum the Gilbertian ditty under their breath:

Behold the Lord High Executioner!

A personage of noble rank and title –
A dignified and potent officer,
Whose functions are particularly vital!
Defer, defer,
To the Lord High Executioner!

They were jealous of him; and she recognised that, because she was a little jealous herself.

'Being kind to Mr Blore' had been the beginning of it all; she now believed that this being kind was her function in life, her avocation. After the fiasco on the opening night of *The Mikado* all those years ago, there had been much to be kind about. There were men to whom it would not have mattered. They could have laughed it off. Everyone had been embarrassed, but her childish heart had been torn, by the determined way he had stood there in the middle of the little stage, his ill-fitting wig awry, and said to the audience, 'Ladies and gentlemen, we're going to try that chorus again.'

'*Ladies and Jantelmen* . . . .' her brothers had hooted afterwards. But it had been such a very brave thing to do. From then on, the challenge of loving Mr Blore had become the great adventure in her life. To hear her mother speak you would have thought it was a leaping of the class barrier, to rival elopement with a coal-miner or a navvy. She had been innocent of such things at the time. It was only later that she realised what they were on about. He had been to Oxford, hadn't he? Oh yes, but 'Pot Hall'. Her brothers and her father had been to Trinity, Cambridge. They had also been to Eton, whereas Derek had been to a school in North Devon called All Hallows. No one had heard of it. This she considered snooty of them.

Derek's father had been the assistant manager of a bank. One of his grandfathers had been a clerk in an insurance firm. The other, by his own quite unnecessary confession, came from 'varry humble origins indeed.' Merciless questioning by Priscilla's mother discovered this to mean that one of Derek's ancestors had been a draper's assistant.

Her family's extraordinary interest in these details made her even more determined, during the summer of 1957, to be kind to Mr Blore. He needed no prompting to be kind to her, in her pleated tennis skirts and her tightly waisted evening frocks. Drinking shandy with her, having energetically jived to 'Rock around the Clock' at the Young Farmers' Dinner Dance; or sweaty from mixed doubles,

33

drinking lemonade after the tennis tournament; or driving back from the local rep in his dilapidated Riley having seen *Arms and the Man*, Derek would often explain his ambitions to her. Having been Librarian to the Oxford Union would not, he had repeated, 'do him any harm.' Priscilla, knowing nothing of these things, had felt childishly compassionate. There was no more chance – she thought – of Derek getting into parliament than of men landing on the moon. But he had it all planned out: to get himself a constituency, to reckon on losing the first election he fought, winning the next and of being Shadow Cabinet status by the next. Thus he had spoken, over the tomato sandwiches and the potato crisps in those innocent days of her late teens.

Mummy had been quietly horrified when she knew that Priscilla had decided to marry Derek. Daddy was not. That should have been an early-warning signal, for Daddy had never liked anyone in his life without the knowledge that some good would come of doing so. 'Got a lot of good ideas', had been Daddy's earliest comment on Derek: no allusion to his vowels or the draper's assistant. Of course, no one would have been seriously, or even overtly, beastly about these. But she knew that Mummy had them in mind when she said, 'And I thought you were so fond of Guy Lumleigh' – a well-bred young man who lived nearby and was all the things Derek was not. Priscilla had, of course, been 'so fond' of Guy. She found it hard not to be fond of everyone. Derek had been something rather different. He was a frog who could be relied upon *not* to turn into a handsome prince. Always, she had felt with the sunny confidence of seventeen years, Derek would aspire and fail. People would not, really, defer to the Lord High Executioner. He would always be embarrassing the audience by saying that they would try the chorus one more time to see if he could get it right.

And then, little by little, Derek had become a success. If she had thought about it, on her wedding day, she would have predicted that he would spend the next thirty years defending shoplifters in the Crown Court and representing the guilty parties in uncontested divorce suits. As it happened, they only had a little over a year of uninterrupted country life. Within twelve months he had got himself into chambers in the Inner Temple, acquired a number of interests in the City, and been adopted as the parliamentary candidate for a marginal seat in the West Midlands. Rather to everyone's surprise, he became an MP in 1959. By the time he had increased his majority in 1964, he had also consolidated his career outside parliament. He was on the board of an insurance company; he held a number of 'consultantships'. His reputation as a company lawyer brought valuable cases his way. Priscilla grew to sense that he had no shortage of money.

Her instinctive reaction to the transformation – or revelation – of Mr Blore into a character to whom it was no longer necessary to be kind was something which disconcerted her. Why could she not share the glee of her mother? Her father, until his death, could never conceal a vulgar satisfaction at her foresight. How clever, both her parents seemed to imply, she had been to spot Mr Blore's qualities when she had been kind to him all those years ago: seven, twelve, eighteen years. Priscilla, who could see that she should have been gratified, felt a contrary sense of embarrassment. She found herself saying that she was proud of Derek, or that she *admired* him enormously. It was not untrue; it was merely odd that she should have wanted to articulate these sentiments. Being married to him had certainly brought its rewards: two admirable children; the Old Rectory at Willerton St Leonard's; the house in South Eaton Place; for what it was worth, the 'status' of being attached to a rising star in the political firmament. In turn, she had been an exemplary wife. Apart from these unnecessary expressions of admiration for her husband, she had not, like some political wives, been anything of an embarrassment. Her beauty and her poise seemed, if anything, more assured with the years. She could entertain the constituency and the journalists and the parliamentary colleagues with a graceful aplomb which was the envy of many of Derek's associates. If she seemed a trifle intimidating (partly explained by her height) this was no bad thing in the wife of a man who was already being spoken of by some commentators as of an ideal age and experience to be the next Leader of the Party.

Knowing Derek, she realised that this meant running the risk of his being 'the next Prime Minister but three', like the young man in the rhyme. It was not that she minded the thought of standing on the steps of Number Ten Downing Street, waving as other spouses had waved, when Derek went in to take office. It was quite simply – and this was what appalled her – that she felt cheated and envious.

When she married him, she had felt that there was an unspoken recognition on both sides that hers was the role of rescuer. In emotional and social terms, she was to be the success story. The

35

glowing smiles of her mother as Derek chalked up yet another triumph had been to Priscilla like a succession of wounds: Parliamentary Private Secretary to the Minister of Agriculture; a member of this important committee and that; the move to the Treasury; the first appearance on 'The World at One' on the radio; then a television interview on 'Nationwide'; and Under-Secretaryship of State. And then, after the election defeat of his party, a position in the Shadow Cabinet. At every stage, she had been simply, disgracefully jealous; childishly jealous in a way that no self-reminders of her own good fortune, good looks or good friends could appease. It was her darkest secret, scarcely voiced even to herself. There was no hint of it in her dealings with him; no breath of it this evening, as she crossed the kitchen to greet him with a kiss on the cheeks.

'You are looking ravishing,' he said.

She experienced the little thrill of amusement which flattery from her husband was still able to inspire. 'Do you want to do the wine?' she asked.

Six bottles of red wine had been placed in readiness the evening before, in order to give them time to reach room temperature. The white was in the fridge. Nevertheless, he chose to rehearse the guest list and the menu.

'What are we giving the Levines to eat?' he asked.

'Nervous?'

'Of course not. But it does no harm to give a good impression to such people.'

Rachel Levine was an American journalist who had lived in England for some years. She made a speciality of writing 'profiles', often of politicians, for one of the 'serious' daily newspapers. This was to be her first meeting with Derek, and, after dinner, they were to discuss the outline of her article. In addition to the Levines, they had invited Derek's constituency agent and his wife; Derek's own Parliamentary Private Secretary and his wife.

'And Feathers will probably look in,' said Priscilla quickly.

'To keep the other journalists happy. Yas, Yas' – Derek also allowed the matter of Feathers to be accepted with as little comment as possible. He did not like Feathers. He considered him an oaf. For some reason, this drunken hack was thought charming, and one met him in the most exalted circles. Derek, whose social antennae were very dull, chose to accept the fact that, if one were rising in the world,

36

one had to accept the presence of Court Jesters. At least there would be no danger, if Feathers were coming, of Rachel Levine imagining the household to be stuffy, or stiff. It added to the evening a bohemian flavour on which he had not been reckoning.

'And to eat?' he asked. It was the fourth time he had enquired: twice the day before, and once at breakfast that morning.

'There's an avocado mousse. Then we're having saddle of lamb.'

'And good old pud?' he asked.

'Crème brûlée.'

'I think we'll do some serious drinking tonight,' he said. 'Whyever not?'

The answer to this question, which neither of them mentioned, was the possibility that Feathers might stagger in, already well-oiled from a couple of hours in El Vino's.

'Whatever you like. The Chablis is in the fridge.'

Derek opened the white enamelled door and peered at the bottles in question. His action somehow suggested, playfully, that the little woman couldn't be trusted where the delicate matter of wine was concerned even to remove the bottles from the fridge without making some monumental blunder.

'Juan likes doing the wine,' said Priscilla. 'I'm not going to touch another thing. Maria can do it all.'

A Spanish couple were employed to assist with dinner parties.

Derek ignored the reminder. He had forgotten to chill any white wine himself, so it was Priscilla's choice that he stared at now, gathering about itself a frosty haze. To accompany the mousse, he would himself have wanted to show off some of his excellent (and remarkably cheap) Sancerre, bought the previous summer. It was a relief, at any rate, that she had not brought disgrace on the household by chilling that Frascati she was so fond of.

'Puligny Montrachet,' he said triumphantly.

'So?'

'You said Chablis. A white Burgundy, like Chablis, but not, technically, a Chablis. Still, admirable, admirable. I thought that when last sampled it was coming along very nicely. We must drink our way through it this year. It will be past its peak by Christmas.'

'I'm going to have my bath,' she said.

'We'll have a sensational Sauterne with the pud,' he called after her. 'But I'm keeping the identity of the red wine a mystery.'

He fussed with corkscrews and decanters while she lay in the scented waters of her bath. When she emerged, he went up to the bedroom to chat with her. She told him a little of her day; and he a little of his. They both felt the compulsion, each evening, to chatter about their day. It sometimes seemed the primary reason for their being married, apart from the house, and the children, and Derek's career.

# Four

While they indulged in this conversation, Juri Kutuzov, who had been arrested in Piccadilly Circus an hour before, sat in a police station. He was charged with indecent exposure. It was an uncomplicated case. He had cried, protested his innocence, and said that he was a Russian who wanted asylum in the West. This outburst caused merriment among his interrogators. But the charge had no sooner been drawn up than the desk sergeant entered the interview-room and whispered to one of the detectives. There was a hurried telephone call, and Boris was told that he could go. With somewhat heavy irony, the detective who had arrested him apologised for the inconvenience, and said that there had evidently been some mistake.

A large black limousine was waiting for him outside the police station. It swept him off through Knightsbridge and up Kensington Church Street.

A yellow Volvo was waiting at the lights opposite Barkers as Boris was driven northwards. The car contained Rachel Levine and her husband, Hughie Duncan.

'Do you think it will be just us?' Hughie asked his wife.

'I don't think so. I'm not going to be interviewing Blore tonight. Like I told you, he just wants to check me out before he says he'll do it.'

The Volvo shot forward, and they were silent while Rachel concentrated on her driving. She had a pale intelligent face, fundamentally oval, and serious, but broken by a large, sensual smile. Hughie, by her side, watched his wife's profile, lit up by the kaleidoscope of street light as they scudded towards Belgravia. He loved to study her features when they were concentrated on professional business. He had no interest in politics, and rather less in the social life of politicians. He was not looking forward to the evening with the Blores. But he admired the serious way that Rachel was going about things.

They had been married four years. Before that, her history had taken place, as far as Hughie gave it a thought, on the other side of the Atlantic. Some years before they met, a husband had been abandoned in New York. Rather than returning to her native Massachusetts, she had decided, with a consciousness which shocked Hughie when he had heard of it, to 'make a new life' for herself.

This novel creation evolved in England, and had been accomplished without brashness, but with a firm confidence of success. She was already a respected journalist – regular columns, her name familiar in the political and literary circles – when her life came to include Hughie's.

Her particular originality, the distinctiveness of her 'new creation', had something to do with her being smaller than the average, inclining to plumpness, with an absence of ostentation in her dress which was almost, in itself, showy. When she turned up to conduct interviews – with half-famous men and women, or with established idols – she often sensed that her male subjects, in particular, mistook her, on initial appearance, for a stenographer, sent in advance of the real Miss Levine to switch on tape-recorders or sharpen pencils. Their eyes implied that her bearing was not simply insignificantly modest, but also inappropriately so. Rachel Levine, the prize-winning American journalist, the sketcher of 'profiles', portraitist of such diverse personalities as the Cardinal Archbishop of Armagh and the Leader of the Opposition: such a woman owed the world a stereotype. She should have had the wardrobe of the Queen of Sheba and the voice of a Broadway musical star. Gold should have glittered from earrings and necklaces, raven hair should have been swept back, in a frenzy of ambition, from a face in whose creation the Almighty had played only the most minimal and necessary role.

And yet, when Hughie first met her, at that party of the Gypsy Baron's, he had spotted at once that she was not English. The tonelessness of her dress – purchased as it happened at Marks and Spencer for its appearance of *anglais* – suggested somewhere even more dingily 'provincial' than England; Ulster, Canada or France came to mind. He dismissed a fleeting thought of the Soviet bloc. For one thing – Hughie, like all the world, believed in stereotypes – she was not smoking enough. For another, she looked permanently amused. The thick, springy mouse-coloured hair and her oval pallor of countenance kept obliquely, perhaps appropriately hidden, even opaque, the 'fact' that Miss Levine, as the world was instructed to regard her, was originally a townswoman of Hughie's most frequently perused, and, in vulgar parlance, his favourite, romancer. She was, in short, a Bostonian, though a reading of Henry James did little to prepare him for what she was like.

Truth, in the perverse way that it has, did not, as is said, 'out' until their third or fourth meeting. Neither Hughie's origin (a country house in Scotland, boarding schools, New College, publishing) nor her own (refugees, musicology, Harvard, a too-early marriage, divorce, escape) had been mentioned until, to venture an inescapably physical crudity which the Bostonian master of words would have found comically impermissible, they had collectively appreciated two prawn pilaws with accompanying chutneys, curries and pappadoms; two veal steaks; a plate of cold tongue with cumberland sauce, and a plate of lamb chops with mashed potatoes; two dozen oysters and a generous supply of brown bread-and-butter; not to mention the tonic waters, ice, lemon, gin, wine, coffee, or the diversions – musical, cinematographic or theatrical – which, to use a prosaically gastronomic metaphor, *sandwiched* this absorption of comestibles.

Prosaic was right. For, in his love for Rachel, Hughie re-entered the world of prose, from which he had been excluded by years of a long love. Here was none of poetry's anguish. Worst of all, they laughed so much. From the beginning, they had laughed. For thirty-five years, he had managed to keep his life fascinatingly mysterious. People believed it was because he had money, on which he was afraid other people would wish to lay hands. Others darkly hinted of a fondness for his own sex. Neither speculation had much to do with the truth. One half of the truth was that he had been happier on his own than he would have been in the enforced company of those whom he would have come to dislike. His solitude was dear to him. Even at work, as an editor in a small, slightly learned publishing house, his office door was kept firmly closed and his 'private life' was mysterious, even to his secretary. He devoted his evenings to concerts and films, and occasional visits to friends. He was not always solitary. But the inner margins of emotion were fiercely guarded against intrusion. The memory of Jane was kept burning, an ever-sacred lamp. Churchgoing formed some part of Hughie's existence, where rites could be found unmangled by the egoism of the modern clergy. But Jane was truly his religion.

This goddess had been an undergraduate contemporary. She had belonged to the phase of life when he was much too shy to be capable of expressing the magnitude of his feeling for her. The world saw a pretty young woman on whom, not unnaturally, young men, Hughie among them, were keen. Hughie saw nothing. As he swirled and floundered in the hopelessness of his love for her, his addiction to 'feeling' became absolute. Jane continued to be part of life after Oxford. There were little walks. Books were lent. The fortnights between each meeting tormented him with delicious anguish and anticipation.

What chiefly tormented him afterwards was the knowledge that Jane had been perfectly fond of him, and, a rather different matter, looking about for a husband. She would probably have married him had he asked; had he ever got beyond the stage of putting a gingerly arm about her waist as they strolled tensely through parks. She could have done so, but she didn't. Jane made a good goddess. He had never met her since her marriage, conspicuously refused any invitation where there was the faintest chance of her being present, nursed and kept alive his wound.

Jane was not in the entourage of the Gypsy Baron. At that party, nearly five years before, Rachel had seen him through a haze of cigarette smoke, and admired the self-confidence with which he stood on his own in the middle of the room talking to no one. He was not paralysed with embarrassment. If anything he had a rather arrogant appearance. The fact that the room was full of people did not alter his desire to stand there, musing and solitary, if he so chose. There was something about his pink cheeks that she had found immediately endearing. She liked, too, the old-fashioned, almost military hair-cut; the long, quizzical, clean-shaven face; the tweed jacket and corduroy trousers; the heavy brown shoes and hand-knitted thick woollen socks.

'You look like maybe you came up from the Shires.'

The thing he liked immediately about her, apart from her beguiling quietness of voice and appearance, was her refusal to ape the locutions and mannerisms of the island where they happened to be standing. She firmly clung to her elevators, closets, pitchers, apartments, trunks, cookies, purses and bathrooms.

'I like to stand still at parties and just watch,' he said, his eyes moist with everyone else's tobacco fumes.

'You looked sort of lonesome'; here he had detected self-parody, and, as if by justification, she had quickly said, 'I'm Rachel Levine, by the way.'

'It's a pleasure to meet you, Mrs Levine.'

42

He had obviously never heard of her. And, either out of awkwardness, or guided by the arcane rules of British etiquette, he had not supplied his own name in return for hers. When he knew her better she learnt that it was nearly always rude to ask questions. 'I hate it at parties when people say "What do you do?"' he said. She never made that mistake again, but she wasn't sure of any good alternative openings to conversation. 'Can't talk be general, rather than inquisitive?' he had asked.

So there was something brittle here, something to get her teeth into. He had not been stiff, or stuffy, though. He had been perfectly prepared, when she boldly told him that she had no one to buy her supper after the party, to take her out for rather a nice meal at Giuseppe's. He didn't seem hung up on sex. But he had not suggested meeting again. Then they had met by chance at someone else's dinner table, and in the course of that second evening she realised that she was in love with him. In a good-humoured, almost amused, way, they had started to meet regularly. Within about six weeks, they had decided to get married.

Hughie had married Rachel because he decided that his life was in danger of getting stodgy, and he thought she would liven him up. He also found her overwhelmingly physically attractive. He had got most of what he wanted out of the marriage. They were very fond of each other. His life was no longer boring. But, as the years had passed, he had discovered in himself the most appalling disappointment with Rachel. He was not, as he had supposed in the first few months, quite in love with her, and it pained him to know that she was profoundly in love with him. Time went by, and the more it did, the more Hughie had come to feel that he had shut the door on Romance. Tweeded and solitary, his bachelordom had preserved Romance intact. When, in the old days, he had gone to concerts on his own, he had been able to wallow in rather agreeable regret for the girl he might have married at the age of twenty-three. He liked violently emotional loud music in those days. It made him awkward to hear it in Rachel's company. His heart had not been given away, and now, if they heard Wagner or Mahler together, he felt almost guilty of an infidelity; for the intensity of the swirling sounds spoke of a world which had momentarily been laid aside for a well-fitted house in Kensington and an endless succession of meals, parties, plays and encounters devised by the Comic muse.

'You had better tell me about Mr Blore before we arrive,' he said.

43

'Which party does he belong to, for instance?'

She giggled and told him. 'He's really a man of the Centre,' she continued. 'He's good at seeming to agree with everyone.'

'Sounds a bit dreary.'

'He's got various eccentricities. I'm told he can whistle every single one of Beethoven's symphonies. He's a great stereo freak, and a wine freak.'

'What about Mrs Blore?'

'Lady Priscilla's a bit of a mystery; very beautiful, sort of statuesque. It's said he married her to give himself a leg-up in the world. It may be true. I'm going to give quite a lot of my attention to her this evening. You learn a lot about a man when you get to know his wife.'

This observation silenced him. He wondered if anyone were to meet Rachel, for the first time, whether they would be able to reconstruct *him* from the clues given out by her social behaviour.

When they had parked the car near the Blores' house, Rachel leaned over and kissed Hughie on the cheek. 'Thanks for doing this for me, honey. I know you hate dinners like this.'

'Not at all. I shall be amused.'

'The trouble is when you're amused, you just sit back and smile and don't *talk* to anyone.' She nuzzled against his shoulder as she said it, her thick curls brushing his face and sending waves of desire and happiness through him.

'Let's go off and wallow in a hotel,' he said.

'You are just *terrible!*'

They were warmly arm in arm against the chilly night air when they rang the door bell. Just before the door opened, she said, quietly and lingeringly in his ear, 'I l o o v e you.'

There was a disconcerting appearance of panic in Derek Blore's eyes which made Hughie suspect that they had come on the wrong night. The rest of his face did its best to hide the terror, his thick, slobbering lips were framed into a determined smile, which creased almost all his facial muscles in an optimistic, upward direction towards scarlet ears and crinkled grey hair. But it seemed like good humour in a crisis. Behind the very thick lenses of his specs were the eyes of a frightened creature. Instead of opening the door to guests, he might have been trying to resist plunderers.

'Ah, yas. How varry, varry nice.'

44

He led them into the hall, and took their coats.

'Mr Blore, I'm Rachel Levine. This is Hughie, my husband.'

He led them into a stylishly elegant drawing-room. Curtains of peach-coloured velvet plunged from thick poles on the end of which were brass pineapples. The painting over the chimney-piece which looked like a Fragonard *was* a Fragonard. But there was nothing too perfect about the room. It felt like the happily lived-in saloon of a great house. The covers of the sofa were not too new. It was a room to put you at ease: a cultivated, leisured, patrician ease which was not, at the moment, displayed by their host. He paced stiffly ahead of them as if something was about to go badly wrong.

'Have we got ice?' It was a bellow to the quarter-deck.

'In the ice box.' It was the first time they heard Priscilla's voice. Its well-modulated tones trilled from another room.

'Guests!' he shouted, in the tones of a man calling for help – 'Fire!' or 'Man overboard!'

As if to be reassuring, Derek, his hands shaking, said, 'Let's get you some drinks.'

Hughie could not 'place' the accent, and when he asked Rachel about it afterwards, she said she had not noticed it. She was incapable of picking up the multitude of signals given out by an English voice. She could just about distinguish between a strong Glaswegian accent and Cockney. But she could make nothing of a wholly self-created noise such as proceeded from the mouth of Derek Blore.

'Gin? Vodka? What'll it be?'

Rachel asked for vodka and tonic. Hughie had whisky. They noticed that there were a lot of glasses on the tray and concluded that other guests were expected.

He handed over the glasses, first Rachel's and then Hughie's. As he gave Hughie his drink, he said, 'I hope that's how you like it,' and then with the hint of condescension one might use to a child, or to someone slightly deaf, he added, '*On the rocks.*'

Clearly he thought Hughie, like Rachel, was an American. For, when he expressed approval of the whisky, it was evident that Derek mildly disapproved of the way Hughie spoke. He glanced at him with faintly hostile suspicion, as though his voice was rather 'affected'.

'Now, who have we got for you?' he said, turning to Rachel. 'Do you know the Sangsters?'

'Your agent?'

'How efficiently you have done youᵣ researches. Yas, yas. Tad's been a good friend.' He listed the other guests: the Sangsters, the Johnstones; but he did not mention the possibility of Feathers looking in.

Priscilla appeared at this moment, shimmeringly tall in a dark red silk dress, and a childish alice band in her blonde hair. Rubies twinkled on the lobes of her ears and round her swanlike throat.

'This is Rachel Levine, and her husband Hughie,' said Derek awkwardly.

There was silence as they watched Priscilla help herself to a drink. When she came forward, it was to speak to Rachel.

'I'm *such* a fan,' she said, in a natural tone, and began to talk to her about her articles and her work.

'I shall be out of my depth in all this literary company,' said Derek. 'A publisher, you say? What is it you publish?'

'Mainly academic books. Some poetry. A little fiction.'

'I get much less time for reading than I would wish. The good old days of the literary man in politics are a thing of the past, I am sorry to say. Roy manages to find time to write books – I'm damned if I know how; and there's Enoch of course. Enoch's scholarship is phenomenal, phenomenal. But they are a dying breed.'

'It seems a pity.'

'So it just has to be a few favourite books for me. Now, you do know a book I've often read? *The Moon and Sixpence* by W. Somerset Maugham. An extraordinary book. That's what I call a real novel.'

Hughie wished he would stop. He would have been prepared to discuss anything – the balance of payments, motorcars, football – rather than listen to this bungling attempt at 'literary conversation'. But it was clear, on the contrary, that Derek was getting into his swing. 'Wonderful stuff,' he was saying, in the tone of one who thought himself so highbrow that he could afford, from time to time, to descend into colloquialism. 'It's based on the Gauguin story, you know, but he's *transformed* it.'

Hughie said that he had read the story.

'You see, there's this artist. Well, *no*, he isn't an artist at the beginning of the story. That's the whole point. He's a perfectly respectable . . .'

The door bell rang and interrupted Derek with a jerk.

'Shall I go?' Priscilla asked.

'I'd better,' he said reproachfully. 'Forgive us,' he said deferentially, as though the ringing of the bell threatened to throw

46

the evening into chaos. There was even a faint hint that it would not have happened but for Priscilla's mismanagement.

She appeared entirely unruffled, either by the bell or by Derek's air of bustle. She continued to nod when Rachel discussed her work. She stared coolly, sadly, serenely across at Hughie, and he stared equally sadly back. They smiled at one another, almost conspiratorially.

In the hall, Derek could be heard implanting a slobbery kiss on a powdered cheek. 'Pam! How nice! And Ted! My dear *fellow!* Come on, now, Ted, let's have-yer-coat' – all this in his mock-jocular voice. 'Come on in and warm yourselves. Now, I don't know if you know the Levines?'

'Duncans,' said Hughie.

Derek blushed, and turned to Priscilla for help.

'That's okay,' said Rachel. 'I always use my first married name professionally. But I'm now called Rachel Duncan.'

The Sangsters joined the party. There was the same air of unnecessary fuss as Derek distributed glasses of spirits. He had no sooner done so than the bell rang again, and the Johnstones went through the same ritual of bonhomie, removal of coats, introductions. Rachel knew who they all were and talked to them animatedly about opinion polls. Hughie found himself standing next to Priscilla. Her huge blue eyes peered at him with what he felt to be satire.

'I didn't realise you were married to Rachel,' she said.

It was a reassuring remark, establishing by the peculiar freemasonry of English conversational rhetoric that she knew 'who he was'.

'You used to know my cousin Janey Freeborn, didn't you?'

'Very well.' He laughed and blushed. The very mention of Jane's name brought back the lost love over whom he grieved in bachelor days, as the tones of Wagner or Mahler swirled in his ears at concerts. 'How is she these days?' was all he managed to say.

'Very rich.'

They both laughed. It was apparent that Priscilla immediately sensed the painfulness of the topic. She was not going to linger on it with blundering cruelty. Having 'placed' Hughie, and expressed, with her great moist eyes, both recognition and sympathy, she chattered to him lightly about a story in the evening newspaper. Hughie joined in amicably enough. It was an amusing divorce case in which a woman had claimed her husband was guilty of 'mental cruelty' because he had forgotten to feed her budgerigar. But he stared at her too intensely as they spoke, and he recognised at once all the danger-signals of Romance stirring once more in his heart. At first, he felt that she had merely awoken nostalgic feelings for Jane, whom he had loved so painfully and so hopelessly for nearly a decade. But the more they talked, and the closer she stood, the more he realised that his feelings for Jane were at last dead. He took in every detail of her appearance as she laughed and stood there: the multiplicities and texture of her hair, thick, straw-like blonde hair beneath the alice band; smooth, mousey little eyebrows, and lashes which were long and silky and untouched by masacara. And by her ears, at the very top of her cheeks, there was the faintest, palest, most delicate down which put one in mind of a baby's neck. The hands were unadorned, save by a single golden ring on her wedding finger. The wrists and elbows could have been carved out of marble, they were so pale and smooth and perfect. The snowy throat plunged down to where three buttons of her red silk dress were undone to reveal a cleavage painted by Ingres. And yet, for all the perfection of her appearance, for all that she seemed like an animated work of art, there was an air of mischief and kindliness in her expression which made it impossible not to be at one's ease, impossible not to be . . . immediately *fond* of her.

As she laughed, in mid-sentence, about the man and his budgerigar, she looked over Hughie's shoulder to the gilded French carriage clock on the chimney-piece and turned questioningly to Derek. He desperately waved his wrist back at her to indicate that it was by now twenty-five to nine.

'It seems very unsocial,' she said, 'but I think we should go in and eat.' And the rather faceless MP who was Derek's political secretary was left in mid-sentence about the minimun lending rate as they glided in to dine.

The dining-room was dazzlingly beautiful. The long eighteenth-century table was laden with silver which winked at them in the candlelight. On the large wall behind Derek's head was a painting of the Battle of Malplaquet. As people sat down to table, there was evidently one empty chair.

'The next time you dine with us,' Priscilla said to Rachel, 'you must come during a recess and then we needn't hurry.'

The Spanish couple shimmied noiselessly in and out with the

avocado mousse and the white wine, which tasted, to judge from the faint curling of everyone's lips when they first brought their glasses to their mouths, a little acerb.

Two conversations loosely rumbled into shape, though they were interrupted by Derek's refusal to relax. ('Everyone got butter? Good, good.') At Priscilla's end of the table, there was a childishly animated conversation about ghosts. It had just the right combination of the comic and the fantastical to allow everyone to join in. Hughie described a cousin in Scotland who had seen the ghost of George V. Ted Sangster, a moustachioed, red-faced and jolly vulgarian, told a funny story about the Kaiser. Mrs Johnstone, on Hughie's right, wife of the dullard PPS, did not have much to say on the matter, but remembered having funny feelings of telepathy when her grandmother had died.

At the other end of the table, Derek told Rachel about *The Moon and Sixpence* by W. Somerset Maugham. And then, when the Spaniards had started to bring round the plates of lamb, he rose to his feet, almost colliding with the manservant as he did so, in order to grab a decanter. He removed the stopper and sniffed the red wine ponderously.

'Now we have an interesting little game,' he declared. 'Ted, old boy (owld bye), Charlie – I wancha to tell me what this is.' He blundered about the table, getting in the Spaniards' way, and forgetting to fill the ladies' glasses first. Only Ted and the PPS appeared, indeed, to have their glasses filled at all. But he relented, with a flurry of apology, and passed a couple more decanters down the table as if they were port. 'Now, then,' he said, 'tell me what your guess is?'

Hughie was evidently not included in the game. Either Derek had forgotten his name; or, still under the impression that he was an American, he thought his palate had been irredeemably coarsened by a lifetime's consumption of Highballs, Manhattans and Coca-cola.

Rather embarrassingly, Hughie recognised what kind of wine it was at once. He was not interested in the exact years or vineyards, but the general provenance of the stuff was unmistakable. He kept silence, though, as all eyes turned on Ted Sangster.

Ted's appearance helped to turn everything into a good-humoured joke. His moustachioes, and his uneven yellow pipe-smoker's teeth, and his rosy cheeks conjured up a world of outmoded raffishness, of seaside piers and landladies and dirty postcards.

49

'Very very nice,' he said, as he swilled the wine about like a gargle within his whiskery chops.

'Come on now, old boy,' Derek wheedled, 'let's have a guess out of yer.'

Ted laughed. 'Not really my sort of game, you know,' he blushed as he said it. '*May* Dock?'

'Wassat, old boy? Oh, Mu-*dock*. Not a bad try, old boy, not a bad try. How about you, Charlie?'

While this ridiculous display continued, Hughie looked at Priscilla who was murmuring polite compliments to the Spanish woman and appearing not to notice. Rachel, on the contrary, was staring at Derek and looked painfully as if she might be about to burst into a fit of giggles.

'Let's throw this one open,' said Derek. 'Anybody, come on now!

'Nuits St Georges?' ventured the colourless MP.

'I'd have said the same myself, old boy, but it's not. Any other bids, ladies and gentlemen?'

It was too much for Hughie. He could see that Rachel might at any moment break into indecorous laughter.

'It's Rioja,' he said.

Derek did not look at all pleased by this interjection. It was a piece of information he wished to disclose himself. He looked at Hughie with undisguised hostility.

'Like to be a bit more specific?' he asked.

'Sainsbury's?' Hughie asked. Everyone laughed. The tension of the moment was broken. As Derek sat down to eat, he was murmuring something about Gran Reserva 1967. 'It's as good as the best claret you can buy, and, fuck me, it's half the price,' he said.

This inclusion in his speech of the coarse tetragrammaton was repeated as he consumed more of the controversial and mysterious liquid. His admission that the wine was rather cheap seemed designed, in some way, to score a point off Hughie, whose mildly offensive joke had not been taken in the light spirit in which it was spoken. For Hughie's part, as he turned back to talk to Mrs Sangster about telepathy, he felt as though he had struck a blow for Romance, the first step towards rescuing the damsel in distress who, so pale and tall and beautiful at the other end of the table, was imprisoned in a marriage to this monstrous buffoon.

No comment was made on the lamentable Sauternes which they swilled with the crème brûlée, when the doorbell rang, and the

50

Spanish maid admitted Henry Feathers. Her faintly flushed appearance suggested that, in the brief time devoted to removing his coat, Feathers had managed to make some amorous gesture in her direction.

Lank hair was swept back from a face which, over the last decade, had grown pinker and plumper, then redder and flabbier. Feathers was on the verge of going to seed. The silk bow ties which he invariably affected had started to fray and grow greasy. The sellotape which held his horn-rimmed spectacles in place looked as though it was to become a permanency. And yet, the collapse of Feathers, who was not much over forty, seemed imminent, inevitable. It never quite happened. Now, as he made his way deliberately forward across the thick Turkey carpets of the Blores' drawing-room, it was fairly apparent that the previous two hours had been spent in El Vino's. But although the carefulness of his gait suggested a man who might be asked to give a urine specimen, and who was trying to walk down the straight white line in the police station, there was a solemnity in it which half recalled a respectful courtier processing to an Investiture.

Feathers was a joke figure to the Duncans. Neither Hughie nor Rachel had known before that he was a friend of the Blores'. Fleet Street was full of stories in which Feathers had behaved like a clown: drink and women usually coming into the set-piece anecdotes. The last time he had been sacked, he was alleged to have sent in his expenses, and claimed the cost of a night in a hotel with his editor's wife. Some spoilt the story by saying that his claim was queried; but no one generally disputed the genius of Feathers for fiddling expenses. It had been years since he paid for anything out of his own pocket. Continental holidays, visits to Newmarket, and evenings taking secretaries to the theatre could all be translated, when he got back to his typewriter, into expenditure incurred in the course of his journalistic endeavours.

Opinions differed as to how self-conscious the creation of the Feathers mythology had been. One thing was certain: it had done him no harm. However often he got the sack, he always appeared to be moving onwards and upwards. Even in periods when he was not actually employed by a newspaper, he had a genius for persuading publishers to advance him larger and larger sums of money to write books about the political scene. The possibility always flickered in Hughie's mind that Feathers was unaware of his comic status in the eyes of the world. For, although he was a man about whom

51

innumerable funny stories were told, he was not markedly humorous. In this, perhaps, he had something in common with Derek Blore. They were both men, it seemed to Hughie, that it would be impossible to take quite seriously. But, beneath a clownish exterior, perhaps they both nursed a wholly uncomic view of themselves, and a will – not ineffectual in either case – to succeed.

Met at parties or in bars, Feathers liked to drop the names of senior politicians, famous authors, members of the aristocracy. Almost everyone who heard these brags, the Duncans included, took his boasting with a pinch of salt. But, here, he seemed almost like a member of the household. When he bent over Priscilla's chair to kiss her, he said, 'Hullo, old girl,' and she smiled in a way which suggested relief to be in the company of an intimate after the strain of having to entertain strangers. The arrival of Feathers made the Duncans feel excluded. Derek he greeted with a squeeze of the arm. He kissed all the wives and, when he came to Rachel, he asked, rather brusquely, 'What are you doing here?'

'Rachel is here in a semi-official capacity,' said Derek.

'A profile?' Feathers asked. There was a faint air of condescension: like a visiting member of the Royal Family asking a woman in a wheel-chair about her handicrafts. 'What's that for – The *Observer?* The *Guardian?*'

Rachel told him.

Feathers made a few 'knowing' comments about the editor (a rumour that he was about to move on) but quickly broke them off before Rachel had the time to reply. He turned to Derek and said, 'No, but look' as though they were in the middle of an important conversation which everyone else in the room had interrupted. There was no doubting Feather's ability, when the need arose, to dominate any assembly he happened to be in.

'Any news from the hospital?'

'Hospital, old boy?' Derek's face darkened. The little conversations which had broken out around the room in defiance of Feathers unwillingly ceased. They all listened. There could not be much doubt that he had guessed that no one had heard the news he had to bring.

'That's why I'm rather late. We are going to have to reset the whole of tomorrow's front page.'

He spoke in a fruity, rather 'upper-crust' tone. A major-general announcing a plan of campaign to a War Cabinet: short bursts of sound from a heavy jowl, weighty beyond his years.

'Don't keep us in suspense, old boy,' said Derek, visibly rattled by the way in which this was becoming so much Feathers's show. 'Who the fucking hell's in the fucking hospital?'

'The fucking leader of your fucking party,' Feathers replied. The eyes twinkled with merriment at this crack, but his lips pursed with the semi-seriousness of the announcement. It was this kind of repartee which formed the stuff of the stories Feathers told about himself, yarns in which he invariably spoke the punch lines. It was fascinating to the Duncans to see one of the Feathers tall stories being concocted before their very eyes.

'Jack?' Derek was clearly dumbfounded.

'Unless you've changed your leader in the last five minutes.'

'Is it serious? What's the matter with Jack?' Priscilla intervened.

'Coronary thrombosis,' said Feathers. 'I'm amazed you hadn't heard. He was giving a speech at the Manchester Chamber of Commerce and blew a fuse.'

'This evening, this was?'

' 'Bout eight o'clock.'

'I don't believe it,' said Derek. 'This is disastrous.'

And yet, as everyone sat dumbfounded by the Feathers revelations, they all knew that, like most calamities in politics, it was not wholly disastrous. Jack and Derek had never seen eye to eye. It was said by journalists and commentators, Feathers among them, that Jack was not primarily a man of ideas: his great virtue as Leader was his ability to hold the different strands of the Party together, to inspire them to unity at the right moments. Now, with surely less than six months to go before a General Election, the Party would inevitably have to search about for a new leader. And no one in the room doubted that, although Derek had no chance of becoming Leader 'this time round', he ought, in his own interests, to 'throw his hat in the ring'.

A telephone interrupted the silence. While Priscilla went to answer it, Feathers advanced towards the drinks, and said, 'Am I offered any whisky in this house?' This rudeness was a part of his social behaviour that Feathers had mysteriously worked out.

'My dear *chap*,' said Derek.

'No, no. I can help myself,' said Feathers. This was overwhelmingly obvious. There was no nonsense about ice, which would have taken up valuable space in the glass. Only a very moderate amount of water was added to the generous fistful of Famous Grouse which Feathers awarded to himself.

'It's for you,' said Priscilla, returning to the room. She went over to the sofa and sat down, quite ashen. Hughie wished, in a moment of absurd fantasy, that he was the only person in the room with her. He wished that he could run over and throw his arms about her, and hug her: she looked so stately and vulnerable. There were tears in her great blue eyes.

'He's dead,' she eventually announced. 'He died about an hour ago.'

The MP and his wife, and the Sangsters, started to jabber embarrassingly. They made little character-assessments of their Lost Leader as though they were talking to the newspapers. They used clichés, but Hughie hardly heard them. Only every other word – 'tragedy' – 'very grim' – 'what a shame he was never Prime Minister' – floated into his brain. He was transfixed by the vision of Priscilla, in sorrow, on the sofa.

Feathers had moved over the room and was talking to Rachel. He appeared to be hinting that this death was something which he had himself foreseen. Hughie stared solely at Priscilla, but she did not return his gaze. She alone seemed capable of the dignity which the news of death demands.

'That was Jack's wife,' said Derek, coming back into the room. His face was alive with an unseemly excitement. He started to list the names of colleagues in the Shadow Cabinet.

'Poor Dorothy,' said Priscilla quietly.

'She was everything a politician's wife ought to have been...,' began Ted Sangster.

'Gerald already knows. I don't know about Tom. It's going to be on the late news. Gerald. I shall ring up Gerald,' said Derek.

'I think I ought to get down to the House,' said the colourless MP.

It was evidently a signal for the dinner party to be brought to a conclusion.

'I wish we'd had more chance to talk, and get to know each other,' said Priscilla to Rachel as they were going. 'And,' she added with what Hughie prayed was a studied casualness, 'and I'm so glad we've met,' when she touched his fingers on parting.

'Can we give you a lift?' Rachel asked Feathers. Everyone else was by now in overcoats. Derek, having waved perfunctorily at them all from the telephone, had, in the event, been the first to leave, swanning off in a taxi in the direction of the Shadow Chancellor's house in Chelsea. The Sangsters were going back to a hotel; the colourless ones to the House.

'I'll be all right,' said Feathers. He alone had made no gesture towards leaving. 'I'll stay and help wash up.'

It was only as they emerged into the piercingly cold dark mist that the Duncans recollected the Spaniards, who had knocked off about half an hour before. Such washing-up as remained – a few whisky glasses – could not have needed the assistance of Feathers. It was anyway unlikely that he was adept, even when sober, at this domestic function. But something prevented either of them from talking about it. Feathers had ceased, quite, to be so much of a joke.

As they were driving away Rachel said, 'I guess I was the last person to do an interview with the Leader of Her Majesty's Opposition.' She gave the title its full weight of irony, but there was an unmistakeable tone of triumph in her voice. Doubtless the glossy magazine for whom she had done the interview would 'bring it forward', and ask her to rewrite the introductory paragraphs to fit the lugubrious new situation.

'Very nice for you,' said Hughie, noticing with quiet distaste that she did not sense his tone. Only Priscilla had reacted to the news of this death in a remotely natural way. She had said, 'Poor Dorothy.' She had expressed at least a polite feeling of sympathy for Jack's widow. In the morning – and this sickened Hughie – they would all be poring over the obituaries and giving 'tributes' of their own. Everyone would have been saying what a fine Party Leader he had been, what a pity that he could not be the country's next Prime Minister. And the figures who were loudest in his praise would be those, like Derek Blore, who stood to advance their careers by this coronary failure in a northern hospital.

Hughie did not deceive himself. He had no sentimental attachment to the Leader of the Opposition. When he thought about him at all, it was usually as a faintly ridiculous figure, the photographs in newspapers being blended in his mind with the caricatures of cartoonists and satirists. But the inhumanity of everyone except Priscilla's reaction to this death made Hughie feel bleakly uncomfortable.

He knew that he could not possibly talk about this to Rachel. She would not understand what he was talking about. Her father, whom

55

he seldom met, had practised some religion, but, from Rachel's accounts, it had largely extended to dietary fuss and synagogue attendance. Even had she practised her faith there would be no reason for her to think of life beyond the grave. It was one of the great gulfs between them.

Hughie had not been a pious Christian for years. Only now and again was he able to find a church where they had not wrecked the liturgy. When Rachel fell in love with him, and he got married, he had been so caught up by the delights of it all, that had anyone suggested to him that religion was a barrier between him and his wife, he would have thought they were joking.

Nevertheless, for a number of reasons, he had more or less given up going to church since his marriage. This was partly because they lay late on Sunday mornings; partly, in the initial stages, in deference to Rachel, whose agnosticism found religious ritual unsympathetic. He did not feel he was missing much in these years of absenting himself from the increasingly maimed Anglican observances. He had never been sure how much he *actually* believed of the old verities. Now, as they drove back through the darkened streets of London, he contemplated this death, of a man he had never known, of a man by whose existence he was unaffected. He thought of Derek, whose gleaming ambitious eyes behind the spectacles hinted that he was a step closer towards becoming Prime Minister; and, if this were so, then all the people in the room were affected by it. They were his courtiers and hangers-on. Rachel, likewise, saw the death, not partly, but wholly in terms of her own personal ambitions. He stared at her self-confident profile as she parked the car now, and he felt vaguely terrified by how alien she seemed.

He knew that his reaction was irrational. The death of a public personage was inevitably to the benefit of their rivals and juniors. Derek and his mates rushing off to the House of Commons was no less absurd than Falstaff and Justice Shallow and Pistol and Bardolph all rushing to Westminster on hearing of the death of Henry IV. There was nothing modern about this. And yet the secularism of it all suddenly overwhelmed Hughie. Priscilla's 'Poor Dorothy' had at least suggested a heart. But no one's reaction had been (was he tight?) *solemn* enough.

'Are you going to sit there all night, or shall we go in?' Rachel was jangling the car keys. They both sat silently in the stationary car outside their house in Kensington.

'No, I'm coming in,' he said abstractedly.

He thought of the poignant music of The Dream of Gerontius and all those grand effects, and massed choirs and angelic voices were involved simply in the death of one old man. In Rachel's view, the Leader of the Opposition's heart had stopped beating, and he had ceased to exist. In Edward Elgar's view, his soul had begun its final journey to God: it went in the name of Princedoms and of Powers, of Thrones and Dominions, accompanied by its guardian angel to the Throne of Judgment; it glimpsed the beatific future before the purgation began.

'That was a very interesting evening indeed,' said Rachel. 'I hope you weren't too bored. You seemed to like Priscilla Blore, at any rate.'

'I don't know what you *mean!*' he hugged her and laughed. She often teased him about flirting with other women. At any one time, she had a list of 'rivals' with whom she taunted him. It was a game she played. This time as she said it, however, he had a chilling sense that, guiltily within his breast, and without his being able to do anything about it, a new love was dawning.

They both gazed about them at their own residence and were struck by how impoverished it seemed after the luxuriance of the Blores' Belgravia establishment. In fact, it was a comfortable enough little house in a mews off Kensington Church Street. There was a pleasant small sitting-room; a dining-room which Rachel used as a study, a couple of bedrooms. Most of the furniture was good, solid stuff, slightly too big for the place, which had been inherited from Hughie's father.

'Let's have a drink before we go to bed,' said Hughie.

'You can, I've drunk enough.'

As he helped himself to whisky, slowly, deliberately, he could hear his wife preparing for bed upstairs – a gurgle of taps, a flushing of waters, an opening and shutting of sliding wardrobe doors. He knew that she waited for him lovingly in the large double bed where so many happy nights had been spent. He knew, equally, that a great change had come upon him.

He switched on the turn-table and placed a gramophone record upon it.

*Sanctus fortis, Sanctus Deus,*
*De profundis clamor te:*

*Miserere, Judex meus,*
*Parce mihi, Domine . . .*

The swirling, repeated tones of Gerontius's soul on the point of death filled the house. Hughie felt they were a requiem, not only for the Leader of the Opposition, but for the deadness of his existence with Rachel. He had tried to put by the world of daydreams and romance which he had been inhabiting until he met her. The lonely evenings at concerts and the occasional visit to church, the memories of the Love of his Life; these all seemed more real to him now as he drank his whisky and listened to the music, than the stranger in his bed upstairs.

The 'real' feeling, the triumph of the heart over senses and 'Sense', was complete by the time his glass was empty and the record had finished. Extinguishing lamps, he staggered up the stairs and into his pyjamas without cleaning his teeth. He flopped down into bed, ready for sleep.

Rachel lay beside him, enchantingly pretty, her round, bare shoulders freckled against the white of her nightdress, her hair a brown fuzz spread against the pillow. She did not pretend to read. He knew from her expression that she wanted him to make love to her. In the circumstances, the marital routine was unavoidable. But afterwards, Hughie felt that even this, the sheer physical competence of it all, was flatly disillusioning. He could feel the room turning slightly as he lay silently with his wife's head on his pillow. He knew that she was asleep, glowing with sexual satiety. He knew that he should be the happiest man in London. He thought rather of the lonely beauty of Priscilla, and the doctrine of immortality.

# Five

Gingerly, over the space of ten weeks, the days had lengthened. Snowdrops, crocuses – at last, daffodils and narcissi had sprouted in the parks and gardens of the metropolis. The April novels were piled on the tables of Heywood Hill's Bookshop in Curzon Street. Next door, at the barber's, Hughie Duncan and Mr Van der Bildt sat in adjoining chairs. Since they did not know each other no greeting was exchanged between them. They each stared impassively ahead at their respective looking-glasses, vaguely aware of the supreme artistry and conversational skills of their barber, but each given up to interior reflection.

Mr Van der Bildt had just suffered an awkward interview at the Embassy. He was not often summoned there. More usually, the Professor, as his unnamed contact preferred to be known, met him on neutral ground; and they discussed any necessary business, or exchanged money, while lunching at a restaurant or walking in the Park.

Mr Van der Bildt had very little notion of what, precisely, the Embassy required. He supplied them with tapes, and photographic evidence concerning some twenty men. Some of them were eminent in public life. There were a couple of policemen, a judge, a headmaster. He had no political function, as he had stiffly needed to remind the Professor. He was a businessman. Among various commercial interests there were some which, of their nature, attracted clients who wished to be discreet. And a man who needed to be discreet had something to hide and could therefore be persuaded to pay to keep these matters a secret. Had it not been for various accidents of birth, and the discovery of a number of skeletons in Mr Van der Bildt's own cupboard, he would never have got sucked into doing this extra work on behalf of the Embassy. It terrified him. The stakes were too high. Let them concoct a political scandal if they liked, but keep his name out of it.

Three things had come to complicate the existence of Mr Van der Bildt. One was the manner in which the Opposition Party had rallied behind their new leader. One English Party was much like another, as far as They were concerned. That had been his opinion. Apparently he was wrong. In various crucial areas, the Embassy preferred the Party of Government to the Party of Opposition. South American grain, the price of base metals, and North Sea oil had all been mentioned in the Professor's staccato tones. They were hoping for an electoral defeat for the Opposition. Now that one of Mr Van der Bildt's clients, Billy Bunter, had risen to such a position of eminence in his party, this was one area where they could surely discredit the Opposition. But it would have to be done cautiously. There were, it was averred, other considerations.

There was, for instance, the embarrassment of Juri Kutuzov, congenitally indiscreet, inefficient, lazy and promiscuous; neither side in the great ideological conflict felt much desire to take responsibility for Juri. He was very small fry indeed. And yet, in so far as he was a ballet dancer, and in so far as his brushes with the London constabulary were of a sort to appeal to the vulgar Sunday newspapers, he had to be watched. Each side knew perfectly well that the other was paying Kutuzov to keep quiet. He was at present in Switzerland. An English 'lecturer' imprisoned without trial in Stettin had, by mutual compromise, been released. But the Embassy now wondered whether it might not be possible to kill two birds with one stone. The Professor's heavy well-tailored shoulders had shrugged. He had implied that he was merely the servant of the hare-brained schemes of his superiors. But this girl, with whom Billy Bunter was so unwisely involved. Might it not be possible to establish some link between her and Juri Kutuzov? They had been through all Billy Bunter's business interests. Unfortunately he had not sat on the board of any companies which had been involved in fraud; no bank accounts in assumed names, no bankruptcies, no markedly dishonest dealings could be attributed to him. The Embassy found it hard to interest themselves in hanky-panky, pure and simple. Were the Opposition Party to win the election, it would do them no harm to lose a Secretary of State through yet another minor sexual scandal. The public were sated with sexual scandals. Any Government could afford to lose the occasional Cabinet Minister through indiscretion of this nature. The flurry of excitement it caused never lasted more than a few weeks. But the hint of a 'failure in security' was a different question.

Mr Van der Bildt had tried to point out that Bernadette was not the woman for this purpose. She was quite amazingly dim. Nor was she even very good at her job. The Professor had asked what objection there could be to her *meeting* Juri when he was brought over to London. They could at least *try*.

Mr Van der Bildt did not like it. Not one bit. The Embassy could have no real idea of what risks they took. His had been a simple existence until his diplomatic involvements began. When he was obliged to take risks in his own chosen avocation, he had heart and nerve and sinew to do it. He had been importing obscene material into the country for the previous ten years; and this was never without its risks, particularly the material relating to children. There had been commercial risks too: he had a chain of shops and cinemas, and that sort of enterprise, during rough economic periods, is not kept going without an iron nerve. And, of course, he was prepared to dabble a little with blackmail, as well as with what the law called 'immoral earnings'. This was all, however, in the way of business. Juri Kutuzov was not. Van der Bildt foresaw, with the true businessman's eye, that the combination of Juri and Bernadette would be disastrous. Disaster, of course, of one kind or another, was precisely what the Embassy wanted and demanded. But why, oh why, did it have to involve him?

He looked at his own face in the glass as the man rubbed the sides of his head with a towel. The blue eyes, red face and unusually long nose all had a faintly military bearing, still, though it was fifteen years since he had been in the South African Army. *One day*, his frightened eyes, staring back at him, seemed to say, *one day, Van der Bildt, you will go too far.*

A schoolmaster had said it to him, thirty-six or thirty-seven years before, in a pleasant suburb of Johannesburg. How true it had been. In one way or another, he had been going too far ever since, always with the heady sense that he would get away with it. He had risen to the rank of major very young; too young, some said. The sexual indiscretions, and the very minor embezzlements and frauds in which he had been involved, were never openly discovered. He still did not know who it was who had spied on him and found out. Once confronted with the choice, however, he felt that he had no alternative. Either he would be exposed, or he would be available to give information.

61

The proposition had been put in so very polite a fashion that he had genuinely supposed himself to be working for the British. He had left the army when his father died, and taken a directorship, having sold the family firm, in a diamond company. Every now and again, he was 'approached' in this new job and asked for information. He always handed it over. They wanted quite specific information: the exact state of certain mines; labour conditions, profits, percentages, forecasts for the future. Sometimes he was asked questions about gold or about oil; usually diamonds. He always gave them an answer.

It was only when the chance came of moving to London that he realised that he was not spying for the British. This fact now seemed fantastical to him, but it was true. The trickle of information which he had been giving over the years would have been enough to damn any future chance of life, let alone wealth, in South Africa.

The pornographic interests – using interest in its purely commercial sense – had developed 'naturally' after his London posting. It was obvious that it was an area of expansion. London was set fair to rival Paris and Amsterdam, and become the porno-capital of Europe. It was foolish not to cash in on this fact. A judicious purchase of down-at-heel properties, and a bold disregard for import laws, made Van der Bildt's fortune in a couple of years.

By then, he knew who 'they' were. When directorships came his way in the City, he was obliged to take them. 'They' insisted. The information which he leaked to them was all highly detailed and, for the most part, trivial. He knew by now that he was technically involved in the world of espionage. But it did not feel like that. Only the latest episode of Juri Kutuzov had begun to smack of cloak and dagger.

Mr Van der Bildt turned his eyes in the glass a little to the left and watched the face of Hughie Duncan. It seemed to Van der Bildt a smug, very English face. When the barber said things to Duncan, he drawled non-committal replies which somehow passed as conversation. When *his* barber spoke to him, Van der Bildt felt called upon to make an effort.

'Looks like an Election, then, sir.'

'More or less inevitable,' said Van der Bildt.

'We had the Home Secretary in here yesterday morning, no, I tell a lie, day before yesterday.'

'Is that so?' Clearly the wrong thing to say. As the most distinguished barbers in London, they found nothing to boast about the simple fact of cutting the Home Secretary's hair.

'And he seemed,' the man ignored Van der Bildt's naive interruption, 'raring to go. Not that he would say, of course, sir.'

'So you think the Government will win?'

'Anybody's guess, sir. They say in Ladbroke's down the road that it will be the closest run election for years. We might even find ourselves with a coalition, sir, or – heaven forbid – another hung parliament.'

'Yes,' said Hughie's barber, catching up with his colleague's conversation, 'we had the Home Secretary in yesterday morning, and if you ask me, sir, he's a worried man.'

'Oh yes.'

'They're not going to have it easy, sir. Mind you, since the Opposition have only just got a new leader, we're none of us too sure, are we, sir?'

'No.'

'That was a very interesting leadership contest, wasn't it, sir?'

'Mmm.'

'It was your wife, wasn't it, sir, who wrote the article – was it in the *FT* or the *Economist*?'

'Which one?'

'There were a couple. One about the late leader of the Opposition – and profiles of all the candidates in the leadership election. *Economist!*' The barber laughed at his own absent-mindedness and named the actual paper where Rachel's articles had appeared. 'I shall forget my own name next.'

Hughie had his hair cut at this establishment regularly. He had not realised before that they connected him with Rachel.

'Yes, it would appear that Mr Derek Blore is a man to watch, sir. Not this time, but the next time, would you say, sir?'

'Mmm.'

'Your wife was really quite taken with him, if I got her right, sir?'

Hughie smiled, just the right smile; completely non-committal.

'His policies, that is to say, sir . . .'

The haircut proceeded at a stately pace. The back of Hughie's neck was once more slightly cold, as the powder was squirted on to it. He was handed the napkin himself, a part of the ritual he never quite understood. They had already wiped him, brushed him, scraped and preened him so much that to rub himself further with the face towel would have seemed superfluous. On the other hand, not to use it at all would have been churlish. He usually gave his neck the briefest flick with the towel before handing it back to the barber.

He paid the extremely large sum of money demanded by that establishment and was soon standing outside in Curzon Street in the spring sunshine. Shortly afterwards, Mr Van der Bildt followed him out, and crossed the street. Van der Bildt disappeared through the low arcade which led to Shepherd Market. Hughie consulted a pocket watch which was suspended from a leather strap in the lapel of his tweed coat. The haircut had taken twenty-seven minutes. It was 10.27. He walked briskly up through Mayfair in the direction of Bond Street, with the compulsive, earnest steps of a man in a dream. He had long ago ceased to ask himself whether there was any sense in this ceaseless pursuit, these pointless perambulations. He moved automatically, hopelessly. A day in which he did not glimpse Priscilla at all had become intolerable to him.

There were, of course, such days: Saturdays and Sundays when she was out of town; or, worse, when he and Rachel pointlessly drove to see friends. There were painful days when, however hard he tried, he simply failed to 'sight' her. But at the beginning or end of most days there was a chance of a glimpse at least. And on other days, like this morning, there was really quite a stroke of good fortune.

He had got to Priscilla's front door in South Eaton Place at about 9.30, having telephoned to his office to say that he had a dental appointment and would not be there until after luncheon. He had only to wait in the back of his taxi for about six minutes before she emerged. For a horrible moment, he thought she might cross the road, ask the waiting cab if it was hired, spot Hughie, and wonder what on earth he was doing there.

With a part of himself, he wanted this to happen. At the very least, a lie could have been concocted, and he could then have said, 'But, please, do use this taxi: where are you going?' And she would say where, and he would say, 'Astonishing! I'm going that way too, we can go together.'

Alternatively, had he been feeling bolder, he could have used the discovery to declare himself there and then. 'I have been waiting outside your front door merely hoping for a glimpse of you. I love you besottedly' – and here she would put her arms round him, and perhaps cry a little.

None of this had, however, happened. She had hailed a taxi almost at once and Hughie, feeling absurdly like a man in a film, had asked his own driver to follow her.

Both taxis had lurched north-eastwards until the SW became merely W1. Priscilla had been dropped in Piccadilly on the corner of Old Bond Street. She had fluttered a five-pound note through the window of her carriage. Hughie, keeping his distance behind her, had followed her up the street, waited, breathless with adoration, as she had sometimes paused to look in the window of a gallery. Glimpsing the pictures for himself a few moments afterwards, he was slightly disappointed that she had not, particularly, paused by *nice* pictures. The ones of horses seemed to have engaged her longest attentions.

To walk up Bond Street, on a bright morning of spring, with Priscilla in view all the time! He could hardly believe his luck, his happiness. She was dressed in a pale blue coat and skirt, of a light linen material, and she was carrying a rather large black handbag. Yesterday, she had been wearing boots. Today, it was the dark blue court shoes but with (unless his eyes deceived him) a new pair of tights, blue again, but paler than the suit. A pretty yellow silk scarf flapped at her neck in the morning breeze. He did not see her face; only her wonderful blonde hair, blown by the wind invitingly in his direction.

At about ten to ten she reached a doorway and disappeared. When he dared to come up to it, he realised that she had gone in to have her hair done. It was the second time in ten days. He had not followed her the first time; merely noticed that she had had it done when he spotted her (a chance sighting, doubly exciting) at the theatre.

'Isn't that Priscilla Blore?'

'I didn't see her.' It spoilt the romance if Rachel could see Priscilla too. They were in the crowded bar of a theatre during the interval.

'That man's not her husband, that's for sure,' added Rachel, crudely. It was a remark that had provoked in Hughie a cold sweat. He praised heaven that he had been able to answer back, truthfully, 'No, it's her brother.'

'How come you know that?'

'I was at school with him.'

'You were at school with him? Hughie, you are extraordinary. Why don't we go over and say hello?'

'Because I don't know him, and besides it would be embarrassing.'

'You were at Eton with him and yet it's embarrassing to say hullo

65

to him when you meet him in the theatre. How come you never said you were at Eton with Priscilla's brother?'

Hughie, in common with many people who had been educated at that school, never used the phrase 'at Eton'. He saw nothing wrong with doing so; it was simply not something he said, it sounded oddly to him when his wife said it.

'It's a large place,' he had said, 'anyway, that was the bell. Act Two in five minutes. Enjoying the play?'

'It's so *funny*. That bit where the...' She repeated what she considered the funniest episode of Act One. Hughie was normally capable of enjoying comedies. Opinions of this particular play had been golden. Tonight he had been unable to enjoy himself. But the glimpse of Priscilla had transformed the evening at the theatre into a semi-religious experience.

He knew that Rachel had noticed that he had been 'funny' of late. She was not slow to notice these things, or to comment upon them. She was a warm, outgoing, friendly person, and she loved him. He knew these things and they pained him. He could not bear it if her warmth and common sense and her love barged in, as it were, on his feelings for Priscilla. She had kept up her teasing for a few days after the Blores' dinner party ('pining for her ladyship' had been the phrase which had made him flinch the most). But then she had got absorbed in her work again, and been pleased by the amount of attention that her series of 'Tomorrow's Men' had received. He would tell her what the barber had said. It would please her.

As he stood in Curzon Street, then, at 10.27 a.m. he realised that he had ample time to walk back to Old Bond Street and watch Priscilla come out of the hairdresser. As he did so, he thought of his wife with a great wave of disappointment, pity and contempt. It was impossible not to *like* Rachel, and yet the more he liked her, the less he wanted to be married to her. Why had his married life, hitherto serene, become suddenly intolerable? Was it just because he had fallen in love with another woman? He felt there was more to it than that. Rachel, he realised, had never allowed him any *privacy*. He did not mean by that 'freedom to commit adultery'. He meant a sort of mental space in which he could be entirely alone with his own emotions. Until he married, he had never reckoned up how much time he spent, entirely alone, daydreaming or listening to music, or walking silently along the streets of London. Rachel only knew about his solitary visits to concerts, his solitary meals in restaurants. She

66

did not know the half of his solitariness. She had persuaded herself that he was lonely, and of course there had been some truth in this. What neither of them had realised was how much he depended on his solitude. It was not merely that he liked reading or playing gramophone records, or walking, or doing anything else which was best done alone. It was that he needed solitude in the same way that he needed sleep. It refreshed him. For over ten years, he had been besotted with love for Jane, and for nine of those years she had been married and he had not seen her. The love was an expansive necessary part of his inner life. When he married, he had put it aside. He had told himself that it was unhealthy and fantastical. Doubtless it was. But he could not live without this inner life. In some nebulous way, Rachel was the enemy of his independence, his solitude. It was as though his thoughts could only function when locked alone in an inner chamber: but that she had insisted on taking the key of his spiritual sanctuary. It was not that she intrusively burst in upon those thoughts. Since he spoke less and less, she could not possibly know the half of them. It was merely that she was *there*.

He knew that, if one devoted one's life to Romance, marriage was the cardinal sin. And he had committed it. Marriage was for the common-sensical, it was for those who took short views, or no views at all; it was for those for whom life was largely a matter of meals and clothes, orgasm and real estate. For anyone who nurtured Emotion as the centre of existence, and who felt the permanent pull of an unseen, spiritual or cerebral world, the quotidian triviality of married intimacy was bound to be intolerable. So, in practice, it invariably was. Not only were the married lives of most poets and musicians intolerable. So too were the lives of religious mystics if they made the mistake of getting married. As often as not, this category of person sensibly opted for a celibate existence. But there were enough cases of unhappily married mystics to substantiate Hughie's conviction.

He was neither a mystic nor an artist. He was merely a man with an overdeveloped inner life. He was a junior disciple of Romance, he knew it. For Rachel's affection, her intelligence, her good cooking, he ought to be, was, extremely grateful. When he thought of her handsome alien face, crinkled with amusement at his disgruntled features, he felt twisted with the most painful, affectionate pity. But he paced on obsessively, nonetheless, towards Old Bond Street to await the emergence of the goddess.

The intent perusal of silver forks and cream jugs arranged on blue

67

velvet took up no more than the next eighteen or nineteen minutes. His eyes only dwelt on the silver in the shop window fleetingly. They were concentrated firmly on the reflection, in the glass, of the opposite corner of the street, which gave him a perfect view of the hairdresser's doorway.

When she came out, he felt as though he were falling in love with her all over again. He had not, of course, forgotten what she looked like, in the forty or so minutes since he last set eyes on her. But he thought, as she stood there in the sunshine, that he had never taken her beauty in before.

The hairdresser had streaked her hair with platinum 'lights', the silvery blonde providing the perfect complement to her large blue eyes which he could not resist turning to look at across the narrow street. When their eyes met, her face creased into a magnificent smile and her eyes arched with surprise.

'Hullo! Nice to see a publisher so busy of a morning,' she said.

'Priscilla.'

'Isn't it a heavenly day? I've just spent the earth having my hair done, isn't it awful? You've just done the same by the look of you.'

Rather to his amazement, her long white fingers had stretched forward and were touching the bristly new-shorn back of his head. 'Makes you look *frightfully* old-fashioned.'

'Sorry,' he managed to inject irony into his voice. So long as comedy could be sustained on life's surface, Romance could seethe undisturbed beneath.

'*Hate* long hair on men,' she said, as they swung along. 'You'd be amazed at the length of hair on some of Julian's friends. And Kate's last boyfriend was an *ape*; hair *every*where, still I think we are through the worst.'

Whether hair fashions in general, or unsuitable consorts for her daughter, she did not specify.

'I'm so worried about Kate, though. She's with this rather beastly family in Paris and I don't know what to do about it; they don't give her any time off, they overwork her . . .'

'Can't she just leave?' He did not want her to be talking of her family. He wanted them to drift along in a silent, sultry, suggestive haze of unresolved emotions, or else to be caught up in a conversation of operatic emotionalism. And yet, every word she spoke, however trivial it might look when written down, filled Hughie with a happiness which it would not abuse language to call ecstatic.

68

'She can't leave because the family are friends of some very good friends of ours in the French Board of Trade . . .'

He didn't like that 'ours'.

'I saw you with your brother the other evening,' he said.

'At the play? Wasn't it a *hoot*. I laughed myself silly.' She specified for mention the very scene that had amused Rachel so deeply. 'You should have come and had a drink with us at the bar. Were you at school with Rory? I forget.'

'We overlapped – but we didn't know each other.'

'All the same . . .'

For a brief second, he could see that she was running out of things to say, and that she might, at any moment, jump into a taxi and go off to Belgravia again.

'Got a moment,' he asked, 'to look round this exhibition?'

He hovered in the doorway of a gallery in Cork Street. He had been ambling quite arbitrarily. The gallery was chosen with equal disregard for subject matter.

'Kinetic art? Perhaps I'm wrong. Perhaps you're not old-fashioned,' she laughed.

'Aren't there some pictures as well?'

The gallery was tiny, little more than a small shop, and the prickly young pansy sitting at the white-topped desk in the corner greeted them as though they were expected to buy the objects and pictures on display. He thrust a typed 'catalogue' into Priscilla's hand.

'D'you know those slinky toys?' she asked.

'Slinky?' Hughie didn't.

'Sort of coil things. You put them at the top of the stairs and they sort of slither down on their own one stair at a time. Rather fun. Julian had a great craze for them at one time; they get broken very easily.'

'No, I've never seen them.'

'That bit of sculpture over there looks a bit like one of them when it's been bust. D'you know, I think it *is*.' They went over to examine it. 'It *is* one, Hughie. I don't believe it.' She spoke without any sense of shyness. The young man hovered at his desk, smiling contemptuously at the philistines who could not recognise art when they saw it.

'Fifteen *hundred* pounds,' she whispered to Hughie, full of amusement, and as she did it, she leant towards him and some of her hair, only a few strands of it, very faintly brushed against his face. He

69

knew that he was blushing terribly and that he could not really speak any more. He felt so childishly happy in her presence that he was not *thinking* about anything. But, in so far as he was forming impressions, they were that she sensed his adoration, and rather liked it. He sensed the possibility, too wonderful to absorb, still less to contemplate, that she might fall in love with him.

After a while, they both started to laugh at the metallic, widely spaced and overpriced objects on display in the gallery. They perhaps only spent five minutes looking at them, but when they were outside on the pavement again, Hughie felt that a new intimacy had developed between them. Nothing momentous had been said. But he felt it was mutually recognised that he had stumbled into the gallery, not because he was a follower of kinetic art, but because he wanted to prolong his encounter with her.

They stood now and looked into each other's faces, he entranced, she smiling.

'Time for a drink?' he tried to keep earnestness out of his tones as he said it.

'I *mustn't*. As you can imagine, things are positively *frantic* at home. Poor old Derek hasn't slept for two nights.'

It was double dutch to him. It wounded him bitterly that poor old Derek was being brought into his idyll to wreck it. An image of the politician's face, frog-like and vaguely obscene, flashed before his inner eye.

'I'm going to have a drink anyway,' he said. 'Just a quick one.'

'This is frightfully naughty.'

It appeared that she was, after all, consenting. It was days since he had read *The Times* properly, or listened to the news, or taken in anything that Rachel was saying about the political situation. The Government was having 'a rough ride'. In two all-night sittings, the Energy and Transport Bill had come close to being defeated in its first reading and only the tattered support of Celtic nationalists, Independents, Liberals and others was keeping the Prime Minister in Downing Street. The Opposition, under its new leader, was doing well. He had been elected in the end after a three-cornered fight and got the necessary number of votes after the second ballot. In the first ballot, Derek had got twenty-three votes, a derisively small number, according to most commentators, but enough, according to others, to show that his future in the Party was to be taken seriously.

Hughie knew about this, but only in the vaguest terms. It meant nothing to him. In so far as it preoccupied Priscilla, and threatened to sweep her into an unapproachably 'important' sphere of life, he could not bear to contemplate it, so the mind blotted it out.

Outside the pub, although it was still hardly warm enough, office workers were mingling with tourists at tables set out on the pavement. Inside, it was comparatively empty. Priscilla asked for a large vodka and tonic, Hughie drank whisky.

'We're all desperately hoping the Government won't collapse until the autumn. It would be too tedious if we have to spend June electioneering,' she said. 'We've planned to go over to France in July, and rescue Kate from this frightful family. But we can't do it until Julian's term is over. Then we're going to drive down to Avignon for a week, and then on to the coast. If there's an election I just know it will all be cancelled, or I shall have to go without Derek; and I hate driving long distances on my own.'

He could not be receiving clearer signals that she was wholly committed to her family, to her husband's career, to a way of existence which completely excluded his devotion. And, at the same time, her eyes and her smile seemed to be *allowing* him to love her; teasing him, almost, with the thought that there might exist a magic area where his devotion would not be despised. Still, he was unable to be rational. He basked simply in her company. In the long hand, and the wrist which clattered with silvery bangles as it held her icy vodka glass, some three and a half inches away from his own hand.

'It was a pity you and your wife came on that ghastly evening when Jack died,' she said. 'I feel we didn't get a chance to talk. If there's a moment during the summer you must come down and stay in the country.'

'Won't you be in France?'

'Not for more than three weeks. Then we'll be in Herefordshire.'

'At Great Willerton?'

'Willerton St Leonard's. We have this nice house three or four miles away from Mummy. Used to be the rectory when I was a little girl. It's sad that they are selling all these old places, but when it came up for sale we felt we simply had to buy it. We couldn't afford it, of course, but I don't know how we would exist without it now. Derek and I are getting too old for London.'

There seemed something worse than an absurdity, almost a wickedness, about her pretence to be the same age as her husband. Derek was surely over fifty. She could not possibly be more than

71

thirty-five. The daughter, now working as an au-pair in Paris, did nothing to shake this conviction. He did not know why it mattered. But he wanted her to be as young as possible.

'My wife isn't a great country-lover,' he said.

'We'd try not to bore her. It would do her good. *Do* bring her down. Tell her I suggested it, won't you?'

To his horror, he found that she had managed to finish her drink, and was standing up.

'*Wonderful* to see you, Hughie,' she said. Were they going to kiss? He was not sure that he could quite bear their first kiss to be a trivial little thing in a public bar. He merely waved a confused sort of blessing, and said to her, 'I'll stay here and have a Scotch egg, I think.'

'Don't forget to tell Rachel. She's very welcome.'

Hughie felt crushed, stunned, by the weight of emotion which hung over him when she had disappeared. He did not want to be seen to follow her. But, as soon as she had gone, he did follow, at a discreet distance. He saw her stretch an arm in the air. Obedient to her whim, a taxi pulled up almost at once, and bore her off into the lunch-time traffic of Piccadilly.

# Six

As the taxi drove along, Priscilla felt buoyed up and pleased – by the vodka, by the hair-do, and by her encounter with Hughie. She liked men to fall in love with her, and had enough self-confidence to handle it all decorously and good-humouredly. There was in her nature both a tremendous toughness and a deep ordinariness which made her the perfect politician's wife. She had known so many people who were incapable of dealing with good looks. The knowledge that they were beautiful made them retreat into a Garbo-like shell, or worse, to be brazenly conceited. Others, bored by the continuous and flattering attention which the accidents of nature guaranteed them, deliberately allowed their beauty to *go*. One could easily spoil the nicest looks: a failure ever to be quite clean; an excessive indulgence in food, alcohol or cigarettes; a persistent inelegance of wardrobe; best, a combination of all these things could reduce the handsomest features within a matter of years to the happy position of being presentable at parties without the risk of a single 'attempt'.

Priscilla's generosity of nature, combined with a perfectly controlled vanity, would have made this line of retreat impossible. She had been made beautiful. It was her duty to keep her appearance *up*. And it was the necessary consequence of it, that men would enjoy her beauty and fall in love with her more easily than if she had bad breath, a double chin and spots. As it happened, her good looks did not damage her life-long dedication to the task of 'being kind to Mr Blore'. In this morning's encounter she felt she had struck a great blow for the cause. Hughie would inevitably go home and implore his nice American wife to write more nice things about Derek. And the more friendly publicity he received in the coming months, the better.

He had not done well in the leadership election. Nor had he done so badly that he could be dismissed altogether. When he threw his full support behind the candidate who would almost certainly be the country's next Prime Minister, there was a dogged common sense, an admirableness in Derek's position. Many people would have noticed its eirenical implications. It was not a concession of defeat. On the contrary, it showed that he had his eye on an important Cabinet post.

*Ladies and Jantlemen, we're going to try that chorus again.*

She knew by now how passionately ambitious the Lord High Executioner was: that nothing would stand in his way. It did no harm to her vanity to recognise that she was 'coming up in the world'. It amused her considerably. Long ago, in the government of Lord Palmerston, her ancestors had been briefly 'powers in the land'. The rewards of it all had been money, and a peerage, and a good marriage, and Willerton Abbey. In the four generations since, the family had sunk into pleasant obscurity. Much of the money had disappeared. Elder sons had continued to inherit Willerton and make occasional appearances in the House of Lords, though her brother, the present holder of the title, spent most of his time at the merchant bank where he worked, and her father's last speech to his peers had been in 1952 when he had made a brief and characteristic campaign for 'a lavatory in every lay-by'.

How odd it was that her quixotic desire to be kind to Mr Blore should mean once more that a member of her family would be having to do with affairs of state.

She sighed, thinking of Kate's misery in Paris, and of Julian's last letter from school. For most of Priscilla's waking hours were devoted not to her beauty, nor to the men who fell so easily in love with her, nor to Mr Blore, but to these children. Childless people found it tedious that parents should be unable to prevent themselves from talking endlessly about their children. They talked endlessly because they thought endlessly, *felt* endlessly. She had a great deal of emotional energy, and poured it out prodigally to friends and husband and family. But what she poured out to the rest of the human race was merely the left-over trickle of affection, preoccupation and obsession that she felt for these two individuals.

'Whereabouts in South Eaton Place, my lovely?' asked the taxi-driver.

She told him the number, ferreted in her purse for another five pound note and realised that, since leaving the house, buying cigarettes and sitting under the dryer, she had parted with nearly £50.

Closing the clasp of her handbag with a click, she was about to put her key in the lock when she realised that an extraordinary-looking young woman was standing outside the house. Most unsuccessfully

74

hennaed hair lankly hung around a fat face whose poor complexion no amount of make-up could conceal. Heavily mascaraed eyes and bright-red thin little lips suggested the tart. So did the laddered fishnet tights which showed over the cheap boots and beneath the green PVC mackintosh. They did not usually hover for trade in that part of London. Priscilla thought instantly that this girl might have something to do with Derek, but dismissed the notion because she looked so cheap. A huge number of the politicians known to the Blores had the weirdest and most sordid sex lives. Priscilla had long ago made up her mind that, if Derek were no exception to what seemed such a common phenomenon, she would have to live with it and go on being kind to Mr Blore. The numbers who got into the newspapers through some silly indiscretion or another were only the smallest percentage. She knew that. In the previous government, of which Derek was a Junior Minister, there had been two practising homosexuals, at least five habitués of brothels in Paris or London, two men and one woman who were known to be having love affairs of a more emotional nature while keeping their marriages going for the sake of public appearances. There had even been a Secretary of State, well-known to everyone, whose chief diversion had been riding about naked on a tandem with the divorced wife of a duke.

These things must be taken in the stride of a politician's wife; and, though Derek had a reputation which was boringly impeccable, Priscilla was perfectly prepared for the day when she knew that he had something to hide. But this little scrap of a thing outside her house was not that thing. She felt certain.

'Can I help you?' Priscilla asked.

'I'm looking for Mr Blore,' said the girl.

'He's very busy,' said Priscilla. 'Have you an appointment? It's more usual to see him at the House of Commons, if it's a matter of business.'

'It's about me stamps,' said Bernadette. 'I've just got married, see, and I'm worried about the stamps.'

'Do you live in Wheatbridge.'

'You what?'

'Do you live in Mr Blore's constituency?'

'Hackney,' said Bernadette. 'I live in Hackney.' The perfect poise and smiles of Priscilla were frightening; and her good looks made you feel a mess.

'Well, shouldn't you go to your own MP if you are worried about something? Why bother Mr Blore about it?'

'I think he'll see me if you ask him,' said the girl archly.

'You'd better come in.'

The two women stood in the carpeted hall. From the back of the house, they could hear Derek's voice, either speaking on the telephone, or addressing his secretary, Edna Philips.

'Quite imparrative,' he was saying, 'to get inflation down, to get unemployment down, to get public spending down, before we can start spending *again* in all those great areas that have been neglected for so long...'

He had been speaking in this vein for weeks. Priscilla recognised it as one of the hazards of a 'run up' to the General Election.

'I'll get him for you,' she said quietly, and then called out, '*Darling*! Someone for you!'

'Who is it?'

'A young woman!'

'I'm varry varry busy!' he called back.

'What's your name?' Priscilla turned to Bernadette and smiled.

'Bernadette Woolley – well, Bernadette Kutuzov now.'

'Mrs Kutuzov!' called Priscilla.

Derek flung open his study door and faced his wife. 'I'm sorry, Edna and I have an enormous amount...' When he saw Bernadette, he blushed crimson and was reduced to an immediate silence.

'Hullo, there,' said Bernadette.

'I'm not sure if we've met before,' he hedged. He stared rather desperately at Priscilla. What had she already been told? What had she guessed?

Since the Leadership contest, in which he had come modestly before the public eye, Derek had made a resolution. He would no longer visit Hackney. He would see how things went. If he found that he could not get by without the gratification which only schoolboy shorts, and a cane, could provide, then some casual arrangements might occasionally be risked. But he had suddenly panicked about Bernadette. As yet, he had told himself, she did not know who he was. Sooner or later, however, she would suspect something. He had decided to abandon her forthwith, and without explanation. Punctilious, always, on his visits to her Hackney abode, he had never carried so much as a cheque book which would disclose his identity; no credit card, no ticket from a dry-cleaner's would ever be found had she gone through his pockets. How then ... how the *hell*?

He looked at Priscilla, tall and amused, whose features were screwed up into a mixture of curiosity and apology, as though to say: '*Tried* to get rid of her for you.'

Momentarily, Derek was frozen. He felt so suddenly weary that he might collapse. After two all-night sittings in the House, and a morning dictating letters and speeches, he was anyway in a shaky condition. Now his stomach heaved with fear and all the hairs on the back of his neck stood up. This was the worst of nightmares: Bernadette in Belgravia. The most respectable, the least respectable sides of his life clashed together, noisy cymbals. Bernadette stood beside Priscilla. He was afraid as he had never felt fear before. This was not the exquisite, artificial, toy fear for which he had left cash sums on Bernadette's dressing table week after week over the previous few years. It was a terror which threatened his whole political future, his reason for existence.

'It's me Social Security stamps,' said Bernadette. 'I come to ask your advice. I been to the offices in Hackney, and there's this Paki, see. He gives me all these forms and that, but you don't always know what they mean . . .'

This at least was a way in. The mention of 'Social Security' allowed Derek to fall back into a more or less public self. He would be 'the good constituency man', a reliable figure, 'good with people': a figure who, for all his luxurious lifestyle and economic expertise, still kept the common touch.

'Ah, yas. Social Security. Always causing problems, isn't it? Leave us, my dear. I'll talk to this young lady in the dining-room.'

Priscilla shrugged, and walked up the stairs with a flounce and a giggle.

'Have we had the pleasure of having met before?' Derek was asking in a loud voice. 'You have been to my weekly surgery perhaps? You must forgive me. I haven't slept for fifty-one hours.'

'What a one!' said Bernadette, as she followed him into the dining-room. It did not occur to her that all this sleep might have been missed in ways other than in the pursuit of pleasure.

'I didn't come to no surgery,' she added.

'I thought you might have done. Do you know that, in the last twelve months alone, over a thousand people have passed through my surgery? You just can't remember all the faces.'

'I been to the clinic,' she said, affronted that he should imply a knowledge of her medical history. She knew when they said it was all anonymous that they was lying, but she wondered how Billy Bunter had pried into it.

'You'd better come in and sit down and explain your difficulty.' For they still hovered in the dining-room doorway, conversing for the benefit of eavesdroppers. He drew up a Sheraton chair for her by the glistening mahogany table. He saw her gazing about her at the épergne and the silver candlesticks on the sideboard; at the oil paintings, and the thick velvet curtains. They were intimidating to her, and that put him in an advantageous position. He decided to be firm.

'I do not know how you came to have my address, nor my name,' he said. 'I assume that you've come for money. That I will give to you. That must be the end of the matter. If you bother me in the future, I shall call the police and I can assure you that you would be in very bad trouble.'

He sweated a lot as he said these words. His shirt and jacket clung to his shoulders and he could feel a little flood of perspiration cascading from his brow and temples. But he was pleased with his performance. She looked blank.

'I haven't come for money. I've come for Social Security. You see, Juri don't understand it either, being foreign, even though he gets *his* little bit of benefit. I kept telling you though you wouldn't listen,' she suddenly sounded rather cross. 'I haven't paid my stamps and I don't want to go to prison and I thought how since you was who you was you might be able to get it all sorted out nice and proper like.'

Not fooled by this sort of talk, Derek continued. 'There was absolutely no need to come to me about this matter. There are perfectly good channels by which inquiries can be made about National Insurance, which is what I take it is bothering you. If, in addition, you require assistance – unemployment benefit, rent rebate and so on, you only have to ask for them in the proper way and through the proper channels.'

'But you said you'd help,' she whined. 'I can't get on with the Paki. He'll ask me why I haven't been buying my stamps all these years and then he'll find out where I live.'

'Come now,' said Derek. 'You must have managed to save up quite a lot. I have paid you £50 a week now for several years. You are not going to pretend to me that I have been your only client. I should think that at the most conservative estimate you have been making two or three hundred pounds a week. At least that sum. You can't have spent it all, now, can you? Now, if you're so behind with your National Insurance contributions, all you need to do is go to the relevant office and *say so*. They will allow you time to pay any sums you owe, though probably you are in a position to pay them a capital sum.'

She blinked at him uncomprehendingly.

'I never made that much money,' she said.

'I'm afraid that's impossible to believe.'

'Stan'd have murdered me if I'd have kept it,' she blurted out. 'I don't want to be doing this job, not now I'm married, even if it was Stan as arranged for us to meet. But I need to have paid my stamps. Say I go along to a shop and ask for a job: they're going to want to see my cards from me last job. And then I'll have to go back to the Paki and that would mean being sent to prison.'

'Wait a moment,' said Derek, 'You are telling me that, all these years I have been coming to see you, you have been paying the money back to a *man*?

'It was Stan as told me where you was living,' she said simply.

'Stan did, did he?'

'Mr Costigano,' she added, deferentially, as if the use of the Christian name had been presumptuous.

Derek felt the gates of the cage click. He was trapped. And, for the first time since he had gone to Bernadette, he wondered at his own extraordinary folly. For years now, he had led this double life with such correctness, such panache, that it had never crossed his mind that, all along, someone knew his secret. Mr Costigano, Stan, loomed up out of the mist and threatened to destroy everything.

'He made us get married,' she trembled. 'I didn't want to. I'd only met him over a couple of drinks, like I'd met a lot of gentlemen,' she said.

'I can well understand.'

'Funny really, when you think. All those fellas, and the one man in the world I've never been touched by is my own husband.'

Derek was prepared to concede that life was full of ironies, but he could not understand what she was talking about.

'You and Mr Costigano are now man and wife?' he asked.

'He told me it was only to get him a *passport*, see. They did it with the hookies years ago.'

'Hookies?'

'Quarter to twos, Stan calls them,' she laughed. 'You know. Get

79

them a passport if they can marry one of us. To escape Hitler. Well, that's what I done.'

'I'm sorry, you aren't making yourself clear. Have you contracted a marriage to give Mr Costigano a passport?'

'He got two passports, one Irish and one English, like me mum has. She's going to flay me when she finds out it was in a registry office. Flay me alive.'

The flow of irrelevant autobiography which poured from her lips in fits and starts made it hard to concentrate on the purpose of the visit. Presumably, she was trying blackmail. Given the present political situation, the fact that they were in a run-up situation before the Election, it was not bad timing, presumably on Costigano's part.

'Funny thing is, I didn't want to get married to him. It was all formal and cold and it didn't seem right.'

'Speaking purely personally,' said Derek, 'I deplore using loopholes in the law in this way. The man you have married, I take it, belongs to one of the, let's put it this way, ethnic minorities?'

'You what?'

'No, don't get me wrong. The contribution made to this country by the immigrant population has been simply marvellous. Great people. I don't know where we should be without them. I detest discrimination and prejudice – in whatever form – ' his jowl shook pompously, – 'whether it be the employment sector, whether it be in housing. But we must have a firm rule of *law*.'

'He said he was a ballet-dancer, but he's more of a stage hand. Can dance, beautifully. Mr Costigano says as how he'd never want to lay a finger on me.' She flipped her wrist in a camp gesture.

Derek grinned to show that he, too, was a man of the world. 'Obviously not.' He supposed there were Indian ballet dancers. He had never heard of them. Looking back on it afterwards, he did not know what had put it into his head that she had married an Indian. 'It would be purely a marriage of convenience. I see that. There would be no need to consummate the marriage.'

'He's nice,' she added irrelevantly, 'ever so dishy. He's forty-three, but I like an older man.'

'In their country, arranged marriages are part of the normal, the perfectly normal structure of society,' once more his jowl shook pedagogically. 'But that is not so here. It is going to be a major social problem in the years ahead, and we are not going to get around it by burying our heads in the proverbial sand.'

80

'Stan made me do it. Said my life wouldn't be worth living if I didn't turn up at that registry office.'

'Now, look here. This is a free, and, let us hope, a democratic country. As I say, we live here, by the *rule of law*. If you felt you were being har*assed*' – he put the emphasis on the last syllable of the word – 'or pressurised into marrying this Mr Costigano, you should have gone to the police.'

'The fuzz?'

'Of course.'

'Don't be stupid. There's dozens of girls inside for what I done. They'd just put me inside, that's all they'd do.'

'There I think you're wrong,' he said. 'We all know, incidentally, that prison is an entirely inappropriate treatment for this particular social problem. The reason that girls get taken into custody from time to time is for their own good, their own protection.'

'They torture you in there,' she said.

'That is very far from the truth.'

'Them guards, they're just a load of old dykes. Charmaine – that's a girl I know, says they flick you with wet towels in there. I'm not going down the bloody nick for my protection. I'd tell on you before they took me.'

There was silence between them and they now confronted each other as equals, not quite as enemies. It was more as though they were wrestling gladiators caught in a net of Mr Costigano's devising.

'That is blackmail, as I suppose you know,' he said. 'Of course, I realised that was the reason for your visit.'

'That's not fair. If I can get help with getting my security sorted out, me and Juri is going to leave London altogether. I'm going to live with him now that I've married him. We don't know what we'll do yet. We might travel. We might open a jeans shop.'

She had mentioned her husband's name before but Derek had failed to take it in. He was very tired, and it had been a bad enough blow when she made her first appearance, with Priscilla, in the hall. It was only a quarter of an hour ago, but it already seemed as distant as a golden age, an age of innocence. The pain of seeing her standing there beside Priscilla had been nothing compared with the exquisite torture of knowing that his secret was out: that there was a man called Costigano who knew of his surreptitious visits to Hackney. That meant the end of Derek's political career. Or so it had seemed at the time. Five minutes ago. Now, it was knowledge he could almost live with. He felt that there was room in the world for Mr Costigano without doing damage to his chances, one day, of occupying Number Ten Downing Street.

But, out of all the incoherent staccato chat, had now emerged this worst of all blows. He felt almost choked by the realisation of what she was trying to tell him.

Ballet. *Juri*. It seemed such a bloody cliché. It must be someone's idea of a joke.

'Your husband,' he inquired gently. 'What country does he come from?'

'Like I told you, he's a Russian.'

Derek buried his face in his hands for several minutes of silence.

# Seven

The eyes which surveyed the file of Juri Kutuzov in an Embassy in Kensington had read many more important documents in the previous seven days. In the scheme of things, Kutuzov was insignificant enough. At that moment talks were going on to reduce the nuclear arms race; world currencies were jumping up and down, and there were nasty rumours about a rise in the price of oil; Soviet gold reserves were low; pointless little wars were ruining the lives of Africans, Central Americans, and portions of the Moslem world. In this painful and extended melodrama, Kutuzov had not so much as a walk-on part.

Neither side had ever dignified him with the name of 'agent'. He was too unreliable ever to have been entrusted with important information. But the nature of his work in the Ballet, when he bothered to turn up at the theatre and was not having to be helped out of a bar or bailed out of a police station, meant that he visited most of the European capitals, and this made him a useful postman. In his time, he had been a little more than this. But it had never been his task to photograph documents, tape conversations or commit murders.

Intelligence work depended upon human weakness to ensure its effectiveness. Human weakness was messy, and Kutuzov was part of that mess. Perhaps the most useful 'work' he had ever done had been when his bare thighs appeared, slightly blurred, in a compromising photograph of Vassall. But, since then, he had been nothing but trouble.

He had been too undisciplined to have been a ballet dancer. While the others in his troupe had worn themselves out with their grotesque daily exercises, he had fooled about, and then had been disgruntled when he was thrown out. Somehow the Ballet had found that he would not go away. It had appeared, after all, he had not wanted to be a dancer. He was to have been a great director, a new Diaghilev. As a theatrical jack-of-all-trades, he had made himself gradually useful.

He knew a bit about everything. When lighting needed to be fixed in a hurry, when the Company was on tour, Kutuzov could usually improvise some arrangement. If a flat needed repainting, he could do it. He could even mend costumes. He was an accomplished needleman. But then, in Rome or Hamburg or Paris or Glasgow, there would be another arrest. The obvious thing to have done was to send him to some provincial town in eastern Russia and let him grow potatoes for the rest of his life. But the Embassy were not trained to do the obvious thing. The indiscretions had their political usefulness. In more than one political capital he had found his way into the bed of an army officer, or a policeman, or a businessman, who had subsequently been useful to them. And even the new, and rather ludicrous, 'dissident' persona created an atmosphere of muddle on both sides which was not without a very occasional serviceability.

The occasions were few in recent years; Kutuzov had never regularly been on the pay-roll. He had simply been paid piece rates for the small tasks he performed. When it was discovered that he had failed to deliver his envelope in Rome some years before, there had been moves to have him 'dealt with'. Minimal as his importance was, it was now recognised that he was playing a double game. On the other hand it was pointed out that he was known to have had 'dealings', if not actual 'relations', with an eminent figure in the British Labour Party. He therefore possessed enough embarrassment value to be worth leaving alone to pursue his own chaotic course.

There was nothing much in the file after the Rome incident, in which Kutuzov's 'cover', in so far as he had ever needed one, was 'blown'. On a previous visit to London, some five years earlier, he had presented himself in an hysterical state at a police station – the usual indecency charge – and asked for asylum. His country was suppressing his rights of expression, apparently. He was no great loss, and they had allowed him to stay in London as an exile for that season. The British had not been anxious to grant him citizenship. He had been back in Moscow, grumbling about the inadequacy of his fellow-technicians, the following winter, and at the same time complaining about the depraved commercialism of the West.

And now, this. The British were going through one of their routine expulsions of Soviet agents following a security leak. Kutuzov, no longer useful to them, was being threatened with deportation after a series of little incidents in London. There had been a tearful scene at his own Embassy when he had said that his future depended on being allowed to finish that particular season at the Wells. Could nothing be done to help him stay in this Godforsaken capitalist country just a few weeks longer?

The scene had taken place less than an hour after an interview with Van der Bildt, who was bringing helpful supplies of filth in an attaché case in exchange for his monthly retainer. Two and two had ponderously been put together. It was all far from being important. But it was surely worth everyone's while if the pot could be kept well-stirred. There was a whore; a hopeless character from Van der Bildt's description, but involved by chance with a rising British politician. It was feared that she was not tough enough to be a blackmailer; Van Der Bildt was understandably anxious that his name should not be brought into it. Why not arrange that the whore marry Kutuzov to substantiate his claim for a British passport? It could do nothing but harm. So the scheme had gone forward.

The large, soft brown eyes gazed at the file through a haze of cigarette smoke (Player's Capstan) and pushed it away. It was a gamble. With luck, Kutuzov and the whore, trivial little people, would soon be forgotten in the immensity of other events. They might worry the politician concerned. At the moment they scarcely posed a threat. If Blore were confronted with them too soon, then the whole little scheme would be wasted. Some of the truth of this must be conveyed down the line via Van der Bildt and his moronic henchman in Soho, Costigano. If Bernadette and Kutuzov were to be serviceable, it was essential that they hold back until Blore had an established position in the British Government. Then the thing could go either way. Heads they won; tails Blore lost. If he lost, it would be another little scandal, an embarrassed letter circulated to the Press, a resignation from the Cabinet, a brave little photograph of him driving away from his London house with his pretty wife. But, if they won, the winnings were rather higher. Should his party win the Election, it looked horribly as though there was going to be a Cabinet which contained not a single Soviet agent or sympathiser. Was his craving for office stronger than patriotism or principle? What sort of mettle was he made of? Would he be prepared, when threatened with exposure, to work for Moscow? A few secrets would be enough. It was the familiar gamble: more a question of nerve than of principle. Some men, foreseeing the years of uncertainty, fearing that they were being vetted or spied upon by their own side, were prepared to abandon their political ambitions and retire into obscurity. Others, with a stronger nerve, stayed on. What sort was he?

The hand was brown, nicotined at the index and gold-ringed on the little finger, which stretched out across the desk and opened a file labelled BLORE.

Driving past the Embassy, Feathers said, 'I wonder what little plots they are hatching in there.'

Rachel had bumped into him at a party held in the Ritz to launch the memoirs of a Trade Unionist magnate. They often bumped into one another in this way. Sometimes, if one or the other was at a loose end, supper would be proposed. They drove now to meet Hughie at their favourite Italian restaurant in Charlotte Street. As always, Feathers had his appearance under control. The apparent touches of decay, the bad teeth and the grease of hair or worn silk tie probably served the hidden movement of his own self-advancement. Rachel, relaxed by the alcohol, and pleasantly shocked by the splendour of the Trade Unionist party – endless champagne, salmon in aspic – continued to muse about the Russians and their Embassy.

'It's funny how different I feel about them now that I live in Europe,' she said. She ignored his hand which occasionally strayed from the gear lever of his battered Saab, finding, with an inebriated uncertainty, now her handbag, now her knee. 'If you'd had a good liberal upbringing like I did . . .'

'Ah ha! Very dangerous things, liberal upbringings . . .'

'But it's true. You know, I grew up in the McCarthy era. All my father's friends, or friends of friends, found themselves being suspected.'

'Were they very un-American?'

'That's not the point. They'd come out of Europe to escape persecution, and what did they find?'

'That entertaining interests inimical' (he just managed the word, suppressing a belch) 'to the country of one's adoption was as unacceptable to the Americans as it had been to the Germans and the Poles and the Hungarians.'

'Feathers! How can you say that?' She secretly rather enjoyed his outrageousness. 'But anyhow, like I said, the Russians just never meant anything to me until I came here. So, there were agents and fellow-travellers. We never saw them at Harvard. How d'you know an agent if you see one?'

'False beard, dark glasses . . .'

'It's all sort of different here. You know, they feel close here. The Russians, I mean. Is it any wonder my poor old country makes such a mess of its foreign policy; it's so goddam far from everywhere.'

In the pause which ensued, she asked, 'Seen anything lately of the Blores?'

Feathers noted that it did not take much, these days, to get Rachel on to the subject of the Blores. It was becoming an obsession.

'D'you think he'll get the Chancellorship?'

'Who –Derek?' There seemed something defensively blasé about Feathers's air when discussing the Blores.

'Sure.'

'Not a hope, I'd have thought. The best he can hope for this time round is Secretary of State for Trade.'

'He certainly didn't shape up any too well in the Leadership contest.'

'Eleven votes! Good old Derek. But you see, that's typical of Derek. Why do you stand in a leadership election?' – Feathers was moving into the pedagogical exposition of politics which made it so easy for him to write his columns week after week. 'You go in either because you think you're going to win, right? Or you want to embarrass everyone by standing out on a limb and drawing away a handful of votes from either of the two main candidates – Enoch technique; or you want to lay "markers" for the future. Now, obviously Derek was never going to become leader, and he's never had a distinctive or courageous thought in his life . . .'

'Feathers!'

'It's true. He'd never be the Archbishop Lefebvre of the anti-marketeers in the Party; or set up the Downham Market of the Gallow-birds.' His allusiveness, particularly his habitual likening of political life with ecclesiastical, was quite often hard to follow. 'No, the only reason old Derek wants to waste everyone's time in a leadership election is to lay down a few markers. Now, if you do that, you have to take soundings first.'

'Otherwise you'll look foolish.'

'Correct. But when did Derek ever *not* look foolish. If he'd asked around in the lobbies, he'd have known he couldn't possibly hope for more than fifteen votes – and it's not really enough.'

'But he didn't get fifteen votes.'

'I know he didn't.'

'He got eleven votes,' she persisted. 'Only eleven MPs were

prepared to say they might, one day, think of Derek as leader of the Party.'

'But he's got push, you see. That's the sort of vote which would crush most MPs. Not our Derek. He'll push and he'll fight until he rises through the ranks of that bloody party.'

'I thought you were his friend,' she said reproachfully.

'Derek's? He doesn't have any friends.'

'Do you mean that?'

'Like most politicians he has a bit of a self-created entourage. But the way he's picked up you and Hughie is entirely typical.'

Feathers spoke as though he were in a slightly different category.

'Presumably he picked you up too?' she said.

'He likes to have a few journalists, a few MPs, a few technical advisers hovering about the house. It makes him feel important. But, you see, how well does he know you?'

'As well as you can know someone you've met six or seven times, always with other people around. But does he really have *no* friends?'

'Does it surprise you?' He spoke impatiently as though he wanted to get the subject out of the way.

'How about Priscilla? You see, from the moment I met Priscilla I felt she was my friend. In one way and another we've met her quite a lot since. Hughie was at school with her brother – typical of him not to mention it before . . .'

'Ah! That Old Etonian mafia . . .' Feathers's voice trailed away. It was never immediately clear where he had been to school. On different occasions the Feathers mythology demanded that different messages be given out. His rather blimpish voice suggested one of the older boarding schools. But he liked to appear as a man who struck solitary poses, belonged to no clique, no in-group. In this, as in several other respects, it seemed to Rachel that he resembled Derek Blore. Derek had almost got to the top by the dogged pursuit of respectability. Feathers, in a less respectable profession, had unquestionably got on by his heavy cultivation of the seedy role.

'We've grown quite close to the Blores,' she said, even though Feathers did not appear to be listening. Perhaps he was the only one allowed to befriend rising stars in the political firmament. 'Close to Priscilla, at any rate.'

'A perfect couple,' Feathers said.

'Priscilla and Derek? You surprise me. It's been a mystery to me ever since I met her why she married him.'

'Don't you think some women need a man to whom they can feel perpetually superior?' Feathers asked. 'Patronage is the only form of love some of them know.'

'I don't think Priscilla's patronising. She's so natural, so out-going. So, so . . .'

'How American of you. You think anyone with Priscilla's background is wanting to gaze down their noses at us plebs and republicans.'

'That's what *you* implied.'

'No, no. Not Priscilla.' He whistled between his teeth, trying to find a parking place in Charlotte Street, but indicating that he regarded the conversation as over. She would not be deflected. She felt mildly cross with him for the way in which he was dismissing the subject as though it were dependent on a grasp of English mores and manners too complex for the crude transatlantic understanding.

'Why, then,' she pressed on as he locked his car and they walked to the restaurant, 'Why did she get married to him, d'you think? Priscilla to Derek?'

Feathers blinked crossly at her – as at a child who asked too many questions. The furrowed brow was perhaps brought on by an inebriated half-memory of what the conversation was about.

'These women,' he sighed, seizing the lintels of the restaurant door for support to make his declaration. 'These women would marry *anyone.*'

They marched on into Giuseppe's. It was the usual clientèle. Mrs Jonquil Yates, the famous mystic, waved noodles in the face of a clergyman near the window. Hughie, with a look of sadness, sat at the next table and lifted his glass of Campari in greeting. Rachel was made to feel guilty by her husband's grumpy features. Perhaps Hughie, she reflected, found Feathers less amusing than she did.

# *Eight*

The Blore family holiday, planned for July, was not, in the event, disarranged. The hung parliament came unhung before the end of April. There was an unusual event in British politics, a defeat for the Government in a vote of no confidence. The next few weeks were busy ones for Rachel, for Feathers, for Derek Blore, for all those involved in the changing pantomime of political life.

Rachel was there in the House, watching from the Press Gallery, when the no-confidence motion was discussed. The quaintness of the over-excited atmosphere appealed to her sense of the ridiculous. Hot, bespectacled faces gathered in corners of the tea-room. The Chamber, which was full for most of the night, seemed no bigger to her when packed to capacity than the debating hall of some private High School. There was noise, inebriation, bad temper, exhaustion. It was the House's confidence that was on trial. For most of the day, however, the Government Whips had been wooing the confidence of a tiny number of eccentrics. At one point.there was a rumour that Derek Blore had been offered a peerage in order to abstain.

'He wants power, not grandeur,' Feathers pontificated to fellow-journalists who had not made Blore's acquaintance. 'They'll never woo him away to the Lords.'

At a later stage in the evening, there was a rumour that the Liberals would vote for the Government in exchange for a reform of the entire electoral procedure. But then, as Rachel was quick to observe, such a reform would, if implemented, put the Party of Government out of office for the next twenty years. The Ulster Unionists appeared to hold the balance. Rumour flew about the corridors that they had been 'bought' by one party or another with promises of vast public expenditure in the Province. Then it was discovered that someone on the Government back benches was still away on holiday in Jamaica and refused to come back. This threw all calculations into confusion. It meant that the Government would certainly lose, until – happy hour – an Opposition backbencher was rushed off to the Westminster

Hospital with a bursting appendix. Then the thing was once more in the balance. More brandy, more tea, more unfounded speculations were swapped and absorbed. More red faces huddled in MPs' rooms. More telephone calls were made to the constituencies. Then the surprise of the night came to everyone. The Manx Nationalist and the Independent Member for Launceston West were both wavering. The Government Chief Whip was known to be relying on them. The Independent Member for Launceston West was frequently on his feet in the Chamber throughout the hours of darkness. He knew that he would never get such publicity again. Any General Election, held at any time, would certainly cut his slender majority of 215 to nought, and send him back to private schoolmastering near Polperro. So he stood up and sat down; and irritated everyone by raising points of order with the Speaker. When his turn came to speak in the debate, it was the oration of a lifetime. Its elegantly turned quotations from Hawker of Morwenstow and its allegedly withering (actually rather feeble) attacks on the Leader of the Liberal Party were not what most members wanted to hear at half past three in the morning. But they provided Rachel with copy for one of her most pointed pieces of political analysis. She had written a profile of this minor eccentric only the week before. She would now be able to say that the Monarch was being forced to change her ministers because they did not command the support of this Celtic exhibitionist, and had failed to promise a Cornish Television Channel and confiscation of the Duke of Cornwall's estates.

By the time the Government actually fell, light was beginning to appear in the sky. How odd, it seemed to her, that so many major democratic decisions in the country of her adoption were taken when Members of Parliament were too exhausted to think. It was a thrilling day, as the weeks which followed were thrilling. She and Feathers appeared on chat shows, and toured the constituencies to catch the national mood. And the mood appeared to be that of the Independent Member for Launceston West. For reasons equally arbitrary, though less esoteric, the inhabitants of these islands were going to vote for a change.

Rachel, who had seen the Blores about six times since her first dinner there with Hughie, realised that this meant she would soon be the friend, or close acquaintance, of a Minister of the Crown. Once more, this did not excite pride so much as a wistful blend of melancholy and amusement, for she knew that evenings with the

91

Blores did nothing to alleviate the intense glooms into which Hughie had fallen during the previous three months. She feared very much that this melancholy madness was caused by love for Priscilla. But, in the excitement of the Election, Rachel managed to be distracted from the pain caused by Hughie's infatuation. As she ate her railway meals, telephoned her copy to offices, and chattered to other journalists in pubs, she even persuaded herself that she had got the thing out of proportion. What had begun as an elaborate marital tease had assumed the character in her own mind of a cloud which threatened to obscure all her happiness. And yet these cascades into melancholy could be averted when she reminded herself that Hughie had never *said* anything or done anything to justify the intensity of anxious feelings she allowed herself. When she was away from him for a few days, she forgot, sometimes, what it was that made her so anxious. Taciturnity was a feature of his character. The long silences with the whisky bottle, and the diminutions in physical affection, did not necessarily suggest an unrequited passion. When they did make love, things seemed as happy as before. And, as she told herself repeatedly, if there were anything 'between' Hughie and Priscilla, they would surely be unable to brazen out the social encounters which had taken place when they were all there together, the four of them, Derek and Rachel as well as the guilty pair? Rachel pinned much on Priscilla's manifest niceness; on her common sense; and, not to gild the lily, on the woman's obvious ambition on her husband's behalf.

Hughie himself, however, had become so engrossed in this new religion and worship that he gave almost no thought to what his wife was thinking. Nor did the political drama touch him except when it demanded exits of Priscilla in order to smile on platforms with her spouse. Hughie had discovered a masochist's delight that he was as capable of suffering aged thirty-seven as he had been at the age of twenty. This proud little secret had beguiled him through the initial weeks of the preoccupation until the matter was beyond his control. He was back again in the clutches of Romance. Once more, in solitude, he could pace the streets of London, sit wretchedly at the back of empty churches and drink too much whisky while Mahler or Brahms blared from the electric turntable. Again, in the office, he could close the door on the jabbering chat of the secretaries and devote anything up to two hours to contemplation of Priscilla's photograph, or to repeated copying of her name on his blotter. The

92

letter P itself became invested with an arcane charm. He caressed it while making proofs or correcting typescripts; he bought himself handkerchieves and pencils embroidered or marked with it.

Time had allowed one improvement since the days of Jane. In the case of his old love, it became so intensely painful that it was almost unendurable, and ultimately impossible, to speak to her. This was not so with Priscilla. When they encountered one another, as now and again they did, at parties or dinners with the full connivance of Derek or Rachel, it was possible to keep up, still, a level of mannered chat. They did not frequently direct words to each other. But they were often now part of the same gaggle. Words which fell from the lips of the Beloved were cherished for days afterwards, remembered, even quietly intoned, on those days when Rachel too was out of London pursuing the fortunes of tomfool politicians, as he sat at concerts or went to church.

He had not lost his affection for Rachel. He was unaware of how many hours he spent in silent contemplation of the new mystery. When he surfaced, he managed, or so he thought, to be perfectly cheerful, as conversible as good manners required. Domestic evenings had always been spent quietly, chat an interruption of books or music. He could still look up at his wife's pallid and ironical features and smile at the things she said. He fought against the temptation, which the new feeling brought in its train, to regard his wife with contempt. It would have been different, if he had never felt for her an even fragmentary echo of what he felt for Priscilla. Then one love, withered, would have to be abandoned for the new. The only extent to which he resented Rachel, or tempered his resentment to feelings of pity, was when he considered that the previous four years had been a blasphemy against Romance; that too much of Rachel's cool pleasantry, or too frequent reverberations of her dangerously infectious laughter, might shatter some quietly inward vision of the goddess which the silent mind might in repose have deliciously and poignantly created.

His feelings towards Derek Blore, however, were less coolly controllable. The shackling of the pale divinity to the red-faced buffoon was probably a recurrent joke in the pantheons of the world, a stand-by in Olympian comedy. This could not prevent feelings of uncomplicated hatred for Derek welling up inside Hughie whenever he met the man. It was not difficult to put him down in conversation; to correct him on points of fact, to say things, less to 'make Derek look silly' than to show up his incontrovertible absurdity.

The only speech which Hughie hated to recall from the lips of Priscilla was this: 'I know it's awfully embarrassing when politicians' wives boast about their husbands. But I really admire Derek.'

She had said it one evening to Rachel, across a dinner table, Derek not having been present. Details had followed, too painful to recall, concerning Blore's self-created triumphs. As she had said them, Priscilla had been looking, not at Rachel, but at Hughie himself. There had been a quality of serious reproach in her stare; reproach and warning, as though she sensed his adoration, and was flattered by it, but was unable to tolerate it if it could not absorb subscription to the cult of being kind to Mr Blore.

Those words came back to Hughie, months after they were spoken during a very nasty moment on the nine o'clock news, when Derek, in his recently acquired position of power, faced reporters in Brussels at the end of a Common Market Conference of Ministers.

Everyone agreed that had the previous PM been able to call the Election a fortnight later, his Government would have been returned for another term of office. As it was, Derek's party were in the ascendant once more. The campaign was short and hard-won. Derek had taken part in one of the TV party politicals. Outside his own constituency, he made speeches in Nottingham, Dudley, Finchley and Southampton; and this extended work on the part of the party probably explained the slight fall in his personal majority. To everyone, as Derek said in his victory speech, he owed debts of gratitude. To Ted, well goodness, where would he have been without Ted? To all the secretaries, and campaign organisers; to all those who had trudged the streets and canvassed on door steps. To his own private secretary, Edna Philips; and, above all, he would like to thank his wife and his children for all their support.

'You know,' he had added in a personal note which he thought was really rather moving, in that victory speech: 'the longer I'm in politics – and I hope to be in politics for a long time to come (CHEERS) the longer I realise that this is what it's all about. Politics isn't just about economics – though, with this new government, we'll see inflation and unemployment down in manageable figures by the end of the year (CHEERS, BOOS) and it isn't just about the law – though under our new Prime Minister I have no doubt that the firm *rule of law* will be (HIS VOICE DROWNED IN CHEERS) . . . but

94

you know, at the end of the day, all that this amounts to is that politics is about family life, and about people; and if, like I do, you have a wife and children who support you in what you do, you feel (VOICE SLIGHTLY BREAKING) well, pretty grateful.' (RAPTUROUS CHEERS.)

In spite of his public tribute, Derek had felt edgy in relation to his family throughout the summer. Kate, who had disliked living in Paris so much at first, now pined to stay on. Obviously there was a boyfriend in the picture. She had picked up a lot of rather embarrassing Euro-Communist ideas about the Stock Exchange, disarmament, the police. Julian, with whom Derek felt such an affinity, had seemed such a stranger too, when they last took him out to luncheon at a hotel in Malvern. Only eleven, but he already had that habit of reproachful silence which Derek associated with adolescence.

To Priscilla, too, Derek had felt awkward; for months now, ever since her encounter with Bernadette. Derek suspected that she half-guessed that the girl had come to blackmail him. It would have been the moment to make a clean breast of things with Priscilla, but she, too, seemed remote from him. The moment for such a disclosure had never seemed right. He had decided, instead, to confide in Ted Sangster, who would be sympathetic, sensible, practical. Once they had worked out what to do, the two men together, Derek would manage to put it out of his mind for the duration of the campaign. As it happened, though, he never found a moment when he was drunk enough to brave a confession – even to good old Ted. He trusted rather to Good Luck and kept his fingers crossed that Bernadette would not recur.

But a chilliness had descended in his domestic life which was not dissociable in his imagination from the sordid figure in the PVC mackintosh standing in his hall, and the look of *loftiness* in Priscilla's eyes as she smiled. The 'concessions' made to Priscilla since the half-revelation had all been unspoken. More time had been spent with her family. Political associates had, on the whole, been seen off home territory. She had kept her supportive role in the Election campaign – or so it seemed to Derek – to a minimum. In his first Election, he remembered, she had listened to every speech he had made; she had hung on every word, winced at every heckler, and scowled whenever he was asked a difficult question. This time, she had only sat on platforms with him about two-thirds of the time.

And then, he recognised, there was the strange development of her friendship with Rachel and Hughie. Derek had not known what to make of Rachel's article when it appeared. It was flatteringly long, but it did not take him quite as seriously as he would have wished. There had been something a little cheap, he felt, about describing his reaction to the death of a Party Leader, still more about the comparison with Falstaff rushing to London to cash in on his friendship with the newly-crowned Prince Hal. He did not know where she had got hold of some of the anecdotes about his relationship with the new Leader. It was most unfortunate that his joke about the Leader's – now the PM's – 'Mussolini pose at Euston Station' had been allowed to circulate. And yet, all his advisers told Derek that Rachel's article had done him nothing but good. Hitherto, it was claimed, he was a bit faceless, as far as the General Public went. Now there were little things they could associate in their minds with the name of Blore; the interest in wines and music and the fondness for Somerset Maugham; the hint of a faint froideur between himself and the PM. None of this did any harm at all, according to the experts. Whether it did harm or no, Derek suspected it was somehow inevitable that the Duncans would still have started to be part of their lives. Rachel, together with Feathers and one or two other journalists, had stayed quite close to Derek throughout the Election campaign. He had found their traipsing about after him rather touching. It meant, inevitably, that they had come to inhabit that uneasy category which in other people's lives would have been designated friends. Blores and Duncans had now supped together, probably, six or seven times.

There were journalists you could respect, for instance Henry Feathers – men who were highly astute politically. Derek quite liked Rachel, and felt that it would be worth cultivating her; or, at the least, not hurting her feelings. About Hughie he was altogether less sure. An antipathy had been manifest from the moment, ages ago now, when Hughie had deliberately made Derek look ridiculous by suggesting that the Rioja had come from Sainsbury's. In Derek's view, a joke in the worst possible taste; simply bad manners. It had been extraordinary to him that Priscilla had laughed at the rudeness. Now the woman seemed to have any amount of time for Hughie. They had all half-known each other before, of course. Priscilla's brother had slightly known Hughie at Eton. He had been in love with her cousin Jane (as if that wasn't enough to put you on your guard – what an awful woman!). Priscilla had prosed about it all on several occasions during the private sessions of marital gossip.

Of Priscilla's fidelity to him, Derek had never been in the slightest doubt. He knew quite well that she would never be vulgar or cruel enough to *go to bed* with Hughie Duncan. In the frank and manly way Derek liked to put things to himself, he would have preferred it if his wife *had* gone to bed with little Duncan. In fact, this was nonsense. He would have hated it. But he hated, too, the sense of exclusion which assailed him whenever Priscilla made new friends. They nearly always turned out to be connected with old friends; to be first cousins once removed of Priscilla's mother; or best friends of someone she had been at school with; or related to one or another discarded wife of her brother. His own social pattern was, and always had been, a series of random leaps and encounters. Priscilla was a whole series of interlocking pieces, in which all the characters were united, whether by blood, or divorce, or common attendance at a tiny number of educational establishments. It didn't matter, as Derek furiously viewed it all, it did not matter that Hughie was only five foot six, and probably earned about as much as a curate, publishing books that nobody wanted to read; it did not matter that Derek, on the contrary, was rich enough to educate two childen, to maintain two fat establishments in London and the country, to dress Priscilla in the most lavishly expensive clothes ... Oh no, he had fumed inwardly. However unsatisfactory Hughie was, and however worthy, obviously worthy, he was himself, Hughie would always be allowed to sit in his house and make jokes about the wine. Hughie, and the likes of Hughie, despised Derek. In a red-faced way, he was determined not to bloody well care.

His Election campaign had been a good one. Whatever journalists thought about the froideur between himself and the Leader, his usefulness and his economic skill were never more needed than at present. He had hoped, right up to the last minute, that there might be a switch of mind, and that he might end up as Chancellor of the Exchequer. He had spent an unpleasant few days (after Rachel's article appeared) when it was rumoured that the Leader was considering landing him with Northern Ireland. But, as it was, he couldn't have a more appropriate or a more stimulating role than he enjoyed at present.

With what joy he had moved into his new rooms – the spacious panelled room in the House, with its huge desk, its portraits, its little

97

view of Palace Yard from the windows; and the room in his Ministry, the very seat of power. Derek respected civil servants. He liked order, he liked detail. He liked to think that they knew where they stood with him. His Head of Department, Sir Magnus, was known to be stubborn, but if you leant on him hard, you got the required results. In his present visit to Brussels, for instance, Derek had told Sir Magnus that he needed much closer briefing. It was no good simply arriving with a generalised picture of the Common Agricultural Policy. How much had we actually spent, in the previous year, on Butter? How much on Lamb? How much on Wheat? and so on . . . Sir Magnus had been impressed by this, Derek could see.

In fact, the visit to Brussels, which he had represented to his friends as yet another tiring piece of business, was quite a welcome little holiday. The meetings did not go on all the time, as they did in London. In the previous week, he had had to sit on the Legislation Committee; he had a great deal of departmental work; and he found that Cabinet took quite an extraordinary amount of time. Not only did Cabinet meetings (already very acrimonious, and the Government only a few months old) seem interminably long. They were invariably followed by hours on the telephone in which one or another of Derek's Cabinet colleagues would ring him up and conduct a post mortem on the PM's behaviour.

Power and business had come Derek's way. Fame – the really big fame for which he felt a perpetual longing and hunger – had so far eluded him. That was another reason for feeling pleasure at the Brussels Summit. He was here representing his country. In fact, all his utterances, made through interpreters, had been tediously bland, but he had allowed it to be known, through aides, camp-followers and journalists, that something exciting was brewing. In consequence, when he had finished his luncheon on the final day, he found himself surrounded, at the plate glass door, by a satisfying crowd of popping flash-bulbs and TV arc-lights. Microphones were temptingly pushed towards him, like bananas in the hands of schoolchildren, thrust through the bars of a gorilla's cage. 'Varry, varry stimulating of course. Varry exciting. And, hopefully, varry productive.'

'Mr Blore, is there any truth in the rumour that you are trying to renegotiate the whole Common Agricultural Policy? . . .'

'Now, thank you, thank you varry much. I've answered all the questions I can.'

'Is it true that the French Foreign Minister has accused Britain of double-crossing the Community?'

'Thank you varry much. It's all been most stimulating.'

'Secretary of State . . .'

'Please, please. No more questions.'

As they bustled about him, Derek could already picture the snatch of film, starring himself, on the evening news. He hoped that Priscilla would be watching, and his son Julian. He hoped his constituents were watching, and the Prime Minister. He hoped that they all appreciated the tough, and yet good-humoured, way in which he deflected all the assaults of the reporters.

When the scuffle and banter were over, and the photographers had departed, Derek turned his attention to the matter of recreation and the next three hours. The Summit Conference was drawing to a close, which was why the journalists were so anxious for a story. So far, it had been a dull affair in the eyes of the newspapers.

A little to his surprise (there had been interesting conversation at the luncheon; they had talked literature, Derek had recommended *The Moon and Sixpence* to the Italian Prime Minister) he found himself solitary for the afternoon. Even members of his own delegation appeared to have ploys which excluded him. There had been much dashing off in taxis after the coffee had been consumed.

It seemed that everyone but he wished to cram the last remaining hours in Brussels with activity. He had already sampled two restaurants, admired the variegated Gothic of the Grande Place, black and gold, defiantly medieval amid the city's surrounding modernity. Beyond this, there seemed nothing much to do in this city except stroll through the sumptuous Edwardian arcades of the Flower Market. This he had done. Chocolates, lace, almond paste and other local specialities had already been purchased, for distribution to appropriate recipients on his return to London. He did not share the desire of some members of the party to visit the Beaux Arts. A French attaché, trying to be clever, had said to Derek, 'Your famous poet, T. S. Eliot, was it not, has written about the painting there of Breughel's Icarus.'

This might very well have been the case. Derek would have preferred a visit to the town's red light district had it been possible to arrange discreetly. Even now, as it happened, he half-suspected the gaggle of agitated attachés who had followed the Frenchman to the

Beaux Arts of feasting their eyes on something more fleshly than the accomplishments of the Flemish masters. That being the case, he felt even more hurt at their exclusion of him from the party. It could not, he realised, have been a personal matter. On the contrary, he had gone out of his way to be charming to everyone. This 'hiving off', leaving him on his own, had a distinctly political flavour; childishly so, in his view. The Minister from Luxembourg, accompanied by a civil servant in Derek's own department, might at least have cast a look in his direction as they drove their hired car so speedily down the hill. They believed there was time to see the field of Waterloo before the plenary session at the end of the afternoon. Well, he saw distinctly that there were two empty seats in the back of the Fiat. Not that he liked to be seen driving in the back of foreign cars; not that he remotely wanted to see the field of Waterloo. He might, quite simply, have been asked.

As it was, he stood rather disconsolately on the hill and thought, with three hours 'to kill', what an unutterably dreary place this was. The eminence on which he stood, Berlaymont, belied the picturesqueness of its name. Impersonally pale concrete soared expensively towards a grey sky. Beneath, down the steep slopes, a few little patches of Brussels maintained, as far as the eye could discern, some of their ancient charm; an avenue of planes, a church spire, a domestic gable reminiscent of the pleasanter suburbs of Leamington; even, towards the centre, a certain royal grandeur in the Parisian manner. But these were tiny, isolated, and surely accidental survivals in a great scheme of fast roads, advertisement hoardings, traffic signs and block upon block of offices, flats and garages.

Had he been better informed he would, he boldly thought with a private smirk, 'have been only too happy to be left on his own three hours'. Not without a reckless hope that something of this nature might turn up if he were 'out and about', he set out for a solitary walk over the brow of the hill, as the grey sky darkened and threatened rain.

As he paced, he wandered out of the Parc du Cinquantenaire and into the Parc Léopold. In Brussels, it seemed, one park was very much like another. Beyond this one, the tower blocks and the railway bespoke an even dingier life style, the arterial roads which screeched up the opposite hillside showed an even more frenzied desire to be out of the place, as lorries honked and Renaults raced their way to Aachen or Berlin. Within the park itself, there was a pond with civic, doubtless Community, ducks; a playpen and a multinational sandpit; and on the far horizon some large buildings, museums and medical schools, reproachfully beautiful and decayed palaces in the late nineteenth-century manner.

Puffing – for they gave you far too many potatoes to eat, and they drank as greedily as they ate, these miserable Belgians – he stood and surveyed the park, with the knowledge that if he walked down the slope towards the sandpit he would only have to come up again. He walked instead along the upper reaches of the garden until he came to the terrace outside the Natural History Museum. And it was there that he saw Bernadette and met her husband for the first time.

That they met by chance was inconceivable. He realised as soon as recognition dawned that he had been walking carelessly, and in a daze. They had probably been tailing him ever since he left Berlaymont. His instinct was to make a quick getaway; to pace forcefully down through the Parc Léopold and hope that a taxi would be passing the great iron gates at the bottom of the hill. But a mixture of fear and curiosity held him back. He allowed himself to be approached.

Bernadette no longer pretended to smile, apparently. Her face seemed to have hardened. She had lost all touches, not of innocence – for he had never seen that in her visage – but of approachability. She wore a white raincoat, green stockings and black patent-leather shoes. The hair was browner, and less hennaed. Though she was not tall she towered several inches above the stocky figure at her side, a man in early middle age, swathed in a crimson plastic jacket which simulated leather; and corduroy trousers of slightly too bright a blue. The face which turned towards Derek's combined an arrogant beauty with a failure to sense its own comedy. There were large dark eyes, thick brows, wide nostrils and wider, sensually thick, lips. Abundant curly black hair was flecked with white.

'Mr Blore, good afternoon to you, sir,' he said.

'Hullo, there,' said Derek, suspicious of Juri's accent, guessing at once who he was.

For months, this had hovered over him. The Secret Life had been abandoned before the General Election. Derek believed that, in time, the thing would probably blow over; he knew that he wasn't the only man in Westminster with a few skeletons in the cupboard. It seemed to have been the right policy. Derek had heard nothing of, or from, Bernadette, throughout the Election campaign. He had heard

101

nothing of them during his first few months in office. There had been periods, sometimes whole days, when he lived without the conscious dread of exposure. And yet he had been living like a man who knew he was sick, though his illness had not been officially diagnosed. He had not been free, ever since he knew that Bernadette was the mere puppet of blackmailers. Who were they? It had been only too easy to supply the answer, since she now appeared to be married to Juri Kutuzov.

They needed so little money, Bernadette had pleaded, Juri's employers in the theatre did not pay him enough. She intended to escape her life of vice and pursue respectability and obscurity. All they needed was a start in life. Juri would really turn over a new leaf. So would she. If only he would help her with her stamps.

He had been rash. He had promised to investigate her position vis-à-vis the Department of Health and Social Security. He had taken the risk of writing letters to the Minister, and to the civil servants responsible. They had been able to supply no information which had not been given with perfect accuracy and courtesy by the Pakistani of her first inquiry.

He had taken the further risk of paying them a large sum of money. Yes, *them*, he realised now, as he confronted the pair on the terrace. It was starting to drizzle. By clearing out his current account and selling a handful of shares, it had not been difficult to lay hands on £2000 in cash within a week of his painful interview with Bernadette. He had tried to be jocular about it in the letter, but he had been equally firm. *Teacher is very tired and I know that she needs a nice long rest. Her obedient pupil sends this token of his esteem. Teacher must now go abroad.*

With wordless agreement – for it was now coming on to rain quite heavily – the three of them entered the museum and found themselves at once in a huge cathedral of a place, populated by the gigantic skeletons, which the Belgians had painted sombrely black, of extinct monsters of prehistoric times.

'Are they models?' Bernadette innocently inquired.

'They have been dugged,' said her consort, 'though many of these is phoney, no-good fake.'

'They are certainly a varry varry imprassive sight,' said Derek, genuinely awestruck by the size of the iguanadons and by their age. A million years had passed since these obsolete jokes of Nature had clumped about the world's swampy surfaces. It was not a fact which could be absolutely consoling, but he knew that it should set his

102

present troubles 'in perspective'. He glanced nervously about the museum. There were some children with their mother; they all sounded American. A punctiliously neat little man with a stiff collar, and wire-rimmed spectacles, a brown pinstriped suit, furled umbrella and a brown trilby hat was conducting an equally respectable and ancient spouse beneath the tusks of mammoths. It looked as though it was a regular part of their lives, this prim perambulation among the bones, as though the visions of creatures so old renewed their youth before they returned to their lace antimacassars, their potato-laden soups and their chocolatey puddings.

No one here looked in Derek's view 'suspicious'. He ventured to speak to them, but his voice seemed suddenly loud and echoing, the archdeacon bellowing a hymn number.

'I don't know what you want, but I think on the whole it would be a better thing if we didn't meet,' he said.

'You are Mr Blore?' asked Juri, surprisingly late in the conversation.

'I think you know who I am.'

'And you, with my wife, had visits, often, in Hackney.'

'This is not something I wish to discuss. There is nothing to say.'

'Come off it, Juri's only trying to be friendly. And we got something for you, haven't we, Juri?'

'You visit my wife for game. You make my wife a filthy whore. You call her teacher.' The words were not delivered angrily, but coaxingly, cooingly, echoingly. There was a coarse leer, a display of appalling teeth, a smell of halitosis as the Russian spoke.

'A little less loud, please,' whispered Derek.

'You exploit my Bernadette.'

'Now look here,' said Derek, whispering with sudden anger. 'You can believe and say what you like. I have no idea who you are. I do not even know whether you two are actually man and wife or whether you are playing some elaborate game.'

'You, it is you who do play the game.'

'This young lady came to me in difficulties about her Social Security,' said Derek awkwardly. 'As you probably know, she intimated to me that she was in financial difficulties.'

'She hit you with canes and this gives you erection. She strike you. You are a little boy in the shorts and she is the teacher in her black raiments, and she strike you. When you write to her with the money,'

103

you say *Teacher must now go abroad.*'

'This is something I wrote?'

'Oh yes. We forget. It conveniences us always to forget. I say you, my friend, there is no bloody point in pretending. You pay this lady two grand, two thousand pounds. Do you do this with every lady who come to you and say you she has no stamp-security? Kindly pull my leg, please.'

'I have no recollection of paying the money,' Derek said suddenly, conscious that there was almost certainly a tape-recorder in Juri's pocket.

'Ah, but Bernadette, she remember.'

'Course I remember. You sent it in that envelope like we agreed and the night we got it me and Juri escape, didn't we?'

'And you, sir, you have a passport?' Derek sounded suddenly threatening.

'You admit you pay Bernadette the money?'

'Course he admits it. Can't deny it, can you? Why d'you want to deny it? It was really generous, that was. I got away from Hackney and Mr Costigano. Juri got away from his boring job. We're free now. We've worked, saved up.'

'What doing?'

'Hotel work,' she said quickly.

'We want to show,' Juri faltered, with an air of humility which was completely convincing, 'that we stand in our own bloody shoes. We grateful.'

'Are grateful,' corrected Bernadette.

'We do not ask for you to give money. Sit down, please.'

From where they sat the darkened bones of monsters swooped in Gothic arches towards the high ceiling above their heads.

'We save, we work, we are not ashamed. I work with bar, I wait at table. Bernadette, she wait at table, she make beds, we save money.'

'What Juri's really saying is, we want to pay you back. Just a bit, like, now. More later when we can afford it.'

This was such a surprise that Derek had no response for it. £500, in sterling, held together by an elastic band, but enclosed by not so much as an envelope, was being pressed into his hand by Juri.

'Go on,' said Bernadette. 'I won't pester you. Only, see, I want to go straight. I want to get it all sorted out. I want to pay you back.'

As non-committal as possible for that tape-recorder which he still half-suspected to be concealed there, he grinned and said, 'Yas, yas,

104

yas.' A mean instinct made him grab the money and put it firmly into his inside pocket. He suddenly wondered with a burst of ludicrous rage against Bernadette, why the hell she *shouldn't* pay him back. The knowledge that she existed, however, that Juri existed, that they were married, that they were able to materialise from nowhere and pursue him through the Parc Léopold, all this was enough to bring him out in a cold sweat, a self-absorbed state of panic which made him fail to suspect the presence, behind the iguanadons, of a dapper little man in a brown suit, carrying a tiny camera.

While Derek sat in the aeroplane that evening, and drank whisky for the short duration of the flight to Heathrow, Priscilla lay naked in the arms of her lover. He was no good at it. This fact alone excited her pity and allowed him to return, as he had done now so often, to her crisp, cool, white linen sheets, to her long pale arms, and her thin hands which stroked his head which bobbed up and down between her bosom and her shoulders. First fast, then very fast. Then his cheek flopped as on a pillow against her breast.

Of course the attentions were flattering, and gave some pleasure. She had tried, during his initial advances, to hold out against its ever reaching this stage. But she had simply allowed it to happen. Priscilla knew that, if she had a fault, it was this acquiescence in events; and that, if she had a virtue, it was her ability – usually at least – to use her pliability to good purpose. This was not the first little unfaithfulness. But her discretion and common sense had never allowed her to get entangled with a man where her heart was too fully engaged. Nor would she ever have admitted a man to her bed if she feared that 'heaviness' was threatened. She could not have borne public declarations, elopement, operatic absurdity. After all, Derek's career was her achievement as well as his own. A divorce would wreck it. But now, she was – had been for some months – worried to the point of indiscretion. For it was not just from a desire to distract her mind from the unsatisfying gyrations of the present coition that she shared her worries with Feathers.

Feathers was always over-excited with Priscilla. It made him go too fast. Years later, when the affair had become reasonably common knowledge, a colleague had remarked that Priscilla's beauty was almost immaterial to Feathers. He was both so much a snob, and so much a hack, that dalliance with her would have been excessively stimulating even had she been as ugly as sin. The admission into her intimacy carried all the excitements rolled into one of turning the pages of Debrett's and bagging a journalistic scoop.

'That was nice,' she murmured kindly, and played with his ear. Perhaps, like King Midas murmuring his secrets to the earth and stones, Priscilla needed a confidant who would be ultimately unreliable. There were many, many people with whom she could have discussed the problem. Instead, she chose to talk to Feathers, as he rolled back comfortably by her side, allowing her to breathe freely once more. She hugged him as she did so, because she did find him so very, very reassuring, the little scrubs of hair on his flabby shoulders, the alcoholic aroma about his sensual lips, the jerkily automatic nature of the most intimate of his approaches.

'How much longer have we got?' he asked.

'Derek will be back in about an hour.'

'That *was* nice,' he echoed.

'I'll get us drinks,' she said. Feathers thought, as she stood up and strolled across the room, that good humour was the basis of their compatibility. Her lanky strides somehow suggested the Captain of Lacrosse *en route* for the showers; it was a thought he found purely amusing. And yet amusement had its place in the erotic life, rather than posing a threat to it. Feathers heard about falling in love. Since regular sex had formed a part of life, he did not think he had ever been 'in love' in the sense that adolescents or nutters like Hughie could be in love. You fancied a bit of pussy, in the Feathers scheme of things; and you tried your luck. If you got the door slammed in your face, then you moved on up the road. In the course of this ramble, he had managed to keep the friendship of most of the women who had good-humouredly obliged him, and it had all 'meant' about as much or as little as the provision of regular meals would have done.

Priscilla lolloped back. More hung and quivered from the naked frame than one would have predicted, gazing at it in its expensive arrays of shimmering fabrics. It was a sensible body that had been kept well in trim but which could not pretend to be younger than its forty-odd years.

'Look, Feathers, I want to talk to you about Derek for a minute, and I want you to promise me that you won't go blabbing to anyone.'

A sly grin animated his features at the notion of his blabbing.

'No,' she prodded his furry little belly, 'I really mean it.'

He sipped the refreshingly icy vodka and extended the hand not occupied with a glass towards her breasts.

'I think he's getting himself into trouble,' she said. 'I don't know anything. He's been stupid enough not to tell me. We had a visit from a whore, you know . . .'

As she spoke, she watched the hairs stand up on Feathers like quills upon the fretful porpentine.

'Now this is for private consumption only,' she said. 'Private, see.'

'Derek's whore came here? Blackmail?'

'I expect so. You see, if he could bring himself to tell me, we could work out a plan of campaign. He wouldn't be the first Cabinet Minister . . .'

'Indeed not.' Feathers laughed at all the fun there had been in Fleet Street the last time it had happened.

'I just think it would be *rather* a pity for Derek if it all burst just when he's starting his lovely new job,' said Priscilla. 'And I wondered if you could do anything to sort of stop the story spreading.'

'Has it started spreading?'

'No, but it's bound to, isn't it? Politicians can't keep anything to themselves. You know that. But I'm sure you *can* control what goes into papers.'

'Me personally?'

'You personally, journalists generally.'

'You have a very exalted view of my power if you think I can stop things going into the *Express*, say, or the *Mirror*, or even my own paper come to that.'

'All the same, I know of quite a few people whose stories didn't get out . . .'

'There's usually a reason for that.'

'I don't know, but, Feathers, it *worries* me. It is usual for Cabinet Ministers to be vetted?'

'What d'you mean?'

'You know what vetting is. To make sure they aren't spies or pooftahs or anything.'

'It has been known in the past. Usually the Cabinet Ministers in question were both and nobody did anything about it. Some people in political life are *above* suspicion; but there is another, equally useful category of people who are *beneath* it.'

'But blackmail is how they go to work, isn't it?'

'They?'

'The Russians.'

'It must be a long time since anyone bunged information their way

107

for purely ideological motives, certainly. But you never know. Is there any reason why you should suspect Derek of being mixed up with anything dangerous?'

'Her name.'

'What was it?'

'The whore's name, I mean. It's ridiculous, isn't it. A whore comes to this house, Derek's whore. That's obviously who she was. And I haven't been able to talk about it to anyone for four, nearly five, months.'

'But what was she called?'

'It was a Russian name, Bernadette Kutuzov, Kutzov, something like that. She only said it to me once, and then Derek spirited her away into the dining-room. That's what made me so sure she was his whore – or had something *on* him. Normally, he fights off time-wasters quite mercilessly.'

'What was she like?' Feathers was entranced. He had put his spectacles back on. Although naked, like her, he sat up with the detached and unerotic excitement of the fully clothed.

'Please don't smoke in the bedroom, there's a *duck*,' she said, planting a little kiss on his forehead. 'It's something I never do, and there is no point in arousing Derek's suspicions.'

Feathers looked, while gulping the vodka, as if the conversation could not really go on unless he smoked. But he longed for it to go on. He wanted to extract every detail from her. He wanted to know why she thought a girl called Bernadette was a Russian spy. Because she had a name ending in *ov*. Kutzov, Kutov; sounded painful. The whore lived in Hackney. Where in Hackney? How long was Derek likely to have been her client? Why did he go to Hackney? How did they first meet? These were all questions which Priscilla had asked herself again and again in her mind. But while there was no answer to most of them, it was a comfort to ask them in the presence of someone else; a giddy comfort, too (whence its comfort derived, she did not know), from discussing the matter so freely with a man who could ensure that it was on the front pages of all the morning papers.

'This is fascinating,' he said. 'Look, I'm going to have to have a cigarette.'

They got dressed. The dressing, afterwards, was always the most ignominious part of making love, an archetypally depressing activity, a crestfallen reminder of Adam and Eve's improvised stitching of fig-leaves.

Once clothed, Priscilla could not emerge from the bedroom without several minutes before the looking glass. Stuff had to be applied to eyelashes, cheeks and lips. Hair had to be patted and combed. She took infinitely longer to be 'ready' than Feathers.

'You see, if he has been vetted, and they have found something, it could explain why he feels there to be this coolness between himself and the PM,' she continued when the glasses had been refilled.

'You mean they wouldn't trust him with a really risky position.'

'I don't know what I mean,' she said despondently. 'It haunts me night and day. I think how terrible it's going to be for Derek if a public scandal breaks. I shall be all right. But his whole *life* has been a preparation for this. It would be so cruel to take it away from him. So terribly cruel. You'd never do that, would you, Feathers?'

'I keep telling you, Priscilla, it isn't in my control. I write one column – well, two if you count my occasional bits in the weeklies. I earn my living. I know lots of journalists. But I could no more stop them printing a story like that than . . .'

'I know. But you can assure me that they are not very likely to print it, can't you?'

He sighed and inhaled deeply on his cigarette. He smiled at her as he said, 'You know as well as I do, don't you? It's bound to come out.'

She had not smiled back. He'd been asked to stay for dinner: Rachel and Hughie, friends of the hour, it seemed, were coming, and her brother and new sister-in-common-law. Derek, she cheerfully said, would have to lump it.

Feathers, glowing with secret knowledge, felt for once in a while that he was actually entitled to claim the taxi fare from South Eaton Place to El Vino's on expenses. He took his time with the story. He wasn't going to blab it to anyone. Only when a group of quite distinguished editors, political and gossip columnists were gathered about at the far end of the bar did Feathers lean against a cask of sherry and declaim, 'Friends, what do we know of the sexual predilections of the Rt Honourable Member for Wheatbridge East?'

# Nine

The next night, Derek told Priscilla that he was having to work late at the House. There was, he said, an impossibly large amount of work piling up before the summer recess. Once he had used the phrase 'aftermath of Brussels', he had a sense that she had stopped listening, and that she feared a catalogue of farm prices. He was not lying, altogether. There was work to do when night eventually fell, and the lights burned in his large panelled room to be glimpsed, high Gothic shapes of gold, by the duty policeman in Palace Yard.

But he dined at the club. Its dingy ancientness did something to give him confidence. A large glass of whisky in the smoking room soothed his panic a little, before Ted Sangster's head appeared at the glass door.

'Tad; my dear fellow! Good of you to come!' The moustachioed agent felt his hand being wrung while drink was brought to his side by a Latinate waiter, in a crimson nylon coat.

Derek, in the previous twenty-four hours, had racked his brains about the right man to choose as confidant. As the professional Blore-watchers had cruelly discerned – Rachel Levine, Feathers and the rest – Derek did not, in the strictest sense, have any friends. In his dogged view of the universe, men who had friends were 'cliquish'; and Derek disliked cliques. He justified his apparent unamiability by a creed which contained phrases about the virtues of standing on your own two feet, and not – a precarious accomplishment, even when avoiding this sturdily pedestrian stance – being in anyone else's pocket. And yet, at times of trouble such as this, it would perhaps have been helpful to belong to a clique. Such a group existed, of course, around the Prime Minister. Some of them were Cabinet Ministers, some were peers, some were contemptuously dismissed in Derek's mind as 'hangers-on'. He would have given anything, as it happened, at that moment, to have hung on to the Prime Minister. A telephone call, a little chat one day after Cabinet, and the matter, if not cleared up, would doubtless seem less alarming. Even now, he felt that he would not have the courage to brave a frank admission of what was going on if it had stayed at the level of Bernadette, blathering about her National Insurance and reminding him of his peculiar sexual adventures.

They now, those mornings or afternoons in Hackney, could be viewed with a blend of anger with himself at his indiscretion, and simple nostalgia. Regrettable as it all was, he had enjoyed them so very much. And it was hard not to view with a certain wistfulness a period of life, so recent in time, so remote in feel, when he could spare the hours for indulgence of any kind. Now, his secretary could account for every overcrowded minute of his day. Only on visits abroad (Brussels, the most recent; there had been one to Stockholm; flights were booked later in the year for Rome and Tokyo) was there the remotest chance of an unscheduled pleasure. While in London, the paper-work, the Cabinets, the Committees, the sessions of the House, the meetings with civil servants took up, as he was fond of saying, 'more hours, frankly, than I have in a day'.

This alone was a reason why it was almost impossible to get hold of anyone to discuss his little problem. But had he done so, what could he say? We had doubtless, he bluffly told himself, grown up a lot since the days when politicians had to quit the scene for some amorous peccadillo. Everyone knew that the House was full of men and women who were guilty of one misdemeanour or another. As in any good club, they all covered up for each other. And no newspaper was going to risk a libel action accusing Ministers of sexual misconduct, so long as those Ministers had the support of a Cabinet and the Prime Minister. That was the rule of the game. But he felt there was no one he could approach about this little Russian. That really was too hot to handle. If he went now to the PM, the best that he could hope for would be a resignation without publicity. And he had scarcely had three months of the job. His appetite for power was whetted. It was impossible to relinquish it now.

It was for this reason he turned to the only man he could talk to: Ted Sangster, his faithful old agent, who now stood politely though slightly humourlessly awestruck, by the atmosphere of a 'gentlemen's club', and swilling his gin while Derek talked.

'Something cropped up, old boy, and I want to talk about it over dinner.'

'Something in Brussels?'

'As it happens, yas.'

111

'You came over very nicely on the news last night. Very nicely indeed.'

'Thank you, Tad, thank you.' Derek gave a lordly little wave to Sir Jorrocks Monteith, an elderly member of the club who was passing towards the centre table in search of the *Spectator*.

'So when you've finished your drink, old boy. No hurry!'

They made a stately progress up the gentle staircase and along the carpeted landing to the coffee room, where the pale blue paint was flaking off the walls, and where the gigantic portraits of the Duke of Wellington and George IV were failing to hide patches of damp. The place was less populated in the evenings than at luncheon. The grandiose crystal electroliers twinkled over the heads of no more than a dozen men, most of them huddled in dark suits at separate tables, perusing newspapers or library books. Only at the Monsignor's table did anything like conviviality flow as they passed about decanters of wine and the ecclesiastic chit-chat.

'We'll go over here,' said Derek, finding a cobwebby corner that felt to Sangster as though no one had sat there since the reign of William IV. When the Thai waitress had brought menus, Derek said, 'Have exactly what you want, old boy, exactly what you want.'

The menu did not make provision for this limitlessly hedonistic imperative. In the event they both settled for potted shrimps, pork chops and a bottle of burgundy.

'Thing is, old boy, I'm in a spot of trouble,' Derek said. 'Now, Tad, I know you and Pam are a happily married couple, and so are Priscilla and I.'

'Priscilla's not leaving you, is she?' Sangster asked hastily.

'What makes you ask that?' Derek snapped back at once. He regretted bringing their wives' names into the conversation.

Sangster, for his part, suppressed the memory of constituency gossip about Priscilla's lovers.

'I can talk to you,' Derek asserted, though everything about his bearing suggested that he was finding it difficult – taut lips, glistening forehead, blustering irrelevancies of diction. 'How long is it we've known each other, Tad?'

Ted told him.

'The thing is, Tad, that a man can be perfectly happy with his wife and still need a little bit extra on the side.'

'Tarts, you mean?'

'Exactly, old boy.' Relieved to have the first difficult confession

112

over, Derek beamed. Ted's expression was less sanguine.

'What's happened? You got found with a tart in Brussels?'

'Not exactly, old boy. It's a thing of the past. Let me emphasise this. We're talking history. But, I have to admit it, there is this young lady. She's called Bernadette . . .'

'That's a good one . . .'

'Beside the fucking point, Tad. What I want to say to you is this. She has started to make trouble. She came to my house once, and I gave her some money.'

'How much?'

'Two thousand.'

'Two *thousand*! For one visit?'

'Keep your voice down, old boy. I'd made pretty frequent visits to her. Even so . . . She was in difficulties with her National Insurance stamps. Now this part of the story is something that I can tell in public without shame.'

'I hope to God you don't.'

'But I could, Tad, if it came to it! She came to me, and needed help, and I tried to give it to her. She has only met me once again, and that was yesterday in Brussels.'

'What the hell was she doing in Brussels?'

'Tad, I must ask you not to speak so loud.'

'Brussels!' he hissed through his whiskers.

'I don't know, Tad, what she was doing there. The point is that she has subsequently got married to . . .' He sighed and drank his wine.

'Who to, Derek? You'll have to tell me now.'

As he continued with the narrative, Derek felt his nerve failing him. He was unable to tell Ted that anyone else was in on the secret. Bernadette had specifically indicated that she was in the hire of a man who would almost certainly use his knowledge of her liaison with Derek. This was somehow too shaming to confess. As he told the story, even in its doctored form, Derek's own folly seemed to himself almost unforgivable. He could not understand, now the confession was being made, how he could not have seen the risks he was running.

'The point is, I insisted that she stayed abroad. I wrote to her, with the money, to that effect a few months before the Election.'

'What did you say? In the letter. Because she's going to sell that to the newspapers, you know. And you still haven't said who she's married.'

113

'One point at a time, old boy. And what do you think of this wine, incidentally?'

'Never mind the wine,' said Ted impatiently. 'You've got to tell me now, Derek.'

'I didn't say much in my letter. I put it in a sort of code...' Once again, as he gave utterance to what he had done, it seemed unimaginably foolish. 'The words wouldn't mean anything to you.'

'What were they?'

'Something like, *Teacher must now go abroad.*'

'*Teacher?*'

'A little joke,' Derek added lamely.

'She wasn't kinky, was she?' Ted snapped. Derek felt angry with him. He was expecting sympathy; not this reaction of panic and reproach. 'I mean, it was just a straight screw – in these ancient history days we're talking about when you used to go to her?'

'Not exactly, old boy. There was an element of, well, harmless fantasy, I'd call it...'

'Oh, my God.' Ted's voice had sunk to a whisper. 'You mean she dressed up as a teacher, don't you? Did she hit you?'

'Sometimes.'

'Christ! With a cane?'

'As I said, it was all a piece of harmless fantasy. It's all over, Tad, I can assure you.'

'Oh God, we are in the shit,' said Ted as he sawed at his recalcitrant pork chop. 'Go on. What about her husband? What's he? Russian spy, I suppose.'

'Why d'you say that?'

'Calm down, Derek, it's a joke.'

'You're too fucking right it's a joke,' muttered Derek. ''Cause he *is* a Russian. Now, don't get excited, Tad. We're not in the world of George Smiley here. I've met this man once. Yesterday, in Brussels. I've no idea what he does. Bernadette says he works in the theatre. Ballet, I believe.'

'One of those as well? Oh, my God, you haven't been...?'

'Of course not, Tad, of course not. My point is that there might just *conceivably* be an additional danger here. So long as they're both abroad, I don't see that we are in any danger. But the fact that they wanted to contact me might mean that we are in for a rough ride.'

Fascinated, and horrified, by what he heard, Ted Sangster was also extremely hungry. Before replying, he scraped the last little pieces of

114

mashed potato from the metal serving dish and worried the final fragments of fat from his chop-bone with the voracity of a starving vulture.

'Well, of course, you know I will stand by you, Derek,' he said at length, wishing his tongue could reach up and lick some of the gravy which was lodged in his moustache. It seemed a waste to be wiping it on the napkin.

'Good man, Tad, good man. Goodness me, one of the best.'

'But it's not that simple, is it, Derek? I mean, you have always been a very good constituency member; we've always known we can rely on you.'

'Yas.'

'The by-pass scheme...'

Derek nodded. He was proud of his part in that thoroughfare, but now was scarcely the moment he would have chosen to discuss it. He wanted to put to Ted his scheme about Bernadette.

'And there are a lot of people in the town who remain very grateful to you, Derek, for the part you played in the seat-belts campaign.'

'Yas, yas, yas.'

'Then again, we are looking to you to put our case about unemployment in the town...'

'Look, Tad, I think we'll have to go down and have some coffee. Sure you've had enough to eat?'

To Sangster's dismay, Derek had risen to his feet. He had himself eaten less than enough. He had even built up in his mind the possibility of a pudding as well as the biscuits and cheese. But the coffee room was filling up. A pair had arrived at the next table – Sir Anthony Peverill and the financier 'Pimlico' Price – and Derek was not anxious to be overheard. They all smiled at one another as Derek squeezed past the end of the table, muttering something about his never needing to eat much in the evenings.

On the leather sofa of the cavernous smoking-room a few minutes later, Derek resumed his murmurings.

'As I say, Tad, at the end of the day it's all too fucking *petty*. I mean I'm sure it won't come to anything, sure.'

'If it only got to the Press, that would be the end of everything,' said Sangster quietly and gloomily. He was lamenting more the loss of his pudding. He thought of all the work he had put into this man, the ceaseless constituency activity, the organisation of meetings, the sealing and unsealing of brown-paper envelopes, the rallying of

115

voluntary workers at Election times, the raising of funds, the fêtes and Christmas parties. 'Everything,' he repeated.

'That's what we've got to stop,' said Derek deliberately.

'What happens when she asks for the next £2000 – and the next?'

Derek sighed. 'I don't think she is as poor as she told me. As a matter of fact she paid me some of the money back yesterday afternoon.'

'Paid you *back*?'

'Funny, wasn't it? We met in this museum. Extraordinary. Some of those prehistoric monsters are over a million years old.'

'Prehistoric monsters?'

'In the museum where we met. It was a natural history museum. And she paid me back £500 in used notes, Tad. Made me feel almost criminal.' He grinned. 'You may be right though. It could be that she will regret doing so. But I think in a funny sort of way she felt *obliged* to me. I really do.'

'You don't mean you took the money?' Sangster's concern was renewed. 'You took money from a Russian in a public place?'

'Don't get excited, Tad. It was money I'd given her, don't forget. A quarter of it. I'm not a rich man.'

'Don't you see what that's going to look like?'

The silence which ensued, broken only by the slurping of coffee, and the distant rumble of other conversations in distant corners of the smoking-room, suggested by its painful duration that Derek had not appreciated the construction which could be placed upon his acceptance of the cash.

'No one saw, Tad, no one saw,' he added hastily.

'Oh, we are in the *shit*,' Ted moaned.

Feeling that he was fast becoming the junior partner in the conversation, Derek assumed a masterful tone.

'The reason I've asked you here, Tad, is to lay my cards on the table. The potential dangers of the situation are varry grave, varry grave indeed. But what I want to emphasise to you, Tad, is that we are still at a varry early stage. We're not dealing here with an experienced blackmailer. Personally, I think we can regard this Russian character, whoever he may be, as an irrelevance. Bernadette is varry categorically not a girl who has the wits to exploit this situation.'

'And Boris Karloff?'

'Forget the Russian, Tad, forget him.'

116

'Look, Derek, you can't just forget a bloody Russian. You are a senior Cabinet Minister. You can't sit around in museums taking £500 off Russians and then tell me to forget it.'

'I'm sure no one saw, Tad; quite sure. I'm not wat behind the ears, you know.'

This was the reverse of the truth, as Ted observed. Derek was wet everywhere, glistening with anxious sweat. His red face gleamed with it, and nervous moisture was running down his wrists on to his hands.

'My view,' he said decisively, 'is that we should nip this thing in the bud.'

'And how do you propose doing that?'

'Nothing dramatic, Tad. But I think we should make it quite clear to Bernadette that we all speak the same language. There are to be no more contacts, no more money, no more meetings. I'll have nothing more to do with her.'

'And what if she doesn't agree? What if she thinks it might be a good idea to go into some newspaper office and tell her story? *He called me Teacher.* Oh, my God – how could you be so *stupid*?'

Derek looked into Ted's eyes. If this was the reaction of his closest friend and associate, how was it going to appear to the rest of the world? He longed for Ted's features to melt, just a little, into a more sympathetic attitude. And yet, when they failed to do so, Derek felt a strange thrill pass through his stomach of a kind which he had not experienced for weeks, not since the last fantastic hour in Hackney, when he had implored Bernadette to be merciful, and still, relentlessly the rod of correction had fallen.

'I don't think it would take much to shut her up, quite frankly,' he said quietly.

'What are you thinking of now, Derek?'

'Here we are, Ted, two quite clever men. It shouldn't be beyond us to think of a way of getting rid of this girl if she starts to cause trouble.'

'What are you saying?'

'I think you know what I'm saying, Tad. Lat's have a brandy.'

The Latinate waiter in red nylon was summoned, globular glasses were brought to the table, the fumes of the spirit brought excitement to Derek's eyes.

'Think of the world that girl must inhabit, Tad. It must be a miracle she has never been finished off before now.'

117

'Now, steady on, Derek. This isn't funny.'

But Derek was no longer listening. He was speaking with the quiet intensity of the possessed.

'I can't go back to that house in Hackney. If I could, I would. But my position makes it impossible. Frankly impossible.'

'At least you see that.'

'You, on the other hand . . .'

'Look, Derek, what are you expecting me to do: go along and hit her on the head? I've never met the woman. Don't know what she looks like. You're getting carried away, Derek. I think you're forgetting a few facts.'

'She's not a big woman,' said Derek.

In the very long and shocked silence which followed, Ted Sangster thought of the many evenings he and Pam had spent, being patronised by the Blores. He thought of Pam's smilingly innocent features, her false teeth, her terriers and her pleasure in grandchildren. He thought of Priscilla's kind nature – something you always had to take into account when you felt intimidated by her voice and manners, or when you heard stories of the string of Lotharios who had trooped in and out of her life over the previous fifteen years. He thought of Derek's frequent references, in private conversation and in public speeches, to the virtues of family life. He thought of them all lined up together in the pew, during the recent Election, putting in their appearance at Wheatbridge parish church, shaking the parson by the hand after the service, chatting up the old ladies and the punks afterwards in the shopping arcade. Could the Derek Blore who had been the centre of this multiplicity of remembered scenes be contemplating murder by proxy?

'I don't think you quite know what you're saying,' said Ted.

'We live in a tough world, Tad. Think of all we've been through together, you and I. If I go down, you'll gat dragged down with me, you know that.'

There was a measure of truth in this.

'I'd get dragged down further if I was had up for doing a girl in,' Sangster ventured.

'Look, Tad, I'm determined to squash this matter. We're not going to be ruined by it, you and I. There must be ways of getting rid of her without actually . . . Goodness me, Tad, I'm not suggesting . . . with your own bare hands . . .' It was hard to know exactly what he was suggesting.

'And then there's your Russian,' said Ted. 'I know you think he doesn't matter. But do you honestly suppose that they've kept this thing to themselves? Do you? What good would come of killing one of them? You're going to need a whole squad of killers, if that's your solution.'

'Good heavens, Tad, I'm not talking about *murder*.'

But he was, and they both knew it. There was not much more to be said to a man in Derek's condition of mindless panic. When they stood up some twenty minutes later and parted, Mr Van der Bildt noted expressions of fraught anxiety in the eyes of both men.

Mr Van der Bildt was at the opposite end of the smoking-room, seated at a window seat, his handsome blond head silhouetted against the leafy gloaming in Carlton House Terrace. Like Derek, to whom he was unknown, he found the antique dinginess of the club provided a suitable atmosphere for confidences. His guest was the 'Professor', the man from the Embassy. They had not gathered specifically to discuss Derek Blore. Many topics had been aired between them in the previous two hours: the fortunes of South African gold mines, the stability of a particular firm of City brokers, and the private life of the leader of the National Union of Mineworkers. The man from the Embassy had prosed enthusiastically about an anticipated holiday on the shores of the Black Sea.

It was only as Derek and Ted Sangster passed that Van der Bildt realised that it would be necessary to discuss the Blore business. He did so with reluctance. His world was that of commerce and money. Sexual vice provided an amusing, not to say lucrative, sideline to these austere subjects of meditation. But, when the political world intruded, he was anxious.

'There goes our friend,' murmured the Man from the Embassy. His heavy, ashen, fleshy face was always swathed in cigarette smoke. The abundant white hair which sprang back from his brow was streaked and yellow with nicotine, as were his thick brown musical hands.

'And his agent,' added Van der Bildt. It was all very well for the Professor. If a scandal blew up around Blore, the anonymity of the diplomat's life would go untouched. Van der Bildt was less safe. He deeply regretted ever having met the girl. The Man from the Embassy had insisted that he did so to make sure that she was the gem that Costigano had described. True enough, she was. She had seemed to swallow, without a grain of scepticism, the notion that he, Van der

Bildt, had the power to make her famous on the big screen. But even a moron would recognise him again. It was unthinkable to his egoism that his features could ever be forgotten. Probably Stan had told her his name. Supposing something went *wrong*. Given the crew of clowns assembled, partly by chance, and partly at the instigation of the Embassy, it was hard to imagine anything going *right*. What did morons invariably do? They accepted money from the newspapers. So, a reporter would hear her story and, before anyone knew what was happening, the police would have Stan Costigano for living off immoral earnings.

Mr Van der Bildt 'had' quite enough on Stan to discourage him from blowing the gaff. But, what if the truth were forced out of him against his will? Stan owned the lease on one tiny 'Adult Bookshop' in Frith Street. It was essential for Van der Bildt's purposes that this should be so. It was he, of course, who 'ran' Costigano, he who owned such a sizeable number of amusement arcades and other rackets in Soho. That he did so under an assumed name, that the profits from these concerns were moved with rapid regularity from bank account to bank account, that he had in his pay two members of the Metropolitan Police's 'vice squad', did not at all rule out the possibility that he might, one day, be rumbled. No one would bother to unravel all the pseudonyms, fraudulences, and currency deals if it was just an ordinary criminal case: if the bent policemen were exposed, for instance, or if obscene material were seized from one or other of his concerns, such as the Gobi Club. But it would be a different matter if national security was at risk. A political threat to the Government would mean, inevitably, a full-scale investigation by MI6. They would certainly discover his own part in the Blore affair. And, even if this did not lead to a full discovery of all his racketeering in Soho, it would obviously do no good to the 'respectable' side of his business life, when he met in panelled rooms off Lombard Street for luncheon with liverymen and merchant bankers.

'Yesterday went well,' said the Man from the Embassy. 'We have a completely clear picture. He took the money back from the girl.'

This was frankly astonishing. Mr Van der Bildt thought it was the oldest trick in the book. He thought that no one, even on the fringes of public life, liked to be seen receiving cash.

'I think we are almost ready to approach our friend,' said the Man from the Embassy.

'We?'

120

'It would be very natural that you, the director of a City firm should . . .'

Sir Anthony Peverill and 'Pimlico' Price, who sat on the same Board as Mr Van der Bildt, nodded to him as they came in to consume their coffee. Mr Van der Bildt thanked God for the unsocial conventions of his club. This was not some chatty, arty place, like the Garrick, where bores could way-lay you for hours. The convention was firm. No one spoke to anyone else except by some esoterically tacit consent, a thing of eyes and mood and gesture. Every armchair had a book-rest. One entered the grandiose classical portico to retreat from human intercourse. Peverill and Price saw that their young friend had a guest. They did not approach.

'Don't you see that this would put me in a very delicate position?' Van der Bildt asked. 'Supposing he says No. Supposing he calls my bluff? Then the cover is blown.'

'Is it likely – with all that he has to lose?' The fat pianist's fingers removed the lingering Player's Capstan from dry lips, using its remaining embers to light a fresh cigarette from the packet.

'He'd have more to lose if he said Yes,' said Van der Bildt.

'You mean, he would have to decide to work for us, and that is more dangerous than being guilty of . . . indiscretion?'

'Of course that's what I mean.'

'In that case, he fails to recognise that he is already working for us. He has received his payment yesterday. The little pooftah, you see, has still some use in the world.'

'It seems to me fantastic that we should be leaving a delicate operation like this in the hands of Kutuzov and . . .'

'The seedier they are, the better. What if you are not right? Supposing Mr Blore is a man of honour? I am afraid, too, that you may be right. Supposing he does not want to play ball? Why waste a good agent? Kutuzov, in any case, has come to the end of his usefulness. Even if it were not for this business, the British authorities are not going to allow him to remain in London much longer.'

'But is he in London? I thought you sent him abroad . . .'

'London is still his base. But there is no justification for his being here. That makes them suspicious, you know. And it also makes Moscow suspicious. I have arranged everything, of course. Normally a man in his position would never be allowed to spend such extended periods outside the Soviet Union; particularly after he made such a complete fool of himself over Solidarity . . .'

'The rally in Hyde Park . . .'

'How many Soviet citizens would tell an English newspaper they supported the Polish nonsense and expect to get away with it? And, in the same rally, he is picked up by the police behind some bush. It is really too ridiculous. London does not want him; Moscow does not want him. To link him with Mr Blore was my little moment of inspiration . . .'

'Thanks.' There was something a little too loud about the guffaw which Van der Bildt gave out. 'You also linked him with me . . .'

'Don't worry. We'll soon send him away. Some nice little provincial town in Georgia. I see him as a post office clerk, perhaps. A happily married man, too, we gather . . .'

'I refuse to meet Blore,' Van der Bildt said with a jerkiness which emphasised his unwillingness to let the matter slip. He did not need to finish the sentence.

'Very well,' said the pianist from the bronchitic depths. 'Very well.'


When Derek got home that night, after two hours at his grandiose desk in the House of Commons, he found that his wife was asleep. His head ached, and he feared the onset of a cold.

The Blores were in the habit, when a sore throat or swollen glands threatened the advent of infection, of bombarding their systems with effervescent vitamin C tablets, and he searched about in the bathroom for some. There were several of the metallic cylinders in the medicine chest, but they were empty. He did not want to wake Priscilla up by opening the drawers of her dressing-table. Some, he knew, were often kept in the drawers of the table in the drawing-room where Priscilla wrote letters.

In stocking-feet, he went in search, a glass of water in hand: he put the glass on the blotter and opened the drawer. Sure enough, there was such a tube, and he soon unfurled the silver paper within, extracted two tablets and put them into his beaker. The house was completely silent, so that the hissing of the prophylactic was as loud as the bubbling of an alchemist's retort. When the bubbles had ceased their most eruptive spraying, he raised the glass to his lips and imbibed deeply, superstitiously, sure that if he drained it all off in one gulp he would prevent himself having to spend the next nine days snivelling into paper handkerchieves.

It was only as he came to close the drawer that he saw the letter. So much else was on his mind that he did not read it in a spirit of investigation, he simply picked it up because the handwriting was unfamiliar. Even as he perused it, he was wondering how much of the Bernadette muddle he could tell to Priscilla. Sooner or later she would have to be informed. He wondered if it would be possible to represent his persistent visits to Hackney as a very occasional aberration. What made him feel guilty, in relation to Priscilla, was not the element of sexual infidelity so much as the regularity of payments made in this expensive quarter. Fifty pounds a week for two years. There had been some gaps, of course. But he must have spent in the region of £5000 on Bernadette: money which could have been devoted to Kate's future, or Julian's school fees.

These thoughts strayed inconsequentially through his tired brain before he began to focus on the words written with such pinched and painful elegance on the thick white paper in his hand.

I have been thinking of you without cessation for four weeks, now. Darling Priscilla. Please let me write to you and say this. Letters are a terrible intrusion, aren't they? But I now have gloomily morbid thoughts: what if I were to die, and had never told you how much I am in love with you.

Yes. You have known of course since our eyes met at your dinner party. And I have told myself again and again that I must not be a bore, and mustn't tell you. I don't often fall in love like this, which is why I am thrown into a state of complete adolescent turmoil by the experience.

Then we met in Bond Street and I managed to persuade you not to be the dutiful politician's wife. Just for a little bit. And even when you said 'this is frightfully naughty', I could tell it made you happy. So take pity on me, dearest Priscilla, and be 'frightfully naughty' again with me. On Tuesday? 11 o'clock. Outside Asprey's, as before. Hughie.

Derek folded the letter with deliberation and put it back in the drawer. When, pyjama-clad, he crept into bed beside Priscilla ten minutes later, he knew that his head was churning with so many and terrible blows that he would never sleep. He was wrong. Priscilla was soon able to open her eyes, stop pretending to be asleep, and lie for a few luxuriously insomniac hours staring into the darkness, listening to her husband's snores.

# Ten

Bernadette still, after two months of wedlock, felt an intense shyness in her husband's presence, an awkwardness not diminished by his evident fear of her. They huddled together, chance refugees from life's tempest, and hardly able to communicate. The silences, though, at least as far as Bernadette was concerned, were welcome. For the first time in her life, she was enjoying the virtues of courtesy. Juri's stiff awkwardness might have been embarrassing to many women, had they found themselves thrust into marital union with a stranger. Bernadette sensed that she had found in him an oasis. Existence had never offered such quiet, undemanding and well-mannered companionship. The first seventeen years were now, in memory, a catalogue of insults and reproaches from her mother. The few little days after her escape from Bognor Regis, there had been the bed-sitting-room in Notting Hill. But sounds and persons had soon enough intruded upon her; invaded her, kidnapped her. Since the arrival of Mr Costigano, it had all been noise and lack of privacy. The solitude of Hackney had not been a restful solitude. At any moment, Costigano might burst in upon her, to insist upon compromising poses with clients. The pleasure of Juri's companionship was surely a little like having a domestic animal. Only the most rudimentary, frequently one-sided conversations were possible. And yet his presence was reassuring.

They had been in Brussels a week now. Bernadette had not stopped thinking about her National Insurance stamps, but it had ceased to be an immediate worry. After paying for *demi-pension* at the modest suburban hotel where impeccable English was spoken, there appeared to be money left over. Juri was entitled, it seemed, to a small Government pension. She had not quite understood what it was he said; but apparently in Russia they respected artists. This was something of a revelation. She did not know whether this somehow risible category of person were respected in England or not. She was scarcely aware of their existence, except in so far as you see examples

124

of their endeavours suspended from park railings all the way down the Bayswater Road of a Sunday morning. It was always possible that these artists had been prudent enough to buy the Stamps and were now living off the State on some artist's pension. Juri doubted this. England, he said, treated the oppressed working people like pigs.

Sometimes it worried her that he missed home so much. Nothing about Western Europe seemed quite right for him; the food, it stink; the vodkas, the bloody daytime burglary, no problems; the trains, they filthy; the theatre, how they not see that Juri was just too fucking good for them, no problems. The preponderance of Jews, blackamoors and Asians in the various European capitals of his acquaintance dismayed Juri as much as their indigenous cultural inadequacy. And yet things were apparently worse in Russia. There were frightening stories of queueing all day for a small quantity of meat and being turned away empty-handed from the butcher, with perhaps only a little how you say, *saucisson*. No problems, in the cities, they were lucky. In the country, the poor people never see so much as a *saucisson*.

Bernadette was surprised with herself by the swiftness with which she discarded the notion that Juri was on one side or the other in the great ideological conflict which divides nations. She sensed with complete correctness that he was not on either side, although, so mysteriously, he had been caught up in the struggle on one side or the other for the last fifteen or twenty years. He spoke to her about the possibilities of going to the new world – to Australia, to Canada, to the USA. He wanted to get away from the loneliness and failure of his life. So, okay, he had done wrong in the toilets; for this they arrest him in so-called free bloody democracy. No problems. She too had her past. He no judge. No way. They could fool the whole bloody lot of them if they simply stick together.

It was not an amorous contract. In their hotel bedrooms, they lay happy and with the relaxation of full repose in their separate twin-beds. Bernadette made no advances to him, nor he to her. She sensed at last the vision of a future without the wearisome ignominies and pain of copulation. In the intervals when he was not with her, she made no enquiries. They were allies, and their alliance was to be kept a secret, for the time being. The big bloody fools, they think they can push anyone about like a pounce. Pounce? She had no idea what he was saying, but his big square hands, thickly hairy at the wrists, had gestured a difficult chess move, while his heavily browed features had parodied Korchnoi devising a master-stroke. *Pawns*. An idiomat, he explained, from the game of chess. These fools can no longer use him, Juri, her, Bernadette, as their small pawns. There was always something bigger than chess master. Karpov tries to make his excuse, and so does Korchnoi. They say the other side cheat, pass messages even in the carton of yoghourt. They do not see that men are not the bloody Almighty. Our destinations are not controlled by the masters, this bugger from the embassy; or the Jew who try to sell her the stamps for her ID card. The human spirit was free. In Russia, again and again, they had tried to crush the human spirit. They can not. They tell people there no God, but people no such bloody fools.

His toleration of religion, his apparent embracing of it into the scheme of things, provided a curious link with the world of her mother. From Julie's place, years ago, there had been the idea of Colette and her going to mass at the French church off Leicester Square. In the event, they had not gone; gradually, religion, never important to her, had faded from view. Juri, on the contrary, appeared to regard it as part and parcel of the secret scheme which he lacked the linguistic mastery to adumbrate, but which she generally understood to mean *flight*. In Brussels, he had insisted on their walking, hand in hand, around the Cathedral, and lighting a candle at the statue of Our Lady. The gesture recalled Bognor Regis, the fierce maternal catechisms, and she had tried to explain that she would like Juri to meet her mother; if possible to reclaim the innocence of her lost years, and create a reunion at the seaside resort where she had spent her childhood.

Juri had been pliable. Sure, they go to Bognor and meet her mother, no problems. And, after that, he will explain. There are things it no safe to say, but don't worry. Everything, it going to be all right.

# *Eleven*

It was a time for re-examining personal relationships. Change was imminent. Life with intimates was never to be the same. A show-down, however undesired, must be faced.

The commercial astrologer opined all this and Rachel Levine smirked, the evening newspaper propped against the tea tray before her, with an oblique melancholy upon the discovery that she was taking his words seriously. She was on the point of taking a transatlantic flight. Some rudimentary purchases necessary for the three-week adventure had drawn her to Barkers, and she now sat in the cafeteria, her face almost level with the spire, beyond the window and across the High Street of Kensington, of St Mary Abbots Church.

A show-down! It was hardly an imaginable enactment in her house. The success of the thing – and she was a modern enough American to gauge marriages a success or failure – had depended upon obliquity. Neither she nor Hughie had demanded to know all where all could not be known. They had respected each other's inner sanctum of private thoughts and feelings. They had strung together their conversational unions with a pearly rope of allusions and ironies. They had brought to each other laughter, shared friendship, sensual satisfaction and, above all, an obliteration of that fearful sense of being alone in a bleak universe. Why, then, as she nibbled her Danish pastry with no keenness and sipped her lemon-tea did Rachel feel such agitation, so apprehensive an idea that a blow was about to fall?

All that was to happen was that her husband, having finished work early, was to meet her in this cafeteria, and for this ceremony. (Since marriage, she had prided herself on her English addiction to breaking the afternoon in this manner and, when out of the metropolis, took note of the towns in England where it was scarcely possible to do so, where 'tea was going out'.) And yet, that morning his 'Look, I think we ought to talk about this' had sounded such a blast of menace.

'This' being the flight to Boston, booked months ago, the three weeks in her parents' house, the visits of aunts, the short excursions, possibly to Vermont or Cape Cod. For four years, this had been part of the marital routine to which Hughie had submitted quite readily. Her parents were fond of him: he, apparently, of them. Such visits, moreover, always seemed as though they could be invested, for Hughie, with some professional or commercial usefulness. Luncheon with fellow publishers or literary agents had often, in the past, punctuated the heavy programme of Levines and Schultzes. He had never previously wanted to 'talk about this'. It was something that happened. The astrologer, however, predicted today a show-down.

Rachel was fully aware that all was not well with Hughie. She veered between suspecting great financial worries and an emotional attachment elsewhere. But either or both of these depressing possibilities would surely in the course of the months in which he had seemed 'funny' have begun to yield evidence; telephone messages, letters, even telegrams. In fact, there had been nothing. This had aroused much deeper fears. A few days previously, the thought dawned on her that he might be very ill. Normally a hearty eater, even inclining to overweight, he had pushed away a delicious plate hardly touched at a dinner party. It had been a convivial gathering of old friends and new: Mark Wisbeach, with whom Hughie had been 'at school', and Mark's pretty wife Sarah; his sister, Priscilla Blore, and her husband the Cabinet Minister; a couple of poofter actors, one mildly famous. It was the kind of dinner which Hughie made a fuss about hating, but in fact enjoyed. Derek Blore, of whom in a ridiculous way Rachel had grown fond, had left promptly at ten thirty, to return to the second reading of the Electricity and Gas Bill, oblivious to why anyone laughed, still less at his brother-in-law's advice, bellowed down the stairs, that if Derek did not pay it soon they would send a little man round to cut it off.

Hughie had laughed with the rest of them, but there had been something *solemn* about his behaviour all evening. Priscilla, whom Rachel loved now almost as a sister (it was impossible not to), had been light, funny, beautiful. When they had first met the Blores, Rachel had teased Hughie: she had even half-suspected him (quite seriously) of being in love with Priscilla. After all, if rumour was only partially accurate, many men were so enamoured. Rachel could see why. She was almost in love with Priscilla herself. There was so much animation there, so much emphatic fun, so much mischief without malice. Hughie certainly had shown no signs of enjoying it that evening though. He had been sullen, almost ill-natured. Afterwards, in the Volvo, when she had asked. 'Are you okay?' he had not replied.

It was then that the whole likelihood of a dangerous, and perhaps mortal, disease had dawned upon her. Their discourse drew, she recognised, on an almost purely humorous area of rhetoric. He had, perhaps literally, no language in which he could tell her that he was dying. It was this, surely, which explained the painfulness of the previous few months. The other explanations (that he loved another, that he was on the verge of bankruptcy) were not wholly dismissed. But it was this, the medical diagnosis, which came to find most favour in her tortured mind.

If it was possible, she thought, sipping her tea and watching the cotton wool clouds sail past St Mary Abbots' spire, she loved Hughie more than ever; more than, in the days of their apparent serenity, she would have dreamed quite possible. Over-scrupulous, as ever, about the exact state of her own mind, she tried to work out whether it was truly an increase of love, whether such an increase was possible; or whether it was fear that she was about to lose him. At the thought of this something inside her chest hurt bitterly – it was as though someone were kneading fistfuls of muscle and tissue – and she felt that her heart would, literally, break. Sentimentally explained, she would say that she first loved Hughie for his sad face; that, now he was even sadder, she naturally, consequentially, loved him the more. But she knew no such rational parallelism explained her mood – any more than did the faint, if not absolute, cooling of their physical intimacies.

He seemed lost in a world of silent melancholy which no one else could penetrate. Even as he made his way towards her now, between the tables of the tea-room, he looked like a somnambulist. She watched his stumbling, enchanted pace, first in the reflection of the window, then, turning, directly. He smiled at her, but it was almost the smile of a lunatic. His eyes were elsewhere.

'Hi – your tea's getting cold.' She gripped his finger-tips, he leaned over and kissed her hair.

'Been busy buying knickers?'

'Uh huh. Panty-hose, and I've gotten mother a little lamb's wool twin-set for her birthday. It can be,' she added – interpreting a bewildered brow as the thought that he should have made some purchase to celebrate the seventy-second year of his mother-in-law's existence, 'from both of us.'

'It'll have to be. Rachel, I *can't* come to Boston,' he said suddenly.

Her lids, usually lolling lazily over her green eyes, on the verge of closure, opened in astonishment.

'You can't *come?* When the flight's been booked and my parents are expecting you . . .' She had meant, when the almost expected disclosure was made, to have been sympathetic and asked at once intimate questions about his health. This explosion of emotional tension was not helpful. It prompted a flood of absurd lies.

'You know how August is a busy time: we've had a lot of trouble with the printers – two of our most important titles for September haven't appeared yet – everyone else is on holiday . . .'

'*Exactly.* And you should be, too. You haven't looked well at all lately.'

'Rubbish.'

'Oh, *Hughie!*'

The tears, which burst from her, almost as though someone had squeezed them, at pressure through some air-filled device, shocked him.

'Come on!'

'Look, I know,' she interposed, 'damn well that nothing goes on in that office of yours in August.'

'This year's different.'

'You can say *that.*'

'I do say it.'

'Hughie, if you're sick, don't you think you owe it to me to tell me.'

'Sick?'

'You heard me. Look, darling, if you're keeping something back from me, it's not very clever – not if I find out in my own way.'

'There's nothing to find out,' he said stiffly.

'My parents would understand,' she said. There was so much more that she wanted to say. She wanted to allude to the fact that Hughie had not properly looked her in the eye for three or more months. She wanted to say something about his hunched shoulders and his silences. But how to describe this enchantment, this gloom, from which she was so conspicuously exiled?

'They'll be pleased to see you on your own,' he said.

'They *like* you.'

'That won't stop them being pleased to see you.'

130

'*Hughie!*'

'What?'

'Stop kidding.'

'Look, it isn't just the three weeks away,' he said. 'It's all the work which will have piled up before then. Which I should have been doing in July – it's the thought of piles of manuscripts accumulating on my desk—it's the thought of a whole backlog . . .'

'You're not usually this much of a workaholic.'

'I don't usually have this much work. Since Maisie married we've been one short – I keep telling you.'

'But three *weeks*.'

There was a silence at this, at which his round features looked flushed. Apart from 'odd nights' when she had been away, conducting an interview, or following an Election campaign, the Duncans had never been separated in the whole of a four-year marriage. A severance of twenty-one days was an unpleasant novelty.

'Look, lovey,' he said, 'let's not talk about it. My mind's made up. I'm *not* coming to Boston.'

She managed to restrain her features into an attitude of wry composure until she reached the ladies' room. Once there, the face which stared back at her from the glass, though very pale, was hot and quivering. Tears now ran freely down the cheeks and she indulged herself a moment in looking at them. She would herself, in that moment, have forgone the visit to Boston, had she not been overcome with sudden homesickness. There were plenty of people in England whom she designated, quite accurately, good friends. But in a marital crisis no one can 'help'. She did not need counsel, or advice. Hughie, having been mysterious, was now being cruel. She could not tell why, and it did not make her love him any the less. But she pined for the company of her parents and nothing but home, at that moment, would have done. The recognition of this brought a desire to go to Boston which was stronger than her anxiety about Hughie's secret. Kleenex was applied to the corners of her eyes. Cheeks were bathed with cold water. By the time she returned to the tea-room, and watched him paying the bill, she knew that there would be no further discussion of the matter. She would go, on her own. Their marriage in consequence would never be quite the same again. An edge had been knocked off its newness. She overreacted, she felt sure, because of her previous and wounding experience of the matrimonial state. Hughie had *moods*. Could it not all be as simple as that? Was it not

131

tyranny to insist on the Bostonian pilgrimage year by year? She tried not to show evidence of her grief as she resumed her place at the table.

He, noticing the red eyes, felt plunged into a silent guiltiness and wished that a topic could be found which would rescue them from it. The joke, in that week's issue of *Private Eye*, was what Rachel seized out of the air.

'Derek's quite pleased by it,' she said, 'that's the odd thing. They're a very strange breed, politicians.'

'I don't even understand the joke,' said Hughie. 'Does it mean that he is excessively pedagogical?'

'No, I reckon it refers to his contribution to a debate in the last parliament about whacking.'

'"Derek Blore is an old-fashioned disciplinarian. It's thought he's going to give the EEC six of the best" – did anyone really say that?' Hughie asked. The periodical, produced from Rachel's basket, was now open at the 'Grovel' column.

'No, I'm sure not. Many of the jokes in that thing are so obscure I guess only five or six people understand them.'

'Here he is again in the Glenda Slag column – *Derek Blore – dontcha love him. Those big sensual lips and the wise owl specs.*'

'That was the bit Priscilla said pleased him.'

'Priscilla?' He stiffened and bridled.

'Yeah, she gave me that thing. I dropped by this morning for coffee to tell her we were going away.'

'You *did*?'

It seemed an odd thing to have done. Their intimacy with the Blores had surely not reached the point where it was necessary to keep abreast with each other's movements. Was Rachel really spying on him? Had she called at South Eaton Place, hoping to find him and Priscilla locked in a conspiratorial kiss?

'I don't know why I called. I've gotten sort of fond of her. Perhaps you don't understand that?'

'It's understandable.'

'I'm sorry, *honey*. You were unfriendly, though, to the Blores, the other evening at Mark's.'

'Was I?'

'I went over—not to apologise—but to show that we still liked them. Politicians, like I say, are a strange breed. If they think a journalist likes them, they'll let all kinds of little tidbits fall their way.'

'So you are cultivating the friendship of Priscilla because you want information out of her husband?'

'Put that way, it sounds crude,' she smiled.

'It isn't *without* crudity, surely.'

'How you hate journalists.' She patted his hand, delightedly, the pains of his cancelled visit to Boston put momentarily on one side, their old tone resumed.

'I do.'

'Hughie, you know it's not like that at *all*. Derek happened to like the piece I wrote about him. It turns out you knew Priscilla's family *anyway*.'

'In a most marginal way.'

'It was inevitable we'd make friends. Besides, Priscilla's so friendly. They've cultivated *us* more than the other way around.'

'I haven't been aware of the Blores badgering us.'

'When did we first go to dinner there – January?'

It was January 17, but he was not going to disclose the exactitude with which he recalled the evening.

'Sometime like that.'

'It was when Jack Lupton died – end of January. Anyway, I reckon we've seen the Blores two or three times a month ever since and I don't think it's been all accidental.'

This remark had a strange effect on Hughie. It came to him with the directness of a message from Priscilla.

'You may be right,' he grinned, confident at last that she did wish to encourage his attentions and that, once Rachel was out of the way in America, there would be nothing to prevent the Love Affair from getting under way.

'Do you know what Priscilla said?' Rachel asked. A great relief had descended on her features. Lighting the king size Silk Cut which she occasionally inhaled, she felt that she had exaggerated a marital squall into a tempest and that everything was going to be all right.

'No,' said her spouse. 'What did Priscilla say?'

'She said that Derek was really *pleased* by *Private Eye*. She said that fame really *mattered* to him: that, if he couldn't get famous, he'd settle for being notorious. Aren't politicians the *end*?'

133

# Twelve

Derek Blore felt that, even if reason and conscience allowed him to go through with the interview, the body was going to rebel. Even those early, and presumably formative, days at his first private school – queuing outside the headmaster's study and hearing the swishing of the canes, knowing that one's own turn would come next – had not, so far as memory was accurate, produced such gulpings, sweatings, heavings and shakings. His mouth kept filling with gallons of spittle; the heart-beat was not merely insistent, it shook the whole rib-cage, as though he had swallowed some malign goblin whole and it was punching to be let out. String vest, shirt and jacket were sodden with anxious moisture. Sweat even poured in runnels down his legs. At the same time he felt cold and it was hard to stop his teeth chattering as he stood there, absurdly self-conscious, in the Egyptian Room of the British Museum. If somebody saw him? He had implored the Man from the Embassy not to choose the museum. After the Belgian iguanadons, it seemed dangerously repetitious. A hotel bedroom, even a visit to his own house in South Eaton Place, would have been preferable. Vanity made it impossible to believe that, of the milling school parties, foreigners in anoraks, squabbling families, there should not be a single individual who recognised the Secretary of State.

He was still stunned by the speed with which things had begun to move. After his most unsatisfactory evening with Ted, Derek had begun to hope that he had got the matter out of proportion; that it would 'blow over'. There had then come the telephone call. He now did not doubt that it was designed to cause maximum embarrassment. He was in conference with one of the Permanent Under-Secretaries in his Ministry and had only allowed them to put through the call because they claimed it was a message from his wife at the Middlesex Hospital. This had been sufficiently alarming to cause him to shake even before the trick was exposed.

'Mr Blore, we have not met, but I think we should do so this

134

afternoon at three p.m. in the Egyptian Room of the British Museum.'

'Hallo. Hallo. Who is that, please?' He had felt the beady suspicious eyes of the Permanent Under-Secretary fix themselves upon him.

'I have some interesting snaps of our paying you some money in Brussels.'

'Oh yas.' Then was the moment, of course, to have called their bluff. He saw that now. But he had allowed the voice to continue.

'And I want to share with you some of the delightful views of Hackney which our researchers have provided.'

'Very well then.'

'Three p.m. in the Egyptian Room. I will approach you. You will be wandering about quite naturally.'

'All right then. Three o'clock this afternoon.' As he put the receiver down, he had said, by way of feeble explanation to the beady-eyed civil servant, 'Meetings, meetings, meetings.'

'You won't be attending Question Time?'

'Alas, it would seem not.'

'Won't it look a little odd? At least two of the tabled questions, although they are to be answered by the PM, come well within your sphere, Secretary of State. The one, for instance, about the rival claims of Oil and Fisheries as major areas of capital investment...'

'I can't help that,' he had snapped.

Later in the morning, Ministry staff had asked about his wife. The rumour had flown about that she was in hospital. This was hellishly frightening. If that much of the telephone message had been intercepted, then all of it had probably been heard by at least one switchboard operator. At best, it was now the tittle tattle of the building that he was spending the afternoon among the mummies and the pharaohs. At worst, the information would already be filtered back down the line to our own Intelligence.

The morning was crammed with business, the rush precipitated by the advent of the Summer Recess. Heat did not make it any easier to work. The heaviness of a London August was about to descend, clammy and thunderous. Luncheon with an all-party informal group of back-benchers could not be got out of. It was precisely the kind of engagement which meant most to Derek. He was all too painfully aware that he had failed to attract much support in the last Leadership contest. This would not happen again. He would, in

135

future, be the man they all remembered as 'available' when they wanted him; the Minister who had not forgotten what it was like to be an ordinary back-bench MP; the wag of the smoking-room, the comrade of the tea-room; the brilliant economic mind which did not distract him from his human warmth. Derek Blore will always remember a face...

Such was the point of this tedious little luncheon. He had not managed to eat much in the course of it, nor listen much to things that were said to him. They had all assumed that he would be lingering about the House, as they all were themselves, for the last PM's Question Time before the Recess. An end-of-term atmosphere encouraged their silly opening of more wine, the back-slapping and cliché-swapping.

But at a quarter to three he had risen. The Treasury ... cuts ... no recess for the wicked ... laughter. He had almost managed to suggest an important meeting. A taxi had conveyed him northwards. He had strong hopes now, as he contemplated the mummified relics of a sacred cat, illumined in their plate glass, that he would be back in the House in time to hear the last of the Questions.

'It is, to me, one of the most attractive forms of religion, the worship of the cat,' said the voice beside him; 'and you call me Professor and we walk about quite naturally for a moment.'

'Ah, yas. Professor...'

Derek had not noticed his companion slip up on him. He was a man of about sixty, perhaps. A large loose-fitting pale grey summer suit hung from fleshy shoulders and haunches. A pale face sagged in a way which echoed the folds of the suiting. A belly, and a striped tie reminiscent of a cricket club, made of the plain white shirt a spherical protuberance beneath the double-breasted coat. A species of panama was held in one hand and used as a fan. Above the crinkled brow, very thick white hair was brushed back, streaked with what Derek took at first to be blond dye and then recognised as the stains of nicotine. There had been an old woman who kept a sweet-shop, a Mrs Carpenter, who had had hair just like that in his childhood. It was the discolouring of the habitual smoker.

'You are familiar with the different techniques of mummification?' pursued the Professor. 'And with the variety of theories which have been advanced as to the theology behind it? Those who thought it naïve...'

'Are we going to talk?' Derek asked impatiently.

'That is entirely for you to decide, my dear Mr Blore.' There was only precision in the voice, not strictly an accent. The slightly exquisite refusal to elide the words marked the speech as foreign; but in no word was the pronunciation noticeably at fault.

'I'm not given a choice, am I?' said Derek.

They had stopped their pretence of peering into glass cases, or looking up at the great stone obelisks. As fast as the heat and the milling crowd of tourists would permit, they were waddling at quite a rate back through the classical sculpture and towards the great entrance of the museum.

'A taxi,' said the Professor. 'If you think yourself in danger, I can assure you that I am equally compromised by our being seen together. It is hardly my custom to...'

'Where to?' asked Derek.

'Just so that we can talk. No one can overhear us – except the driver, and a driver chosen at random can not be a worry to us.'

Out in the courtyard, descending the gradual Grecian steps and feeling their way through the coachloads which continued to spill out towards the museum, the Professor spoke more relaxedly. A Player's Capstan was already ignited between his lips. He did not remove it as he spoke.

'I am relieved you came,' he confided. 'It makes life very much easier for all of us. You need not worry. This sort of cloak and dagger will not be necessary in future. But it was necessary, you see, the first time. To establish you as *bona fide* ...'

'First time? Now I think, at once, I ought to make clear that this is not, as far as I am concerned, compromising either me or my position in the British Government.'

'Oh come on, Mr Blore. We both know that you have been compromised. We are simply meeting to decide what to do about it.'

'There are three taxis there if you want to climb into one.'

'We won't take one of those,' said the Professor. He did not give them a glance. The idea that an agent might have been planted at the gates of the Museum, on the chance that Derek and his companion might climb into a cab, seemed a little fantastical. But it was presumably the risk of such a calamity which made them stalk down Coptic Street, along Bloomsbury Way and through the charming little arcade called Sicilian Avenue before they felt safe to hail a taxi in Southampton Row.

'London Bridge,' said the Professor.

137

'Station, guv?'

'If you please.' To Derek's disgust another cigarette was ignited. They settled back in the seat, Derek and the Professor. From the inner pocket of the double-breasted suit, the heavier man produced an envelope.

'I think you should peruse those,' puffed the Professor; the offending object danced on his lips. Derek said, 'If we could keep this interview brief; I need to be back at the House by four . . .'

While Derek stared at the photographs, the Professor leaned forward and said to the driver, 'On second thoughts, could you make it Dulwich?'

'Bit out of my way, know-what-I-mean,' began the cabby, until £5 was passed through the glass.

Derek was not listening to this exchange, his eyes were fixed on the ten exposures, black and white, which the envelope contained. The two most innocent photographs had been taken very recently in the Parc Léopold in Brussels. But even they made it look as though both Bernadette and the Russian were fawning upon him as he pocketed the cash.

The other photographs would be less easy to explain away if they arrived on the desk of a newspaper editor. There were two of him kneeling on the hearth-rug in Ardleigh Road, clad only in a school-boy cap. Others were even less seemly.

'You may keep them if you choose,' said the Professor. 'I imagine you would rather not.'

Derek handed them back silently.

'This is always the worst part of an interview,' said the Professor. 'Once we have established where we stand, there is far less unpleasantness. Let me say at once, that I do not expect you to work for nothing. On the contrary, I think you will find that the arrangement will be mutually advantageous to us both.'

'I take it you are the KGB?' Derek asked baldly.

'There, as it happens, you are wrong.'

'Damn it, I've got to know who you are.'

'It wouldn't be easier for you *not* to know?'

They sped on, over Clapham Common, without saying anything.

'This isn't the way to London Bridge,' said Derek. 'Now look here, I have to get back to the House of Commons at four.'

'We need a little time to talk. Do not waste it by bluster,' said the Professor.

Derek had not been cast by nature in the heroic mould; he now believed, in addition to all the other horrors which had been heaped upon his head, that he was being kidnapped. A sudden *Boys Own Paper* bravado overtook him.

'You can't get away with this, you know,' he said. 'Hi-jacking a Minister of the Crown in broad daylight ... I mean, it's preposterous. Moreover, no one is going to believe these photographs. It's perfectly well-known that you can fake such things. I ought to warn you that I have only come to meet you out of curiosity. As it happens, ever since I had that meeting in Brussels which you engineered, I have been in touch with our own Intelligence service and the Prime Minister.'

'How interesting,' grumbled the Professor's voice from the midst of a nicotine cloud. 'If you wish me to tell you who I am, I shall. My own view is that you would prefer not to know. You can, if you wish, spin this cock-and-bull story about the Prime Minister being informed. Meanwhile, I am obliged to point out to you certain facts. One is that we are in possession of a number of incriminating photographs of yourself; and, I might add, tapes of your conversations. They record predictions about the dates of British Elections, speculations about the contents of the Budget and about the composition of future Cabinets. These speculations were all made, you understand, to the fiancée (now the wife) of a Soviet agent. These things are automatically recorded. There was no attempt to get at you personally.'

'And if I believe you,' said Derek. Just for a moment, the heroic pose seemed to him not only the most honourable but the most sensible. If they 'had' as much as this 'on' him, he himself was without future. Better to go honourably, it seemed. Better to make the brave choice ...

'I am sorry to say that we are running to a rather tight schedule,' said the Professor apologetically. 'A collection of these photographs, and an explanatory letter, is stamped and ready for the post. It will be sent to the editor of a London newspaper by the 5.30 post. In order to prevent it being dispatched, you must ring this number' – he produced a card – 'and say that you are going to play. There is no need to reveal your identity on that line. Just say, *I agree*, or *I play games*.' The faint faltering in syntax, if not of accentuation, perhaps suggested that, in spite of the calm bulk of his cool exterior, the Professor was not without anxiety. It was not presumably every day

139

that they recruited a British Cabinet Minister. And there was the frightening possibility that he would refuse, and accept the idea of a scandal. If so, as Derek was being slow to realise, there was as much to lose on one side as on the other.

'What is there in it for me... ?' Derek asked. 'If I accept?' He caught his breath, chiefly for fear, but in part because the confined space of the taxi was now thick with tobacco smoke.

'Silence,' growled the Professor. 'We do not let people down. After a year, I guarantee that you will be given all negatives, tapes, all documentary and photographic evidence. Surely this is worth it? You will be able to go on then, with a clean slate. By then, it will be old history. Besides, you will be strongly placed when the next Leadership contest comes round. You will be able to be the next Prime Minister, perhaps...'

'And the girl. What is to stop the girl?' For his mind still buzzed with the indiscretions of Bernadette.

'She is really very insignificant,' said the Professor.

The suburbs were becoming leafier now, the gables more unashamedly neo-Tudor, more usually than not fitted with burglar alarms.

'Whereabouts in Dulwich, guv?' asked their driver, sliding back the glass panel.

'The station,' said the Professor.

'If,' he pursued in a low voice to Derek, 'you are still worried about her, there would be ways of guaranteeing her silence. But that would depend upon your willingness to work for us.'

'What ways? You mean?...'

'I mean that she would be silent forever,' said the Professor. 'But you must first agree by telephone, at half past five this afternoon; or before.'

'It leaves me an hour and a half,' said Derek, looking at his watch.

They paid the taxi-driver at the station, bought tickets to Victoria and were soon pacing the wooden suburban platform, whose boards scorched in heavy July blaze.

'I shall leave you at Herne Hill,' said the Professor. 'A Ruskinian destination.'

'Sorry?'

'What we need is occasional information about Cabinet documents. You will be consulted, I should conjecture, no more than once a month.'

'Oh, no. I'm afraid . . .'

'Fuller access to documents in your own Ministry would be appreciated. But we do not want to have so much information that suspicion is aroused. We would naturally wish to make specific inquiries from time to time. But for the most part we should content ourselves with material you chose to pass our way.'

Derek was unable to reply. He could not quite believe he was having the conversation. Had anyone told him, six months before, that a Minister of the Crown was being approached by a foreign power to spy against the State, he would have been astonished. Moreover, he would not have thought that there could be any doubt of his reply. He must, of course, say no, without regard for personal consequences.

'You are taciturn,' said his companion, as they boarded the suburban line train and sat side by side beneath the string netting of the old luggage-rack.

'It is difficult to take it all in,' said Derek blankly, less to the Professor than to the world at large. The train was largely empty. Several seats away some children were ragging, and drinking something fizzy from tins.

'All you have to do is ring that number,' said the Professor.

'It would not be possible to wait until the morning?' asked Derek.

'Regrettably, that is the case.'

'The girl,' Derek said at length. 'It would depend on getting rid of the girl. And of her husband?'

'Everything would be arranged,' said the Professor with the quietly reassuring tone of a man sealing a package holiday.

The Ruskinian destination was soon enough reached.

'You wouldn't forget . . . let me down . . . the girl . . .'

As soon as he had stood up, bulky and grey in the small confines of the carriage, the Professor seemed like a stranger. He made no response to Derek's imprecatory tones. Derek watched him pace, like a resident of the place, towards the ticket barrier. He did not look back as he lit another cigarette and walked out of the little station and into the respectable anonymity of the sticks which wallowed in the heavy afternoon sunshine.

It was nearly a week since Rachel had left for America. Hughie, waiting in his office, could not concentrate on proofs. *She* had said that she would ring at four. It was now ten past. He had already told himself that she would not ring, and yet had now decreed to himself that he had made a mistake and that she had promised to ring at a quarter past four.

If she had time after visiting an aunt, Priscilla was going to ring him up at the office and they were to have a cup of tea together, or perambulate the pretty, hospital-dominated square in Bloomsbury where he worked. The minutes ticked by. Each arranged meeting with Priscilla – there had been three of them now – had been more painful than the last. She kept saying that it would probably be kinder *not* to see him, and then breaking her word by consenting to a tryst. The first time, in Mayfair, she had been able to treat his advances as good-humoured flirtation, and they had kissed on parting. Now, they realised that even to hold hands would signify too much. They sat far apart on park benches, or opposite one another in cafés, awkward with his agony.

She only saw him to be kind. That was the dreadfully obvious truth. Perhaps this afternoon, however, she was to deliver the ultimate kindness of dropping him altogether. She had explained exactly why it was. She was flattered by his attentions, but, she said, she owed it to Derek not to have love affairs. Derek, Derek, Derek. All too many of Hughie's precious moments with Priscilla were dominated by reflections about the admirable Derek. He heard about his distinguished early promise in an amateur production of Gilbert and Sullivan, about his legal and political expertise, about his skills as a father, his directorships, his palate, his ear for music.

The rest of the time, she prattled about her children. Kate had caused them terrible worry when she had hated France. Now that she liked it, they were even more concerned. Julian was their consolation – good at games, promising at maths, handsome, his mother's description made Hughie loathe him. He pictured the little brat as a grotesque mirror of Derek.

Hughie did not know what, quite, he hoped to get out of these encounters with Priscilla. His mind was now devoted to her almost all the time, only distracted by the most persistent conversationalists and the occasional intrusions of physical need, as when he ate or sat on the lavatory. Even then, the image of Priscilla could swiftly come back to mind, and stay there fixedly for hours upon end. Of course, he loved her in every possible way; and he therefore hoped, when she did consent to see him, that she would fall into his arms, say that she had changed her mind, and that she loved him to distraction . . .

142

The telephone trilled and he sprang to answer it.

'Call for you,' said the toneless voice of the girl on the switchboard. There was a clicking, during which he wanted to be told from whom the call came. But he had little doubt and said an enthusiastic 'Hallo!' in readiness for Priscilla's voice.

It was not Priscilla. It was the author on whose proofs he was meant to be engaged, an uninspiring treatise on the German Army during the Second World War. It was the fourth of such titles to come from this particular bore. Hughie was aware of sounds coming out of the receiver into his ears. Every so often, he made some appropriate response. On occasion, when asked for a detailed reply about a mistake on some particular page, he was able, absently, to turn the awkwardly floppy unbound leaves, locate the misprint and assure the old man that it had already been noted. He was further able to make intelligent punctuation to the fool's happy memories of the days of hot-metal printing; assure him that he was not saying something he had said before, and make a reasonable attempt at laughter when a tediously familiar anecdote had been repeated.

By half past four the lengthy conversation was over. In the course of it, Hughie felt certain, Priscilla would have called, and gone away discouraged. Enquiries revealed that there had been two calls while the old general was on the line. One was from a literary agent and the other from America.

Despondently he accepted his lot. He recognised that it was, in a way, deserved. He had sprung too much on Priscilla too quickly. Had he received a similar declaration of love from someone he had not met often before he would, he recognised, have felt embarrassed, not to say hostile. But the nature of his feelings for Priscilla made concealment of his love impossible. It would have been worse to flirt with her; to chase her; to make passes at her, and risk a rejection in that way. For then, she would never know how important his feelings had been for her, and were he to reveal them after an unsuccessful seduction scene, she would obviously conclude that he was simply inventing a grand passion to increase his chances of breaking down the walls of her castle.

He recognised, in any case, that she was impregnable. He believed, with all the irrational certainty of a neophyte, that she was stonily chaste. In dreams, and fantasies, she melted, just for him. When asleep, he had often seen Priscilla naked, sometimes sitting on the altar of a church like a demure nude painted by Lord Leighton,

143

sometimes running Chatterley-like through woods. In daydreams, too, he envisaged his hands reaching round her snowy neck and unbuttoning the dress; silk shimmying from ivory shoulders on to some half-visualised bedroom floor. But he alone, as chief priest and votary of the cult, would be in the position to melt her. For the rest, he was certain that she had been loyal to her husband throughout their years of marriage; and he was equally certain that she had only ever made love to Derek rarely and irregularly. The (frequently inaccurate) tittle tattle which flew perpetually in gossipy little gusts round London concerning Priscilla's love life had never reached his ears. And, as if to protect himself, he no longer wanted to know anything about her from other lips. He had hated it the other day when a friend of Rachel's had described Priscilla as a 'beauty'. The phrase implied that some initiated catechumen had presumed to peep into the sanctuary.

As he sat there, loving her, and hating the old man who had rung up (he was convinced) in her stead, her voice said to him, 'Are you *furious?*' And there she was, her blonde bob and her hilarious teeth twisted round his door. 'My dear, I couldn't *move.* I've been sitting in Theobalds Road for half an hour – I couldn't get out of the car to ring you up, I couldn't . . .'

He wanted to bring the catalogue to an end. 'How was aunty?' he asked playfully.

'Aunty was *frightfully* well, and starting to be fractious, which the nurses say is a good thing. They think it was really a very mild stroke.'

'Is she your father's sister?'

'She's my *mother's* aunt.'

'Aged a hundred and fifty?'

'*Twice* that. Oh but look, your *office!*' She strode in, rather like a mother seeing her son's dormitory at prep-school. 'Love seeing where people work,' she said.

'Nothing very special about this.'

'And you have a lovely view. What's that?' She was peering out of the window beyond the plane trees.

'Directly opposite is the Hospital for Nervous Disorders. Over there is the Ospedale Italiano.'

She let out a guffaw and said, 'I'll *happily* spend a few weeks there.'

'Look, what's the time,' he said quickly. 'Let's go out and have a stroll . . .'

144

'*Can't*, and you're working. No, really mustn't,' she said, starting at the horrified pain on his face.

'But you can't just come and go.'

'Yes, I can.' But this was too much, and she added, 'Oh, *Hughie. Please.*' Shutting the office door firmly, she walked farther into the room, keeping her distance from him. 'It's not *worth* torturing yourself.'

'I can't help it.'

'Oh God, what are we to *do* with you?'

She stood, and he sat, staring at each other with hideous melancholy. The awful thing was that she thought he looked so *sweet*. But this kind of display simply could not be lived with.

'And, Hughie, there's another thing'.

'What?'

'Don't write to me.'

'Oh.'

This was a crushing thing. He had been told that he *could* write if it helped.

'I'm sure Derek has seen one of your letters. He's been so very gloomy and edgy of late. I haven't asked him, of course.'

'Did you leave it lying around? . . .' In a way Hughie hoped that she had done so. When he wrote his letters, he liked to imply that a rather greater intimacy existed between them than was in fact the case, on the principle of staking out territory. It thrilled him to think of Derek being infuriated.

'Derek has been such a very kind husband to me,' she said, oddly. 'I would hate him to be hurt, that's all.'

'Not a postcard?'

'Hughie, there's no point, is there? You've got your lovely Rachel, and I am married to Derek. How can we be such babies? What good would come of your being in love with me?'

'I *am* in love with you, Priscilla, don't you see that? I am in love with you as I have never been in love with anyone before . . .'

She looked away, towards the Hospital for Nervous Disorders and said, 'Oh, you poor darling.'

'Yes.'

'You'll get over it,' she said. 'One always, always, *always* does. You know that. Think of the horrors of one's youth. One gets over *anything*.'

'I don't.'

'That's just silly. Supposing I said I'd run away with you? Where would be the good in that? Derek's career in ruins – oh yes, it would be, even nowadays, if there were some little scandal like that. And could you really be so unkind to Rachel?'

'Forget Rachel.'

'How could anyone? She *adores* you; and you know that she does.'

The truth of this infuriating assertion silenced him.

'So it's much better for us not to go on behaving like donkeys and meeting, and letters and everything.'

'Don't be cruel to me, Priscilla.'

'Hughie, I've got to be. You can see that, *surely*? Anyway – where's the fun of meeting like this? It doesn't make you happier – does it?'

'I love you.'

'Goodbye, Hughie.'

She was gone so suddenly that he hardly took in that it had happened. He did not care what the secretaries in the outer office thought of him as he ran past in his shirt sleeves to the lift. It was already going down, and he tried to catch it by running down the stairs. He failed. She waved casually, as she drove away down Great Ormond Street, leaving him desolate on the kerb.

# *Thirteen*

The Parliamentary Summer Recess had begun, the first of the new Government. And England, Scotland and Wales stewed, with the Province of Northern Ireland, beneath the thunderous haze of early August. In London, the Dean of Westminster, in collaboration with those members of the Chapter who were not on Hellenic cruises or cooling themselves on the Norfolk Broads, continued to aver that he, and they, had erred from the divine ways like lost sheep; while beyond, in Ashley Gardens, the nightly choir continued to call down mercy from the Lamb who could bear the sins of the earth.

Beneath the heavy heat, sin went on being committed, in thought, word, and deed. The sea mist which enveloped Bognor Regis could not cloak it, nor could the inhabitants of Bognor dissemble before the face of the Almighty. And it was this theological truth which brought Mrs Mary Woolley, day after day, to the bleakly modernised Roman Catholic Church not far from her place of work. She was able to attend the early mass before going on to the hotel, where it was her task to Hoover corridors and bedrooms, and to change sheets.

The words of the modern-English rite caused offence or bewilderment to those who, in London, sought out the Latin chanting of Westminster Cathedral. Mrs Woolley did not give thought to the beauty or otherwise of the words. She had known them by heart now, for about ten years; they formed the structure and pattern of her existence.

As she stood in her bench-like pew and heard the words for the two hundred and fifteenth time that year, her mind did not dwell on the words, but fixed itself on their inner meaning. She thought of the mass as a washing line on which she was permitted to peg out her own fears and preoccupations. In the three-fold confiteor at the beginning of the service, she always offered up each part of the petition for a member of her own family. *You were sent to heal the contrite* . . . and here she prayed for her husband, who had abandoned her over twenty years ago and was still, for all she knew, with the floozie in

147

Blackpool. *You came to call sinners* . . . the words were associated with Bernadette, who had gone to London and gradually, mysteriously, 'lost touch' . . . *You plead for us at the right hand of God.* She prayed for herself, for all the staff of the Excelsior, especially Mr Gates (as though anyone couldn't see he was making a fool of himself with the sweaty little Italian maid) and for all those whose rooms Mrs Woolley would that day clean out. During the responsorial psalm, Mrs Woolley's mind usually wandered. The priest read out a verse and then, today, they were meant to reply, *Lord, who shall be admitted to your tent?* She forgot the words on the first repetition and, by the time of the second, she was wondering whether to ask Mrs Kennedy, who knelt in front of her in a mantilla of black lace, to keep two chump chops for her when she returned to her husband's butcher shop.

After the Gospel came prayers made up as the priest went along. Father Colvin was away on his holidays, and there was a replacement priest with a beard. Mrs Woolley wondered, as he asked them to pray for the republics of Central America, what happened to the Precious Blood, drops of which would inevitably be soaked into his moustaches when he drank from the chalice. The prayers for the world did not mean all that much to her. After all, you could get it all just as well on the news. But she shut her eyes tight when they prayed for the sick and suffering, rattling through the names of bad backs, weak hearts, varicose veins and haemorrhoids of her acquaintance. And then the Faithful Departed, in which she prayed for her parents, the stillborn child she had had before Bernadette, her grandparents, aunts and uncles, her brother Reg, all those killed on the roads and drowned at sea. During the Hail Mary she prayed once more for Bernadette, reminding Our Lady of Lourdes that the child had been dedicated and entrusted to her.

Then there followed the Eucharistic Prayer, in which the priest consecrated the bread and wine and made them into the Body and Blood of Christ. Communion, silence. This period of seven or eight minutes was not often devoted to specific thoughts or prayers, as were the opening moments of the mass. Mrs Woolley preferred rather to allow all her previous thoughts to be gathered into a concentration on the person of her Redeemer, of whom there was a representation suspended from the beam over the Holy Table. Today, however, as she received the Host, Mrs Woolley made the specific prayer that she could receive the most holy on behalf of Mr Woolley in Blackpool and of Bernadette in London, that whatsoever

148

sins they had committed would be forgiven, and that they could be gathered into divine mercy, whatsoever good they had done, whatsoever evil they had endured.

There was no complication in Mrs Woolley's faith. She had only occasionally committed mortal sins; even these had been nothing more serious than missing mass or shop-lifting. The former was explained by previously awkward hours at the Excelsior, and the latter by an irrational desire to see if she could get away with it. In both cases, she had been to confession within twenty-four hours of committing the offence, and had been absolved. Father Colvin said to her – for she was a frequent penitent – that there was no need any longer to think in these categories of *mortal* and *venial* sin. He sometimes spoke as if there was no *need* to go to confession at all. But Mrs Woolley knew that there was. She knew that life was a spiritual obstacle race in which the risk of toppling into hell could only be averted by frequenting the sacraments.

It terrified her to think of what might have happened to Bernadette in London. She had managed to find out from the mother of Wendy Jenks, with whom Bernadette had originally left home – five, six years before – that the shop job had not lasted long. Long after Mrs Woolley knew this to be the case, she still received sporadic and illiterate epistles from her daughter describing work in the jeans shop. The mother feared the worst without knowing what the worst could be. She poured forth prayer for her daughter's purity, and lit candles with the intention that, if she had been led into sin, she should be led with equal expedition into penitence, and that, in the former instance, the sin should have been committed with a person of European and preferably Catholic extraction.

But the prayers, day after day, week after week, year after year, had not been answered by any visible sign. This did not diminish the fervour of Mrs Woolley's faith. She knew that there were two possible answers to prayer – *Yes* or *No*. She also knew that prayers could be answered without our knowing. She also knew that God and Our Patron Saint and Our Guardian Angel protected us and kept us whether we asked them to or not, so long as we were Catholics.

The time had passed since Mrs Woolley had felt Bernadette's absence. The upbringing of the child had been burdensome. They had been stuck in too small a flat, and the expense of heating, clothing and feeding them both had hardly been covered by what Mrs Woolley had been able to earn by hotel work. Bernadette had not been good, as the years progressed, at any of the domestic arts in which her mother ineffectually tried to train her. Cooking was not part of Mrs Woolley's life – things were thawed, fried or re-heated, or bought ready-cooked from fish-shops. But she could iron, she could sew, she could polish. Bernadette had left the hot iron face-down on a pile of shirts during the phase when Mrs Woolley had had to take in washing.

Her mother was not one to notice much. The two had quarrelled a lot, particularly as the girl grew to womanhood. There had been, as far as Mrs Woolley discerned, no filth, no boyfriends, though it was on her conscience that Bernadette had not been to a Catholic comprehensive. The girl's slowness, lethargy, lumpish absence of enterprise had provoked in her mother her besetting sin of wrath. Mrs Woolley was still half-conscious of the fact that, for the last six months of Bernadette's residence in Bognor, railing at her had become a habit. What had she been angry *for*? Mrs Woolley no longer remembered. All she knew (and she knew it a little less each day as the memory mercifully blotted it out) was that she had been a cross-patch, moaned at Bernadette for the state of the house, recalled that at her age she was employed gainfully, asked whether there was nothing better a young woman of sixteen could do with a morning than masticate Chewies and peruse the periodical *Bunty*. This unanswerable line of disagreeable enquiry had been what led, in the first place, to the flight of Bernadette. And Mrs Woolley knew it. Day after day, with guilt she half-acknowledged it, as she watched the priest lift up the white sphere of water.

Today was the feast of St Jean Vianney, better known as the Curé d'Ars. She remembered a sermon in her youth in Liverpool about him, from a proper priest in lace and a biretta. The Curé d'Ars had been so holy that he had sometimes eaten nothing but a raw potato all day long. He had slept on the floor and fought off visions of demons and seen telepathically into the inmost souls of his penitents. Mrs Woolley prayed to him fervently now, before leaving the church, asking forgiveness for her uncharitable thoughts about Father Colvin whom she was sometimes guilty of thinking an idle basket even as he was in the act of absolving her from all the previous week's sins. *He* had never seen telepathically into anything.

She genuflected, and remembered to ask Mrs Kennedy about the chops before she walked out into the Bognor air. The heavy sea-mist felt almost hot, even though it was not half past eight. Several people

150

saw her walk along. There were old men, clad as for bowls in white caps and blue blazers, walking pert dogs or decrepit women past well-trimmed privet hedges and low garden walls, over which one could glimpse the neat rows of lobelia, dwarf salvia and marigolds. Some of the old men touched their caps, or even removed them, when she passed. She did not know whether they were being forward; or whether they were guests in the Excelsior whom she had failed to recognise; or whether they belonged to the generation and category of persons who salute almost everyone they pass, particularly of the opposite sex.

She did not quite acknowledge their salutations, whatever the motive for them. The lines around her mouth were deeply puckered, betraying a lifetime's habit of pursing the lips with annoyance and disapproval. Her brow was similarly knit. Her grey hair was rather savagely cut and her clothes did not look as though they had been chosen to allure the world. The square, splashy blouse made no attempt to disguise its origins on the jumble stall. Nor did the skirt pull in her figure, which slouched lopsidedly, one arm carrying a plastic handbag, the other free to hold the Woodbine which she normally inhaled after her morning devotions. The whole of her appearance – face, shoulders, legs, crumpled old shoes, down at heel – carried a look of strain. Her eyes were half-frowning all the time, half-peering out to some far distance without any expectation that they would be pleased by what came into focus.

What these eyes saw standing on the steps of the Excelsior was the figure of her son-in-law. But she did not register the fact, largely because she did not know Bernadette was married, and partly because she never entered the Excelsior by the front. She got to her brooms and mops and electrical devices by a side door, and through the kitchens. She took, in fact, no notice when the head waiter stupidly told her that she had a visitor. It was some pleasantry, she concluded, to do with the gentleman in Number 32 or 33, and therefore to be ignored. She had set to work, roaring down the corridor, manoeuvring the inflatable bag and the extensive flex of the vacuum cleaner with the wary aggression of a sapper handling a mine-detector. She made no effort to avoid scuffing the skirting-boards or knocking and bumping with her equipment against the doors of the idle or fornicating guests who angered her sometimes by being able to afford the twenty-eight pounds for bed and breakfast.

When Bernadette came down the corridor towards her, Mrs

151

Woolley took her for something she should not have been. Partly, of course, the girl walked down with the light behind her – the big window of the landing, edged with red stained glass. But, even so, the shape, the feel, the appearance of Bernadette were not reassuring to a mother's eye. For one thing she had put on so much *weight*. When she had left home – six, was it seven years ago? – she had been just a slip of a thing. She was now undeniably stout. The dress was short; far too short, and low-cut. Her legs, exposed generously, were like jellies around the knee-caps.

'Hallo, Mum.'

Her little voice was not heard above the roaring of the Hoover, and Mrs Woolley was going to pass her daughter by in the corridor. By then she had recognised her, and felt a reluctance to do anything about it. If *that* was what she had turned out to look like, Mrs Woolley felt, she wouldn't greet her daughter. She felt immediately cross again. Her anger was not diminished by the difference between the Bernadette for whom she had so recently offered up prayers, and the lump who stood in her way now, probably in need of money.

'Mum!' wailed the figure again.

Mrs Woolley kicked the pedal which made the whirring subside.

'You're a stranger,' she said. 'This is a funny time to call.'

'I've brought my husband to see you, Mum.'

'Husband, is it?'

'Mum.' Mrs Woolley stiffened slightly as she felt herself being kissed. It was dreadful, the way the girl had just let herself *go*. Her hair when she got up close to it was scrubby. Dyed.

'Well, it's nice to see you: but I mean . . .' She gestured to the tangle of flex, the yards of unswept carpet, the empty laundry baskets afar, awaiting the dirty sheets.

'We went home, but you'd gone,' said the girl.

'Mass,' said Mrs Woolley. 'It's very early, for you,' she added, 'for you.'

'We came over on the night boat to Portsmouth.'

'On the boat?' asked Mrs Woolley. 'He's foreign then?'

Bernadette laughed lightly, in acknowledgement of the fact.

'So you've been abroad all these years?' asked her mother.

'Just a few weeks.'

'What you want to marry foreign for?'

Bernadette tried to explain. All night, inarticulately on the boat, she and Juri had tried to murmur their plan. It would be said that

152

they had met . . . how? By chance? A disco was eventually selected as the likeliest venue for such an encounter. He was fond of dancing, so it fitted in well. His nationality could not be concealed. His convictions in police courts could; so could the mysterious international work which Bernadette failed to understand. For her part, she would blot out the whole of existence since she left the jeans shop. She would say that she was out of work at the moment, but had been working in a variety of shops in London. No one would check.

Mrs Woolley needed time to collect herself. She must, she insisted, finish her work. Bernadette knew that, surely, by now. She must take her husband – what was his name again – down to the Front or something.

Juri, sullen and leather-coated, had let himself be led off to the amusement arcade on the front. They spent half an hour and a few pounds playing bingo. Juri had won a bread knife which they agreed to give to Mrs Woolley. They ate ice-creams and gazed at the ruins of the old pier which appeared momentarily clearer against the Channel as the mist lethargically lifted.

When introductions had been affected, Mrs Woolley realised that a celebratory mood was required of her, and they had all adjourned to a pub. Juri had paid for the drinks. Where was his money *from*, Mrs Woolley had wanted to know: she had asked. There was no point at all in beating around the bush. Her frankness had elicited a similarly open approach from the young people. They wanted to emigrate. America or Australia were the places, with a faint preference for Australia. They would like to stay with Mrs Woolley until the final arrangements for this life in the new world had been made. They were acutely conscious, Juri especially, that it was wrong not to have told her about their wedding. It had only been a registry office.

Mrs Woolley did not consider that nuptials *could* be performed in a registry office. In the days that passed, her routines did not much vary, but she did not feel able to ask the bearded priest about it. Had Fr Colvin not been on holiday, it would conceivably have been possible to discuss the matter with him.

They lingered, as it was. Mrs Woolley came, in time, to disbelieve their intention to emigrate. She seethed with crossness to have them under her feet all day. No proper explanation was made of her son-in-law's identity. He sat in the front room smoking and appeared to claim that letters had not been answered. But he was a Russian. They couldn't go to Australia just like that. Mrs Woolley was not a fool, even though her daughter evidently was one. Before long, they would be having babies. Already they had asked her for some money. She saw no end of it.

While Bognor contained them, messages had gone forth from the Embassy. The Professor had explained the matter to Mr Van der Bildt. He was much to be congratulated. No more than that. Explanations were not offered, but a very considerable coup had been effected. All the Billy Bunter material was to be handed over to the Embassy: films, tapes, black-and-white stills. The operation was, in so far as it affected Mr Van der Bildt, finished. One small thing remained. The girl was to be found.

And, when found, she was to be murdered. It was much better that Mr Van der Bildt arranged this last, small, tidy detail. At second or third hand, the murder, if successfully investigated, would not 'get back' to the Embassy. The whole success of the operation would be ruined from the start if the murder were connected in any way with Billy Bunter. Costigano must do it.

Van der Bildt informed his henchman of the painful necessity of this operation on the feast of St Jean Vianney in the back room of his shop in Frith Street. There was no need of further discussion. Costigano had protested. Why should he do such a thing, even if he could find her? The flat in Hackney was empty. Van der Bildt had cleared it out. It was not to be used for other girls. The whole show was to be wound up.

Bewildered by this interview, Stan Costigano had closed his shop early, and waddled out into the fetid heat of Soho. He had eaten a pie in a pub, drunk some beer and slumped into the car in a mood of despondency. When he reached Julie's establishment in Shepherd Market, she thought his features were troubled. His lower lip pouted. The brow beneath the Brylcreem line was furrowed.

'What's bothering you, darling?'

'Nothing,' as he slurped lager. In the little bar where French tuition was offered, they all reclined in a stupor of perspiration. Heavy weather was no good at all for business, as Julie often told the girls. You heard a lot about the sultry climates of the Mediterranean exciting desire. But she had known whole weeks pass in August in which you hardly earned a bean. It was the last thing you were thinking about when your limbs were all floppy. A nice sharp autumn

154

frost and all the regular customers were back, merry as crickets.

So Tina, Cindy and Jackie could think themselves lucky that three obese adolescents of Chinese origin had come into the club bursting with five-pound notes. While they began their professional entanglements with the young men, Julie could give herself over to cheering up poor old Stan.

'It's the weather I'd say,' she mused. 'Gets you down.' As she spoke, she dabbed at her face with a wodge of paper tissue. Beads of sweat appeared on her nose, cheeks and on the balder bits of her brow as soon as they had been mopped up. Stan made no attempt to stem the flow of his body's moisture. His shirt, which had been pale blue when he put it on in the morning, was now dark, patched and blotched with wetness. His face was glowing, awash. The pungent odour of his body blended unpleasantly with a cheap unguent.

'Whatever happened to little Saint Bernadette?' he asked.

'You liked her, didn't you?' said Julie.

'Nothing special.'

'I felt sorry for her going up and doing all that kinky work. She always said she was a loner.'

'She's married now,' Stan informed her.

'Get away!'

'Thought you knew.'

The quainter arrangements were kept from Julie, who could hear of nothing without jabbering about it to the next person she spoke to.

'Yeah, foreign bloke.'

'You might have told me, Stan. I liked that kid. We could have given her a little party or something. Oh . . . "I'm getting married in the morning" . . .'

It was too hot for this throaty bellowing.

'No, just wondered, like, whether as you knew her address.'

'You're a fine one to talk,' said Julie. 'I didn't even know the kid had got hitched. Is she still working?'

'No.'

'Was he a client?'

'Who?'

'The bloke she married, dopey.'

'Oh. No. Yeah.'

'One of Stan's little secrets!' she taunted him. 'Bognor it was she come from, little Saint Bernadette,' she continued, less to inform Stan than to refresh her own memory. 'Bernadette Woolley. I

155

remember her telling me all about it. Her mother worked at one of the big hotels as a chamber-maid. You know a funny thing about that kid, Stan? She was a complete innocent. She'd never even been *kissed* before she started on this racket.'

'Yeah, well...' He scratched his neck awkwardly. Julie's narration was helpful in its way, but in another way it was not making things any easier...

'How come then you know she's married, but don't know where she is?'

'Doesn't seem to have come back from honeymoon,' he muttered.

'Are you expecting her back in Hackney?'

'Nar, finished, innit?'

'I didn't like it, Stan,' she said with quiet earnestness. 'I mean' – she gestured towards the semi-spherical Chinese youths entwining themselves around the models at the other end of the room. 'Bedtime, boys!' she called out gaily. As they sluggishly responded, she added to Mr Costigano, 'It's just natural, this, isn't it? My old mum would never touch anything in the sado-masochistic line. Wouldn't *touch* it.' She lit a menthol cigarette and, when the boys came to the bar, she said 'It'll be another forty for the rooms.'

'But we pay thirty for our drinks.'

'Come on, lads, don't be mean. They're all lovely girls.'

When the money had been reluctantly put down on the counter, and the girls had gigglingly withdrawn with the customers, Julie continued her meditation.

'Mind you, you do some funny things in your time. I remember one man come in here just after the war with a bag of cream buns. I nearly died. I took him on myself. I still worked in those days and we were, you know, like busy. He took me up those stairs, and I don't tell a word of a lie. He takes off his trousers and tie and that and folds them ever so neat. I thought the buns was just what he'd bought, you know, to eat afterwards, perhaps take home to his wife. I know I can always eat a bun. Big cream buns they was, all bursting out in the middle. And, "Don't you get undressed," he says. "I'd like you to see me with no clothes on." So he takes off every stitch, and I have to throw those bleeding buns at him. I'm not lying, Stan' – she dabbed her eyes in tearful merriment as the anecdote came to an end.

'No, no,' he said. Whether she was lying or telling the truth, he did not care; she had told him the story dozens of times.

'Cream bleeding buns, though.' She refilled the vodka glass.

156

'Cream buns.'

A week later, and a mile or so away, Derek Blore sweated in his study in South Eaton Place. It was his last day in London. Priscilla and Julian, their son, had already left a week before, for Worcestershire. After their sojourn there, a fortnight in France was in prospect.

The previous weeks had provided strains of an intensity that he had never experienced before. He found that he was tired all the time. This was, of course, partly attributable to his ceaseless toil as a Cabinet Minister; meetings, paper-work, train journeys and air-flights had crowded existence. In normal circumstances (here was the bitter thing), this would have given Derek nothing but pleasure. His 'normal' life was dull enough. Filling it, cramming it with bustle, had been one of the great rewards of power. But now, at the back of his mind, there had been an aching sorrow. He had an uncomplicated love of England. In pious mood, he genuinely believed that it was patriotism that had led him to enter political life. He had discovered that he loved power more: power and position. Besides, as he had reasoned after his colloquy with the Professor, there would be no honourable way out now. They would not let him fade obscurely from the scene. If they could not have the high prize of an agent in the Cabinet, they could make him pay for it, by making certain that the story received the most lurid covering in the popular press. A resignation could never be effected quietly in such circumstances.

So, he had acquiesced. A typed letter had been sent to him. He had been obliged to sign it, promising them any assistance they required. It was now in their files. There was no going back. Moreover, he had begun to feed them their first trickle of information. They had the month's trade figures three days before they were released to the popular press. Notes on recent Cabinet meetings had also been sent to them, and a character analysis, as requested, of the senior civil servants in his Ministry. Had this really been necessary? he inquired. Surely they knew about Sir Magnus? All, more than, there was to be known about him could be discerned from the entry in *Who's Who*. But they obviously delighted in making him work for them. So that now, on top of his heavy load of ministerial work, he found himself copying drafts for his new master.

And by the lunch-time post he had discovered that they had played him false. He had made it a condition of his work that Bernadette,

157

and her husband, should be removed effectively from the scene. The Embassy were to call them off; if necessary silence them forever.

To this, the Professor had verbally given his complete reassurance. There would be no more bother for the Blores. How was it, then, that he held in his hand this illiterate scrawl: *Dear Mr Blore, I wouldn't write to you if I could get help any other way, and that's the honest truth. Juri and me is going to Australia to start a new life. But I need HELP. Juri has written off to the authorities and it's three weeks now and we are desperate. They've found out here that I've not been paying Social Security, and I can't understand the forms and they seem ever so difficult. Juri says can you please clear this up for me? Also, get us passports and we promise never to bother you again. We only wants a chance. B. Kutuzov. (Woolley.)*

As Derek said later on the telephone, 'It simply won't do, I'm afraid. You agreed to silence this girl and what do I find?... Well, then, I can tell you her address. I'll tell it to you now.' And in clear tones he enunciated the name of Mrs Woolley's residence in Bognor Regis.

Stan Costigano had decided to forget, when Julie had told him, about Bognor Regis. 'One of the big hotels' was scarcely a specific enough address if you were doing a delicate thing like a hit job. Thus he had reasoned and, with a combination of idleness and compassion, he had let things slide.

The shop, meanwhile, prospered. He was happily tinkering with a faulty video machine in the back room – one of his floating assistants in the front serving the customers – when he received a surprise visit from Mr Van der Bildt.

'Stan, look,' said the young man, with the arrogant colonial drawl which his voice could never quite shake off.

'Wonderful invention, the cathode ray tube,' said Costigano, not looking up from the video machine. 'Amazing, really, innit? I mean, some girls get screwed in the fetid swamps of your studio in Copenhagen and you can go on seeing it all on your video as often as you choose to rewind the tape. I mean, it's one of the miracles of modern science.'

'You're off to the seaside, Stanley,' said Mr Van der Bildt, impatiently.

Costigano took a stubby little comb from the pocket of his short-sleeved shirt and began to comb the thick oily locks back from his forehead. He found this action soothing in moments of stress. He knew at once what Van der Bildt meant by the seaside.

'They're getting rather impatient,' said Van der Bildt hastily, as though he didn't like the business any more than Costigano. 'She's starting to cause trouble again.'

'Aren't we being a bit, how shall I put it, well, drastic, frankly? Aren't we?' said Costigano. 'I mean, it's no business of mine. I've just got to finish the chick off, right?'

'It wouldn't be the first time,' said Van der Bildt savagely.

'Okay, so what if it wouldn't.' He blew hard on his comb, so that globules of spittle and dandruff flew on to the tightly fat trouser-knees. 'It's a question of money, frankly. I mean you said two grand, right?'

'I'm sure we can make it five,' said Van der Bildt. 'But you've got to do it soon. They are apparently thinking of emigrating.'

'*They?*'

'Yes, I think it would be better if you could get rid of Juri too while you are about it. Look, Stanley, I don't like this sort of thing any better than you do . . .'

'Now he tells me. First it's just the chick. Then it's her fucking husband. Like me to do anyone else while I'm down there. Neighbours? Aunts? You know. Just while I happen to be passing, like, so as not to have a wasted journey.'

'We'd give you five grand for them both.'

'Yes, and I'd like to know who *we* is,' said Mr Costigano. But he did not want to know at all. He vaguely suspected the Mafia, but that thought alone was enough to silence any further questions as he pocketed the money, in cash.

# Fourteen

The heat which made London intolerable brightened the rye-fields, and ripened the hops and the apples which Priscilla could see from her bedroom window in the Old Rectory at Willerton St Leonard's. The Malverns undulated in a blue haze beyond the tree-tops. In the opposite direction, glimpsed through the bathroom window and over the barn, the country rolled towards the Welsh Marches. Already, at eight in the morning, the day felt hot. Outside, Julian and his young friend Peterson were splashing in the garish chlorinated pool by the garage.

It was an hour of the day which Priscilla loved. She had just finished breakfasting alone in her room – toast, apples – and was now descending, clad in simple cotton prints, with her tray. The morning was sacred to her. One who gave so much in later hours required this reserve of quietness and solitude; and this Willerton provided. Moreover, it was a link with the past in a way that South Eaton Place could never be; her own past, and the grander things, the business of old tombs, a ruined priory nestling on the hill, the vague knowledge that, on the slopes beyond, the Roman Legions had made their encampments.

Her own past, and this more ancient nebulous thing, were coming together in the comic juxtaposition which village life sometimes demanded. Her mother and the vicar were devising a pageant for November (the church was dedicated to St Leonard, November 6) and already, three months in advance, there were standing committees to arrange catering, stage management, and the appointment of officers. The service was to be evensong – Lady Wisbeach deprecated the widespread cult of Holy Communion at all hours of the day in which so few could join with a ready heart – followed by a pageant, high tea, possibly cider. Everyone was perfectly welcome to come to the manor house. Debates already raged, at this early date. Could the parish stand the social *pace* of another large gathering so soon after the harvest supper? It was

160

assumed they were still having the supper? Why not both? If November, would not something hot be required? Did not casseroles attract bacteria? Now, as to the general conception, was it to be Fancy Dress, or something with a linked historical theme? The vicar hoped for the Crusades. He had given a talk about the anchoresses who used to live in the ruined Priory of Willerton Magna. Lady Wisbeach had thought the suggestion of the shopkeeper and postmistress, Mrs Worrall, that they have the thing in the garb of the Wild West, singularly inappropriate.

Country life thus actively proceeded, while the earth fattened and prepared for its harvest. Priscilla, with the security of her London house, was able to take or leave as much as she chose. She was not, as her mother was, involved up to her *ears*: the WI, the Hunt, the PCC and Meals on Wheels all clashed with Lady Wisbeach's work as a JP and her interest in the WRVS. Now that she was a widow nothing appeared to restrain her.

Derek, expected from London in a couple of days, was vicar's warden of the church. They wanted him to do it even if he could not promise to be present every Sunday. Having the local MP meant something, was how the vicar put it. Priscilla sometimes thought that of all the offices he had held this was the one of which Derek was most proud.

She thought of him, as she stepped out of the kitchen door into the still-dewy garden. It was delicious, certainly, to be on her own, and to be relieved for a little while of the duties of kindness. Derek's triumphs had been hard for Priscilla. They had somehow gobbled up her life. Even when it was not specifically necessary for her to be an MP's wife in a public capacity, the progress of Derek's career had made of her own life almost a non-existence in the previous six months. The visits to Willerton had been snatched, irregular. Less and less, too, had she been able to see old friends. Derek's ministerial absences (official visits to Brussels, Rome) were almost as exhausting as his presence. Priscilla was left to supervise the secretary, Edna Philips. She found herself, oddly, unable to relax in London when he was away. It had something to do with his being a Cabinet Minister. She was not worrying about him; she was not thinking he had been assassinated. She merely felt agitated for no particular reason; and she associated this new experience with his senior Cabinet status.

'Isn't it *frightfully* cold?' she called out to the boys playing in the swimming-pool. 'Come in soon and I'll cook you some breakfast.'

161

Julian's mop of wet hair clung to his delicate skull like a cap. His mother almost gasped with love of him as he sat there on the pool's edge, his teeth chattering; and she thought how odd it was: a stranger would find little to distinguish between Julian and Peterson. They were both eleven-year-old boys, both quite pleasing in appearance. The complete absence of intensity in relation to Peterson showed up the strength of her maternal affection for Julian. Nothing wrong, but she sometimes wondered what to do with it, this overpowering feeling. It was stronger with Julian than it had ever been for Kate (now hiking in the Loire valley; they all hoped to meet up in the middle of the month); but in both cases it was a much stronger emotion than she had ever felt for anyone else. She had never felt, even at her most kind, such wells of affection, a potentially savage, almost tiger love, for Mr Blore. Nor had her other lovers – fewer and further between than gossip suggested – ever seized and gripped her in the way that she loved this child. She knew that in front of Peterson she could not hold Julian in her arms for as long as she wanted; she knew that, even when they were alone together, it did not *do* to be over-demonstrative. It upset boys. Julian was already deep in the stage of finding parental embraces repulsive. Derek now shook him in a manly fashion by the hand. Priscilla was not expected to do this too, but she felt a tautening of the skinny little frame when she *did* kiss him; and 'honestly, Mum', he would say if it went on too long.

At the gas stove, she fried bacon, mushrooms, tomatoes, eggs, while in another saucepan baked beans gurgled. Peterson precociously had instant coffee; Julian, the duck, was still brave enough to say he wanted milk. It gave her deep joy to prepare this meal for the children, as they rushed upstairs in their swimming drawers, and thundered down again two minutes later, hastily dressed, tousled hair, to help themselves to packeted cereals from the kitchen table.

And another nice thing about the companionship of the children was that you could love them wholly, undividedly, and yet give your attention to other things while in their company. Julian's conversation could occasionally demand complete attention, as when he repeated some tedious anecdote of boarding school life, the tale of some cricket-match, the absurdity of some schoolmaster. Last night they had all hooted over the tale of the new master, Mr Shotover, and the water butt. But, for the most part, there was less need to listen, or even to talk, in Julian's company than in a grown-up's.

Why, as the bacon spat, she wondered, do men require the passive audience, the ear of a woman? Derek did it to her all the time; he rehearsed whole speeches in front of the bedroom looking-glass, he kept her awake with rehashing Cabinet meetings or repeating verbatim the telephone calls he had had that morning with constituents, civil servants, Treasury officials. To a lesser extent, Feathers did it too. In his case, there was an obvious desire to be congratulated. On their last encounter, after the usual bedroom procedure, he had confided that he had a new and wonderful job. The newspaper editor who had hitherto thought so poorly of him had suddenly changed his mind. Priscilla did not know, did not inquire, what had brought this volte-face to pass. It had been told in the smug tones of Feathers at his most triumphantly annoying.

Priscilla, like all women, found Feathers annoying. It was odd that she allowed him into her bed. She thought perhaps that when he got back from Italy (where he had taken a villa and a party of friends) she would bring the thing tactfully to an end. Nothing, perhaps, need even be said. They had never really been having a love affair. It was that which she found so relaxing about it all. Whatever Feathers' physical shortcomings, it was a relief to find a man who only wanted you for your body. Here were no agonised scenes, no embarrassing letters, no demands for affection. A simple buttoning and unbuttoning. Perhaps, after all, the Feathers business would drift on in the way that these things did.

'D'you want to go into Hereford with Granny this morning or stay here with me?' she asked. 'Either way we would have a picnic lunch in the orchard.'

The children hummed and hawed. There was a game of 'Monopoly' unfinished.

'If you were going into Hereford you could do some shopping for me.'

This seemed to decide the matter. Arrangements were made to ring up Granny, who would pick them up in an hour or so's time. Priscilla loved the fact that the boys could waste so much of their time during the holidays. At prep-school, she felt sure, they were kept needlessly busy.

Before Granny, Mrs Hartley came to clean, the boys had started a rudimentary game of tennis on the courts, and Priscilla herself had gone to the herbaceous border to gather flowers for the drawing-room and bedrooms: tufts of Cupid's dart, their purplish blue contrasting prettily with the pink and white of clarkia and the spindly little gypsophila. For the rest, lilies filled her trug.

When the boys and their grandmother were gone, and Mrs Hartley was 'doing' the rooms, Priscilla went to skim the surface of the pool. As she did so, the cool water was so obviously inviting that she entered the little bathing-hut at the pool's edge and donned the outfit suspended there from the peg. She dived vigorously into the water and, in the first exquisitely cold minutes, all thoughts passed out of her mind: Feathers, her mother, Derek, the fête, the children, Mrs Hartley were all subsumed by the intense physical sensation. A little breast-stroke, and then, turning over in the blue liquid, she floated, enjoying the feeling of her thick wet hair floating beyond her head like seaweed. The sun rose higher. The sky was bright. Inevitably, Priscilla shut her eyes, and only half-opened them to the figure by the pool. The postman? Mr Dishman to discuss the pageant?

'Don't move,' Hughie said. 'Let me look at you floating there for a little longer. It's like Millais's "Ophelia."'

'My *dear!*' she pealed. 'You gave me the shock of my life! What on *earth* do you think you are doing?' For the horrible truth was that, embarrassing as she found this matter of Hughie, and much as she chose to shove it to the border of her mind, even out of her mind altogether, she also found it deeply flattering and touching.

She stood up in the pool and shook herself. 'It's lovely,' she said, 'Do come in.'

'I've no things.'

'I *insist* on you having a bathe. There's bound to be a pair of drawers hanging up in the little hutment.'

He was strangely compliant, and emerged soon into the sunshine. Priscilla was always amused by the sight of men without any clothes on; the scrubs and patches of hair made it impossible to revere figures who when swathed in shirts and suits made claims to be taken wholly seriously. Hughie really had quite a tum. Derek's briefs were not too absurdly large.

He jumped into the water and splashed playfully. The pool was almost too small for a pair of grown-ups. A few strokes of crawl took him from one end of the bath to the other, and the tempestuous stroke splashed the water over the edge.

'But what on earth are you doing here?' she asked. 'You turn up in the least expected places.'

'I've come to see you.'

'That's very flattering.' She could not help it showing, so why conceal it? But it was provocative perhaps to continue: 'The boys are out, Derek is still in London. I'm afraid you find me all on my own.'

'Priscilla.'

He held out his hand to her in the water, and oblivious of the interested attentions from the lavatory window of Mrs Hartley, working with Harpic, Priscilla allowed herself to be kissed, and enjoyed the sensation of her own breast squeezed against his beneath the chlorinated surface.

She burst away from him quickly, splashily, as though it had all been a little joke. But the look on her face told him that the period of jest, of cat and mouse, was over; that she was, at last, prepared to take him seriously.

'I couldn't stand being in London without you any longer,' he said. 'The office is hell, everyone's away. I just drove down this morning on impulse.'

'You can't stay,' she said suddenly. 'Not the night... The boys...'

'I thought I'd put up at the local pub.'

'Oh, Hughie, *please*.'

She heaved herself out of the water and shook herself with almost canine vigour. An elegant towelling gown had soon been taken from the shed. Hughie was left to shiver, semi-naked on the concrete.

'You don't really understand, do you?' he said with a sort of lunatic intensity.

'I think perhaps that I do.'

'But if you did...'

'You poor old sausage. But I was right, you know.'

'When?'

'When I came to the office that day. It can't make any of us happier. The whole thing is doomed. God knows, I'm sorry for you, and I think it's heartbreaking...'

'You speak as though I had got some disease which it was not in your power to do anything about.'

'Perhaps you have.'

When he had been given time to rub himself with the damp towel, used already by Peterson and Julian, Hughie was brought into the kitchen and offered tea or coffee. Priscilla nervously burbled. She told him about the St Leonard's pageant in the autumn.

'The Church is a thousand years old,' she prattled. 'Mr Dishman

165

thought we ought to mark it. Mother thought a *son-et-lumière*, but you can't really have that in the autumn – winter by that time.'

'I am going to leave my wife,' said Hughie. His face had a manic intensity which she kept trying not to notice.

'Hughie, you *can't*.'

'I am going to write to her. When she gets back, she'll find I've moved out.'

'Write to her? Where is she?'

'She always has a fortnight or so with her parents at about this time of year. Boston. We normally go together, but this year I couldn't face it.'

This was dreadful news, terrifying.

'Don't you think you are being rather cruel?'

'I don't think so . . .' It was an impossible thing to deny. He hated the way she harped on it.

'Hughie, this is a very difficult thing to say. But I am not in love with you. I can't allow you to . . .'

'I don't believe you. In the pool, just now.'

'Yes?'

She was sitting with a mug of instant coffee at the kitchen table. He could hardly go down on his knees before her on the vinyl. Nor could he take her in his arms. He bent over her awkwardly and tried to kiss her again.

'Don't, Hughie, don't.'

'Why not?'

'Because Mrs Hartley . . .' But it was too late because already that person with mops and looks of disapproval had entered the kitchen and was making her way to the sink.

166

# Fifteen

On the day of the crime, Bernadette and Kutuzov went to London. He filled up with waiting waiting all bloody the day long for they to answer letters. She, for her part, had no objection to a jaunt in town, and wanted to settle the matter of Australia.

They went, without telling Mrs Woolley, by a morning bus, intending to be back by early evening. Juri had begun to feel touchingly protective towards her. He was afraid that, once back in London, she would be lured into her old ways. With he, different. The fact that he was always, much of the time half-consciously, scouting around for illicit sexual gratification did not affect his courtly resolve that Bernadette should live a life of rectitude. Australia was obviously the place for such a course. But why had they answered no letters?

On arrival at Australia House, they were appalled to discover that their migratory ambitions were not greeted there with enthusiasm. They had quite failed to master the procedure. For Bernadette, some rudimentary reference would have been adequate: but she had provided the name of nobody who could give her a character. In the case of her spouse, everything was much more complex. If he were intending to abandon Soviet citizenship, he must, of necessity, acquire citizenship of some other country.

But for Christ's sake this what he ask. He want to go down under and become Australian.

In which case there were procedures to be gone through.

Neither he nor Bernadette fully understood what was being said to them, but they had a firm sense of the brush-off. Nothing could be promised for at least six months.

By then, they catch up with us. Believe me, beautiful, they find Juri Kutuzov and make the trouble. They kill, these buggers. He no talk only of his own people. He spit on the bloody British Intelligence who leave him in this excrement. He spit on the Ballet. He spit on the copulating Australia House.

167

Such contemptuous salivation and expectoration, though good for the spirits, would not, Bernadette avowed, get them anywhere; and she had the firm sense that, like the little children on the Start Rite shoe box, they were making a progress, these two. The trouble was that the money had dried up. An application to South Eaton Place seemed, in the circumstances, inevitable.

A woman answered the door. It wasn't his wife, Bernadette didn't think. His wife hadn't had spectacles. She said that Mr Blore was not in. No, he would not be back that day. Was there any message?

They left their names, but Juri was convinced that he was in and that his secretary was keeping callers at bay. They tried the experiment of ringing Derek's number but, once again, the faithful Mrs Philips spoke, and they replaced the receiver immediately.

All this activity made them both partake heartily of their luncheon at the Golden Egg. The omelette and chips vanished swiftly from both platters, and neither of them felt incapable of devouring waffles and cream, or a second cup of tea.

As the most brutish edge of hunger was appeased they could begin to speak to each other. She reminded him that application *had* been made to the Welfare at Bognor; that she had her little Post Office account (£329.16p) and that Mother could doubtless help. He was thinking in broader, and more ambitious, terms. They must, he insisted, get away. If Australia was difficult, they must go to America. Anyone could go, and if they wandered about from place to place sufficiently often they would not be caught by the Immigration officials.

But Bernadette had not wanted to wander about.

'Maybe it safer for you if I go by myself. I go America. You follow, maybe, later, when it is all safe.'

'I'd rather we stayed together,' she said, touching his hand in a rare gesture of physical demonstrativeness. It was hard to pin down what she liked about being married. But she instinctively felt it was a protection against the rest of the world. She had not let on to her mother that they were not 'properly' married. Juri had to sleep in the box-room since they only had single beds.

'These men, these officials, these bloody Jews,' he fulminated over his tea. 'They exploit me, you, everyone. Why not for a change we make big money, no?'

'How d'you mean, pet?'

'Okay, so you have big story, no? You know all the guilty secrets,

168

yes, of the great Mr Blore. You have some letters, no? The naughty boy begs teacher not to punish him but to go abroad? This is right, is it not? Why we no sell this to the newspapers? We rich. Fifty, hundred thousand pound . . .'

Bernadette was dazzled by the sums named. She had been told by Mr Costigano so many times that, if she breathed a word, she would be beaten, or worse, that it had never crossed her mind to go to a newspaper. How, in any case, would it be done? She had come to dread the intolerably predictable response when any 'official' encounter was embarked upon. Someone asked you to read something, to write something; they were foreign; or they were posh English who spoke words you did not understand. And before long you felt as though you was in the wrong and they was so high and mighty they'd be able to find you out. She dreaded the newspaper scheme. She implored him to put it off for a while until all other avenues had been explored.

Such as? She ring Mr Blore and they get no answer. They call Australia House and he get no kind of reply – it all bloody Dutch. The Ballet are out of town, all his friends who could help.

But why not, she had asked, his own Embassy? And rather to her surprise and relief he had consented to go there. They had given him money in the past. They would surely do so again. He conceded that they would be unlikely to let him down. It was he, Juri Kutuzov, in his pride, who had not *asked* for payment. But they would give him a few roubles.

And so, heavy with waffles, they had made their way to the Embassy. Bernadette had been told by Juri to wait outside on the pavement while he went inside. And wandering up and down by the railings, the police had given her quite a few funny looks. It was a joke really, how as they thought she was soliciting, and she wasn't any longer; just waiting for her husband.

The waiting took longer than she had expected. Half an hour, three quarters of an hour, an hour.

The policeman who had given her such funny looks said to her, 'I think you should move along now.'

'I'm waiting for my husband,' she said grandly.

'Gone in there, has he, my dear?'

'I'm waiting; honest he has.'

But an hour later, when she had run out of fags and started to think they were going to miss the bus back to Bognor, Juri had still not

169

appeared.

Another policeman, taking less interest in her than the first, gazed at her with amused disapproval when she spoke. It was always either this 'Move along', or the hint of satirical lechery. She wondered what it was about her appearance. She had toned it down since she had stopped working. But somehow men *knew*. In her worst moods, she guessed that even her mother had her suspicions.

'I'm waiting for my husband,' she said.

'Oh yes, my lovely. And where's the lucky man been, then?'

'He's gone in there'. A thumb indicated the main entrance to the Embassy. 'There's no back door or nothing, is there? He's been ever such a long time.'

'We could ask for you, my darling, if you wanted.'

She did want, and the uniformed official conversed with another uniformed official at the open door.

'What did you say your name was, madam?'

'Kutuzov,' she said. 'My husband is called Juri Kutuzov.'

But there were bewilderment, shrugs, expressions of sympathetic concern. She must have been mistaken. No Mr Kutuzov had called that afternoon. No Juri either. If she had seen him enter the building with her own eyes then her own eyes were mistaken. There was no Juri Kutuzov there.

The English constable looked prepared to take the matter kindly, but she felt too distraught and too alarmed to press the matter.

'Perhaps he's gone out the back,' she said. This turned out, eventually, to be true. But she never learned the truth of what happened to him. She did not know that he was flown out of the country that night. She did not know whether he was alive or dead. She was exhausted and tear-stained on the bus back to Bognor.

Mrs Woolley came home at her usual hour to find a man on the front door-step. She was tired from work, and she was afraid that she was going to lose her temper with Juri. She had already tried to offer up her annoyance in reparation, to smother it. But she was afraid that, if his frayed leather jacket were hanging from the corner of the settee, this piece of spiritual mortification would avail her nothing, and she would fly off the handle.

The man provided distraction from these thoughts. Short, dark, stocky, he had the air of being on official business; he carried a small attaché case.

'Yes?' she enquired of him. She knew that she had paid the electricity if that was what he was come for.

'I'm looking for Bernadette Kutuzov,' he said.

It took some getting used to, your own flesh and blood having this surname.

'Come in, then,' she said, fumbling for the keys. 'She'll be in the yard, I expect.'

A couple of folding chairs were indeed sweltering in the small paved patch of ground at the back of the house. But they were empty.

'Bernadette,' she called up the stairs. 'A gentleman!' She turned and asked him, 'Was she expecting you?'

'It's to do with her National Insurance,' said the man. 'Just a routine call.'

'Well, do sit down,' said Mrs Woolley.

'She came to the office about a week ago,' said the man.

'I know. I sent her. I can't be keeping her and her husband. Not now she's married.' She spoke with the tone of suspicion which she felt appropriate for conversation with one in authority.

'She said she had lost her cards,' said the man. 'That she was an air hostess who had been made redundant.'

'She said that!'

'Mrs?'

'Woolley.'

'Mrs Woolley, we have reason to believe that Mrs Kutuzov's affairs are not entirely in order.'

'She's my daughter', she explained. 'Didn't see her for seven years and then she turns up with a husband. What am I to do? Air hostess! The silly trollop.'

'The Social Services exist to help people, Mrs Woolley, but we do need to have a certain amount of information about them. When she came to see us, her story was, frankly, confused. She told us that she had approached an office in London with a view to drawing supplementary benefit. But there is no record of this in the office she named. She said that was some years ago. Then we gather she had her spell as an air hostess.'

'It's all lies,' said her mother. She felt herself boiling with anger, to the extent where she did not wish to protect Bernadette. Let her stew in her own juice. 'She was never an air hostess.'

'Frankly, we guessed as much. Of course, giving false information of that kind is a very serious matter. But, before we proceeded

171

further, I wanted to find out . . .' He hummed and hawed.

'Yes?' she said sharply.

'Well, to be honest, Mrs Woolley, your daughter seems rather confused. I mean, is there any history of mental disturbance?'

'Has she been in the bin, d'you mean?'

'We can find no trace at all on our computers that she has received benefit in recent years. Nor is there any evidence that she has paid her contributions. I wondered if she had been out of the country.'

'She went to Belgium,' said her mother. 'I can't think where she is now. BERNADETTE!' (As if shouting would make her materialise.)

'You see, if she wants to claim unemployment pay and supplementary benefit, we have to be in full possession of the facts,' said the man. 'Frankly I'm very glad to have found you in, Mrs Woolley. I wonder if you could give me all the details I need.'

'What like?'

'Simple things. Her date of birth, where she has been living lately, that sort of thing. It might be an idea to make sure that everything she's told us is, well . . .'

'And you'll be wanting tea.'

'That would be nice.'

She heaved herself into the kitchen as though this request were the last in a series of outrageous demands and put a greasy kettle on the gas. He stood over her as she did so, with a clip-board open and a ballpoint poised. The strange gap in Bernadette's career was not something that Mrs Woolley could help him with.

'When she was in London – working at the jeans shop,' he said, 'didn't you go and see her?'

'Me?'

'Yes,'

'Me? In London, is it now?'

'I thought, perhaps, when you became worried that you didn't see her . . .'

She knew that she was not two hours from Victoria Station. But she had always felt afraid of what she would see if she got there. It had been hard to explain this, even to Father Colvin. To the Man from the Inspectorate, or whatever he was, it was impossible.

'So when was the last time you saw your daughter after she left home?'

'I didn't see her, did I? She'd left.' She hazarded a guess as to the date.

172

'And then seven years passed, and she just came back.'
'Yes, that would be right.'
'And you didn't think it was odd?'
'She'd just got married. She wanted me to meet him before they went to Australia.'
'Australia? She's going to emigrate.'
'Her husband has written about it. They haven't got a reply.'
'So they have really come to say goodbye to you?'
'They don't know when they're going.' She brought the steaming kettle to the brown pot on the Formica-topped kitchen table and stirred in the bags. 'Just leave it to infuse,' she said.
'And her husband – he is a foreign gentleman, is he?'
'Name like that?' Her tone implied, 'silly question'.
'Now, would he be a Russian?'
'He is.'
'But where does he come from, Mrs Woolley.'
'Russia. That's where Russians come from, isn't it?' The man had the brain of a potato.

He sighed and thanked her for the tea. Two biscuits were offered, wrapped in cellophane; pinched (a venial sin, different from stealing) from the Teasmade in one of the bedrooms she had done out that morning.

'But you understand, don't you, Mrs Woolley, that the Russians can't just go and live in Australia? I mean they live a very restricted life. You have to receive permits to move between one Russian town and another. They have very strict rules about emigration.'
'But he's here now.'
'Yes, he is. But, I mean...' He sighed and once more sipped. It seemed too complicated to reiterate the facts. Besides, he was not sure of them himself. But it was impossible, surely, for a Russian to be in Bognor Regis, contemplating a move to Australia. 'His passport,' he ventured. 'He has a Russian passport?'
'I don't know. I never saw it.'
'You don't suppose it's lying about...'
'I could look.'

He followed her as she heaved herself up the stairs. The smell of men's feet dominated the landing. There was no sign, however, of anyone being about. The little box-room where Juri was put to sleep was a tangle of unwashed shirts, socks and vests. No personal documents of any kind appeared to be lurking there. They searched

173

with a shameless thoroughness. Mrs Woolley wanted to go through pockets for French letters, and the presence of the Man from the Inspectorate somehow diminished the prurience of this exercise. To her satisfaction, she found none, though it made it all the likelier, as she realised, that Bernadette was pregnant, and that she would have the girl back on her hands until the child was fully grown. Fifteen more years of servitude seemed a hard thing to place on her tired shoulders. It would take her to sixty-four. She mentally offered up this fact.

'Well, I'm sorry not to be more useful to you,' she said, flinging open Bernadette's door, but the word finished on a yelp when she saw that the room was inhabited. Sitting on the divan was the heavy little figure of Mr Costigano; the counterpane crushed by the weight of his amply-filled porcine check trousers.

'Sorry to cause you any distress,' he said measuredly, for she was wailing the Holy Name and calling upon the Mother of God.

Stan Costigano made a dash for it, and met the man from the Social Security, a Mr Bracket, on the narrow confines of the landing.

'Just visiting like,' he said. 'Excuse me.' He tried to elbow past the Welfare functionary, but felt a hand on his shoulder. A little struggle ensued.

'Not so fast,' said Mr Bracket.

'Who the fuck d'you think you are, then?'

'That sort of talk isn't going to get you anywhere.'

Mrs Woolley had hidden herself in Bernadette's bedroom and slammed the door. They could hear her heaving furniture against it to forbid entry. A recitation of the Sorrowful Mysteries of the Rosary had begun its rapid progress.

Mr Costigano forced his knee with some force into Mr Bracket's groin, and pushed him against the framed representation of Our Lady of Knock which was suspended from the wall at the top of the stairs. But Bracket pushed back, the pain causing him to butt Mr Costigano's chest. Both men stumbled against the banister, and when Mr Costigano righted himself he was holding a gun. His exit was still prevented by the form of Bracket, crouched or slumped at the top of the narrow staircase.

'Pray for us sinners now and at the hour of our death,' said Mrs Woolley.

'Now, you let me pass, see,' said Stan.

'Put that down,' said Mr Bracket.

'I'll use it unless you get out of the way.'

'Don't be a fool.'

'Come on, I haven't got all day.'

Mr Bracket lurched forward to grab the weapon, and it went off. The short silence which followed was broken by Mrs Woolley, who was screaming out of the bedroom window. On the landing, no one had been hit. The bullet had lodged itself in the plaster-work above the lavatory door.

'I'll kill you,' said Mr Costigano. 'I'll kill you.'

And then he did, quickly, and at short range with the automatic pistol which he did not relinquish at Mr Bracket's request. He stumbled over the recumbent body in its executive suit, and went downstairs three at a time. There was a small party of people at the gate, their attention drawn by Mrs Woolley's caterwauling. He made his way swiftly to the back of the house, and stood for a moment in the yard. In a next-door garden, someone called out, 'There he is!'

He was trapped. In the labyrinth of little roads which surrounded Mrs Woolley's residence, there would have been no hope of escape without the car. And that was at the front. There was only one thing for it. He must make a dash. Panting, he stomped to the front door and faced them. There were a few kids; mostly, they were OAPs: a crowd of perhaps twenty people.

'I warn you,' he shouted. 'This thing's loaded. You're going to let me through, see!'

They were. Most of them started to run as he advanced down the path, and held the gun aloft. They let him get into the driving seat of his car and start the engine. He narrowly avoided killing a cat as he reversed with recklessness on to the front lawn of the next-door neighbours, but by then he could hear the police sirens. The chase was hardly worthy of the name. The white panda car forced him into a cul-de-sac not half a mile away, and he realised that he was lost, finished, done for.

The officer who made the arrest noted that Mr Costigano said, on being apprehended, 'They're going to bleeding murder me.' The remark was not explained in the subsequent interview down at the station.

# Sixteen

Summer scattered them all. By the second week of August, they were in different countries, different continents. Juri Kutuzov, his head shaven and his body aching from the torture of electric shocks, had begun his life-time's imprisonment in a 'psychiatric' hospital some twenty miles from Moscow. He was already half witless, and did not know what further experiments his tormentors had in store for him.

Derek Blore was in France with his wife and family. Henry Feathers spent an energetic time, travelling on crowded trains between Bognor Regis and Victoria. It felt as though he was endlessly on the train, taking refuge in first class compartments from the howling families who, laden with buckets and spades, made their way to the coast. When not so wedged, he was on the telephone – to lawyers, to editors, to agents, to American publishers, to film directors. He was about to make his fortune.

The story had everything. Writing it for an allegedly 'serious' Sunday newspaper, week by week, he was able to play up its high political significance. But he was not appealing to anyone's interest in higher political theory as his tale unfolded in weekly instalments. There was a murder. There was a vice ring; more than a hint of sexual scandal; there was a Russian agent; and, inextricably mixed up with it all, there was a high ranking political figure (as his readers learnt in the first week); a Cabinet Minister (as they learnt in the second); and by the third week, they knew who it was. The scandal had broken, and the Blore Affair had begun.

The Bostonians of Massachusetts, being a fastidious class of reader and knowing little of Bognor, were slow to be excited by the death of Mr Bracket. Rachel read about it piece-meal. The murder itself had only been reported on page three of the *Daily Telegraph*, an edition of which she had happened to purchase from the vast array of papers on sale in Harvard Square. It had passed her by, for her parents produced in her a haze of boredom which made her cut her visit short by a week. Existence without Hughie was, she discovered, simply unendurable. Phrases such as *at loose ends* came to mind. But they were too mild. While she helped her mother to bottle berries or heard again her father's dull memories of ancient faculty feuds, Rachel's ends were so loose as scarcely to exist. She wandered about by the river, up and down Memorial Drive. She made wholly unnecessary visits to stores which took up whole mornings. But she could not pretend that these outings had a purpose and she rarely *bought* anything. She picked up books which she had always meant to read, and abandoned them after the twentieth page. The time was still not ripe to tackle *The Ambassadors*. Though Henry James would hardly have recognised her immigrant parents as true Bostonians, Rachel felt that they were all equally boring. No wonder Hughie could not face dinners with her parents' friends, or discussion of their favourite television programmes, punctuated with interminable and largely ignorant conversations about the nuclear arms race. But the absence of the man she loved from these occasions made them more dull, not less. It awoke in her an unwonted callousness. She thought that she *needed* to see her parents. She found herself for the first time despising them.

Cambridge, moreover, became no more agreeable. On each new visit the road works and the building had got further out of hand, and the violence, which made Boston itself almost uninhabitable, had started to creep nearer home. A youth was stabbed in the bus queue in Harvard Square, not half a mile from her father's house, while she was staying there. No wonder Hughie had not wanted to be there. The melancholy of her husband was in these days rather forgotten. She remembered not the silences of the immediate past, but the shared laughter of comparatively recent times.

Boarding the airplane for Gatwick did much for her own spirits, and it was only when they had been flying for two hours that she had read through the huge pile of English newspapers bought for her flight, and, like an archaeologist discovering by russet smudges the date of an ancient fire, come to the layer of Derek Blore. She had been reading, avidly enough, of a worsening economic depression, threats of strikes in the next few weeks, and a possible Cabinet reshuffle (notwithstanding the fact that the Government was very young) in the autumn.

Her heart leapt up at the word *autumn*. She would always palely, doggedly smile as she persisted to say *fall*. But it was the users of the

177

word *autumn* with whom she was in love. Each time she revisited the States, she felt more alien there. Her body had become accustomed to English food, English weather, above all to an English *scale*. Her eyes pined for evidence of the past: of real past – more than five hundred years, and not in museums. Her mind teemed with a gossipy professional desire to know what was going on in the public scene – since her absence.

Since the TUC conference was enough to excite her most passionately anglophile interest and curiosity, it may be imagined with what excitement she began to uncover, peeling one paper open after another, the extraordinary story. A very small item, on the centre pages of the *Telegraph*, told readers that Mr Bracket's murder was without explanation. The man who was helping police with their inquiries did not appear to be doing so with any enthusiasm. Why was the owner of a pornographic bookshop in Soho sitting in the upstairs bedroom of a Bognor chambermaid? Mrs Woolley, 52, was still shocked when she spoke to reporters, two weeks after her ordeal. She had nothing to steal, and it was only the prayers of the Mother of God which kept her alive.

That was Saturday's paper. But Sunday's, which she had bought at the same time, carried a much fuller report of the matter, and her heart quickened to see at the top: *HENRY FEATHERS asks some awkward questions which are already sending tremors through Whitehall.*

Murder stories were scarcely in the Feathers line. Even in the more exotic cases of *crime passionnel* they rarely provided the opportunities of self-advancement, and for mixing with the famous, which were the hallmarks of his journalism.

'STANLEY COSTIGANO,' he wrote, 'is the proprietor of a shop called ADULT BOOKS in Soho's Frith Street, the kind of joint patronised by the down-market dirty-mackintosh brigade. At the moment he is charged with the murder of ROBERT GARETH BRACKET, a 42-year-old employee of the Department of Health and Social Security from Bognor Regis. It is alleged that Mr Costigano was waiting in the upstairs bedroom of the house of MRS MARY WOOLLEY, 52, who works as a chambermaid at the EXCELSIOR Hotel, Bognor Regis. Why was he there? Why was Mr Bracket shot, in cold blood, three weeks ago today?

'There now seems little doubt that the murder of Mr Bracket was a callous blunder. If anyone had wished to murder him, there would have been easier ways of setting about it than by concealing

178

themselves in Mrs Woolley's house. No more than a handful of people could even have known that Mr Bracket intended to call on her that day.

'Why was he calling? To visit Mrs Woolley's daughter, Mrs Bernadette Kutuzov, 23, about a matter, which remains swathed in mystery, to do with her National Insurance contributions. Here the plot thickens. For at the very moment that someone was waiting in Mrs Kutuzov's bedroom with a gun – the gun that killed Mr Bracket – another mystery was taking place. Mrs Kutuzov's husband, a dancer with the Bolshoi Ballet, disappeared without explanation in London. He had gone to the Russian Embassy. Mrs Kutuzov said he had gone there to apply for permission to visit Australia. She says that two English policemen saw him go into the Embassy. The Police have made no comment about this.

'When I telephoned the Embassy last week, their response, too, was a firm *No Comment*. So, just what is going on? And just who is telling the truth? Mrs Kutuzov, who alleges that her husband has been spirited away by the KGB?

'Here the matter would rest if it were not for a further very disturbing coincidence. There is reason to suppose that Mrs Kutuzov's name is linked with that of a very high-ranking British politician. There are some worried faces in Whitehall this week, and when Parliament reassembles in two weeks' time it is likely that there will be more than egg on the faces of a few front-bench MPs.'

She smirked at its sensationalism. Feathers was capable of better than this. But, once again, he seemed to have landed on his feet. This looked like a scoop. None of the other articles she had read made the chain of connections which Feathers had done. She wondered who had tipped him off. His normal forte was pugnacious comment on facts which other hacks had burrowed out after a lot of hard work. It was unlike him to have been sober enough to conduct an investigation himself. She wondered if, in the phrase, he was simply flying a kite. It was easy enough to say that Bernadette's name had been 'linked with a very high-ranking British politician'. That libelled no one and simply sold more copies of the newspaper.

It was upsetting of course. Rachel had come to form more than a slight affection for Priscilla; and she was, apart from Priscilla, one of the few people in the world with an admiration for Derek Blore. And yet, it was impossible not to snigger, just a little, at the thought of Feathers. It was only as the plane touched down that a further

peculiar thought struck her. England must by now be buzzing with
Blore-talk. She had, the previous day, spoken to her husband on the
telephone, told him when she was going to come home. How odd –
how simply extraordinary of him – not to have mentioned *anything* of
this scandal – nor to have alluded, by so much as a word, to Derek, to
Feathers, or to Priscilla.

Ted Sangster had read the Feathers articles as they unfolded. And
it was he who was largely responsible for sealing the last link in the
chain of innuendo. The article in which Feathers was still dangling an
un-named and high-ranking politician before the public nose lay
unread in the Sangsters' sitting-room for the whole of a Sunday
morning. Draped over the arm-chair, he did not turn to it until he
had perused a number of other papers and remarked to his wife Pam
on their poor coverage of the cricket.

Pam had been following the murder of Mr Bracket, and read
Feathers's article entirely from the point of view of Mrs Woolley.
When Ted asked his wife, 'Did you see this?' she replied, 'Awful for
the woman, isn't it.'

'Eh?' Ted was too stunned by the article to pay much attention to
the plight of Mrs Woolley. His eyes kept returning to the paragraphs
in which the terrible connexions were made: between the prostitute,
and the Russians, and the 'very high-ranking British politician'. He
tried reading them in a different order. But however hard he tried, he
could not forget his evening at Derek's club. And the conclusion
which Feathers forced upon his readers was the inescapable one.

'If I came back and found a man upstairs with a gun I think I'd go
potty,' said Pam. 'And then that nice man from the Social Security.
He had two children, too.'

'We met him, the bloke who wrote this,' said Ted, shaking the
paper at Pam with jerky, almost threatening movements. 'He was the
one who told us Jack was dead – that night at the Blores.'

'So he was. *Knew* I knew the name.'

'And who do you think the senior politician is?'

'No idea. It's crazy, isn't it? Why do people who go into public life
take such risks, for heaven's sakes? I mean fancy going to bed with a
Russian woman! I suppose he met her on some trade delegation in
Moscow. Well, it's well-known, isn't it? They set these things up.'

'Yes, I know.'

'I mean, he's probably perfectly innocent. I never know why they think there's a security leak just because a bloke's been to bed with someone. The last thing you'd be talking about, I should have thought, as you found yourself tucked up with Olga the beautiful spy. And yet they always seem to think these blokes have been telling state secrets to their floozies.'

'Pam.'

'Yes, love?'

'There's something I never told you about Derek Blore.'

Her eyes opened girlishly and she cackled uproariously. 'Derek *Blore*! You're not going to tell me that he's been...' It was too funny. She hooted.

But, when she had recovered, he told her about the evening with their MP at the club. That he had been involved in some form of kinky sex with Bernadette Kutuzov, the girl in the story.

'You're making this up,' she said slowly, placing a king size cigarette between her lips to calm herself. 'I just don't *believe* it.'

'That's not all, I'm afraid, love.' And, with a tragic flourish, he wiped his nose and played around with his bushy moustaches. 'You see, the reason he wanted to tell me was that he had this scheme of bumping the girl off.'

'*Derek* had?'

'I'm afraid so. I thought he'd gone stark staring bonkers, to tell you the truth. He sat there as bold as brass – in the middle of his gentlemen's club, mark you – and asks me if I'll arrange for her to be done in.'

'Asks *you*!'

'I know it sounds fantastic.'

'What did he say?'

'I remember him saying, "She's not a big woman." I honestly think he wanted me to do it with my bare hands.'

'What did you say?'

'I told him he didn't know what he was saying. He denied he was asking me to murder the girl, but I couldn't put any other interpretation on his words.'

'But you don't think?...'

'I don't know what to think. It's *haunted* me, that conversation. I haven't felt able to talk to you about it. But ever since I've known about this girl, I have known that sooner or later there was going to be trouble. I must say, I felt that evening he was serious. He genuinely wanted her to be killed.'

181

'And now when there's a bloke who's burst into her house with a gun...'

'Exactly, pet.'

'Oh, Ted.'

They sat so long that the roast potatoes spoiled. And much of the time they said nothing. And, when they did speak, it was in panic-stricken little bursts. Pam felt terribly cheated, and said so. The tart, and the murder: of course, they were terrible. But she felt it was so very, very mean of Derek to have done this thing to *them*. Ted had slaved for that man in the constituency. Derek had swanned it to the House of Commons at Election time. But it was not Derek, month in, month out, who posted all the letters, arranged his 'surgery' on Fridays, liaised with the other party workers at the time of local elections, canvassed on doorsteps. Twenty years of Ted's life had been devoted, very largely, to promoting the fortunes of Derek Blore. And this was all he had to show for it.

'I think I'd better ring the police, don't you,' said Ted, when they had joylessly pretended to eat lunch. He too had caught the mood of Pam's fury, and his own inherent anger flared up once more. 'I mean, a man's been killed.'

'Poor Priscilla,' said Pam, 'and Kate, and little Julian.'

Feathers named Derek Blore in the newspaper of the following Sunday. Hughie was probably the only man in London not to read it over his breakfast. He always saw all the Sunday newspapers in his office on the following morning. Rachel's absence gave him the pleasant excuse not to clutter his house with them on the morning of publication. He allowed himself a Sunday morning which recalled his bachelor existence: an early start; bacon and eggs, toast; oat crunchies; a huge pot of tea and Henry James's *English Hours*. Then, a leisurely tube journey from Notting Hill Gate to Bond Street, a sunshiny stroll down the deserted pavements of South Audley Street, followed by sung mass at the Grosvenor Chapel. The unhurried dignity and perfection of the liturgy took Hughie out of himself; the chanting of hymns and propers; the orderly locomotion of celebrant and servers; the sheer beauty of the building, where the sun shone through eighteenth-century windows and caught the billows of incense in its beams made Hughie forget everything. It was ecstasy in the correct sense of the word.

When he found himself being accosted afterwards by Priscilla's mother, he momentarily blinked, finding it hard to fit her into place. She often made little sorties to the capital, but he was not to know that. In a hat, and a smart pink coat, he took a moment to recognize her.

'Mr Duncan? Hughie Duncan?' she said imperiously, as though he were just as puzzling to her, and it was somehow his fault.

'How nice,' he said vaguely. It was odd to think that this squat and pop-eyed figure had given birth to Priscilla's elongated elegance. Lady Wisbeach's physical attributes – she was short and round and fat – were not underplayed by her clothes. For, beneath the pink summer coat, there were loud splashes of jolly silks. She had a mischievous face, and, unlike Priscilla's, a malicious one. Something in her beguilingly glossy, faintly protuberant eyes suggested an earlier age of Counter-Reformation intrigue. In spite of the Angela Thirkell clothes, she had the face of a villainess in Webster: her gleaming eyes conjured up a world of arrases, eavesdropping, poisoned paintings; mysterious deductions; hellish plots. At any moment, she might pierce the shoulder-blades of some devious cardinal with a bare bodkin.

Lady Wisbeach was a pillar of the Church of England – and high – so it was no surprise to see her at the Grosvenor Chapel.

'I'm kidnapping you,' she said, taking Hughie by the arm. 'We'll go and have a cocktail.'

'How nice.'

'No. We'll go and have a cocktail, we'll go and have a . . . because I want to get your *line* . . . you know what about – get your *line*.'

Her conversational technique established supremacy by claiming as much ground as possible – as it were, bagging all the chairs in the room. That is, even when she had nothing to say, she used up the silences which might have been filled by other people's talk by repeating herself, either in snatches or whole sentences.

'Cocktails,' she repeated, 'and we'll walk down to the Ritz, that's what we'll do – why not, hardly *ever* come to London, the Ritz, or get a cab, kidnapping you, and you can tell me *all you know*.'

A taxi had materialised. Hughie had the embarrassed certainty as he squashed in beside the dowager that he was going to be given a 'talking to'.

As an erotic expedition, his visit to Willerton St Leonard's had scarcely been a success. Not only had a sniffy domestic found him attempting to embrace Priscilla in the kitchen. But that had been his last chance of doing so. Children had shortly crowded in followed by Lady Wisbeach herself who had just taken them on an expedition to Hereford. He had been offered luncheon, but taken merely sherry. The arrival of neighbours was threatened in the afternoon. Derek himself was promised the following day.

Priscilla in short was impregnable. Before she left for France, he had rung up several times but she had greeted him each time with a re-emphasised impatience. Cousins were to be entertained, or visited. Her son was to be escorted to the houses of his friends. Had he any *idea* how much time it took up, having a family? Certainly, for Priscilla, having ties of blood appeared to be a full-time occupation, entire of itself. But he now knew (the kiss in the swimming bath) that this was merely a device, and that a feeble one, for keeping him at bay. When she returned from France anything might happen.

The thought overpowered him, drove out all other preoccupation. He knew that if he were sensible now would be the moment to leave home, while Rachel was in America. Several letters were written, never posted. The practical awkwardness of finding a new place to live during a London August was in part what held him back. Perhaps in a very minimal way common sense played a part. But, also, the very object of his devotion distracted him from flat-hunting, letter-writing or, indeed, any form of activity whatever. He lived in a mystic daze in which he thought only of Priscilla. By night, he dreamed of her, so deeply and intently and repeatedly that it was often impossible, by morning, to believe that the dreams had not been real. Even the most bizarre nocturnal visions – Priscilla sitting quite naked on the platform of Sloane Square station and telling him that if he made love to her there and then he would be allowed to marry her – seemed so solid in waking retrospect that he found himself adjusting his rational perceptions of her true nature by the experience of his own figments. The fantastical Priscilla was a more abandoned creature than her Herefordshire equivalent. Now, to encounter her mother was to feel an irrational fear that the half of his fantasies were public knowledge. At best, as he sat in the taxi, he felt that she was aware of his devotion to her daughter. There could be little doubt that in Lady Wisbeach's eyes – those dark, globular, emotional wells which so readily registered gossipy astonishment at human misdemeanours – he was 'pestering' Priscilla.

'I felt I *had* to go to church this morning, but I couldn't face St George's, Hanover Square – lovely church – three out of my four

184

great-grandfathers were churchwardens there – I used to go to the Grosvenor Chapel in the old days, but, my dear, I'd no idea. That,' she glossed, '*sermon!*'

'Fairly absurd,' Hughie acknowledged.

When they were settled with the champagne cocktails on which Lady Wisbeach insisted, she said, 'I need this to get *through*. You must tell me – was it you – your wife, I mean? Everyone talks of her things. Says they're wonderful.'

'Lady Wisbeach, I don't think . . . I mean . . . what?'

'Of course I rang up Priscilla at *once* this morning when I'd read the article and she was astonished. They're about twenty miles from Cannes – takes three days to get a paper there, twenty miles, and I rang her up and of course she behaved well, but she was naturally *astonished*.'

'Has something happened?'

She stared at his pink, round innocent features with the air of a startled toad.

'Oh, come! You've seen the morning papers.'

'I don't buy papers on a Sunday.'

'My *dear*, this is too priceless.'

She was evidently finding it hard to believe and was ready to put down his air of bewilderment to a carefully-feigned lack of involvement with an enterprise of which evidently all the readers of one Sunday newspaper were now familiar.

'Priscilla said you knew Henry Feathers.'

'Yes . . .' His features continued to express cautious puzzlement.

'I pressed her, d'you see, she said you knew him. I pressed her really very hard. How could the paper *think* of publishing such a thing – I mean, a Cabinet Minister. I mean, how could they possibly think? Of course I wanted to know if it was *true*. And, whether it's true or not I want to know how this Feathers character . . .'

'Lady Wisbeach, *what* is it? What is the story?'

A waiter was despatched to bring them the newspaper. It seemed hardly bearable to hear of this forceful virago badgering Priscilla down the telephone. At the same time Lady Wisbeach could not quite bring herself to tell Hughie the nature of the story. All that he gathered was that Feathers had found out something scandalous about Derek Blore and that it was printed as an Exclusive in one of the Sunday papers.

His initial reaction, of pity for Priscilla, blended quickly into a

185

sense of elation. By the time that the newspaper was brought – *THE DEREK BLORE I KNOW – Former Model Bernadette Kutuzov talks to Harry Feathers* – Hughie felt an almost childish certainty that, since Blore was in disgrace, it was only a matter of time before Priscilla fell into his arms. There he sat, in the Ritz – incongruously surrounded by the fantastical splendours of that place, with the large eyes of Lady Wisbeach firmly fixed upon him.

'Absolutely will... I mean, ridiculous in a way but you *know* them – how much of all this had *you* known?'

Reading the Feathers article *en famille*, and three days late, in France, brought with it a strange sense of solidarity to the now united Blores. They knew what to expect. Down a crackling line direct from her London hotel, Lady Wisbeach had expressed horror. The day before – they had all been content to wander about on their own, if wandering was possible in so densely-packed, and over-heated and over-populated, a heap of sand. Kate, fresh from Paris (but without the boyfriend), had been the quickest to rally behind Derek. She had thrust her arm through that of her father as they paced the esplanade and gazed at the syrupy blue of the Mediterranean, and this physical gesture of solidarity counted for much. Since cutting off so much of her hair, she had grown to resemble her father much more markedly. There was the same heaviness of lip and jowl; the same sense, thrust upon any seaside observer who noted either the English Cabinet Minister or his daughter, of the unwiseness of shorts.

Eleven-year-old Julian had, until the article appeared, been tending to wander by himself in amusement arcades, sometimes imploring his mother to accompany him. Now that Feathers had dealt his blow, the little boy, following some unspoken lead from his mother, trooped round with Derek – into cafés – in and out of the sea – back to the absurd hotel which Derek persisted, inappropriately, in claiming 'did you varry varry well.'

Neither son, daughter, nor even – a rare occurrence – wife could discern from his features how much of the Feathers article was true. The small hat of woven green plastic raffia, the jazzy short-sleeved shirt (fundamentally orange), the pale blue shorts, were not garments conducive to dignity. Derek would need a grey suit, and an audience, before a reply to Feathers was possible. Now it was simply a matter of 'this is ridiculous, frankly... Oh, *really*,' and when he had reached the end, 'Wall, this is all actionable.'

186

The paper had been bought, read, re-read. Conversations had happened down the telephone to England, but none of the family knew much of what had passed between Derek and his solicitor, his PPS, his PM, his constituency agent, his secretary.

'Frankly, I'd thought Tad was a friend – Tad Sangster. I'd never trusted Feathers but I'd thought Tad was a friend' – was all he would say, coming back from the telephone, in front of the children.

Julian and Kate assumed, both, privately, and severally, that Derek was talking about the matter with their mother. He was, but only a little. Between them had grown up a gulf of diffidence. He did not know, with certainty, whether he *should* tell his wife. He knew that from a legal point of view he was safe and that, whatever he told her, wives cannot give evidence against their spouses. He was afraid, simply, that if he told her the full truth, she would not be able to forgive him, and without her presence he did not think he would be able to weather the storm. She was already being gently angelic. She had expressed horror at Feathers's article. She had fully supported Derek when he said, 'Of course I shall be obliged to sue.' But she had not *asked* him anything. Her mother had reduced her to tears on the telephone.

'Mummy. Of *course* it's not true.'

'I mean, have you *asked* him? Thank God, your father . . . I mean about the spying. I mean about the visits to prostitutes . . . It would have broken his heart – surely a wife's entitled to know, darling, if the readers of the Sunday papers are told. If you don't ask, I shall. Who would know? That nice American girl. Jewish name – you introduced me at Mark's house, married to the second Duncan boy.'

'Rachel Levine. They're in America.'

'I think we ought to find *out*.'

Between the telephonic intrusiveness of her mother on the one hand, the solid bull-like immovability of Derek on the other, Priscilla felt guiltily paralysed. She dared not ask too many questions of Derek lest he ask questions of her. And it was all, all her fault. In serener moments, she realised that Feathers himself was partially to blame. It was so deceitful, as well as so very unkind, to have written the article. In fact, it was so unkind that Priscilla could not understand it. Whatever Derek had done, could it be bad enough to merit the public pillory which Feathers had made for him? Did Derek, who had worked so hard and been so dutiful and so ambitious, now have to bow out because Feathers had said vile things about him in the paper?

187

It did not look as though he was going to resign without a fight. *Ladies and Jantelmen, we're going to try that chorus again.* Poor, poor Mr Blore. Priscilla wept and moped for him and hated herself. She wondered, repeatedly and obsessively, how she could have been such an *idiot* as to tell Feathers about Bernadette Kutuzov. It was an act of pure madness.

'*The name of Derek Blore had already been linked with that of Bernadette Kutuzov,*' he had the cheek to write. *So, when a mysterious and peculiarly bloody murder happened in her mother's house in Bognor Regis, I naturally felt the matter needed further investigation . . .*'

Priscilla, who had never hated anyone, rather hated Feathers as she walked alone, in the early morning, to the tobacconists, or sat, in the middle of her solitary afternoon walks, beneath the shade of church porches or spreading branches of olives. But her self-hatred, guilt and self-reproach were much the greater. There were – contrition did not allow her to be blind to the fact – dozens of men in love with her: men like *nice* Hughie Duncan, married to nice wives. But she had nearly always chosen as lovers, not the men she liked most but the ones who had tried the hardest. Feathers – the drunkenness, the affectation of learning, if not erudition, the shiny toes of his repulsive old suede shoes – had seemed at first a Bohemian figure slightly – only slightly – out of her world. Cousins whom she faintly envied had joked about him, had him to stay. With other cousins he had been at Oxford. When he had made his so-obvious pounce, two or three years before, she had felt flattered, amused and not remotely threatened. Contrary to what was popularly supposed, Priscilla did not sleep with every man in London. When Feathers seduced her, it was a whole eighteen months since she had been unfaithful to Derek, and she had recognised at once, in Feathers, all the necessary qualities of coarseness and emotional independence. Marriage was the last thing he wanted. She had been stupid. Stupid. Stupid enough to forget that he was professionally committed to finding out secrets. But was he? What *purpose* did it serve?

Oh, she had wrecked and ruined everything. And in her despair she felt unable to reproach Derek for one single aspect of the affair. It was all, and so directly, her fault. She dreaded the legal proceedings. She dreaded the look on Derek's face when, having sued Feathers for defamation of character, he discovered the offensive article could never have appeared in print without the indiscreet co-operation of his wife.

188

The whole French holiday was wrecked. Within days, they were back in London, and under siege. Feathers, who had enriched himself so enormously, had alerted the world's attention to a story in which most of the newspapers, and many of the TV stations in Europe, were deeply interested. Bernadette could not be found in Bognor. But the Blores braved the gazed-upon existence of celebrities – notorieties, more like – in South Eaton Place.

# Seventeen

For Julian Blore, there was no worse agony than the day he had to return to school. And the beginning of an autumn term was always worse than the others. The more the long summer holidays allowed him to re-establish the roots of home affection, the worse was the wrench when they ended. And, instead of the merciful ten or twelve weeks of other terms, he had fourteen weeks of exile stretching ahead of him.

The agony began about a week before the day. On this occasion, it was the very day they got back from France that his mother began to prepare the packing of his trunk. He dreaded it being brought down from the attic. He loathed the last-minute visits to Harrods which followed the perusal of the clothes list, the purchase of dull grey socks, grey shirts, sleeved vests, serge football shorts.

And, this year, the family was in turmoil about Daddy. The newspapers said that he had done something very wrong. Julian had read the articles avidly as they appeared. His father had visited a prostitute and had been a spy. It was quite obvious to Julian that this was true. He was almost pleased to read it, for it justified his sense, never admitted to himself before, that Daddy Spoilt Everything.

Julian was convinced that if it were not for his father, and his father's career, he would not have to go away to school. Mummy, he was sure, would have allowed him to go to the Hall, and then on to Westminster like everyone else. It was Daddy who had found out this hateful prep-school in Malvern, and Daddy who had ambitions later on to send him to Repton, where none of his friends were going.

While the trunk was being packed, items on the clothes list ticked off (*One Teddy Bear: First Term Only*), Mummy was brisk, trying to avoid the pathos of it all and Kate (home for a week or two) was positively exultant. His elder sister smoked Gauloises now as she strutted about the house in her scarlet romper-suit and her espadrilles.

'Honestly, Julian, I think you're *really* wet, never *known* anyone

190

make such a fuss about going back to school.'

'You don't have to go to Hillbury.'

'Mine was just as bad. All schools are foul,' she puffed and belched. He hated her for it. This term was Rugger. One would get back and see with dread the H-shaped goals established on what had been the comparatively civilised cricket pitch. Fourteen weeks of it stretched ahead, each colder than the next; games every afternoon; runs on the Malvern hills; cheesy milk drunk out of third-pint bottles; the grazing of knees on coconut matting as one jumped from ropes in the gym; the drab melancholy which hung over *everything*.

In normal circumstances, his mother took account of his misery, and treats were devised to lighten the burden of those last few days. The trunk was dispatched to Paddington days in advance. Tickets for shows would be purchased, knickerbocker glories consumed at Fortnum's, tense little games of 'Monopoly'. Always, there was the sense that his mother had the power to save him from his impending fate; always, it was a sense which he did not dare to put to the test. If he made her fight for him, his father would be foul. The household had to revolve around Daddy's needs. Julian, certainly, in this particular week, was the least of everyone's consideration. Poor Daddy must have breakfast in bed; Daddy must see his solicitor; be quiet *do*, Daddy is trying to work on his papers. This tending of the lecher and the spy superseded any claims Julian might have had on his mother's time. She asked Kate to take him to the cinema; they went a couple of times. The first, it was stupid, because she took him to a French film at an Academy cinema and you had to follow what was going on by reading the sub-titles. She laughed a lot, too, which was annoying, because there was nothing funny in the film at all. In fact very little happened in it. There were a lot of close-ups of dustbins and dew-drops. When he had registered disapproval, she had taken him off to a really childish Walt Disney film, which he had seen most of anyway in excerpts on 'Screen Test'. So they were miserable, miserable days. On the last evening, which Mummy would normally have spent with him, they went out together to a State Banquet. She had held his hand before they left and looked intently into his eyes.

'Daddy needs me to help him now that these horrible men have said such wicked things about him,' she said. 'We've got to go out to show them that we know they aren't true. If I didn't go out tonight, everyone would say it was because I thought Daddy had done all

191

these *terrible* things.'

'Are you sure he hasn't?' Julian asked.

Her great blue-grey eyes had not flinched as they stared back at him. There was reproach in their steely strength.

'Julian, don't ever ask that again.'

'But are you, Mummy?'

'Of course I'm sure,' she had said; but she had looked away again almost at once.

'It would be very bad if they caught him, wouldn't it, Mummy? I mean, if they proved he really *had* done those things – been spying for the Russians and everything?'

'Julian, they are not going to catch him because he is *innocent*. You really mustn't talk in that way. When you go back to school tomorrow, you must be terribly careful what you say to people. You will, won't you? You promise me?'

'I never talk about Daddy at school anyway.'

'Look, *darling*. We've spoken to the headmaster, and he is going to make sure that no newspaper men talk to you or anything like that. But, if any of the other *boys* ask you about it, you won't say anything, will you? You see, there are some really *awful* people in the world. They would even use *boys* to get information about your father. You know, they might ask quite casually where you spent your holidays, or something like that.'

'Can't I even tell them *that*?'

'Of course you can. It was a silly example. I just mean, be careful. If they start talking about your father . . .'

'*Mum*-my. No one talks about their dads. I keep telling you.'

'Let's hope that's true,' she said, and kissed his forehead. He hated, in these latter days of home, to be kissed. The time stretched ahead in which there would be no hugs, no kisses; in which her lovely face, and the smell of her, would be miles away, and he would be imprisoned in a vile dormitory full of children discussing masturbation.

'Mummy.'

'Yes, Julian.'

'I was just thinking.'

'Yes, darling.'

'I mean if it's so dangerous for me to go back to Hillbury; I mean, if you think I might be tricked into saying something about Daddy . . .'

'Oh, *darling*.'

192

She hugged him so closely now that he started to cry. She had seen through the ruse at once.

'I really thought that was a good idea too,' she said over his shoulder, stroking his hair. 'But Daddy thinks we've all got to be brave, and behave *exactly* as normal. Think how awful it is for him at the moment.'

'But, Mummy, it's his fault.'

'If someone told lies about you, would you say it was your fault?'

'No, but it wouldn't be. I don't believe you think he's telling the truth. I think you're just covering up for him . . .'

'Oh, Julian, you *mustn't*, not even as a joke.'

'I'm not joking.'

'Well, well, well, you're keeping your mother from a State banquet, young man,' said Derek, entering Julian's bedroom without permission. To the boy's eyes his father looked frightening in his evening dress. The colours of his countenance were set off by a high white winged collar and white tie. The cheeks were the colour of bricks; the whole head was an even reddish-brown, except for his scarlet ears which stood out like tea-pot handles, and his very pink, moist lips.

'We must go,' said Derek crossly.

Julian reached up to be kissed by his mother one last time. Derek leant forward and implanted a kiss on his son's brow.

'Good night, old sausage. Sleep well.'

It was a ridiculous injunction. Julian couldn't settle the night before term. He found himself hatching escape plots. Supposing he were to ask his mother to drop him at Paddington, rather than actually seeing him on to the train. Could he not then catch *another* train, go into hiding in Bristol or Wales or somewhere; send them a telegram saying he was all right, but that he would only come back if they let him leave Hillbury?

Or he could try a last attempt to *implore* them, to beg them to let him leave. He was still awake when they returned from the banquet. Daddy looked rather drunk, even redder than when he had gone out. Mummy was in a long swooping gown with a tiara on her head.

'What on earth d'you think you're doing?' she said, really crossly, when she encountered him, pyjama-clad, on the landing.

'Mummy, do I have to go back to school, do I have to?'

'Of *course* you do, now *go* back to bed.' She had really snapped. He had mustered so many good arguments while he had been lying there.

He had thought of pointing out that it was much cheaper to go to day schools. Daddy was such a nana that he probably did not realise all the money he'd save. But this very reasonable tactic could not be advanced. It was horrible that Mummy was so cross. It made him wish that he had stayed in bed; because now the whole of his last night at home was wrecked. He was just standing there in tears.

'I know someone who's varry over-tired,' said Derek.

'We're all tired,' said Priscilla. She was really angry.

Surprisingly, Julian went to sleep quite soon after this.

In the morning, she was being nice again. She did not apologise for losing her temper with him the night before, and he half-wondered whether she was going to punish him by getting Kate (an abominable driver) to convey him to his train. But she was not as cruel as that. They expected him to eat breakfast, but the boiled egg made his gorge rise, and it was as much as he could do to stop himself openly blubbing over the toast and marmalade.

'I think you're a real baby,' Kate mercilessly observed. 'I only cried my first term at Cheltenham. You don't cry in your seventh term, for heaven's sake.'

'I'm not crying!' he paradoxically howled.

'Wall, goodbye, old chap,' said Derek. Absurdly, a handshake was thought appropriate as a mode of paternal valediction. That suited Julian. Mummy helped him carry his case to the car. It felt horrible to be in the prison uniform again; stupid shorts, rough grey flannel against chapped legs, a blazer braided with hideous orange, black and white edging, and a tie of the same design around the collar of his grey shirt. On his head, the ignominious cap, with a school shield embroidered on the front.

'We'll come and see you in a few weeks,' said his mother, trying to talk through his grief. He wanted to behave well for her but, now they were alone together, he could not help weeping openly. 'It'll be all right when you've settled in. You say so yourself.'

'It's *not* all right.'

'Darling, we all have to do things we don't like.'

'But why do *I* have to . . .' he gulped with the sobs, 'go away . . . other children . . . don't go . . . away.'

'I went away. Kate went away. Daddy went away.'

There was no answer to that.

'I'll tell you a secret,' she said. 'Daddy hated it, he used to cry, too. But he learnt how to be brave. Don't you *see* how brave he's being

194

now? One day you will. He could be Prime Minister, you know. And that's why these *horrid* newspaper men are spreading lies about him. It's because they want to stop him being Prime Minister.'

If so, it seemed such an eminently reasonable line of conduct that Julian could not see what was wrong with it.

'Will you come next week-end?' he asked.

'There's no exeat the first week-end,' she said. 'You know we're not supposed to come until you've had time to settle in. As it is, the headmaster said I come too often.'

'*Please*, Mummy.'

'And we'll *write* to each other.'

'Sorry,' he sniffed.

As the car approached Paddington, he became dimly aware that too much sobbing would embarrass his mother, and he tried to stem its flow. He more or less had it under control when she opened the flood gates by saying, 'Now, be brave.'

They parked in Praed Street, on double yellow lines. This time, he was to carry his own over-night bag. As they made their way into the great glazed terminal, his eye unwillingly absorbed the sight of a gaggle of Hillbury boys, waiting by the barrier with the master who was responsible for their safe conduct to Worcestershire: Sir Caradoc Pass, an obesely ugly man with whiskers, and a tattered sports coat with pins sticking out of the lapels.

'Mrs Blore,' the master's tone with Pricilla was always obsequious. 'Hallo, Blore,' he said, 'have a good holiday?'

Julian mumbled something inaudible.

'No need to cry, Blore,' said Sir Caradoc sadistically.

'I think I'll go, darling.' She crouched over him in the warmth of her embrace.

'Oh no, Mummy, there's ten minutes before the train goes.'

'You've got all your friends, now.'

'Oh, please don't go.'

He did not want to be making a scene. He knew that he was eleven, and that when you were eleven it was no longer quite natural to cry. But he was clinging to her neck and sobbing, and would not let her go.

She struggled free callously, and ran, not looking behind her, into the Great Western Hotel. Crumpled with shame, his eyes and cheeks stinging with grief, Julian allowed himself to be loaded into the train on Platform Four. When, later, he watched old films of the Jews or

Cossacks being bundled into trains, his disgust was of a peculiarly personal character. When it was airily said, 'Why did they let themselves be butchered? Why did a thousand men and women allow themselves to be put on a train by a handful of bullying sergeants and corporals?' he could not answer the mystery, but felt again the completely crushing power that captivity has over the soul.

Crushed then, too miserable to read or speak, he swayed and rattled towards Malvern. Sir Caradoc sat opposite, playing with the pins in his lapels, occasionally withdrawing one to prick his cheekbones and make them draw blood. The baronet, come down in the world, made no effort to speak to the boys until they got to the station, when he arrogantly said, 'Your family has been in the news a lot lately, Blore.'

It was not the thing to talk about your family at school. Sir Caradoc was hitting beneath the belt. Julian was sure that the other boys would recognise this, but to his horror they didn't. There was a general tittering.

To his shame at being the only one blubbing was added a wounded family pride and a fury with his father for having landed him in this intolerable position. Once back in the hateful confines of the school, there was enough activity laid on to enable him to escape this intrusive line of questioning. There was finding where one's bed was. Julian found that he was in the largest, coldest dormitory in the school, in a house with the least beautiful matron, between two boys he had never liked. There was always a hideous poignancy about unpacking, and seeing the things which had been spread out on the bed at home, piled on the locker beside the cruel little iron bedstead which was to be his resting-place for the next three and a half months. Then there was a diving around the school, unnecessarily seeing what had altered since the previous term. Which corridors had been repainted, which tables revarnished? The notice-board had been re-felted in green baize and the notices were pinned with an unnatural symmetry. There was a list of the names of New Boys, and a new master, Major Stokes, was to teach Geography and PT, replacing Mr Shotover.

High tea was presided over by the headmaster's wife, a well-bosomed sadist whose summer holidays had been devoted, at least partly, to the purchase of new mohair cardigans and auburn hair-dye. The sausages on toast which the boys were required to consume were but half-cooked, but she would not hear of any protest. Every scrap must be consumed. Afterwards, they were to be addressed by her

196

husband.

The prissy-voiced, snowy-haired Scot who enjoyed the distinction of being Mrs Fraser's husband was produced, as if out of a hat, at the end of tea. The image is not wholly absurd, since the white locks and faintly protuberant teeth suggested the rabbit, as did the watch-chain suspended from a dandified fob. He hoped that they would all enjoy their term, and that they would work hard. He would like them especially to welcome Major Stokes. Major Stokes was a stooping, yellowing man who looked like the semi-successful product of an experiment to reanimate the dead. He was to teach, nevertheless, physical training. It was hoped that, under his tuition, they would all become *fit little bodies*. How primly Mr Fraser said the words, and how knowingly Mrs Fraser smiled as they were spoken. There was an old Latin saying, and he hoped they would all be able to understand it. *Mens sana in corpore sano*. And then they had to be asked to bow their heads in prayer and he had thanked, a sure sign in Julian's mind that he was round the twist, God for the beginning of a new term. And then he had said they could go, but that he would like to see Blore.

In the study afterwards, that room of dread, where one normally only went to be caned, upbraided or told bad news from home, Mr Fraser asked Blore to be seated on the sofa. When Julian found himself sinking down into the back of this commodious article, Mr Fraser had joined him, and the tweed of his trousers had pressed most unwelcomely against the embarrasingly bare knees of Blore.

For, he was Blore now. Julian was a label discarded for another few months. It would be seen in his mother's handwriting at the top of a weekly letter. Apart from that, it had no connection with him.

'Blore,' said Mr Fraser, punctiliously, politely, 'we have all watched with very great concern the terrible ordeal that your father has undergone in recent weeks.'

'Yes, sir.'

'I have promised your parents, Blore, that we shall take very especial care that you are not bothered, Blore. You know what I mean.'

'Yes, sir.'

'Don't talk to people about it, there's a good chap.'

'No, sir.'

'Gossip is a very terrible thing, Blore.'

'Yes.'

197

'I'm sure the other boys will be kind to you. It must be worrying to you, Blore.'

There! He had got what he wanted. The mention of kindness was enough to make Blore blub again.

'But you must look on Mrs Fraser and myself as your friends, Blore. And if you are in trouble, or worried, you must come to us.'

He was crying helplessly now, and wishing he could stop, for the more he cried, the more likely it was that the old man would do what he did, in fact, next. An arm had reached round him, and Blore was being squeezed. 'You're growing up into a nice boy,' he said. 'You'll always regard me as your friend, won't you, Blore?'

Blore mendaciously averred that he would, and escaped. An hour had to be killed before the bell summoned him to the dormitory. He perambulated bushes, tennis courts, lawns, round the back of the scout hut, and down to the opposite border of his confines, the drive leading to that happy world outside. In the same way, animals pace around their cage when first entrapped. His hour of solitude was, in the event, too short. In the dormitory, he knew the drill. Clothes were folded neatly on the chair at the end of the iron bedstead. Clad only in underpants, progress was made to a line of basins in the middle of the room where teeth were brushed and faces swilled with cold water. It was a relief to bathe his tear-hot face, but he knew that hours of crying lay ahead. These ablutions were performed in obligatory silence, presided over by a fat matron with a warty face. Silent prayer, again of obligation, was offered kneeling at one's bed. There was then a quarter of an hour for recreational talk or the reading of approved books.

Blore could not understand how nearly all the other boys were able to be so cheerful. Did they not have homes? Did they not love their mothers? They japed and quipped, they hooted and ragged, they cheeked the matron and made faces behind her back, they boasted of their summer holidays.

After lights out, when the noise of matron's footsteps had died away and they knew her to be absorbed in the evening's television programmes, they talked again. Blore lay silent, quivering with grief.

'My Dad took us to Spain.'

'My Dad took us on a Boeing 707.'

'That's nothing. We went on *Concorde*.'

'Has Blore ever been on a plane?'

From Blore's bed, silence. From all the other beds in that

198

darkened room, there were giggles.

''Spect Blore went on a plane to Moscow.'

More laughter. From Blore, more silence.

'Did you, Blore? Did you?'

The chorus grew louder.

'Did you go on a plane to Russia, Blore?'

He covered his face with the coarse linen sheet, but someone was coming over to his bed.

'Did you, Blore? Did you go on a plane to Russia?'

There were several of them now standing round his bed.

'Can't you answer, Blore? Don't you know English?'

'Comrade Blore!'

'I bet he's wanking.'

'My dad says Blore's dad ought to be hanged.'

'Traitor!'

They had got hold of him and were dragging him out of the bed.

He kicked and wriggled, but lashing out only seemed to increase their blood-lust.

'Get a leg, Chester-Jones.'

'I'm trying to.'

They bumped him on the floor, up and down, but it was too benign, too jolly a torture for their tastes. Chester-Jones, the leader of the pack, had forced him face down on the floor and was kneeling astride him now. One of Blore's arms was being pulled up in an agonising half-nelson. Someone else was holding his hair and banging his head up and down on the splintery boards. When they were bored with that, they filled one of the basins with water and ducked him. In the struggles which ensued, his pyjamas were not the only ones to get soaked. His punishment was to be made to eat a bar of soap, and it was only when he had retched up his sausages on toast that they left him to drag his throbbing, aching body back into a bed which someone had, in the duration of the fight, amusingly made into an apple pie.

# Eighteen

In every pub in the land, people were discussing the case of Derek Blore. Everyone had a theory about what had happened. Everyone felt that they knew more than the newspapers were 'letting on' about Blore's involvement with the prostitute. Almost everyone disbelieved the implication that he was mixed up with the Soviet Union. This was, in the opinion of the majority, 'paranoid fantasy' on the part of a few right-wing journalists.

In El Vino's, Feathers himself, the journalist of the hour, had just been boasting of his triumphs. He did not reveal how he had been put on the trail of Bernadette Kutuzov. He did not need to: it was by now common knowledge. As he slurped vodka down his gullet, dribbling on the already damp edges of his greasy bow-tie, his audience, huddled around the bar, were meant to admire what he had done. They chiefly admired, and envied, the amount of money he had already made out of the whole affair. No one knew exactly what it was. But the circle of sozzled, sweaty faces who grinned at the triumphant Feathers were not listening to what he was saying. Always given to offering reminders of his Oxford education, his friendship with the more famous dons, Feathers was in the middle of a pompous survey of the great exposures of history. Blore was to be a name which would in future be spoken in the same tones with which we remembered Dreyfus, Marconi and Watergate. While he gave them this lecture, Feathers was prepared to buy doubles all round, and neither guessed nor cared that all their minds were engaged in mental arithmetic as he spoke. If it was *really* true that he had been given £200,000 for his Blore book; if it was *really* true that they were thinking of a film . . . Fantasy rioted through every journalist's brain as he spoke; they thought of the happy tax-exile which they would enjoy had they experienced the good luck of Feathers.

At length, he importantly consulted his watch, and left the bar with the unspoken hint that he was to meet a Personage of Great Consequence. For all they knew, he was to dine at the Palace. His departure allowed the audience to break up. Rachel, who in any case had to be sitting at a table, found that she and Hughie had been joined by a decaying hack of the old school, whose rain-coat, battered trilby and swollen alcoholic nose recalled more innocent days. None of *his* coevals had earned as much in a lifetime as Feathers had made in the previous fortnight.

'Feathers is a rat,' said the old hack. It was hard to know whether his face gleamed with sweat or with tears, as he applied the Scotch to his lips.

'Okay', Rachel conceded, 'maybe he is. But we'd all have done the same. It's his job.'

'Dear girl, I deny nothing of what you say. But it is impossible to dispute that Feathers is a rat. Thought he was supposed to be such friends with the Blores, anyway.'

'He was,' said Hughie. 'When we first went to dinner with the Blores, he was there.'

'And stayed on afterwards, I'll bet,' said their companion, carefully placing the wrong end of a cigarette between his lips and igniting the filter. 'I'm sure Feathers would help with the washing up.'

Rachel butted in at once with, 'God, won't it be good when we can get something else to talk about?'

Hughie entirely failed to grasp the implication of his companion's innuendo. But Rachel's defensive attitude to it put him on his guard. Within a few minutes, the old hack was going to enunciate the carefully-slurred information which had the power to break Hughie's heart. The first warning-signals were Rachel's refusals to talk directly about her own involvement with the Blores.

'No need to comment, dear girl. Say no more, say no *more*. Christ, these mild cigarettes taste disagreeable. We've all done it to a greater or lesser extent. I know. We're in the betrayal game. Most of us would be content to buy our victim a drink or two, perhaps stand him a meal. But not our old friend Feathers. Oh dear, what a shitting thing to do. No holes barred'. He leered at Rachel, 'If you'll forgive the expression, dear girl.'

Hughie experienced a start of fear when, instead of following up the hint that Feathers had gone too far in some area or another, Rachel tried to start an incredibly boring narrative about transatlantic air-fares.

'Bloody thing's gone out,' said the hack, twirling the charred cigarette into a metal ash-tray. His elbow slouched on the table, and he now spoke out of the corner of his mouth. 'It's the oldest trick in the game of course. *Cherchez la femme*. The old James Bond stuff. Penetration – you must forgive my language, dear girl – of the enemy lines. All that would appeal to our Feathers.'

Hughie was still genuinely baffled by what the Decayed Hack meant. But he knew that Rachel understood. And it was in the moment that she next spoke that the great bell boomed inside Hughie's head and everything fell into place. He had a sudden clear and horrible memory of Feathers leaning over Priscilla, on that first night in South Eaton Place and, as he kissed her, saying, 'Hullo, old girl.'

Rachel was saying, 'Someone would've found out even if Feathers hadn't put two and two together.'

It was horrible. In the first few seconds, the stench of corruption and disillusionment seemed physically embodied in the smouldering ash-tray and Hughie feared that he might be sick. Feathers and Priscilla, naked in each other's arms.

Nothing needed to be said. He could not have endured to acknowledge that he had not *known* all along. Still less did he want to share the moment of shock with this censorious old relic of purer standards and better prose.

'Thought that thing he wrote on Sunday was bloody awful,' said the decayed hack. 'If you do this kind of thing, you've got to do it well. I remember when I was on the *News Chronicle* and all the Mrs Simpson business was brewing . . .'

Hughie tried to avoid showing that he knew Rachel's eyes were upon him. He felt them glowing with sympathy and, at that precise moment, he did not need sympathy. He needed first to be alone; then to be very very drunk; *then* to have the sympathy. The blow which he had just received was far too momentous for any consideration of manners to govern his behavior.

'Then again when poor old Jack Profumo . . .' the hack was saying.

But Hughie was on his feet.

'I'm going,' he said.

'I'm mean, I'm not boasting; God knows, when you've written as many million bloody words as I have, you give up boasting. That's something the Feathers kid'll learn.'

'Yes,' said Rachel, trying to take in both conversations at once. She could not hurt the old man's feelings by simply standing up and walking away. Hughie was already doing so.

'... But a lot of people thought the thing I wrote then ... you're too young to remember ...'

It was a sharp, clear night outside in Fleet Street. One's breath turned to steam. Rachel joined him after a couple of minutes on the pavement.

'I'm going home,' he said.

'I'm *sorry*, darling.'

No, no: he could not bear her to intrude. The last thing he wanted was for anyone to *understand* what this thing had been to him. But he did allow himself to reply.

'I suppose everyone in London knows about this?'

'I'd heard *rumours*,' she confessed. 'And that first night, when he stayed on with Priscilla after we'd ...'

'*Please.*'

The moment had not come when it would be tolerable to name her. When the archangel closest to God fell through the firmament to the pits of hell, he found himself renamed. It was not possible, quite, yet, to hear *Priscilla*. He did not even know if he hated her or not. He only felt – not a metaphorical feeling, but one of actual physical pain – as though he had been stabbed through the chest. There was a terrible ache. He was too numbed to weep, but he longed for drunkenness. The privately formed scheme – solitude, inebriety, *then* talk was something he found himself able to adumbrate to Rachel. At the time, it did not strike him as big-hearted of her to acquiesce. Only afterwards did her perfect behaviour on that evening make the future seem habitable.

'I'll drop you off at home and go to a movie.'

'By yourself?'

'Sure, I like going by myself.'

In an egotistic daze, he complied. His hand moved the latchkey, hung up coat, lit lamps, unscrewed whisky, with the gestures of an automaton. She found him three hours later, tear-stained in an armchair, his brow and cheeks scarlet, some of her cigarettes unwontedly, messily smoked and stubbed into a saucer.

Pale, cool, collected, she dismissed any cowardly way out, a rehearsal of Jack Lemmon's antics, recently enjoyed, or an immersion of herself in the bath-tub.

'It's better to know,' she said.

'I keep thinking' – Hughie's speech did not become slurred when

203

he was drunk; tears fell, but no sobs broke his voice – 'that I could bear it if it was anyone but Feathers.'

'Isn't that better too?' she asked. She was smiling. And, because she smiled, he was able to recognise that it was funny.

'You knew too?' he said.

'Like I said, there were *rumours*.'

'About *me*?'

'No. About Feathers.'

'But I mean, you knew too, what I *felt*.'

'Uh-huh.'

'I thought because we joked about it...' He laughed. Alcohol alone made it possible to be articulate. Hughie's conversational world, when sober, could only enclose unsayable things. Discourse with Rachel was not entirely verbal. Thoughts, nods, smiles did for the most intimate things. Now he began to articulate them.

'I think I am really in *love* with her,' he said. 'Or that I was in love. I don't know whether the person I'm in love with *exists*. You know, all these months, the only thing which kept me sane was the superstitious conviction that she was completely loyal to that jackass. I know people said she was a flirt. They couldn't know what I was in love with. If I'd thought she'd sleep with *anyone*...'

'You'd have tried it on?'

Her tone just saved the remark. Once more, he laughed.

'You can't understand: or can you? I think, my God, that you *can* understand. I could never tell you about Janey, could I?'

'The girl you were in love with as a college kid?'

'Yes.'

'You're a romantic. That's what made me fall in love with you, Hughie.'

'Romantics shouldn't get married. It isn't fair on the people they marry.'

'Romantics shouldn't marry the same sort of romantics. It hasn't done me any harm.'

'Hasn't it?'

She shrugged, with the saddest of smiles. 'I'm alive. Four years?'

'Janey became a habit. Long after the intolerable pain had just turned into a dull ache, I still went on nursing it. That was mad, I suppose. When I...' The sentence evaporated into a sigh.

'When you married me, you decided not to be romantic, is that it? The bedroom slippers, the jokes.'

'I love you.'

There was silence, and she came forward and held his hand, sitting on the floor by his chair. She did not look up at him. She just held the hand and stroked it. She did not want to labour the obvious. For the first time in four years, he had actually said those words: *I love you*. And for the first time he had referred by name to Janey.

'Have I been in love with a phantom for the last six months?' he asked her.

'*You* would know.'

'I felt so certain of her; so sure that she was, well, sensible.'

'Oh boy!'

'But there is something to love, isn't there?'

'Of course. And you know something?' Rachel had entered by tacit understanding into the convention that Priscilla was, for the moment, nameless. 'She's going to need some friends.'

'Are we her friends? *Can* we be?'

The pain which followed these days was quite unlike the lunatic pain which had accompanied the loss of Janey all those years before. It was a stimulant. Hughie felt physically rejuvenated by it. It was pain, just the same, and he was thankful that, in the intervening week, he did not have to see Priscilla. But he found himself walking briskly from the bus to Queen Square half an hour earlier than his wont. Alcohol was no longer necessary. Paper-work was briskly despatched. The manuscripts of three very dull books were punctiliously edited that week. When he gazed out on Queen Square – the leaves ochre with October against pale blue skies – he was not lost in uncreative daydream. Thoughts, rapid, productive, practical, came into his head.

His question – were they *friends* of the Blores? – answered itself in two deliberate and contradictory ways. On the one hand, wherever he went, Hughie found himself jabbering obsessively about Priscilla and Feathers. It was, he discovered, common knowledge. There was not a single person to whom it came as news. At first it was difficult, this rather shrill line of gossip, but it was highly necessary to his plan of laying the phantom. The more he could link her, not in his mind, but in his talk, with Feathers, the more it was possible to view things comically. A healthful coagulation was taking place between Priscilla in his mind, and the Priscilla in his talk. It was almost as though Rachel's initial banter was becoming the true mirror of his heart: he *was* in love; but it was something which could be brought under control by laughter.

In the more charitable area, Rachel had worked harder than he to assure the Blores that not everyone who wielded a pen was their enemy. Priscilla was now unapproachable by telephone. The instrument was permanently off the hook. A note, scribbled by Rachel in a spirit of commiseration, was ignored. It seemed as though Priscilla was withdrawing into the world of her family and her old, trusted friends. For that, Rachel could not blame her. But she wanted them *all* to meet, for Hughie's sake as much as for anyone's, so it was a relief to bump into Priscilla at the hairdresser's.

'My *dear*, how *lovely*, and I meant to answer your note. But you can *imagine* . . .'

They were strolling down the same patch of Bond Street that Hughie had scouted six months before. Autumnal gold now caught the shop fronts, and their shadows on the pavements were long.

'Derek says we've simply got to batten down the hatches. Of course the really painful thing,' she said, lowering her voice, 'was that it was *Feathers*.'

'It must have been.'

'I mean, *any* other journalist.'

Rachel smirked at Priscilla's almost echo of Hughie's words.

'But I mustn't talk about it because of course it's *sub judice*.'

'I wouldn't . . .'

'My dear, of course you wouldn't. Derek, you know, really liked that thing about him; and it's been sweet of you not to make capital out of it since all this blew up.'

'I understand you not trusting any journalists now. It's just nice to *see* you, Priscilla.' There was something so immediately beguiling, so physically reassuring about her. However glossily turned out she was, and however elegant her features, there was something animal (a sexy, but very amiable horse?) about her features which enabled Rachel to seize both her wrists and jangle them affectionately.

'How's Hughie?' asked Priscilla, changing tone. It was the voice for inquiring after someone who had been ill. Rachel felt she understood the anxiety in the interrogative. Priscilla knew, surely, some of the effect that the *affaire* with Feathers would have had.

'He'd like to see you,' said Rachel boldly, to show that she knew what Priscilla meant.

'Well, why *not*? Look, I'm sick to death of being barricaded in that

206

*ruddy* house. Poor Derek, he said this morning we haven't seen anyone for *weeks*. You know how he likes social life. There've been so many concerts and things he's missed, but we simply feel that there's a *limit* to the number of times we want to poke our noses out. I mean, the cameramen are there *solidly*, my dear, day and *night*.'

'Let's hi-jack you both and take you to a restaurant,' Rachel ventured.

It was one of those schemes which could have been disastrous, but which was carried along by the women. Since there was no possibility of confirming the date on the telephone, Rachel agreed to 'hi-jack' the Cabinet Minister and his wife that night at half past seven. Derek squeezed into the back of the Volvo with Hughie, and this was the least painful arrangement. There was something playful about the whole escapade which made even Derek's conversation lighter, funnier.

No 'normal' restaurant would do. In any eating place in central London they would have been pounced upon by foreign newsmen and reporters. They drove for miles and found an excellent Spanish restaurant in Pinner, where Derek could impress the waiters with his taste for Rioja. These functionaries themselves behaved with exemplary discretion. If they recognised Derek, they did not say so.

It was during the conspiratorial gaiety of the evening that the Duncans were invited, and they consented, to go down to Willerton and see the medieval jollifications for the millennium of the local church. Manifestly, this harmless topic occupied a high proportion of the evening's talk.

'Mummy's been working like a *beaver*,' Priscilla expatiated, waving a spoonful of gazpacho.

'She's galvanised us all,' said Derek.

'We've got this perfectly sweet new vicar – queer as a *coot*, but a *poppet* and frightfully high – and between them they've organised this wonderful sort of pageant. We're all going in medieval costume. And then there's going to be a supper afterwards. They're thinking of roasting an *ox* – can you *imagine*! And everyone's coming, not just people who go to church. The whole village.'

'A real slice of English rural life for you.' When Derek leered at Rachel, she wondered why it was so unthreatening. When Hughie's eyes rested on Priscilla they were still glazed with the old passion. After an initial feeling of coldness, even fury, Hughie had found

207

that he did not need to fight his feelings any more. They had changed. The drunken conversation with Rachel had removed the dangerous edge from the thing. There was no danger of total lunacy descending. From time to time, the memory of the ridiculous Feathers pricked the bubble, and he was helpfully able to notice blemishes in Priscilla's appearance to which he had hitherto been blind; the way, for instance, that when she smiled there were little gaps between her teeth at the extreme edges of her lips. In some odd way, the idol had been smashed, and reconstituted. He felt like a heathen at the time when the missionaries had established the Anglo-Saxon church. There could be no doubt that the new religion had vanquished the old. Nor could this prevent him from wandering in the vacant and crumbling shrine of his old devotion, communing silently with the idols that were banished, and even enjoying the nostalgic knowledge that he was the last votary of a now-obsolete faith.

Rachel, for her part, when she looked back on the evening, could not help admiring Derek's professional sangfroid. He had not indicated by the merest hint that he was to give an important press conference on the morrow. She and Hughie watched it on television the following evening.

It was short, and melodramatic. He chose as his venue the conference room of a large hotel in Knightsbridge. His solicitor was at his side: such occasions of public life would, indeed, have been hardly imaginable without his obese form.

Derek announced that he was not going to answer questions. The matters of which he had to speak were of a gravity and a delicacy which made casual questions and answers inappropriate. Moreover, there were certain matters which were *sub judice* and others, of a highly delicate nature, of which he was not at liberty to speak for reasons of public security.

Fiddling with his spectacles, he had then turned down to his typed statement. His plump maw quivered as he held the A4 sheets, and one could see, even on the small screen, that this was the only movement in a crushed and crowded room.

'Following the publication of certain unfounded newspaper articles, I am in the process of instituting legal proceedings against their author, against the editor and against the proprietors of the periodical in question. However, I feel it my duty as a Minister of the Crown to lay rumours to rest which, if left unchallenged, would damage the integrity and good name, not only of myself, but of Her Majesty's Government. I have made a number of statements in the House of Commons. But I wish to make this statement not merely as a Member of Parliament but as a private individual, and I therefore do not claim the privilege of the House on this particular occasion.

'It has been alleged that I had a sexual relationship with Mrs Bernadette Kutuzov, extending over a number of years, she being for some or all of that period the wife of an agent of the Soviet Union. It has been further hinted, though not specifically stated, that I have myself disclosed private information to the Soviet authorities, either directly, or through the medium of Mrs Kutuzov.

'All these wild stories I wish most emphatically to deny. Whether Mrs Kutuzov's husband has had dealings with military or other intelligence I am not in a position to confirm or deny. I do not know him. Mrs Kutuzov I met for the first time at the beginning of this year. She called at my London house, where she was allowed entrance by my wife since she appeared to be in some distress.

'This indeed proved to be the case. She was in difficulties, of a kind which I could not immediately fathom, about her payment of National Insurance stamps. I said that I would do my best to help her, and I lent her a sum of money until her difficulties could be sorted out.

'I did not meet Mrs Kutuzov again until she approached me, in the company of her husband, in Brussels. Their difficulties were by now, as I understood, resolved, and they repaid me in full the money which I had lent to her on the first occasion.

'At no time before or since have I met Mr Kutuzov. At no time since have I met Mrs Kutuzov. The letters which she alleges I wrote to her, addressing her by various nicknames of a kind which are impenetrable to me, are forgeries.

'This is neither the time nor the place in which to present the abundant evidence of the truth of what I say. I merely conclude by taking note of the fact that Mrs Kutuzov has already admitted to receiving a large sum of money from certain sections of the national press for printing this letter which I am supposed to have written, and that she is not alone in having received such sums.'

After this statement, there was hubbub. Several reporters called out questions. 'Do you know Russian?' 'Have you at any time' (an American voice this) 'experimented with sado-masochistic sex, Mr Blore?'

209

But the weighty solicitor ushered him out of view and into the waiting limousine in Wilton Place. There were more people than not who watched the news conference. Derek's ambition to possess a countenance which intruded on the public awareness was gratified that evening if it had not been answered before. They had it turned on in Buckingham Palace. The Archbishop of Canterbury watched it in Lambeth. In blaring technicolour, it stared unaesthetically from the corner of public houses, where the talk in bar parlours was hushed. It flickered in the rest rooms of massage parlours, in Soho; and the same image was repeated in the panelled Common Rooms of Oxford. Dowagers lay propped up by cushions and watched it, fondling chihuahuas. In hospitals, it was seen by sufferers from spina bifida and strangulated hernias. Its flickering black and white image was conveyed to a lighthouse keeper in Cornwall and to the islanders of Lewis and Shetland. In bungalows, old faces tensed before it and forgot index-linked pensions. The prisoners of Parkhurst saw it, and the monks of Mirfield. On their several cathode ray tubes, the Master of the Rolls and the Lord Chief Justice watched it, each forming contradictory opinions about whether it constituted a contempt of court. In a dingy room in the Foreign Office, and in even dingier apartments near the Elephant and Castle, Intelligence officers watched it. And in Number Ten it was seen by the Prime Minister.

The Prime Minister had seen Derek that morning and been informed that the Press Conference would take place. That personage had read Derek's statement, and had been satisfied by it. Between the two individuals, there had never existed any intimacy. It would have pleased the Prime Minister if Derek Blore had resigned weeks sooner, before the whole sorry affair blew up. Now, it threatened to bring the new Government into disgrace. But, as Derek had pointed out, a resignation at this stage would imply an acknowledgement of guilt. There was nothing for it but to brave out the criticisms and to prove them false.

The Prime Minister's voice had sunk low when the next embarrassing question had been put. Whatever personal regard might have been felt for Mr Blore, it was necessary, indeed the Prime Minister's duty, to ask whether there was any substance in any of the rumours. In particular, of course, the Prime Minister had to be satisfied that Derek had had no dealings with the Soviet authorities, directly or indirectly. Derek had been able to give categorical reassurance on this point. When Mrs Kutuzov had visited his house at South Eaton Place, he had no idea that she was married to a Soviet agent. The Prime Minister then reiterated, what Derek knew already, that Kutuzov was known to have the most disreputable character, and that his name had been linked with Vassall and with a senior member of the Labour Party. There had even been suspicion of a liaison with a much-lamented member of the Royal Family.

The Prime Minister had expressed total satisfaction with Derek's replies. Over a glass of not particularly palatable sherry, it had been repeated that Derek was a most valuable, and valued, member of the team. Everyone in the Party, everyone in the House, admired the courageous way in which he and Priscilla were facing up to this terrible personal ordeal.

But there were things that the Prime Minister had not told Derek. Ted Sangster, his own constituency agent, had given the most damaging evidence to the police which had not yet been made public. There was no reason at all to suspect Sangster of malice, and the most thorough searches had shown that he had not been paid by the Press for his allegations. He claimed that Derek Blore had admitted a long-standing love-affair with the girl, of a most peculiar character. Moreover, Derek had tried to persuade Sangster to arrange for the girl's murder.

Van der Bildt, whose name had been given to the police by Costigano after several weeks of silence, had admitted to being a Soviet agent, and had told the Special Branch, and Intelligence, that Derek had, on several occasions since taking office, passed information to the Russians.

The Prime Minister, therefore, knew that Derek was lying. After the programme, the matter was discussed again, with the Head of MI6 and with the Foreign Secretary. Obviously, it was necessary to get rid of Blore. But it was necessary to get rid of him in a way which would cause least damage to the Government, fewest awkward questions in the House. The Press were having a field day, and it would continue until Blore was removed from the scene. It was inevitably going to be asked how such a man could have reached so great a position of prominence in public life without any security checks having been made. The Prime Minister was anxious, if possible, to avoid the embarrassment of a public trial. But the death of Mr Bracket made it unlikely that this could be avoided. Costigano would be tried. Van der Bildt would be tried as an accessory. And it would seem unlikely that the police would want to ignore Ted

211

Sangster's evidence against Derek. In which case, the Government was in the embarrassing position of having to face, at some date in the near future, the prospect of a Senior Cabinet Minister being put on trial for conspiracy to murder.

# Nineteen

The intake of Players' Capstan had increased since the Blore Affair began to break. The Professor, as it is convenient to call him, was now in an agony of doubt. It was quite possible that he himself would be recalled to Moscow. The thing, indubitably, had been mismanaged. He should not have trusted Van der Bildt (who had now been arrested by the police). There were too many risks involved in allowing the cheap little Soho murderer to kill the girl. No one would have predicted that so cataclysmic a blunder would be made. That something messy would happen. A shooting: in a small house in Bognor Regis: it was lunacy! Why could Costigano not have driven the girl out on to the open road and shot her on some heath or moorland? There was no need to lurk in her bedroom and scare the mother.

Then again, so little vetting had been done on Blore himself. Why had no one told the Embassy that his wife – as they now gathered – was in cahoots with the Press: and knew of the Bernadette business all along! They had taken such risks, and made such a failure to suppress the evidence of Bernadette herself. It was of no avail. The lovely Mrs Blore was infinitely more dangerous; and now, since their brilliant journalist Feathers had been alerted to the matter, there was no holding back.

The Professor loathed the Press. He regarded with contempt the reverence felt for it by liberal opinion in the West. They were fools if they thought they would ever get at The Truth by reading newspapers. The *soi-disant* free press reflected only such aspects of the truth as were pleasing to its owners and a certain section of its readership. As much distortion went on in its pages as in *Pravda*. The only difference between the Russian press and the Western press was that in Russia everyone knew what they were getting. In England the illusion flourished that men like Feathers were wizards who could point you to the truth. And, to get their truth, they paid money. The Professor knew the kind of truth you got with money. He had been peddling it ever since the end of the Second World War. It was fragmentary and usually scandalous. Opinions differed about the amount Feathers had paid Bernadette Kutuzov for her letters from Derek Blore. Some said £2000. The Professor had not heard more than £5000 being mentioned. He had sold the serial rights to one Sunday newspaper for £40,000. He had set himself up to act as Mrs Kutuzov's sole agent in the matter. He had forced her to sign all the necessary documents. He was going to 'ghost' her book, for which an advance had been paid of £50,000. Mr Feathers, with his zeal for the truth, had already made the best part of £100,000.

The feebleness of the West in relation to parasites never ceased to fill the Professor with astonishment. It was very hard to see what public good was served by enriching him in this way. Confidence in the Government was undermined: not merely in this government, but in all governments. If one Cabinet Minister can behave like this, why not more? How could a man reach Blore's position of eminence without being checked or vetted? Questions like this were put in the public mind by the likes of Feathers. In other words, he worried them, and stirred them up. For this, the capitalist press magnates paid him sums far in excess of any fee he would have received from the Soviets for acting against Western interests. People went on saying that freedom in the West depended on its free press. But what did Feathers come up with? Great, elevating thoughts, brilliant political or economic analysis? Oh, no: it was this demoralising tittle-tattle.

The cigarette smouldered between the fat brown musical fingers which surveyed the front page of the morning paper. 'BERNADETTE: DEREK BLORE IS LYING. Former model and wife of missing Soviet agent Juri Kutuzov made further sensational disclosures about her relationship with Cabinet Minister Derek Blore. "This country was too hot for both of us," she said last night to Henry Feathers. "Derek paid me to leave the country." In a letter, published exclusively by the DAILY ******* for the first time today, Blore wrote to Bernadette, "It has been very exciting having you as a teacher, but *Teacher must now go abroad.*" Blushing Bernadette confessed last night, "There was a good deal of fantasy in our relationship. Derek had very happy schooldays."'

There were photographs of the cloistered boarding school in North Devon of which Derek was an alumnus. HAPPIEST DAYS OF HIS LIFE? said the headline, in another paper, which had peeped at the Daily *******'s exclusive. The Professor knew, roughly, how much truth and falsehood there was in those stories. He had heard enough on the Bernadette tape, and he had heard enough of Van der Bildt's descriptions, to know that she would have been incapable of speaking the lines which Feathers attributed to her. Why was it necessary to call her a 'model'; and was it strictly accurate to describe the wretched Kutuzov as an 'agent'?

They should, the Professor realised, have brought the girl into the Embassy on the day they took Kutuzov. That would not have stopped the fool Costigano from shooting up the inhabitants of Bognor Regis. But it would have prevented some of this nonsense coming to light.

There would have been no chance, of course, of using the wretched Blore again. It did not grieve the Professor. He had not taken to Blore. He had had friends in the Cabinet of whom he had been really fond. Dear Tom, for instance: always with amusing gossip and nice things to eat; church talk and sex intermingled with stories of High Society. These things enlivened the tedious passing on of information. Derek was going to be dogged; the Professor saw that. But he lacked *charm*. And somehow, by lacking charm, he was less useful to them. Whoever confided in a charmless man? Whoever poured out his griefs, his little resentments, and in so doing let fall that crucial little detail?

No, he had realised at once, in the Egyptian Room of the British Museum, that Derek was not in the Tom league. But he would have had a plodding usefulness, for some years perhaps, had things not gone so disastrously wrong. As it was he was finished, a write-off. God knows how much he would disclose once they put pressure on him. As the Professor had learnt, the researches of MI6 into Blore were being rapid and thorough. The annoying little agent, Ted Sangster, had turned against Blore; even his secretary was giving evidence. They were tracing telephone calls, bugging everything. Now, of course, that Van der Bildt had been arrested, it would only be a matter of time before the Embassy had been drawn into it all. No one involved knew the Professor's name. But there would be embarrassments. He had decided to go home for a year. He dreamed, even, of an early retirement: a little dacha, a grand piano, plenty of *Times* crossword books: he would have been happy. Or would he?

HE WAS MY SLAVE boasted busty Bernadette.

The Professor smiled. It was impossible not to like the English. Without them, would he not be, just a trifle, bored?

215

# Twenty

A Norman, wishing, nine hundred years after the invasion, to retrace the seaward triumphs of his conquering forebears, would find the WELCOME TO HASTINGS PIER eroded by weather as he approached the Sussex coast. The legend, once painted in scarlet against the white of corrugated iron, is now blanched almost out of legibility. The pier, whose southern tip this greeting decorates, has known more populous days. Now, where the orange of rust peeps a disgraceful smear through all the glossy white paint-work, the efforts to keep alive the jollity of more innocent times have been unavailing. The 'Pub on the Pier', open all the year round, daily, fails to attract the *jeunesse dorée* of the district. Spilt out for a few hours of freedom from geriatric nursing, old men in caps sit at the various round tables watching the waves lash the girders of the pier and the pebbles, afar, on the beach, as they overburden their weakened bladders with half-pints of bottled porter. Conveniently close, next door, larger than the saloon itself, a stinking but capacious lavatory pursues its own mysterious life. Whether or not the old men stand before them, fumbling with fly-buttons, the urinals still gurgle periodically, and swill themselves with water.

Further inland, the weather makes a similar asperges, splashing the windows of the glazed corridor, a sort of elongated conservatory, with sea water and rain. The old women sit here, with picnic luncheon on their laps, and the smell is of hard-boiled egg. They stare westward, past the few deck-chairs still left exposed which flap like box kites on the open boards of the pier, beyond the monotonous front of St Leonards-on-Sea, to where the distance of Brighton becomes a grey smudge on the horizon. Rows and rows of the old women sit there, and the old men too enfeebled to reach the bar. Should anyone slide open the glazed door which leads to outside, the sharp gusts of rainy wind blow down the ranks of old women, sending egg-shells, grease-proof paper, newspapers, even wigs, in a tornado course towards the amusement arcades. It happened when

216

Bernadette blundered in to get out of the blowing gale.

Several weeks had elapsed since the last (the final, as well as the previous) quarrel with Mrs Woolley. Existence since then had been peripatetic – a lodging house in Hove, an hotel in Worthing, moving on in each case, when she was approached by the press, or when she suspected that she had been recognised. Brighton had been her refuge for about a week before an Italian magazine caught up with her. Brighton, evidently, was not far enough from the world. It was with no more than a blunderingly happy instinct that she had boarded a bus and alighted, belongings dependent from a shoulder, encased in bright pink nylon, at Hastings. In that ancient port she now wandered, less debating what she should do next than looking, fatalistically, for what might happen. The pier seemed, to her inexperienced eye, a place where activity of a sort might be going on; so, doughnut-replete, she had begun her exploration, seen the rank on rank of old men and women, and walked the length of the century-old edifice on both sides, seeing little but fishermen – boys and old men – who thought it worth tossing their lines and hooks into the driving winds. Now, indoors again, she contemplated the amusements in the arcade which like the urinals (visible as well as audible from outside the open lavatory doors) pursued a bleeping, whirring, autonomous existence which seemed independent of patronage. The pennies and sixpences in Gumpton's Double Falls still shifted seductively about, looking as though the addition of but one more coin would cause a cascade of money to the floor. In expectation of this two bespectacled addicts, sworn enemies for a season, guarded the machine closely, shoving in the occasional piece of silver like votaries appeasing a god, and waiting for their windfall. Around these machines, the bright electronic lights and noises of the others perpetuated the illusion that Four Fun was highly populated. The lights on *Interceptor, Space Race* and *Super Block* danced in vertical and sudden spurts of green or fluorescent pink. Beside them, images of the Prime Minister, Mr Andropov, the President of the USA, and, outmodedly, Idi Amin, twice life size, opened and shut their mouths repeatedly, hungry for the contestants who never came to toss wooden balls at the backs of their throats.

Bernadette, who felt for the first time in her existence rich, allowed herself a few goes on many of these machines. The newspaper for which Mr Feathers worked had given her £2000 on condition that she spoke to no other journalist. The money was amassed in a post office,

217

her account book well hidden in the reaches of her underclothes. She was independent, at last. Her mother had had no call to speak to her in that way, even if the newspaper story had been a shock. Misfortune had made Bernadette wary. A wise instinct told her not to stray far. 'They' would find it as hard to catch up with her in Hastings as they would in Hong Kong. She would live at an hotel until the money started to run out. Then? What?

Had Kathy McKay been doing business that morning – 'Clairvoyante-Palmiste of Celtic Romany origin' – Bernadette would have consulted her. 'With the science of Palmistry,' boasted the sybil's advertisement, 'and the Mysticism of Clairvoyance I will reveal your virtues – failings and future prospects.'

Bernadette would have welcomed some such revelation. Her character, no more than other people's, was not an object of her curiosity. Her failings were obvious enough to her: her mother had spelt them out with her characteristic succinctness. Her virtues were not something she was aware of. But she would not have minded knowing about her future prospects. Was it possible that her husband would, after all, be united to her? She was not thinking of the years ahead. Her time scale was sanely limited. But, say, Christmas. Where would she be at Christmas? How much money, by then, would she have had to have been and spent?

The amplified voice of the Bonus Bingo drew her away from the locked Clairvoyante's cell. A handful of old women, those rich or energetic enough to smoke, sat at the tables while a louche youth intoned the numbers into a microphone.

'On the white, all the sixes, clickety-click; Red, Kelly's eye, blue, you and me, twenty-three; Red, all the ones, legs eleven; Green, as far as we go, seventy-five.'

There was enough distraction here for an hour or so, until the cigarettes ran low and she began to feel again the pangs of hunger. She was aware of the blond youth who was her master of ceremonies – pink cheeks, ear-rings – staring at her. She must have been the youngest contestant by forty years to play Bingo on a weekday morning, since the 'Season' ended. As she played the game, unobservantly, winning little, she felt happy enough. The memories of all the previous few months did not oppress her. She would be able to manage, she knew.

'On your own, then?' asked the youth.

'Yeah.'

'Holidays?' he nodded towards her well-stuffed shoulder bag.
'Yeah.'
'Quiet now,' he said. The dinner hour had been reached. Devotees
of the tables had retired to the snack bar. Bernadette found that the
blond boy was following her.
'Thought you were looking for the job,' he persisted, indicating
the hand-written card on the pole outside the arcade: STUDENT
STAFF REQUIRED.
'Oh, no,' she said.
'Not very busy now till the spring,' he said – her career already
mapped out for her. 'You start in the morning, say eleven, eleven
thirty. You can take a break when you like – couple of hours in the
afternoon – two quid an hour. Can't be bad.'
'Oh, no.'
'I knew you'd see it,' he said.
They had paused by some posters. Genuine Pro-Wrestling
happened on the pier, they proclaimed, every Wednesday at 7.30
p.m. Les Craig was to fight the Wild Man of Borneo; J.J. de Vere was
to be pitted against Warlord.
'How about it then?'
'The wrestling?'
'Sure,' he was chewing on gum. 'I'll take you to the wrestling. But
you'll come and work on the Bingo – give it a try. I get bored on my
own doing it.'
'It'd be difficult with the stamps.' she said.
'Stamps?' he snorted. 'We're paying you cash, aren't we?'
The easiness of it seemed too much to resist. She had not intended
another human encounter. But, within two hours of walking down
the pier at Hastings, Bernadette had found her destiny once more
taken over. Kevin would square it (Kevin was the blond boy) with his
boss. She and he would work together while the days got shorter and
the Bingo addicts dwindled. She was, she continued to aver, a bit of a
loner. She did not need to be having work at the present. But as she
left him – all suggestions 'in the air' – she knew that she would return,
at seven, and meet him in the pub and that the evening would be
spent (today was a Wednesday) watching the Wild Man of Borneo
wrestling with Les Craig. The future, with or without the
clairvoyante's guidance, was already taken care of. This was
Bernadette's conclusion as she emerged from the enclosed pier into
the September gale on the Esplanade and dragged her paces against

219

the wind in the direction of the nearest modest-looking hotel.

Out at sea, the east wind stirred up the Channel into a fury, and all down the south coast of England foamy cascades roared up and down the shingle beaches. The wind that shook the glass of the besieged pier at Hastings howled triumphantly through the ruined ironwork and deserted shell of what had been the pier at Bognor Regis. The front at Bognor was, in effect, closed. Here the amusement arcades could keep up no pretence at an all-year-round service. The Bingo prizes in Bognor were wrapped up in polystyrene for another year. The electronic games were disconnected. It was a full fortnight since any childish finger had forced a fivepenny bit into the fibre-glass dolphin or pink Bugs Bunny to produce a bucking movement on which young limbs could ride for a two-minute space. Even the doughnut machine was still.

Inland, beyond car parks and playgrounds and palm-trees, the wet, salt wind rattled the windows of hotels and bungalows. It shook against the windows of the Excelsior and against the stained glass of the Sacred Heart and Blessed John Fisher in the Roman Catholic church. Mrs Woolley had not been seen in either of these haunts for weeks. Now, she stayed at home, besieged by more than the storm. For, Mrs Woolley knew that she would never be the same again. You couldn't even go to the toilet without seeing where they had mended the plaster and filled in the bullet-hole. They had cut out the stain on the carpet at the top of the stairs and put a piece of matting over it. But this, again, was a perpetual reminder of that moment of horror, Mr Bracket's head at such a dreadful angle to his shoulders, and the blood pouring from his neck, everywhere; all down his shirt, and staining his suit. Everywhere, it went.

They had caught the man who did it, and everyone who had called that day assured her that this was a good thing. Where was the consolation in that? Mr Bracket had been murdered, blood had been shed, on her landing. She could not know the fate of his immortal soul as it so suddenly left the body. Until Father Colvin reminded her, she had rather forgotten to pray for Mr Bracket. She recited the rosary, but she was not really praying *for* anything. It was just a nervous jabber.

The *Stabat Mater* ran through her brain. She couldn't get its tune out of her head. But it seemed like a nightmare, not a song of consolation.

220

*Holy Mother! Pierce me throo-woo*
*In my heart each wound renew-woo*
*Of my Saviour Crucified.*

Father Colvin had brought her Holy Communion, but only once. He had said she really must try to come to mass, try to get out, try to go to the shops as usual. He was sure the Excelsior would let her have her old job back. Any doctor would explain that she was in a state of shock. But she could not move. The chain and bolts on the front door were never unfastened now. In order to persuade her to come to the back door, the milkman and the bread man were forced to call up to her. She would greet them through the closed frosted glass of the bathroom window, and then lower a basket to them on a rope. She lived entirely now on what they were able to provide; raw potatoes, orange juice, yoghourt, sliced bread, custard tarts, Mr Kipling cakes and, of course, milk. She had not had any meat for weeks, and she was not sure that she could face handling it after what had happened on the landing.

Bernadette she had thrown out. She never wanted to see her again. They could deny all the stories until they were blue. Mrs Woolley realised the truth of it. The explanation of her daughter's seven mysterious years in London was something which she had half-known all along. It had been too distasteful to admit it to herself. Her daughter was a whore!

She had had to make her confession before Father Colvin could place the Blessed Sacrament on her tongue, and he had tried to persuade her that she did not hate her daughter. But she did. And she had received Our Lord's body while she hated her daughter; probably she too was sucked down into damnation by it, which made her hate the trollop all the more. Father Colvin told her that Our Lord Himself (he used the Holy Name quite freely, priests did nowadays, but she could not bring herself to do so) forgave sinful women. He was the friend of prostitutes and sinners. It said so in the Gospels. We must not judge Bernadette for what she had done. Father believed that she was still, fundamentally, a good person, and she needed her mother's help; just as Mrs Woolley could perhaps be helped by her daughter...

But it had been no good. Mrs Woolley would not unbolt the door to let her in, not after the first disclosures in the newspaper; her own name in the *Sun*, and the *Daily Mirror* and the *Mail*; what not? She

221

had not trusted the lecherous bespectacled journalist who had come, offering them money. She had known that Bernadette was a fool to have taken the money without some professional advice. She had offered, even, to write to Father Colvin about it for her. But the girl was proud. She wouldn't listen.

Now she could not read the newspapers. She had never been one to have them delivered. There was usually one lying around in a guest's room at the Excelsior. And, if there wasn't, she borrowed someone else's – one of the kitchen staff's – to read over her tea and biscuits at ten a.m.

Now, all over the Excelsior, they would be reading about her daughter's filthiness. They would know that she, Mrs Woolley, was the mother of a common prostitute who had had sex over and over again, spilling the seed of immortal life into little rubber balloons and risking the damnation of her own soul and that of the wicked men who visited her. Mrs Woolley had always hated sex. She hated references to it; she had hated doing it and, after her husband's departure, she hated even the thought of it. When she saw an advertisement on the telly and it was vilely suggestive, it would spoil her whole evening; sometimes, in the middle of the programme, you'd suddenly have a woman in the bath, rubbing foam up and down her smooth shapely legs, and being looked at by a man who smoked a certain sort of cigar or used this or that deodorant. It should not be allowed, that sort of dirt. It made you curl up inside with pain, it was so disgusting.

The night that Bernadette was conceived was the last time she had ever been disgusting herself. She had thought at the time that she might very well die with the horror of it. In the confessional (Father Murphy it had been, who preached so well on the Curé d'Ars) she had told of the sin; and he had told her it *was* no sin, and that she should pray to have a baby and be a good mother. And she had obeyed and lit a candle to Our Lady of Perpetual Succour while she said her penance, and another one to St Joseph to keep her husband from bothering her.

He had gone soon enough. Blackpool! And it had not taken long – sixteen years, was it seventeen? – before all that sin and *bad blood* had come out in the little whore. And she had slaved for her, scrubbed and ironed and washed and Hoovered in the Excelsior, cooked her dinners, mended her clothes for her: for this!

Mrs Woolley wished that Bernadette had never come back from

222

London. She wished that whoever it was who wanted to murder her had succeeded, in Hackton, or wherever it was she lived. She wished she could stop thinking about it all – about Bernadette, about the horrid little man in a leather coat whom she had married, about the Brylcreemed man in the bedroom ... about Mr Bracket, and the bloodstains on his suit, and the warm dripping liquid which seeped through the carpet on to the floorboards. But she did think about it. There was no use Father Colvin coming and telling her to take a grip on herself. She could not. All grip was loosened. She felt herself, in almost every sense, slithering. They would want her for a witness when the Brylcreem man came up for trial. Well, they would have to carry her down the stairs screaming. The letting go of herself had been part of this deliberate policy. Somehow, she believed, they would be less likely to require the evidence of a sweaty, unwashed woman, who had not shampooed her hair all month, nor changed her knickers or vests or stockings. She slept in her clothes. It was not safe to do otherwise. Might she not be surprised in night-clothes? The bedroom had started to reek. She found she did not need to empty the chamber-pots (three stolen from the Excelsior over the years) every day. If she went easy, she could get away with making the hazardous journey of a few yards to the lavatory only two or three times a week. For the rest of the time, the vessels contained their amber or brown burdens, alongside the milk-bottles turning to cheese, the half-finished packets of biscuits and the cartons of orange-juice that developed a thick puckering excrescence not unlike the colour of urine around their torn tops. Perhaps she could have washed up the knives and plates if she had dared hurry along the landing to the bathroom. But, the longer she left it, the less desire she felt to go anywhere near the top of the stairs. Crumbs, therefore, accumulated. The remnants of ginger cake on the knife provided a good sort of fly trap to which adhered rancid margarine, blanket fluff, jam from the lidless pot. Things, in her formerly neat room, seemed to have acquired a rebellious life of their own. She could not be bothered to straighten the bed. Shoes no longer stood neatly in pairs. Garbage, empty plastic cartons, some cardboard boxes, had taken over the surfaces where she might have sat. She found herself squatting on the floor most of the time, staring, she did not know for how long, at the electric fire, and gazing at the luminous souvenir of the Grotto at Lourdes, which had once tinkled *Aves* until the miniature batteries went flat.

# Twenty-one

It had already come to be generally known as the Blore Affair, by the time of the Patronal festival at Willerton Parish Church. Lady Wisbeach had made cautious inquiries, in the village and in the family, about the advisability of Derek attending. But Mr Dishman had resolved it all. Mr Blore, he had said, quite correctly, was his churchwarden, and he wanted him to attend. He had further added that he had complete faith in Mr Blore, as a man, as a friend and as a statesman. The Affair would cast no cloud over what would be a truly festal occasion.

The man of faith could control, in some measure, the clouds cast by Derek's misfortunes. Clouds of a more physical nature were beyond his influence. He prayed for fine weather on the day but a dank drizzling mist hung over the church of St Leonard in the thousandth year of its consecration.

Efforts at a 'pageant' had evaporated into the generalised sense that costumes should be 'medieval'. In the weeks that followed, so swiftly it seemed, the harvest supper, fingers had been busy pasting cardboard shields, adapting pullovers to rudimentary woollen chain mail, running up nylon curtains as veils and wimples. Guests, when invited, had been given the option to 'come as they were'. Rachel and Hughie, out of a mingled sense of malice and a desire to show solidarity, had chosen costumes which would have passed ambiguously in a more Bohemian setting. She wore a long brown woollen smock down to her ankles. He had cross-gartered some old corduroy trousers from the knee and sported a cloak. They made their way to the church with Priscilla, who had done the thing properly and gone to a theatrical outfitter's. No one knew whether some mistake had been made, or whether Derek intended all along to have been clothed as a Viking warrior. He clanked noisily in his boots and breast-plate. His grave bespectacled face was framed by a bronze helmet from which horns jutted out dramatically above his ears.

'This is just a varry normal, pleasant village occasion,' he said deliberately as they left the house, 'and I intend to treat it as such.'

Such was not the intention of the national press, as became apparent when they reached the lych-gate of the church. Flash-bulbs popped, scarcely giving Derek time to remove his helmet. Inside the edifice, it was easy to distinguish villagers, in their gay mantles, cloaks, tippets and wimples, from the more drably attired functionaries of Fleet Street, damp in their heavy mackintoshes.

When the choir had processed, Mr Dishman welcomed them all, and was visibly excited by the crowds and the cameras.

'I need hardly remind you that we are in the House of God,' he said. 'God has been worshipped in this place for exactly a thousand years, and we are gathered together to give Him thanks and praise.'

For Hughie, the occasion belonged to the realms of Romance, and not merely because of the presence of Priscilla, dressed like the object of a troubadour's adoration. The hymn-tune – 'Rhuddlan' – played over on the organ immediately recalled school; the place where supremely in life romantic daydream can continue unhindered. Church could bring back that uninterrupted daydream, in which emotion was all and outward events *remained* outward and distant. There was something rousing about this tune; but it aroused less a desire (as the words implied) to pursue Canon Scott Holland's idea of social justice than the most delicious indulgence of private sentiment.

The scene, too, recalled school because there hung in the air the feeling that one of the boys was in trouble; that someone's 'number was up'. There was that thrilling knowledge, while the evening hymn was sung, that a beating would later take place. Some boy had shirked games, pinched or smuggled some sock and been foolish enough to be found out. Already, perhaps, he had been summoned to the Library and challenged by his accusers. Permission to castigate him would have been sought from the Housemaster. After the evening prayers, when everyone else went to their rooms, the Culprit would be asked once more to go to the Library.

Everyone would know what this meant; and during prayers, everyone in the hall would know that the boy in question was going to be caned. On such occasions, there were certain manly conventions which honour required of the victim. Hughie Duncan remembered them now. He thought of the one occasion on which he had himself been beaten by the Library. He recalled his anxiety, as all eyes seemed to be upon him, not to allow his facial muscles to betray emotion; either during the ordeal of prayers; or afterwards, when, the thrashing done, he had been obliged to stand up and, with politeness and good humour, to wish his tormentors good night.

A glimpse along the pew showed Derek sweating and booming in his position, the stick with a mitre on top, denoting his status as vicar's warden, slipped to the edge of the pew, the Viking helmet cluttering the floorspace along with handbags and hassocks.

> Judge eternal, throned in splendour
> Lord of Lords and King of Kings,
> With thy living fire of judgement
> Purge this realm of bitter things:
> Solace all its wide dominions
> With the healing of thy wings.

Feathers sat in a side aisle where, by an irreverent sideways attitude, he could watch what was going on. He saw Priscilla's eyes downcast to her green English Hymnal, her hair braided into a gold net, blue velvet falling richly from her elbows. He knew that she knew that he was there, and her demure features concentrated on her manual of devotion struck him as having a poignant comedy. He could remember her unclothed, leaning over him with a delicious smile. In his entire career, he had never had such a lucky break. He wished that he had not lunched so very well; and that he had been able to resist those drinks on the train. For this should have been a distinctly memorable occasion, and all that he would remember of it would be a sea of faces and the haunting melody of 'Rhuddlan':

> Still the weary folk are pining
> For the hour that brings release:
> And the city's crowded clangour
> Cries aloud for sin to cease;
> And the homesteads and the woodlands
> Plead in silence for their peace.

When Lady Wisbeach suggested to Mr Dishman afterwards that a more, by which she meant less, appropriate hymn might have been chosen, he had pointed out that St Leonard was the patron saint of prisoners. It was the tune, chiefly, which gripped the congregation. The choir descanted on the final verse, rustics, accountants, hacks and retired schoolteachers, all united in the rich Victorianism of the

226

lyric's aspirations:

> Crown, O God, thine own endeavour:
> Cleave our darkness with thy sword:
> Feed the faint and hungry heathen
> With the richness of thy Word:
> Cleanse the body of this empire
> Through the glory of the Lord.

When the hymn stopped, there was a division in the congregation between those who knelt, or humped themselves awkwardly in semi-prayerful sitting positions, and those who unashamedly jotted in notebooks. *Cleanse the body, sang the Secretary of State, Derek Blore, last night in the parish church of Willerton St Leonard's as his future in politics hung in the balance . . .*

Evensong took its course. They noted that the Almighty had put down the mighty from their seat. They prayed for the Queen, and those set in authority under her. After the closing hymn, they all staggered out for the beano.

In the parish hall, as in the church, newsmen clicked and jotted and noted. To most of the village, it was unquestionably an added excitement, to think that they might be in the morning's papers. A roasted ox had, in the event, been beyond anyone's powers.

Knights, burghers, abbesses and crusaders queued up for their packet soup and slabs of quiche Lorraine. Rachel, in the way that she had, mingled with the crowds. Hughie heard her complimenting some woman on her velvet dress. He stood apart and surveyed the scene with a mixture of unavoidable amusement and poignant sorrow.

Rachel believed that Derek would stick it out, live it down, see it through. The libel action against Feathers would proceed. Neither of them could decide whether this would be just or not. The thing had been so tangled with rumour, speculation, claim and counter-claim that no one, probably, would ever get to the truth of the matter.

Hughie did not care. For him the central question was not whether Derek had or had not had an *affaire* with Bernadette Kutuzov and subsequently been involved in some shady attempt to murder her. He thought only, still, and unavoidably, of Priscilla.

He had told himself that his idol was shattered, that henceforward he would renounce Romance and live only in the world of prose. But,

227

as he watched her helping to distribute the sausage rolls, he realised that Romance was his natural home. The fact that she had been to bed with Feathers would always remain completely incomprehensible to him. The Priscilla with whom he had fallen in love would have been incapable of such banality. Now, in her medieval costume, she was transformed into the appropriate idol of his high ideal. She looked like some heroine in Chaucer or Guillaume de Lorris, a swooping, serpentine creature of white flesh and blue velvet. Her face seemed supernaturally beautiful in the light of the village hall, glowing not merely with a loveliness of physical feature – the bright eyes – the hair! – the extraordinary complexion of the throat and cheeks – but also with the moral strength of a goddess. How could any woman endure it? Her husband had been exposed as a lecher, a liar and, possibly, as a spy and a murderer. Priscilla looked as cool and as dignified and as good-natured as ever. The guts and the panache of the thing made him weak. The thought of any publicity at all struck Hughie as unpleasant. He did not even like to see Rachel's name in print all over her own articles in the press. Priscilla managed to lilt about in the public gaze and lose none of her perfect freshness and strong simplicity.

Derek's features had all the coarse artificiality which Hughie had come to expect of 'famous' or public figures. There was something about a face which was much photographed. In an odd way, it came to lose its edge of reality. It came to be accustomed to posing, to set expressions. Even the complexion of it was unlike that of more private individuals.

Derek was unlike Priscilla, too, in that he could not disguise the strain of the occasion. He himself put this down to the fact that it had been a mistake to wear a real helmet. A cardboard one would have been adequate, indeed more fitting. Priscilla had a way of getting over-enthusiastic about things. He, like Hughie, noted that she was being 'marvellous'. Other women would have cracked up. Not the woman that he had been sensible enough to marry. The gutter press could howl and yell for a week or two. The demeanour of his wife was enough to show the world what sort of a man he was.

In recent weeks, Derek had repeated them so often that he had come to believe his own public explanations of the story. Alone in the wakeful hours of the night, he remembered the reality of the thing. He thought of himself squatting on a hearth rug in Hackney while Bernadette gave him the cane. He remembered the exact quality of her flesh, he remembered the smell she gave off, he remembered the look of misery in her mascaraed eyes, and the relief which spread over her features when it was all over and she could bring him a mug of tea. He remembered that, and he remembered all that had happened since. But, in a public place such as this, inebriated sufficiently with mulled wine, and placed between the doctor's wife and the vicar, he was able to see the whole thing through their eyes. He honestly thought – or very nearly honestly thought – that Bernadette had come to him and bothered him about National Insurance; that he had been foolishly kind to her. He further forgot the Professor, documents which had been passed to the Embassy, the conversations he had had on the telephone. Was it likely that a British Minister of the Crown . . .

'Varry amusing idea, I think, this medieval clobber,' he said to the doctor's wife, who beamed at him to show solidarity, but was trying to think of a topic which had no bearing on 'The Blore Affair'. She herself, in a mob cap and a Laura Ashley evening gown, was scarcely medieval, but it suggested a desire to be festive. Mr Dishman simply wore his cassock.

'Are we going to have a little speech, vicar?' asked Derek.

'I hadn't really thought . . . that is, I had thought a very few words from myself.'

'Certainly, certainly,' said Derek. The sight of the press had excited him. It seemed like a challenge which he could not refuse. They would not make him skulk.

'Ladies and jantlemen,' he called, through the rumbling of conversation. There were murmurs of 'Quiet!' The vicar clapped his hands together ineffectually. 'Ladies and jantlemen,' Derek repeated.

As he said the words, Priscilla's face bore a curious expression of triumphant nostalgia. She was thinking of the Gilbert and Sullivan all those years ago. *Ladies and Jantlemen we'll try that chorus again.* She knew that dozens of photographs were being taken of her, but her features did not register this fact. She leant forward, her lips framed in a kind smile, her whole attention devoted to supporting her husband and being kind to Mr. Blore.

'The vicar has asked me to say a few words, and I shall keep them brief, as I'm sure you all want to get on with enjoying – as I am enjoying – this splendid spread which the ladies have once again provided.'

229

(Cries of 'Hear hear!')

'No, no, it really is stupendous. There's no other word for it. And I do think also that the costumes are all splendid . . .'

Cheers. He grinned beneath the horned hat, an exultant Viking in spectacles.

'You know . . . and I mustn't go on . . . This is what it's all about, isn't it, frankly? A village community, pooling our talents, our resources, our skills . . .'

Opinions very greatly divided, afterwards, over the question of whether Derek *knew* that this was his swan-song. Feathers maintained – it forms the climax of his book – that Blore was aware of everything that was going on, and staged this speech for the benefit of the newsmen. But had this been the case, Hughie protested, he would surely have chosen to say something more memorable. The shuffling, the sheer awkwardness of atmosphere in the village hall while he was speaking, was again something which, afterwards, was subject to a variety of interpretations. Hughie put it down chiefly to the embarrassment of not knowing whether it was polite to eat while the MP was in full flight.

'I've been in politics now for twenty-five years. And I hope I'm going to be in politics for a further twenty-five years.'

Mr Dishman led the clapping at this. Afterwards, people said he should not have done. At a parish supper, this speech had no place. It was not fair to all the women who had baked potatoes and prepared coleslaw, to turn this into a political occasion.

'. . . And I don't pretend they have been easy years, or that we have not had our ups and downs together . . .'

Murmuring; some shuffling by the door; a few popping of flash-bulbs.

'I really don't intend to make any kind of speech whatsoever, and I certainly don't want to keep you from this truly magnificent spread: you've all worked wonderfully hard . . .'

Clapping broke out at this point, not congratulatory clapping, but the sort which announces that an audience has had enough. But he had raised an index to suggest that there was one final point he wished to share with them. Hughie was not the only one who chose to study Priscilla's face at that moment. There could be no doubt that the smile, and the eyes, spoke of loyal support to her husband. But there was room to speculate why, on this important public occasion, she had arranged for Derek's knees to be visible above the socks and

230

sandals: pink, quivering, scoutmasterly knees. Perhaps the breast-plate and the sheepskin jerkin were appropriately martial garb for a man who had been vilified so frequently and so strongly in the public press. And it was, after all, Derek himself, and not Priscilla, who chose to keep the horned helmet on his head as he spoke, rather than hanging it on the pegs with the array of mitres, and other helmets (Balaclava, Roman, Saracen) that had been carried over on other heads or under other arms. Something in the man was determinedly foolish.

'You know, you don't get through these ups and downs without support,' sniffed the Horned Helmet. 'And I think I've said enough to suggest how grateful I am to you all – to David Dishman – a great friend – to Bob, I see over there, to Fran, Phyllis (where would we be without her?) . . . But of course at a time like this a man needs the support of his wife, and his family. And there is something appropriate to me, after a church service, about being able to conclude my few words – and here I really will stop – with a tribute to my wife Priscilla . . .'

Hughie thought that he might be about to die with embarrassment. But what saved him was the sight of Priscilla's uncomplicated pleasure in Derek's words. As the speech at last ended '. . . family life; and, once again, as I think you would all agree, that's what it's all about . . .' she smiled at him with a genuine tenderness, which in spite of himself, in spite of everything, Hughie found deeply touching. In the milling crowd, having discarded his paper plate, he found himself feeling for his wife's hand, and holding the fingertips gently.

Rachel's features suggested that mirth had been hard to keep at bay during Derek's oration.

'Whatever next?' she asked, her ironical green eyes straying upwards towards her curls. She tightened her grip on Hughie's hand. No facial muscle suggested what she felt about this infinitely slight gesture of reconciliation. Hughie could not answer her consequential inquiry. Events did it for her. With an appreciation of local feeling which Derek should, theoretically, have approved, the detectives from Special Branch left it to the local constable to make the arrest. In such a crowd, where every costume was bizarre, there seemed no particularity in the Constable's costume: merely an historical clash as the era of Sherlock Holmes confronted that of Canute.

Even this had the curious feeling of having been staged. Rachel

231

said afterwards that it was like a man being chosen for a television programme called 'This Is Your Life'. Once wind of what was happening spread through the hall, the men of the press, the cameras, and the arc-lights were all directed towards the glistening face of the Norse warrior, keeping resolutely calm, as the officer falteringly read to him from a card: 'Derek Reginald Arthur Blore, I have a warrant for your arrest...'

'Come on now, Pete, what's all this about: a parking offence?' The jocularity struck a false note, as it always did when Derek opened his mouth.

'... and that you did in the company of the persons heretofore mentioned conspire to murder Bernadette Mary Kutuzov; and that you were an accessory to the murder of Robert Gareth Bracket on August 29...'

The whole hall had fallen silent. Nobody afterwards found out why the police chose this public venue for the arrest, but it was said that they feared an escape route had been planned after the parish party was over.

'You are furthermore charged with offences under the Official Secrets Act...'

As the catalogue of crimes was recited, Hughie looked only at Priscilla. Her sadness was so tender, but you could see from the curl of her lips that she would be completely brave. For the first time, standing beside her mother, Hughie could see in her face a hardness of feature which Rachel had remarked from the beginning.

'You are not obliged to say anything. But I must warn you that anything you do say may be used in evidence...'

There, for Hughie, the *tableau* froze, in effect, for ever. The rest of the 'story' belonged to Feathers and his like, who would manufacture their serial articles, their cheap books, and even their documentary films out of the Blore Affair. Hughie had thought, for one dizzy moment before the picture ceased to move, that Priscilla would turn his way. A glimpse, a smile, would have been sufficient to indicate that this catalogue of iniquity had finished Derek in her eyes. Henceforward, the glimpse would be able to tell him, her heart was Hughie's.

Rachel's palm, cool and moist, pressed against his own as he stared at the scene: the vulgar Tyrolean hat of the Special Branch man; the woeful figure of Derek led off to his life of disgrace in the armour of a ninth-century sea-faring warrior; and Priscilla! Ah! She had her hand

232

on his arm. A light touch. But the face, rather than looking strained, seemed almost as if a great burden had been lifted from it. Her eyes were not for Hughie, not for the cameras, not for the village. Some people thought there was a gleam in them, but Hughie knew it was a gleam of kindness, as she gazed so intently at Mr Blore.